DARKEST HEART

P.J. Linden

ATHENA PRESS
LONDON

DARKEST HEART
Copyright © P.J. Linden 2003

ISBN 1 84401 125 9

First Published 2003 by
ATHENA PRESS
Queen's House, 2 Holly Road
Twickenham TW1 4EG
United Kingdom

Printed for Athena Press

DARKEST HEART

Contents

A story told in the form of a Classical Symphony. Macquarie Dictionary definition of *symphony*: from Gk., lit., a sounding together. 1. An elaborate instrumental composition, usu. in several movements.

One: *Allegro Ma Non Troppo, Un Poco Maestoso*

A Classical Symphony will evoke a wide range of emotions through contrasts of tempo and mood. The opening movement is always fast and in sonata form. It is usually the most dramatic movement and stresses exciting development of short motives. Sometimes a slow introduction leads to the opening fast movement and creates a feeling of anticipation.

There is nothing either good or bad, but thinking make it so!

Hamlet
William Shakespeare

1991 – Rick – The Flight South

He sat at the window seat and observed the grey and non-descript buildings of London's Heathrow Airport race past him. The moisture-laden air left streaks on the window as the aircraft gathered speed and started to tilt upwards into the beginning of the ascent. As the engines roared and the thrust pushed all the passengers back into their seats, Rick felt a surge of unease that he always felt as planes took off. It was a slight unease tinged with disbelief that this enormous man-made machine could actually become airborne with its massive load of human cargo and luggage.

England spread out below him. It was a country compartmentalised into lots, fields and holdings by the vicious slashes of the arterial road system, and showing only a winter colour scheme of greys and dull greens. The plane pulled into small wispy clouds and the ever-smaller landscape appeared in two further glimpses before surrendering to the dark grey of the thick cloud covering northern Europe. Rick swallowed to clear his ears and sat back with a sigh.

Rick Graham was twenty-eight years old with shoulder-length straight fair hair that fell on to his forehead from the parting on the left. Dressed in the uniform that his generation had adopted as standard and that hid all nuances of social strata, he wore faded blue jeans, scruffy tennis shoes and a loose heavy knit pullover. With his neatly trimmed beard and slim build he could easily be a postgraduate university student or young lecturer. He had graduated as an architect in London where he had subsequently joined an alternative group practice in the socially mixed community of Clapham.

Now that the outside view was gone he turned to look at his fellow travellers. His companion was a rather mousy and frail middle-aged woman whose large and red-faced husband held the aisle seat. Her handbag's name tag with *A. van der Linden, Nelspruit, Transvaal, RSA* on it, not only gave away their home address but classified them as that reviled breed, the Afrikaners, the white tribe of Africa; the tribe that through its stubbornness and dogged belief in its own moral case had catapulted itself into international awareness and opprobrium. They had also given the world such words as apartheid, Kaffir, sjambok, Sharpeville and Soweto. It now seemed that its vision of gold, tobacco and rugby fields had all turned into killing fields.

The almost unanimous advice of Rick's friends had been against going to South Africa because of the dangers, and because indirectly he was supporting apartheid by being a tourist in their land. The daily newspaper items reporting the ever-increasing spiral of violence between the supporters of the Zulu dominated Inkatha movement and the Xhosa dominated ANC, which now seemed increasingly like a civil war, were indeed daunting. Common sense told everyone that the violence would eventually turn itself around and include the Afrikaners and other whites who had been the power-brokers in the divided land. Rick wondered about his two fellow travellers, and if they felt any unease or if their consciences were clear.

The guttural voice of the stewardess announcing in Afrikaans what he presumed were the details of their flight plan, films and menu, interrupted his thoughts. He had deliberately chosen to fly South African Airways as he had felt that he wanted the whole trip to be an experience, an indulgence to take the pulse of the nation. Having been a convinced follower of Peter Hain's anti-apartheid movement, he had always felt there was a stalling point when arguing about apartheid, and that was that he had never been in the country or observed first-hand its oppression – so how could he possibly know and argue with conviction?

In order to have this first-hand knowledge, this true understanding of the country and the facts, he felt he had to travel and see for himself. He had accordingly resigned his job specifically for this trip. He wanted to travel as a traveller, to shake the tourist tag and truly be unencumbered by time restrictions. Besides, he thought to himself, there was a friend to visit, an Afrikaner with relatively liberal parents who had been at public school with him in Wiltshire. An Afrikaner who had deliberately called himself a Boer.

Tom Pienaar had attended the UK school from the age of thirteen when he had come across from Capetown. He was a jovial extrovert, who excelled at rugby and swimming. Blond and blue-eyed, broad-shouldered and trim, he was the archetypal Boer. Academically he had only just scraped through but Rick had been instrumental in his survival. His grasp of science subjects was tenuous, and only his substantial number of hours spent with Rick swatting prior to exams saved him from being an academic casualty. Most people at school remembered him as the extraordinary wing forward who would break away from the scrum in rugby and if gaining possession of the ball, would somehow dodge and crash through seemingly impenetrable opposition. Others also remembered that he had always been tanned when everybody else was pale, compliments of Christmas holidays in the southern hemisphere.

Rick and Tom had been inseparable, for they had an African heritage in common and somehow managed to complement each other in innumerable ways. Rick had spent the first eleven years of his life in Kenya, and could relate to the people, the colours, the landscape and wildlife that Tom talked of with such passion. In the often rough arena of sport, Tom's protective umbrella always shielded him, to the extent that many of the bully boys tended to keep their distance. The equally rough and cut-throat sparring grounds of academia saw Rick excel and always help his friend along, so that many evenings ended up as sort of extra tutorials for Tom.

Their friendship blossomed, so that they became the butt of

many jokes, mainly along the Tom and Jerry variety. Jokes were also made of Tom's surname, but few dared to say them to his face. With Tom's parents so very far away, Rick's parents had often asked the school for permission to take Tom out along with their son on the recreational breaks allowed at half-term.

The boys had felt that their friendship would last forever, and that it somehow was destined to keep going throughout the trials and tribulations that life would inevitably bring. They had made a pact that dictated that they should always try to see the other one's side in case of a serious argument; whatever became of their lives, they should endeavour to meet every five years as an absolute minimum, to renew their bond of friendship.

Rick smiled to himself as he recalled the youthful idealism they had both so plainly possessed. It had been about ten years since they last had seen each other, and their trip to the Continent had been the summer break they had treated themselves to on completion of their school years.

They had been on a rolling high on this trip. Rick had his place assured at architectural school in London if his grades proved satisfactory, while Tom was returning home in five weeks to see if he could fix up a business MBA course in Johannesburg in order to defer military service. Life's challenges and excitements were out there awaiting them that summer.

Taking the ferry to Calais they had taken the train down to Paris and then attempted to hitch-hike south toward the Pyrenees. They had reluctantly decided to split up when they had spent a fruitless morning hoping for a ride together.

Separately they had succeeded admirably and met up each evening in the next major town. But it was not to be a completely trouble-free trip, for just north of Bordeaux Rick had accepted a lift from an older man in a large dark Citroen. The passage of time had not dulled Rick's impression that the shark-like appearance of these cars was sinister.

The man had been friendly and talkative, but had then steered the conversation around so that he was able to ask a lot of personal questions about Rick's amorous adventures. Awkwardly, he had endeavoured to answer, but was limited by the narrow restrictions of schoolboy French as well a geographical limit of experience that confined him to gropes with a girl, strictly above the waistline. Using a certain amount of bluff and bravado he had feigned a much greater experience and knowledge than indeed was the case.

The car had suddenly and unexpectedly veered off the main road into a heavily wooded, little-used lane. The driver had then auto-locked the doors and, finding a lay-by to pull off the road, had done so. Energetically and with great speed he had exposed himself and tried to pull Rick across to him.

Rick had resisted and during the ensuing struggle, the driver had crossed sides. As they had grappled with each other the seat had unexpectedly gone back and had placed Rick at a further physical disadvantage.

The driver had become incensed and frustrated at the difficulties and with great vehemence had started to throttle his victim. Rick had clawed at the hand unsuccessfully and felt he was about to black out. He was pinioned and trapped and was aware of the stranger's superior strength as his whole body was gripped by entwining arms and legs. Rasping an 'okay!' he had signalled his acquiescence and had gone limp. He had ceased struggling. The driver had smiled, loosened his grip, and patted his victim's face affectionately with triumph written all over his face.

He had unbuttoned and pulled open Rick's shirt and then rapidly and brutally pulled down the jeans and jocks. Gloating with his win, the man had passed his hand over the limp breathless body below him and then, chortling with delight, he himself had started to strip completely. Rick had stared up at him through hate-filled eyes as he continued to gasp and gulp air.

In a decision that was not truly thought out, Rick suddenly brought his knees up with all his might as his assailant straddled him. It brought an anguished cry from the Frenchman, who fell onto Rick doubled with pain and nausea. As Rick struggled to get away from underneath the stricken driver he had managed to open the latch and then the door before falling out onto the grass. The car echoed to the gasps, grunts and moans of his retching assailant.

Picking himself up, Rick pulled up his jeans and ran directly into the dense forest, where he hid for about an hour. Eventually, hoping that the danger had passed, he had cautiously returned to find the car gone and his rucksack on the ground. Walking to the local town, he had caught a bus to the rendezvous with Tom, feeling very shaken and scared; but he was relieved to have not only survived relatively unscathed but also to have his belongings back in his possession.

It had taken a day of talking and discussion before he felt comfortable about continuing the trip, this time with Tom. But somehow the incident had radically impinged itself on his mind. It seemed as if it was the initiator or perhaps was only the precursor of the events that followed that holiday. The events had profoundly disturbed the comfortable mental chart of his destiny and place within the scheme of things.

What a trip that had been! thought Rick to himself. It had been a voyage of discovery that had left unhealed cicatrices to this very day. In fact, were he really being honest with himself...

'Excuse me, sir. Would you like fish or beef for your main course tonight?' asked the stewardess.

Tom (Capetown, South Africa)

Tom was travelling along the beautiful coastal road that went from his new suburban home in Llandudno, near Logies Bay, to the central business district of Capetown. The day was blustery, with the sky dotted with small fleeting puffs of clouds, whilst the bay was speckled with white caps. Looking up toward Table Mountain, he saw the clouds wrapping themselves around the summit and trailing off in wisps. It reminded him of a scarf around a neck blowing in the wind.

He then glanced across to his left as he caught sight of a vessel in the distance. Probably the Blue Star Line ship, he thought to himself. If it is, it will have on board all the computer gear I ordered for the Najee sportswear shops. Rejoicing inwardly, he smiled with satisfaction.

He looked out again, and noticed that Lucinda was also looking out to sea. 'Can you make out what the funnel of the ship has?' he asked her.

'How do you mean, what the funnel has?'

'Well, has it any markings? A blue star, for instance?'

Lucinda peered out again. '*Ja*.[1] I think so. It is not very clear. There is too much spray – or mist or something to see clearly.'

'Good. It probably is the right ship. I'm waiting for a consignment on a Blue Star Line ship. I hope it's the one.'

Lucinda smiled and turned to look out to sea again. Tom looked at her and sighed. She looked so beautiful. Her shoulder length dark hair enhanced her pale eyes. He knew those eyes could really flash when angry and becoming hard and steely, but he also knew that they could give and express great love and tenderness. He knew she was cross, and he was fairly sure it had to do with the arrival of their guest.

'Okay. Okay. I have obviously upset you. What is it?'

Lucinda smiled at him again, and gestured dismissively, making it clear she was not keen to talk about whatever was troubling her.

He glared across at her. 'Shit, woman, what is it? Is it to do with Rick's arrival?'

Lucinda turned to look at him again. She seemed to be deliberating whether she should answer or not. 'Well, if you must know, what the hell are you putting Rick in the servants' quarters for? Is he a friend or not? There is a spare guest room. What is wrong with that?' she barked at him and looked away.

There was silence. In a quieter tone, she then added, 'I just think it is really rude what you are doing. Guests should be made to feel welcome, or they should not be invited.'

Tom concentrated on the winding road, his lips pressed tightly together and not answering. He revved the BMW. *Bitch*, he thought. Somehow these rooinek[2] women were all the same, bleeding heart liberals! A man could not be master in his own house. He could not even do as he saw fit, without being criticised by his lady. A surge of indignation swept through him. She should definitely back off on all decisions dealing with his friends in his house.

'I don't really want to argue on about this, but I think there are two relevant points. First is that it is my house, and that I can do

---

[1] 'Yes' in Afrikaans.
[2] Redneck.

whatever I like in my own place. Second is that he is also my friend, and I know him well, and I feel I'm treating him fine.' Tom stared fixedly ahead. 'He is welcome, goddamn it!' he hissed venomously.

They drove on in silence, each locked in their own private world and mulling over the harsh exchange of words. The big sign ahead announced Kaapstad Sentrum,[3] and they headed off toward the business district close to the Parliament buildings.

'Sorry, Lucy. I didn't really mean to snap at you.'

'It is not important. He's your friend, as you already have reminded me.'

'Would you be able to pick me up at three this afternoon? I have my business lunch at one with Piet, and I shall be finished by three. At the Golden Circle Restaurant, okay?'

'Ja. No problem,' answered Lucinda. 'Whatever time, I'll be there.'

'Don't forget to book the dinner at Groot Constantia when you are in Captour, and pick up any brochures about the city for Rick.'

'Ja, I know. I haven't forgotten.'

'Great. *Tot siens*.'[4]

'*Tot siens*,' answered Lucinda.

He double parked the car, leaned across and gave her a kiss on the cheek. She had proffered her cheek mechanically. Just like an old married couple, he thought. She smiled back at him, with a smile that even if it wasn't forced, certainly lacked any emotion. Leaving the engine running, he got out and watched her move across to the driver's seat. The exhaust gave off some blue fumes as she gunned the accelerator and took off with a slight squeal of rubber on tarmac.

As he was about to turn the corner, he hesitated and then stopped to look back at the car. She was held up at the traffic lights. A white Jaguar was next to the metallic grey BMW. He lingered in order to watch as he was sure she would rise to the occasion and meet a challenge. The lights went green, and with a

---

[3] Central Capetown.

[4] "Goodbye" in Afrikaans.

high-pitched squeal, his car disappeared ahead of the Jaguar.

She's quite an aggressive bitch when she's behind the wheel, he mused. Though he found it difficult to know why, he felt that she'd changed since she'd moved in. Perhaps a stable relationship and marriage are not meant to be my scene, he wondered, for she was an energising and wonderful girl to be with, before she moved in. Could it be that the closeness was swamping her, or perhaps it was the old adage that familiarity breeds contempt? Maybe he should ask her to leave? Perhaps love and passion have nothing to do with stable relationships and marriage…

As he strolled along Bloem Street, oblivious to the milling crowds around him, thoughts bombarded his brain. Was it really love that he had felt for Lucinda? Perhaps it was that heady emotional cocktail of infatuation and near obsession with her trim, boy-like body, easily described as lust. Perhaps it *was* lust, and that because the desired object had become readily available and accessible to him, the infatuation had been removed, and in turn transformed it into… Into what? he pondered.

He remembered describing to Andre that what he felt for her was true passion, a voracious need to be with her, to have and possess her. It was an intense craving, for he felt whole with her, and all the old shadows that danced so ominously on the periphery of his mind were swept aside.

He frowned. Rick, his old school buddy, was again intruding into his world. He had fond memories of him, with his quick wit and easy winning smile. He had been a truly loyal friend all through school, but it was Rick, in the guise of a daemon, who had thrown a shadow across his path. He had never truly forgiven him the incident whilst on holiday that had been branded into him as vividly as any cattle branding iron, and had remained with him ever since.

He turned into his building entrance. Troy, a little black orphan kid who sold papers was in the entrance, waiting for him. 'Goeie more, Meneer',[5] he said. He bowed slightly and handed over the *Cape Times*.

'Morning, Troy,' answered Tom, dropping a rand into his can.

---

[5]'Good morning, sir', in Afrikaans.

He squinted slightly at the boy. The slightly overdone obsequious greeting always struck him as a slight snub, but he was never really sure. That ultimately was the problem with all the blacks, one could never be quite sure.

Tom rode the lift up to the seventh floor, and glanced at the morning's headlines. 'WINNIE TO APPEAL JAIL SENTENCE' stated the paper, and followed with all the details of Winnie Mandela's conviction in the Johannesburg court for involvement in kidnapping, and accessory after the fact of assault. There were a series of photos down the left side of the paper, a Winnie giving a forward to victory sign, a pained-looking Nelson Mandela, the murdered little Stompie Moetketsi, and the Mandela United Football Club member convicted of murder, Gerry Richardson. Justice Michael Stegman's words were caption to Winnie's photo: 'Unblushing, unprincipled liar'.

Tom looked at himself in the mirror of the lift. The suit fitted well and bespoke a quiet elegance. He was tanned and wore his blond hair in a short and neat trim. His clean-cut face looked handsome, but tense. The muscles of his jaw were tightly knotted, and spoke of his inner tension. Looking down to where his hand held the newspaper, he glanced at the upside-down photos he had just been studying.

His lip went into slight snarl as he muttered, 'Fucking baboons.'

The lift arrived at his floor, and swinging around he stepped out with a grin ready to greet his colleagues in the office. The day had begun.

Lucinda (Capetown)

She clenched her teeth together in a mixture of anger and frustration. She felt angry with Tom, and frustrated at their inability to communicate meaningfully together. She remembered reading somewhere that failure was the inability to achieve the achievable, but their living together appeared to be a quicksand pit that threatened to pull them both under.

She glanced in the mirror and saw Tom hesitate at the corner of Bloem Street. She gunned the BMW and deliberately decided to leave behind the Jaguar next to her. She needed to leave tyre rubber on the streets, and rev the car to its maximum. The lights changed and the car lurched forward with a high pitched squeal, predictably leaving the Jaguar behind. She grinned impishly to herself as a sense of satisfaction swept through her.

She realised that she was still clenching her teeth and tried to relax. Doctor Ruben had spoken about this trait of hers, and had warned that great damage was being done to her teeth. She had declined his offer of a bite splint, but wondered if that had been so clever a decision. The problem with Ruben was that he seemed to be stifled by his own grim company, so it was depressing to be with him, and as a result she always felt a need to bolt from the place. She decided to give him a ring as soon as she had returned to the house.

Turning the BMW into the open-air car park near Grand Parade off the Central Post Office, she parked and set off for the Captour Offices on Adderley Street. Rick Graham would be greeted with pamphlets of all the sights and attractions to be found in and around the Cape.

Lucinda Beresford was pretty and was aware of the impact she made as she moved through the crowd, but today she felt too distracted to play to any audience. She was of average height, and boasted a trim and slight figure that she maintained with frequent exercise. Her favourite sports were squash, sailing and scuba diving. At twenty-three she felt on top of the world and was happy with her job as a junior manageress in a chain of successful family restaurants.

Her father was a well-known industrial business personality who spent most of his time in Johannesburg, and seemingly had little time for his family in Capetown. Her two older brothers had proved to be restless souls and had left South Africa to seek fortune and fame in Europe. Her younger brother James was currently in the army, having served in Namibia, before its independence.

She had experienced very little conflict with her family until Tom Pienaar had entered her life. She had sensed disapproval from her parents, as not only was he an Afrikaner, or 'rock spider' as her father derisively called them, but he had been too overtly possessive of her on that first home visit. The first meeting had been a disaster, and Tom and her father had clashed on almost every conceivable topic. It was a repeat of the historical adage about Paul Kruger, the diehard fundamentalist and parochial Boer leader from the Transvaal, and Cecil Rhodes, the well-educated English imperialist, who were deemed to be temperamentally incompatible. To make matters worse, Tom had sensed that the meeting was going badly and had clung to Lucinda tenaciously, almost suffocating her with his embrace and grip. This had only served to irritate her father further, and he'd become louder and more confrontational. When he had finally left, she faced her father's ire as well as her mother's icy silence of disapproval. He had caustically remarked that first impressions could not be undone.

She had never understood why the introduction had been so disastrous, for Tom was normally a diplomat and functioned in a socially active and snobbish business world. She had liked him immensely from the moment they had first met.

It had been a social tennis evening that had been organised to raise money for charity. She remembered so well how she had caught his eye when they were signing in at the register. She had held the gaze of many men, and had been aware of the predatory mental undressing techniques some employed, but this had been different. The look was direct and unflinching and appeared to penetrate to her very soul, which made her fractionally uncomfortable. She had looked down, and then seconds later up again. It had flashed through her as an afterthought that this man's eyes reflected a pain, an inner anguish that was showing through the stern look, and that it wasn't as severely predatory as it initially seemed to be. He was still looking at her, but this time the corners of his eyes were wrinkled in humour, and they glowed with warmth.

When he had looked down at the register to see her name she smiled, and had wondered if her initial flash had been incorrect. She had also looked down at the names and wondered which of the three male names ahead of her was his. She had the choice of Jan Witte, Peter Rushbridge or Tom Pienaar. Using her female intuition she had decided he must be a Peter. He had that clean-shaven look and strong jaw line that spoke of great strength and conjured up a biblical rock.

He had wasted no time, and had come in close to speak almost as soon as she was inside the gates. 'I'm not sure what the L stood for? Is it Lara, Lola, Lillian or Lilla?' he had asked.

'None of them; I'm Lucinda. And you're Peter?'

'No. Tom – Tom Pienaar,' he had replied, and had inclined his head in a slightly old-fashioned nod. 'Pleased to meet you.'

They had joined the same table and had partnered each other in the mixed doubles. They had laughed a lot and lost, mainly because of her inability to come to terms with tennis as distinct from her normal squash, as she found herself continually hitting the ball too hard. They had subsequently met on numerous occasions for outings to the beach or the cinema, and he had been the perfect gentleman. His manner had been courteous and friendly, but certainly not amorous. Time had passed. She was drawn to him. She started to feel desperate that the relationship should develop further.

Eventually, with a sense of exasperation, she had decided to force the issue, and make him notice her: to make a move, or actually reject her. She became mesmerized by him, as if under an undefinable spell that had been cast and enmeshed her in its net. She had to become either completely entangled in his web, or cut loose and be free from the spell. The charm that had been cast had heady confines but was ultimately suffocating.

One Saturday night they had gone out to the cinema to see Robin Williams in *Dead Poets Society*. After the film he had driven her back to her newly acquired flat, where she knew they would be alone. Her flatmate was staying the weekend with her parents in Stellenbosch, so was unlikely to suddenly return. They had discussed the film over Kahlua and coffee, and returned to the phrase *Carpe diem*, the Latin for 'seize the day', and all its implications.

A silence had hung over them, when she had got up and had literally right there in front of him stripped down to her panties and bra. She had done so in total silence, and he had just watched, his glass of Kahlua frozen in mid-space, an inch from his lips. She had lent over to the lamp and, turning it off, looked back at him in the gloom.

Even in the darkness she could make out his eyes following

her every move; they were narrowed, and that combined with the darkness made them difficult to read. She had reached forward for her drink and noticed how he started slightly. A rush of fear that he didn't even find her attractive had swept through her. She had then reclined on the carpet near the red glow of the electric heater and looking up at him had asked, '*Et tu, carpe diem?*'

He had chuckled and sipped his drink slowly, all the while studying her through his narrowed gaze. The music of J J Cale wafted gently over them; it seemed appropriate late night music. She had continued to watch him, as waves of regret, tinged with a slight fear of rejection, jockeyed with the adrenaline coursing through her veins and gripping her in an unbelievable excitement.

He had got up from the table and slowly and silently started to walk around her.

'You know nothing about me; how I love, how I play, nor even how I kiss,' he had said.

'This move is an attempt to find out. Listen, if I'm unattractive to you...'

'No, no!' he had rapidly interjected. 'Well, I've thought of you as my friend, and...'

'Does that cut out being lovers?'

'No, but the relationship is totally different. Friends can become lovers, and if as lovers they remain friends then they have found something special. So what I'm saying is this. Are you sure that the way you are now is due to a reasoned thought process, and...'

'Shut up, Tom! Just shut up. No reason at all, just emotion, man! I know you mean well, but cut it out. I want to know if you want me. I'm lying nearly naked on the floor, and I just need to have a sign, or I might as well get dressed again.'

He had stopped moving and stood in silence. She heard his breathing as he stooped lower. His hand, cold from the chilled Kahlua glass lightly touched her shoulder. She felt goose pimples all over her and a release of pent-up tension, for the wait was finally over. He hand gently caressed her arm.

'I'm a games player,' he had said, and then added as a clarification, 'and I'm not talking about sports.'

She had heard his words and, like a purring cat, had mumbled an acknowledgment. She had briefly wondered precisely what he meant, if he was not referring to sport, before she had surrendered to his kiss.

The lovemaking had been powerful and brought out an intensity of feeling, more so than she could possibly have imagined. It was different. The games he played exhibited a vehemence of feeling and were able to move her into a make-believe reality unlike any she had previously experienced. They had rocked and shocked her, and indeed profoundly altered her, inasmuch as they had become almost obsessional in her mind.

She had reached the Captour offices. She hesitated on the steps before she went in. What was it, she asked herself, that had altered things recently? Was he tired of her already? Was the close proximity stifling him, and literally not giving him enough space? Somehow she felt not; she felt it had to do with the impending visit of his friend.

Unable to clearly come to grips with her thoughts she continued to linger on the steps, staring out down the wide boulevard of the Strand. She felt sure that the profound mood swing he had undergone coincided with the first letter from Rick announcing his visit, and asking if there was any chance of catching up with him. Tom had been overjoyed, and had written back immediately, welcoming him to their house; it was very much a '*mi casa, tu casa*' letter.[6] And then – yes, she could remember it well, he had lost his temper one evening a couple of nights later. He had become increasingly moody and had seemingly lost interest in sex or her, she wasn't sure which.

What did Rick Graham mean to Tom? Why was this friend, whom Tom had only ever referred to once in the past, suddenly seem so important, and why was his visit so negatively disruptive? It also bothered her that he was being relegated to the servants' quarters rather than being put up in the main house, which she instinctively felt was a serious affront to the visitor. No white South African would accept such treatment from a friend, and Tom's reason that it meant he could come and go as he pleased seemed implausible.

---

[6]Spanish for 'my house, your house', welcome.

Lucinda noticed a young black boy shuffling slowly toward her. She felt sure he was watching for an opportunity to grab her bag, and if he did so not even a Carl Lewis would be able to catch him, for the young purse-snatchers were all agile, fast and small and could easily dodge through a dense crowd. Gripping her bag firmly she entered the building, and decided she at least was looking forward to this friend's visit, for he might provide her with answers.

Rick's memories:

...I remember so well how the lead up to it all started, it was purely to do with who should go to the shops for milk. The shops were about a quarter of a mile away from our campsite near the beach. We had bought provisions earlier, and although I had asked him to remind me, we had both forgotten. We squabbled about who should go, till I came up with the idea of flipping a coin.

He got his Italian 5,000-lire 'lucky' coin and flipped it into the air. The coin has always stuck in my mind, as it is one of those remarkable two-tone coins that contain two different metals, rather like a coin in a coin. It's unusual.

Anyway, I called heads, but the coin landed in the sand and to our amusement remained perfectly vertical. We both laughed and started squabbling again as to whether it inclined slightly more one way or the other.

'Okay,' he shouted. 'I've got the solution. If you can catch me and take the coin from me, I'll go. If you can't and I manage to hold on to it, you go. Okay?' He picked up the coin and indicating it was tightly in his fist, set off down the beach at a run.

I was laughing so much it was hard to run at first, but I started to sprint and moving on to harder sand started to gain on him. He saw that I was gaining and started to zigzag before turning and taking off at a tangent toward the sea. I moved to cut him off and attempted a low rugby tackle, which just managed to trip him but not bring him down.

As he ran into the water, he slowed dramatically so that I was able to launch myself at him, and bring him down. We both fell laughing into the small Mediterranean breakers on that quiet Spanish beach. Wrestling in the warm water we tumbled over each other, nearly choking as we accidentally swallowed mouthfuls of brine.

He pushed me back, and although I was gripping his wrist, I was unable to keep my hold. Having managed to break loose, he set off back toward our tent, screaming with delight and triumph. Getting out of the surf, I set off in hot pursuit and managed to catch up with him right next to the grassy area close to our tent.

I leapt on his back and we collapsed in a heap on the grassy embankment. I had now both hands working to unclench the fist that held the coin so tightly. 'Open up, give it to me!' I was chanting as we wrestled together.

As we were both wet it was hard to keep a firm grip, plus he was definitely stronger than I was, so he somehow managed to get up. He started to gain the advantage as we continued. I remember feeling that it was somehow turning against me, and soon I found myself slipping beneath him as he gained the upper hand.

I was forced down on to my back. Just as this was happening I vividly remember this flash of a thought speed through my brain. It was indistinct, and even to this day I rationally cannot fully understand it, but what does come back when I try to recall was this sudden sense of being powerless. A surge of submissive feelings came over me, and I felt a need to give up and say so. It was in tandem with an equally confusing and sudden awareness of his strength, of his very real power, and that he somehow at that same instant knew this and was rejoicing in this novel feeling.

My back was now flush against the ground and he had pinioned me by my wrists to the ground. He sat astride me, grinning down at me in triumph.

'You see, man, you can't do it!' he breathlessly chuckled, but when I looked up at his eyes I knew they didn't laugh. He was deadly serious. 'I demand an apology and a promise to fetch the milk,' he continued, but in spite of the laughter the mood was different now.

'Sorry, sorry, sorry, sorry – and I promise I'll go and get the milk,' I mumbled.

'That's better,' he said. 'But I sure don't feel it's good enough.' He then brought his knees up and used them with his body weight to keep my arms pinioned down. It was undoubtedly easy, as I had ceased to struggle. With his hands free now, he then grabbed my head by the hair with one hand and with the other, dropped the coin into the front of his bathing suit.

I then knew, even before he spoke again, that the apology required had to take a specific form, even if he hadn't clearly thought it out yet. I stared, riveted by the bulge in his bathing suit and his priapic state, and acutely aware of my weakness and apparent inability to fight back, for the catatonia was mental. His hands were now folded over his chest.

Pushed back against the soft soil, I felt vanquished and conquered. His victory was total, and I was now required to do penance. The tight and bulging wet little blue bathing suit filled my gaze. It was if the owner, who had somehow gained this mastery over me, had mesmerised me with his genital pouch. Far from revulsion, horror or shock, I felt that somehow this moment was preordained, a sort of destiny to be fulfilled, and that the pouch dancing before my eyes beckoned me.

I don't clearly remember the mocking words he was saying as he gloated over me; all I know was that in spite of the laughter and jokes, this was far from a game. An act of submission was required of me, not necessarily humiliation, but a definite surrender.

Male chimpanzees bare their rears, as do the females, when in the presence of a dominant male, and that was how I felt; it was just the order of things.

I was in a state of abeyance, and in spite of my inferior and humiliating position below him, strange as it may be to understand – I wanted the moment to linger. A wave of belonging and a peculiar sense of gratitude that this had been shown to me overcame me.

With a sudden effort I managed to raise my head sufficiently to press my head against his wet bathing suit – which was cold – and felt a slight push back... but perhaps it was a reflex? I turned my head and placed a kiss on the bathing suit, feeling his erect member below the fabric, and then sank back to the soil.

Total silence reigned. As the enormity of what I had done struck home a few seconds later, I emitted an involuntary gasp, as if suddenly punched in the solar plexus. My eyes travelled up his body and sought his. They sought his for comfort, for assurance, for confirmation that what had just happened was just a game, a great joke, no more.

His eyes told me I was wrong, very wrong. Those pale blue eyes, embedded in a face that showed bewilderment and surprise, spoke only of elation, at a joy at his success. I always had been able to read them, and although the blue could look so icily cold, I could read the taunting triumph that made them sparkle.

I averted my gaze as abject thoughts crowded my mind. I felt disheartened, humiliated and utterly confused. Distressing thoughts about my sexual orientation and my 'normality' flooded my brain, so I was soon about to howl.

We must have remained frozen in this time warp, immobile, with the victor still astride the vanquished for a good few minutes. Neither of us spoke. I had closed my eyes and had remained with my head turned to one side.

He suddenly climbed off, and set off toward the tent. I sat up and hugging my knees to my chest, sobbed quietly to myself. I felt that I had destroyed everything, and that I was a worthless creature. I even considered ending it all there and then by drowning myself.

My shame and misery had intensified to open and loud sobs, when I heard him shout that he would go and get the milk, and that he needed the exercise.

By the time he had returned I was at least relatively composed, and we continued the holiday without the incident ever being mentioned. Yet I knew that it would never be the same again, for the relationship had altered. I always expected him to return to the topic. I felt sure that he would bring it up and force me to talk about it, about why I had done it, about what it had meant – but he never did.

It left a legacy, a wound in the spirit that has never healed and where daemons have entered and have now established a realm. From their territory, they have constructed a seemingly impregnable fortress, which allows them to make forays and sorties into the settled lands around.

The net result of these incursions are the nagging questions about my sexuality; about my guilt; about my inability to really admit – to myself – that I felt a love or perhaps a secret infatuation for a person… of the same gender.

The fortress has remained, and I've lived in a mortal dread that one day the daemons will take over my spirit and being. I can see them so often, and I curse their foreign presence, but mockingly they assure me they are not foreign, and that they belong where they are. Their presence has coloured so much conscious thought, affected in so many little ways all my relationships, that I do sometimes feel that they will be victorious, and that they cannot be exorcised.

They come into my realm of dreams, so I dread that their domain may expand to become a real empire. Their phantasmagoric presence truly unsettles me. But in final comment, their victory, if ever total, may indeed be a mirage, for I do not know that I could live with it. It would be like the liana that feeds on the tree till it eventually kills it and in the process seals its own death warrant.

Lucifer would have notched up one more soul!'

Two: Molto Vivace

It is in the slow second movement that we are most likely to find broad, songlike melodies.

To live in Africa, you must know what it is to die in Africa.
Ernest Hemingway

Rick (Johannesburg, South Africa)

Presumed Innocent, with Harrison Ford, had been the in-flight film, but Rick had found himself distracted by the tumultuous thoughts that invaded his consciousness. He had eventually decided to ignore the film and listen to the classical music through the same headphones. He had slept fitfully and had awoken with a stiff neck and the woman next to him partly drooped across him.

It was early and the sun was just lighting the cabin with red-tinged rays through the small aircraft windows. A small knot of men was congregated near the food preparation area and were talking together and smoking. They all had the tanned look of people who spend a great portion of their time outdoors. Although two sported beer guts, they all looked fit, and had moustaches. He wondered if they were policemen, or some sort of security group.

He had heard that South African Airways and El Al both carried armed security guards on board, and he wondered if the group up ahead of him was just such a group. Feeling curious he craned his neck to see if there was any clue such as a bulge under the arm or any indication of a concealed weapon.

The lady next to him stirred and, realising she was over on Rick's side, mumbled apologies and lent over to rest her head on her husband's arm. Rick decided to get up, stretch his legs and go to the toilet.

Stretching over the slumped recumbent forms of his two

travelling companions, he got into the corridor and started off toward the toilets ahead of him. The group chatting together certainly noticed him, and a couple watched him move forward. As he moved through them he heard the guttural murmur of Afrikaans. He felt sure of his initial assessment of the group; they looked as if they could kill if called upon to do so.

It was strange how a sense of unease swept through him in the presence of the law. He had always had that sense that he was being observed more closely than was merited, and had often admitted to himself that this was probably due to a guilty conscience that he must permanently have. He himself was not clear why this should be so, but assumed it was a crude linkage of guilt between his anti-apartheid stance at university when he was smoking a lot of dope. The mere illegality of the dope smoking amongst his college friends had pushed him into viewing all law and order with unease.

As he returned to his seat, the stewardess had announced that they would be landing in Jan Smuts Airport in a little over an hour, and that they were currently over the coastline of Namibia and heading due east. The slightly unusual flight pattern was due to many black African states denying South African Airways rights to fly over their air space, thus forcing a lengthier route over the sea.

His travelling companions were also wide awake now as he climbed back into his seat. The stewardess carried on to add that a light breakfast would now be served. Rick pulled the blind right up and looked out. The white fluffy cloud had occasional breaks in it, and indistinctly below in a seemingly deep gloom he could make out a faint pale line that he presumed was the coast. The inhospitable Kalahari Desert began there, the subject of countless Attenborough-style documentaries on its weird and wonderful wildlife, and the recent theatre of a vicious and long war.

He turned realising that he was being spoken to. 'I'm sorry. I didn't hear what you said,' he answered, when he realised that the large man in the aisle seat had spoken to him.

'I was just asking if you could see anything?' replied the man in a thick South African accent.

'To be honest, not very much. I think I can make out the coast, but it's too dark to see clearly.'

'Great country down there. Full of wonderful game and a few wandering tribesmen – mainly Bushmen. The Etosha Oasis is truly a marvel to see. Have you been?'

'No. I'm afraid not. But perhaps during my trip I'll have an opportunity to see it.'

'You're not from SA, are you?'

'No, I'm from the UK in terms of my passport, but I was born and brought up in Kenya.' Rick winced internally, for he recognised that he was seeking approval from this friendly and large fellow traveller. He felt a brief bubbling to the surface of his old insecurities.

'Ja, ja. So you are an old Africa hand at heart?' The man nodded approvingly. 'Breyten van der Linden,' he added and extended his hand, 'and this is my wife Anna.'

Rick smiled, introduced himself and shook Breyten's hand. Since his wife made no move to offer hers, he mumbled a hello and nodded.

'So. Is this your first visit South of the Limpopo?' asked Breyten.

His mind raced to place the river. Did it run into Mozambique from Zimbabwe or Zambia? 'Yes it is. I've only ever been as far south as Tanzania before, and that was really only in the North to see some of the parks.'

'Did you visit the Serengeti?'

'Yes I did. It was really wonderful and full of wildlife.'

'How long ago was that?'

'About ten years ago, I guess.'

'Ja, well, it's all changed now. They have all those Masai tribesmen crawling all over the place now, and professional poachers from Somalia are killing anything with four legs indiscriminately. Great pity. You wouldn't recognise the place.'

'Have you been there?'

'Not likely! I have no desire to go, for the Kruger is the most plentifully stocked game park in the world. Why travel to a troubled country like Tanganyika if I've got it all here?' he laughed.

'What I meant was that I'm not sure that it is as spoilt as you say, for the Masai don't live off the wildlife, as they have their own herds of cattle, and even if the poaching is a problem, it hasn't changed that much.'

'Don't you believe it! Don't you believe it!' said Breyten with great strength. 'I have it as first-hand information.'

Rick was going to add that he had friends who had gone on a safari last year and that their reports differed from his, but decided to avoid an argument, so nodded assent and grinned.

'You'll see for yourself, Rick, don't let me convince you. You must see for yourself. The Kruger is undoubtedly the best-run National Park in Africa. My brother, who is a game warden in Sabie-Sabie, can confirm this – and he has studied the other parks!' said the Boer with an air of finality.

Rick decided to remain silent and listen. He wondered if all Boers were as determined and stubborn as this man obviously was. He made a mental note to steer well clear of all political subjects.

'So what do you do in South Africa, Mr van der Linden? What sort of work or profession are you in?' he asked finally.

'I'm a man of the land. All Afrikaners are essentially that. We love the land even if we wear a suit and work in an office. I'm a tobacco farmer in the Transvaal.'

'Far from Johannesburg?'

'Not so far. More or less five hours, heading east. Not far from Nelspruit, if you have heard of it?'

'No, sorry I haven't.'

'Well, let me ask you – are you going to Kruger?'

'Certainly! It is a must on my priority list,' laughed Rick.

'Good. In which case you must visit us. It is not far from the park and it would be only a pleasure to have you visit. I'll give you my card. Give me a ring a day or so before you come.' He produced a personal card with his name and address from his wallet and passed it to Rick.

'Thank you, that is really very kind of you.'

'Only a pleasure.'

Breakfast arrived, along with a steward bringing entry cards for the Republic. Rick ate his breakfast and filled in the card. He hesitated at the question, which asked what was the purpose of his visit, before putting in 'tourist' rather than the 'investigative travel' that had sprung to mind. His mind raced on to Tom, and he mentally added to the space that the trip was to exorcise a daemon that too long had haunted the playground of his inner psyche.

The plane started its descent and was soon below the clouds, bringing into view the dusty-looking browns and reds of the Transvaal. The messy sprawl of Johannesburg was now visible in the distance, with many street lights still on, giving it that festival air that all cities appear to have when viewed from the air at night. The city founded on gold had a few high buildings lit up by the early morning sun, so that they sparkled and reflected golden hues.

As the plane came closer and closer to the ground Rick studied intensely the country unfolding below him. Some parts did indeed look messy, but it was hard to tell if that was as a result of mining or of the rapid population growth and ensuing chaos. He could soon make out cars, most still with their headlights on, travelling in toward the city.

The touchdown was smooth, and they were soon taxiing to line up with the other large jumbo jets. He could make a British Airways jumbo, a Belgian Sabena jet, a Swiss Air jumbo, a Zim-Air jet and a host of other South African Airways jets. He wondered for a second at the SAL marking, which was different from the SAA he knew, but realised that it was the Afrikaans rendition of the same.

'We have just touched down at Jan Smuts International Airport, where the local time is seven-oh-five in the morning of Saturday the twelfth of November. The current temperature is eight comma five degrees Celsius. Welcome to the Republic of South Africa,' announced the stewardess. She went on to explain disembarkation procedures, customs allowances and immigration regulations.

Breyten leaned across to Rick and gave the thumbs up sign, before adding, 'God's own country. No doubt about it. God's own country!'

Lucinda (Capetown)

She woke early. The sun was just up, and the house still lay in shadows as it faced the Atlantic, western side of the Cape peninsula. One of the best features of the villa was the spectacular view on to the ocean, and the subsequent sunsets that could be enjoyed from the front verandah. The price paid for these sunsets, though, was the deep shadow and gloom that the house was immersed in by the backbone of mountains, in the early morning.

Lucinda felt thirsty, and attributed this to the alcoholic over-indulgence the previous night. They had somehow almost drunk themselves into a stupor, had argued, had sulked, but had not managed to clarify the problem that seemed to be bedevilling their relationship. The more she had drunk, the more daring and direct she had become with her questions in what ultimately proved to be a futile effort, to understand, if not solve, the problem. More than ever, she was convinced now that the problem was Rick, and that he was, albeit probably unwittingly, responsible for the change in mood and depression that Tom appeared to be suffering from.

She had tried to cross-question him about Rick, but had received very simple and uninformative replies. She was already aware that they had been good friends at school, and that Tom had a high regard for Rick's intelligence, and that they both liked rugby. The evening's talk had provided her with a series of stories of their schoolboy antics at school, their trip in Europe, but very little else. He had avoided really talking.

Raising her hand from under the eiderdown, she gently felt her forehead. There was a slight swelling near the right temple, and the skin was grazed. She winced as she felt the raised contours of the bruise. Her head had come off second best in the confrontation with a sofa arm, for the evening had certainly ended differently than it had begun, and unexpectedly.

'A third-rate evening, but a first-class fuck,' she remembered him saying as he had lumbered to his feet and swayed unsteadily over her. She had lain on the sofa and watched him, and had then burst into laughter, for in his crude and drunken way he was of course right.

Earlier, after she had exhausted his stories on Rick, or at least exhausted those that he was prepared to talk about, she had turned to their own relationship. He had seemed equally unwilling or unable to face up to the fact there was a current problem, and that the relationship was not really working. He had disagreed, and fobbed off her criticisms with excuses that his workload was heavy, the economy depressing, politics unsettling, and that he felt it was all getting to him.

Her argument was that it seemed to be affecting him seriously at the moment, to the extent that it appeared as if he was losing interest in her. He had suddenly focused his attention on her and inspected her expressionlessly. She had asked if he had lost interest in her, or if another lady had distracted him. This brought tired denials. Her question as to whether Rick had anything to do with it had in turn brought a sharp verbal rebuke. He had sworn, and then asked her to leave Rick out of it, for his friend had no significance in the discussion they were having.

They were both fairly inebriated by this stage. When she had demanded to know why he hadn't shown any interest in making love in a little over a month, he had glowered at her with what she felt was a look of contempt. His lip had curled involuntarily. He had taken a step toward her in a threatening manner, and then as if changing his mind, had turned around slowly and retrieved his drink.

Downing the contents in a gulp, he had then spun around and grinned with a warm if somewhat lopsided smile. 'You're right, of course. I have no idea why I have been neglecting you,' he had said, and then moved forward to embrace her.

The lovemaking was different from his norm. He had made love in a regular, tender way, though it was characterised by a sense of urgency and as if he was seized in the grip of some great emotion, and was scared. There was none of the games-playing or kinkiness that so placed him in a different category to any other lover she had ever known. As they had collapsed together on to the sofa, she had turned slightly and grazed her head, but though he stopped to momentarily examine the wound and place a tender kiss on the site, he had then continued unabated.

It had been glorious for her; perhaps it was the flood after a long drought, or perhaps it was the alcohol, she wasn't sure which. It had brought them very close together as they lay in each other's embrace, wordless, and remained listening to the sounds of the wind battering the outside shutters.

Lucinda turned to look at Tom. He lay on his front, with his face half buried in the pillow. Raising herself on her elbow, she studied him. None of the worry or even the stressed look was apparent as he slept. He looked at peace with the world, almost as if all her concerns were completely unfounded.

The dryness of her throat and the pressure of her bladder made her move. She slowly and carefully got out of bed. Checking that she had not woken him, she wrapped a kanga around herself and walked quietly downstairs. She put the kettle on and prepared herself a coffee. Her head hurt, though she was not sure if it was from the graze or the alcohol.

The open briefcase took up the kitchen table, and amongst the jumble of letters lay an opened airmail envelope with British stamps. Closer inspection revealed that it was addressed to Tom. She turned it over and confirmed her guess that Rick Graham was the sender. She sipped her coffee and looked down indecisively at the letter. The house was totally silent.

She wrestled with her conscience. Her curiosity was doing battle with the need to keep the sanctity of privacy within a relationship.

Cursing quietly to herself, she turned away from the letter and got as far as the living room, before stopping and listening. There was still no sound in the house. Assuring herself that it could do no harm, and that her actions were justified as it ultimately affected her own life, she turned back and hesitantly opened the letter.

She skimmed through the contents before deciding to read it carefully. It was written in longhand in a flowing artistic style. It was obviously in response to his invitation to stay with them:

> Great to hear from you, and it's great to hear that you are doing well. You sound very happy in your life, and dare I say it ... settled! Your letter from a few years ago conveyed such a different mood. Perhaps living with a lovely lady like you have described Lucinda to be, has had a calming influence on your life.
>
> It would be really great if I could stay with you initially when I arrive – so, yes I'd like to say yes to your invitation – only as long as you are quite sure that I shall in no way be inconveniencing you, or your lady. It makes a hell of a difference if one can start a journey in a foreign land by staying with a local – which I guess you are!
>
> To answer your second question, yes I shall be travelling alone. I've got an on-off relationship with an upper-class English girl called Tash (short

for Natasha), who is heavily involved with the horse scene. Sometimes it seems that 3-day events and dressage take precedence over what we have together. I guess all these establishment types are the same, as I'm sure you remember. When were you last in the UK? I'm assuming it was after school, or have you slipped in without letting me know on some top secret and hush-hush business deal!

So, it seems that by setting off on this trip, I risk losing Natasha – if indeed I ever truly had her! But, such is life – c'est la vie!

The other question is perhaps more difficult to answer. I haven't forgotten the trip, and yes it is strange that we have never really discussed it, but then perhaps we have never really had the time or even necessarily the maturity. I'm sure we shall be able to talk, for I cannot believe that the intervening years have allowed us to drift so far apart. I don't know, but I guess we shall both see!

I'm sorry to ramble on. Looking forward to seeing you and having a good talk, and to meeting Lucinda. See you soon.

Your friend.

She folded the letter and placed it back in its envelope. It had substantiated what she felt, that somehow Rick was the key that could unlock the mysterious change that had come over Tom.

Wind was buffeting the house, and the sea had little white caps that confirmed that the roaring forties were truly blowing. Lucinda shivered and decided it was still worth a quick run out to the end of the drive where the weekend papers would be lying.

She ran down the drive. The wind blew the kanga tight against her body, outlining its contours. As she bent to pick up the paper bundle, she saw a movement out of the corner of her eye. She spun around. The adrenaline was already coursing through her veins.

The neighbour's gardener was standing beside the hedge that separated the properties, with a pair of garden shears in his hand. He was looking impassively straight at her. No emotion crossed his features, not even recognition. Lucinda had always felt that Africans had this peculiar feature, of being able to hide behind a deadpan mask.

One day, Lucinda thought, they'll turn on us with all the fuel of pent-up hatred ready to drive them in an orgy of vengeance. All that is needed is the right spark to ignite the whole inferno. She shuddered involuntarily.

'*Goeie more*, Joseph.'

He inclined his head almost imperceptibly and acknowledged the greeting. '*Goeie more, Miesies.*'[7] His expression had changed to one of slight amusement.

Lucinda felt her kanga flick against her leg and looking down realised that it was now wide open at the front. She hastily gathered it together, and clutched newspaper and kanga tightly to herself. Her eyes went back up to meet his.

They were amused; he could obviously sense her nervousness and embarrassment. He turned and methodically continued trimming the hedge. She ran back inside, and closed the door quietly in order not to wake Tom. She glanced outside one more time through the hall window, and withdrew rapidly when she realised he was looking straight at the window. Joseph had stopped working and was staring at the window. A tingle of slight nervousness again ran through her, for the second time in barely a minute.

There was still no sound from the house, so Tom was obviously still asleep. She decided that she needed to start the day properly, so went to make a second coffee, and gathered the papers to spread them out on the living-room rug.

She turned to the stereo set and flicked through the turntable rack of compact discs. The red cover of a recently purchased double set, caught her eye. It was a 25th Anniversary set of Edith Piaf's greatest hits.

She put both discs into the player and studied the rear of the cover. She found the song she was looking for. She pressed memory and logged in disc 2, song 9, followed by all of disc 1. She pressed play, and taking a sip of coffee, closed her eyes as she lay back to listen to the only song of Piaf's that she knew.

It should wake him she thought, as she set the volume to medium loud. The newspaper could wait till later.

Edith Piaf's strong and vibrant voice echoed through the house in '*Non, je ne regrette rien*'. Is this appropriate, she wondered?

Tom's memories:

...The holiday ended when we found ourselves back in London,

---

[7]'Good morning, madam', in Afrikaans.

right back at Victoria Station. We hadn't announced our coming back to anybody, so there was nobody there to meet us.

Because of Spain, the parting was awkward. I still couldn't believe that it had really happened, and he didn't seem at all willing to talk about it. It was surreal, and somehow seemed as if it was out of some movie, not really a part of us. I regarded it as a sort of alien experience that we had gone through.

I also found it hard coming to terms with it, and resented him in a variety of ways, mainly because I felt he had altered something. I don't know quite what it was, but I guess I feel that he made me feel unclean. Yes – unclean, and here I mean in spirit, not bodily.

A residual level of frustration remained with me, which was at least in part because the holiday had been ruined. That next week I stayed in London with friends in Clapham. It was great as they were a bohemian bunch and were very free and easy, which is what I needed at the time. They definitely weren't my type, but a friendly bunch nonetheless.

I met a whole group of people that I hadn't previously known. Amongst the girls that came and stayed in the flat was a black girl from Ghana – or at least her parents were from Ghana, though I vaguely remember she was born in London. I suppose it makes her English, but one thing for sure she was as dark as any chick from the Transkei.[8]

She was beautiful, with a slim waist and big arse and jugs. Her figure could be described as very 'hourglassish' – if there is such a word. She was studying some useless subject up in Manchester such as galactic cosmology, which I'm sure was being paid for by the British taxpayer!

Anyway, as everybody else seemed to be out all day with studies or jobs, Clarissa and myself were left together and to our own devices. We walked in the park and came back to make large messy omelettes, which made up on taste what they lacked in presentation. It was great.

I soon became aware that she was on heat, for she had that heavy-lidded look about her that Kaffir women have when they

---

[8]Black African homeland.

find themselves aroused. She seemed to be bursting out from her garments, and man, was she curvaceous!

I remember flashing back to Empageni, when Dad had taken me with him to visit his brother, Jan. He had a sugar cane plantation right beside the Tugela River, in the Natal Province. It was bloody hot that afternoon, and my two cousins who were younger than myself were happy to spend the whole time in the pool.

At thirteen I felt older and maturer than my two country cousins, who were then ten and nine, and also I was about to leave for England, so I felt light years ahead of even my peer group. I decided to go for a run as I needed to train for the cross-country back at school in a couple of weeks.

As I ran through the little paths in the cane fields I heard moaning up ahead. I suddenly came into a clearing, and there saw Katie, the Zulu cook, bent over a mound of earth. Two Pondo girls from the farm were holding her wrists.[9] Pule, the headman, along with two other were standing behind her. All the males were naked, as well as Katie – but not the other two girls.

Katie was groaning and mumbling, but making no effort to get away. Her legs were spread, so she was totally revealed. There were marks on her rump that looked as if she had been lashed.

When I ran into the clearing, the quiet talk stopped, and the girls released Katie. Everybody looked shocked to see me. Katie continued to moan and slowly started to push herself off the mound. She still hadn't seen me as she was facing away and looking down.

I had stopped in my tracks when I encountered this scene, and my first thought was that Katie was hurting, and perhaps the Pondos had ganged up on this Zulu lady.

Pule, always a smart Kaffir, rapidly pulled on his shorts and raced forward to me. I gasped with fright.

'Baas, Baas,' he pleaded. 'Miss Katie here, she wants all the men at one time. She is like a big mama to us, which is why we treat her good. See!' He rushed down to Katie and, grabbing her chin in his hands, turned her face to me. Her eyelids looked half

---

[9]Pondo: tribe from Natal Province in South Africa.

closed, almost as if she was intoxicated. She didn't really even seem to notice me, which was strange as she had always been so polite. 'See, Baas. She ready for all men. You like this here Miss Katie, why not you take her now? She not have white Baas man 'fore now.' He chuckled nervously. He seemed pleased with his placatory efforts.

I couldn't help staring inanely at Katie's face. It was normally so expressive, and alive, but now looked so bovine, so subdued. I realised that this was a special state; that she was red-hot and was ready to be jumped. I'll never forget that look for as long as I live.

I turned down the offer and carried on with my run. I saw Katie that night and she said nothing – about the incident that is – and her eyes were back to normal. I've no idea what became of her. The servants were always coming and going, and she was not there when next I saw Uncle Jan, though Pule was still around.

Anyway, the point of this story is that Clarissa had that look. She reminded me of Katie.

I can't actually remember who made the first move, but somehow I found myself embroiled in a jumble of legs, thighs, arms, boobs, everything! Man, did we go at it! That first day we made love at least six times, and I felt myself getting better and better at it, as I seemed to have greater and greater control.

It strikes me as funny that my first sexual experience should have been with a black woman – and it wasn't in SA!

She seemed to know everything about sex, which I guess is not surprising if you think that most house-girls coming from Guguletu or Crossroads have their first pregnancy at twelve. I was happy to learn, and it was indeed a matter of luck that I didn't catch anything from her.

The next day we started early, as soon as everybody else was out of the house. She came to my bed, and we made love then and there. About an hour later we still hadn't left the bed and we began again, but this time, as she was on me she asked me to treat her rough – to be hard, not to spare her. I asked something like, what if I hurt you? Her reply was that she didn't care, and that she wanted to experience everything with me.

Well, I got rough. I turned her over and plunged in and out from behind. Then she said that I should stick it up her arse. I was possessed. Satan was surely in me. I went to do that and she screamed, and tried to wriggle away. I now knew that the game was to subdue her, so I forced her down and pinioned her arms behind her back. She struggled like crazy and started swearing at me, but she was no match. I soon had tied her elbows together tightly, using the belt from her jeans. She seemed to be really fighting in earnest now, so I used my belt to tie her thighs together and stop her kicking me.

I felt absolutely great, for I felt that the game was going well, and here on the mattress was a beautiful African lady who wanted me really bad. I also was aware of the power I had, the dominance I had over her. This actually has nothing to do with my country's politics, but only to do with sexual politics – her being black was only an added turn-on! I hoisted her over the corner of the bed and went up her back passage as she wanted. She screamed so much I had to muffle her with my hand.

Oh man, it sure hurt! That ring was *tight* but it soon became easier, and after some frantic thrusts it was all over. It must have hurt her, but I knew that this was what she wanted. I stayed in her for a long time before I withdrew, and untied her. She got up unsteadily, looked at me with those half-closed eyes, spat and left.

I realised later when I went to shower that I was covered in blood, and its amazing that these women want to go to such extremes. Africa has always been brutal – in nature and in politics, to which I have to add sex.

Clarissa left that same day and I'm sure she was ashamed at how far we had gone, so avoided me. I was after all, only one of a long series of men in her life. It was a stunning experience for me, and I'm really grateful I met her.

What this first experience with a woman did do however, was to cure me of my unease about my sexuality after the holiday. *I felt normal.*

Mozambique

Their leader was Rodrigo. He had not been appointed, there had never been any discussion about it, but the whole group had succumbed to his gravitational pull. He was a natural leader, it seemed, and having the advantage of an elementary education, he was regarded as smarter than the rest. He had other factors that made him stand separate and above his motley band of followers. He was the only one who had lived in a city, and claimed to know the ways of the white men, for he had lived three years in Maputo. He also had been a Frelimo cadre,[10] and at least had some experience as a military man. At twenty-three years of age he had already experienced a lot.

His band of followers numbered only twelve, and included three women, the youngest of whom, Mopete, was only twelve years of age and was under Rodrigo's protective mantle as his girl. Most in the band were from Beria Province, in the North of Mozambique, but all represented different tribes. Although some of the Northerners spoke Swahili, their language of communication was Portuguese, for the former colonists had ensured that their language remained as an enduring legacy.

They all were united in one thing: they feared and hated Renamo. This was the band of outlaws that had taken over the countryside in the fight against the Marxist-dominated Frelimo Government. Fighting with the same guerrilla tactics that were used by the Frelimo fighters a decade earlier, they harassed the government and virtually rendered the country ungovernable. It was widely rumoured that South African money funded the rebel faction in a deliberate attempt to make the communist neighbour unstable. Many of the poorer country people felt let down by the government, so that initially Renamo rode high on a wave of sympathy. The sympathy had rapidly turned to loathing, as Renamo had degenerated into a ruthless and brutal movement. Even its central command appeared to have no real control. They seemed to operate with no set philosophy or political guideline, other than what appeared to be a collective need to inflict as much pain and damage as possible. Villages were raided, and burning, rape, pillage, mutilations, murder and hostage-taking took place.

Everybody in the little band that followed Rodrigo had some harrowing tale to tell. Whilst not everyone had suffered personally at the hands of the Renamo thugs, everyone had lost friends,

[10]Frelimo : Mozambique communist led freedom movement that fought the Portuguese and later became the government.

relatives or loved ones, and all had seen fit to flee from their homes. They were now all living by their collective wits, and subsisting on petty pilfering from fields, as well as theft from stores or shops in the small villages. On one occasion they had held up a small delivery van and, taking only the food, had fled back into the bush. They were frequently mistaken for Renamo guerrillas themselves.

It was dark, and they were all grouped around a small campfire. They were all depressed and quiet. They had managed to steal four chickens from a little village near the highway, but to their shock had been surprised by a local Frelimo guardsman, who was obviously off duty and visiting a relative. He had shot at them, forcing them to flee leaving half the booty behind. One shot had hit Manuel in the knee. He now lay shivering and in great pain, just in the circle of light cast by the small fire.

In a voice that mirrored his despair and gloom, Nkosi, a young seventeen-year-old, shrugged and put into words what everybody had been thinking, 'Where do we go from here? What now?'

'We eat,' replied Rodrigo, who felt instinctively that the question was aimed at him.

'And tomorrow?'

'Another day. We will find food again.'

'But what of Manuel?' moaned Nkosi.

The lady who was crouched and swaying slowly over Manuel's shivering body ceased her hushed wailing and waited to hear Rodrigo's words.

'The hyenas shall not have him.'

There followed a long silence. The only sound to be heard was the crackling of the small fire, and a hoarse rhythmic groan from Manuel. Rodrigo got up and walked over to the injured young man. He pulled back the blanket and examined the shattered knee. Everybody knew that Manuel could not go on. The eyes in Manuel's pain-racked face rolled in fear; the whites of his eyes reflected the red flickering glow of the fire.

Rodrigo turned to look at the group. They were all watching him. The woman next to him, had her hand over her mouth, as if she was ready to scream.

'Woman, hold his legs tight while I fix this knee problem,' he hissed at her. She did as she was told, sending waves of acute pain up Manuel's body.

'Vaya con Dios!'[11] he whispered as he used his body weight to pinion the blanket wrapped Manuel to the soil. There was a quick struggle, a flash of silver, followed by a gurgling sound. Manuel's body arched and attempted to kick, before slumping back. The noise stopped, and Rodrigo got up. He cleaned his knife by stabbing it repeatedly into the ground.

'Sorry compadre,'[12] he said aloud as he stood up. He looked at the group, and read horror and shock on all their faces. 'It is done. Manuel is at peace. We eat. And tomorrow we leave early … in case the guard sends anybody after us.'

As he went to sit down, he noticed a dark form lunge at him. Reacting with great agility, he managed to sidestep, and swinging his arm round brought his assailant crashing down. He jumped onto the crumpled form, and had the knife at her neck.

'*Assesino!*'[13] she spat at him.

'I can cut your throat now, you stupid woman. Manuel could not have survived. I could not leave him to the jackals and hyenas.'

She started sobbing uncontrollably beneath him. 'Não posso mais, não posso mais!'[14] she gasped.

'Estanislao will be your man. Get the blanket from Manuel, and get some food… and no more foolishness,' he added softly. He stood up and released her. She got up and moving slowly did as she was told.

Rodrigo again turned to face the group. 'We will cross borders. South Africa. I will get you in. There is work there, money there, and food there. It is an accursed land, but at the moment… it is where we go. Anybody who does not like this plan can leave in a different direction tomorrow, but if you stick by me… even if it's tough… by the ghost of Manuel, I'll get you out of this shit hole.'

Nobody   spoke.   In   the   silence   that   followed   this

---

[11]Go with God – Spanish/Portuguese saying.

[12]Comrade

[13]Portuguese for murderer.

[14]Portuguese meaning: 'I cannot take it any longer.'

announcement the fire crackled occasionally, and the fat from the chickens sent up little flares of light. The African bush was alive with crickets, cicadas and all the sounds of the night. In the distance their was a yelp followed by the half-bark, half-howl. They all heard it, and all knew it was the spotted hyena. In a land ravaged by war, famine, disease and drought, the wildlife had suffered, but this tenacious nocturnal carnivore had not only survived, but actually seemed to be thriving.

'Evil is all around,' said Rodrigo. 'What has happened here tonight was for the good of everybody. Nobody is to waste effort to bury him, for we all know the dogs will dig him up again. His spirit is free, and released.'

The hyena was definitely closer. Perhaps he already knew that there was yet another carcass, for they had a prodigious sense of smell.

The small group watched the woman, who was still sobbing gently, cross the camp and squat on the ground by Estanislao's side. She was wrapped in the bloodstained blanket that had covered her former protector.

Estanislao regarded her for a minute and then put a protective arm around her shoulder. She gratefully rested her head against his shoulder.

Nkosi got up and pulled the slightly charred chickens from the fire and, using a stick as a fork, sliced them into various portions with his machete. The hard dry soil stuck to the moist portions but nobody seemed to mind.

The group fed voraciously. Nkosi used his panga to gently flick soil onto the fire, so that soon they were in total darkness.

The hyena was now very close. It no longer needed the traditional large predators to kill and provide food for it, for the humans did more than enough killing. The lion had been ousted; he was a new king, and it seemed none dared truly challenge him. He reigned supreme and multiplied, with his new courtiers, the jackals.

Rodrigo shivered involuntarily, and immediately hoped nobody had noticed, for it could easily be interpreted as a sign of weakness. He looked at Mopete. In the darkness she looked even more childlike and vulnerable, a waif in need of protection. He climbed under the blanket beside her, and arranged himself so that she faced the almost dead fire, and he lay on his side behind her. He wanted to watch the group for some time before sleeping. The danger always lay with the humans, very seldom with the wildlife. Tonight he felt that everybody was upset, and apart from his girl, there was nobody he could trust.

Various hours elapsed before he finally succumbed to the exhaustion that was overtaking him. Nobody it seemed, was ready to question his authority.

Tom (Capetown)

The music filtered into the room. Tom forced his eyelids apart and looked across at the clock. It was only nine in the morning. He wondered what had made Lucie get up so early.

Sleep had been so great, so very restful for a change, and different from his sleep of late, which had been punctuated by intrusive and disturbing dreams. Perhaps last night's sex, or the alcohol, or the combination of the two had been the right thing for his spirit.

He suddenly became aware of what the music was, the Edith Piaf song about regretting nothing. He wondered if the choice was purely by chance, or if there was a message in it from Lucie. She had certainly grilled him last night. At one stage he remembered feeling very close to giving her an ultimatum, to lay off or leave that very night, but had managed to keep it all under control. Her unexpected plea for lovemaking had been a perfect godsend.

He remembered grinning at her stupidly as he turned, hoping that she would be infected by his smile. In spite of his inner turmoil, the strategy had worked. She had looked surprised at first, but then had returned a lascivious lopsided grin that showed her wanton side. She was a strange mixture of cultured and basic, fused together in a novel blend.

A flicker of panic had swept through him as he had moved toward her. The old vexing and troubling questions which had pained him so much in the past, had resurfaced like the recurrent bouts of instability suffered by the country – they somehow refused to go away. He had wondered if he could perform normally, without access to any kinky accoutrement. He had wondered if he was likely to be impotent. He had again wondered if he was normal.

He had faltered as they had embraced and kissed. The hints of panic had now turned to a near tidal wave that threatened to engulf him in a sea of nausea, self-pity and impotence. Somehow, and here he felt that the strong Stellenbosch wine he had been drinking had made the difference, he had tumbled on to the sofa, and it had all proceeded normally.

He had moved quickly as soon as he felt fully erect as the possibility that such a state could be maintained seemed doubtful. He wondered if this panic and sense of urgency had communicated itself to Lucie. She was perceptive, he mused to himself, but perhaps alcohol dulled the acuity he credited her with.

Tom decided that he ought to get up. The music was quite loud, and perhaps she was giving him a less than subtle hint that the day had started.

He got dressed in casual jeans and shirt and shuffled over to the mirror to check how he looked. He looked tired, and there were bags under the eyes. 'Not surprising!' he mumbled to himself. He ran his hands through his hair and decided to splash some water over his face before he ventured downstairs. He idly wondered if Lucie was in a good mood.

As he walked into the kitchen, he looked across and saw her reading the weekend papers. Unable to see her face as she was turned away from him there was no way of telling her mood.

He made a cup of coffee and ambled in to the lounge. The music hurt his head. He sat next to the amplifier and reduced the volume before greeting her. She looked so beautiful, he thought. The kanga was tight against her body and outlined her slim, almost boyish figure.

She looked up at him blankly. She remained expressionless with her head resting on her arm. She studied his face in silence till he started to feel uncomfortable.

A smile crossed her features, and eased his anxieties. 'It was different ... and nice,' she said softly.

'What was? The evening?'

'Yes, that as well, but I meant the lovemaking.'

'Ja-nee.[15] It was good.' He nodded in agreement. He continued to sip his coffee, under the searching scrutiny of her gaze.

'Why?'

'Why what?'

'Why were you so different? Were you trying to say something, were you feeling different, were you deliberately expressing yourself in a different—'

'I was feeling drunk!' he interrupted.

'Drunk!'

'Ja. Drunk. Inebriated. Legless. Whatever.'

'That's it. Just drunk?'

'That's it.'

Her irritation was very real now. She sat up and stared straight into his eyes. Her eyes seemed to be blazing. 'Bloody drunk, hey? I'm almost in a state of shock if that is all you have to say.'

She got up and picked up her coffee mug.

'I hoped that for an evening… for just one evening … that perhaps you really felt something for me. That your lack of sensitivity, was due to a lack of ability to express it. I felt that this man, coming from a fucked-up and warped cultural background…'

'I'm not fucked-up!'

'If not you, then your bloody people are. History called you Boers for a very good reason, and none of this Afrikaner whitewash shit changes anything. You may call us Anglos *soutpiels*,[16] but shit, man, you Flemish farmers are truly the insensitive bastards the blacks think you are!'

'You are getting totally carried away. Calm down, damn it!'

'Okay. Okay. I'm sorry I got carried away,' she said, hurriedly, and started to pace back and forth in the living room. 'Look, let me start this again… and more calmly. What I wanted to say was that the evening was very special for me. I've gone through

---

[15]Yes-no, sort of.

[16]Derogatory Afrikaans term literally meaning 'salt dicks'. Applied to Anglos as they have one foot in Europe and one in Africa, so that their privates would inevitably dip in the sea.

bloody weeks wondering what the hell I'm even doing with you. You seem to have lost all interest in me, to the point that I wondered if you regretted inviting me into the house. Do you?'

Now she was suddenly stationary and looking accusingly at him, he shuffled uncomfortably.

'No. No, I don't.'

'Well, you sure as hell act as if you do. I think you must have the courage of your convictions and face me straight with a straight answer. I really don't want to waste my time trying to make a relationship work, if you are suffering under a burden of doubts and regrets. So, if you are under any macho shit illusions that I, as a frail little female couldn't face being given my marching orders, forget it. I can cope, and would rather split now, than drift into something that might ultimately make us regretful and angry. One more time, if you want me out, summon all your strength... like when you play in those brutal rugby games .... and just say, 'Walk, woman!' And believe me ... with no fuss, I'll be gone.'

She turned and walked out of the room. 'I'm going to read the papers on the bed upstairs. See you later.'

Tom felt stunned, and continued to sift through the debris after the mental whirlwind had gone. He wondered if he really had been so neglectful that she was justified in being this fired up, or if something else was really irritating her. He felt sure he didn't deserve the verbal assault he had just endured.

Going back over the last few weeks, he remembered taking her out to dinner on various occasions, once to the theatre, and on at least two occasions had brought flowers back for her. What then was the complaint all about?

Lovemaking, that was it. She had screeched that there had been a drought in that department. Well, I just haven't felt too amorous recently, mused Tom, and I'm fairly sure she didn't either... Perhaps she was using the time-tested strategy of attacking, and assuming this was the best defence. Was she perhaps trying to hide a guilty conscience?

He decided he would later check her medicine cabinet and see what stage her pills were at, for perhaps it was all related to an imminent period, and there was nothing more sinister than that.

'The bad old PMTs,' he murmured pensively to himself.

His mind then turned to Rick. He was arriving on the one o'clock flight. He flicked his wrist over to glance at the time and realised his watch was still upstairs on the bedside table. He felt reluctant to go and fetch it, for he risked an almost certain resumption of the assault by Lucie.

He looked outside and saw that the sun had almost reached the house. It meant that it was almost nine o'clock and that Rick was already in the country.

Rick's letters were friendly and suggested very much that he was still the same person he had been at school. Tom reflected on their friendship, and shaking his head, felt sure that Rick must have changed, but was not revealing anything. Most of their friends had married or were living with their partners, but Rick seemed to be a loner. His choice of an upper-class horsy woman as a girlfriend indicated clearly to Tom that it was all window dressing.

As far as Tom could make out, all English upper-class women had an overbearing sense of social importance and exclusivity that he found impossible to equate with sensuality, or even likeability. He felt quite sure that Tash, the girl mentioned by Rick as his partner, was of the sort that spoke of being 'rogered' by a male instead of being jumped or screwed. The Sloane Rangers were a pet hate of Tom's, and the mere fact that his friend had chosen a mate from that group was perhaps a pointer to how different they had become.

But then he had always known they were different. Perhaps not always, Tom corrected himself. He had known that they were on different paths ever since the European holiday, when he had glimpsed a dark side to Rick.

Perhaps Tash was really what Rick required. She was a front for him, a stand-in girl who could provide the perfect cover of normality, and as such the acceptable residence visa in a hetero world. She would also be non-demanding, as she was heavily involved with her horse-related activities.

A wave of impatience and slight anger passed through Tom as he again glanced at his wrist to realise that the watch was not there. This time, he reflected, I'll have it out with him. There is no way that he will slip through my fingers without him revealing himself in his true colours.

Tom realised he was clenching his jaw. He stood up and decided to go and check that the room set aside for his house guest was properly in order.

Rick (Johannesburg, South Africa)

'Good morning. How is it?' enquired the immigration official as he took Rick's passport. He studied the passport and the completed entry form behind the glass. 'Reason for entry into the Republic is travel, is it?'

'Yes. I felt it would be nice to travel throughout the country, and really get to know the place,' he answered in a friendly tone.

'Have you ever been to South Africa or South West Africa before?'

'No, never. To neither South Africa or Namibia.'

The immigration man looked at him a little more quizzically. The change of South West Africa into Namibia had not gone unnoticed. 'Are you in any way connected with any news corporation, or have you worked as a journalist before?'

'No, never.' Rick started to felt tense. He told himself not to overreact or provoke, for that would mean he was starting with a basic mistake. He knew very well that to come blinkered meant a lot of the travelling was negated, for to have strong preconceptions automatically filtered the story. It would mean he would be confirming what he held to be true, rather than learning all sides to the argument. He expected the next question to be about whether he had ever been a member of any political organisation that opposed apartheid, and wondered what he should say in answer. He decided to be conciliatory and lie, rather than inflame the situation by telling the truth.

The officer seemed to be studying a large book, which Rick took to have names of unwanted people in it. He shifted his stance at the counter nervously from one foot to another, and started to worry that his name had somehow reached the book that the officer was studying so intently.

'You stated that you wish to stay three months. Is that correct?'
'Yes.'

'Are you able to provide proof of your ability to support yourself during your stay?'

'Yes I am. I have nearly three thousand pounds sterling in traveller's cheques.' Rick started to bring out the required proof, and then added, 'I also have some international credit cards; American Express, Visa and Access.'

'That is okay. All I must view is your return ticket, please.'

Rick dutifully handed his ticket across. The officer, with a cursory glance at it, stamped the passport and handed it and the ticket back. 'Welcome to South Africa. I hope you enjoy your stay.'

Rick smiled. 'Thank you,' he said, and taking his belongings passed into the corridor to follow the signs indicating luggage collection.

He went through the green light, 'nothing to declare' line and found himself in a large hall. There were many expectant faces of friends or family of those who had obviously come on the same flight as he had. He noticed only one black family; the rest all appeared to be white. He presumed that this had as much to do with economics as anything else, for it was only the whites who could afford to really travel.

Spotting a Barclays Bank currency exchange counter, he changed one hundred pounds sterling into rands. He then searched for a coffee lounge, and buying the *Johannesburg Star* at a news-stand, took a seat and proceeded to take in his surrounds. He was enjoying having a coffee back on terra firma.

He looked at his watch. It was only half past seven in the morning and the incarnadined sky outside looked magnificent. All the dire warnings and predictions of his liberal friends flashed into his mind, and caused him to smile. He had definitely seen blood red on his very first morning of arrival, but it had not been the streets of Pretoria awash with the blood of the white oppressors, rather a truly magnificent African sky, possibly colour-enhanced by the pollution of the Transvaal mines. The scenes around him were so normal, so deceptively so, that they could be those of any international airport in almost any country.

Rick turned to look at the paper, which carried a photo of the quintessential Foreign Minister, Pik Botha. He was claiming, according to the paper, that he felt no need to resign, as he felt he had involved himself in no impropriety by helping fund the Zulu-dominated Inkatha movement with government funds. The *Star* carried a threat to pursue the truth, so that all would be revealed in the new reformist South Africa that de Klerk was creating. Rick wondered what people like the van der Lindens thought of these scandals currently rocking the stalwart Nationalist Government.

He got up and put his meagre luggage on a trolley. It only consisted of a rucksack and a video camera bag. He then set off to explore the airport.

Jan Smuts International Airport looked clean and lush if somewhat underused. It exuded a sense of wealth, which was something that Heathrow certainly did not. There was the usual array of small shops selling touristy trinkets, magazines and novels to the travellers. All the major car hire firms were represented, as well as offices for various banks. The only area where there was any form of mess was in the corridor connecting the domestic terminal to the international, where some marble replacement work was being carried out. Groups of workers, mostly black, sat around some scaffolding and sipped on coffee from white plastic cups. The two whites in the group were chatting amiably with the blacks.

As Rick ambled past he listened to their idle chatter. It wasn't English or Afrikaans. He supposed it must be Fanagalo, a language from the mines, which had become a sort of Esperanto of the blacks and blended the main linguistic groupings of Zulu, Ndebele, Sotho, Xhosa, Tswana and English.

He passed through the electric sliding doors and was hit by a cold blast of air. Obviously the airport was heavily air-conditioned. A black taxi driver came up to see if he wanted a ride, and moved off when Rick said he was just passing time. The climate was probably close to that of Nairobi, he reflected – in other words, cool at night but hot during the day.

His connecting flight wasn't for another hour, but he thought he might as well go and check in now and not have to push a trolley everywhere. He wondered why the travel agent hadn't obtained a direct flight through to Capetown, rather than have this rather tedious change here.

As he walked back toward the domestic terminal he again passed the workers, though they had dispersed to their respective jobs. Rick noticed one of the whites was actually lifting some marble slabs with a black co-worker. He wondered if this was the norm or was deliberately staged at a highly visible site like this on purpose. He also wondered if he wasn't being too judgemental and critical right at the outset of his trip, and decided that time would tell.

As he approached the counter with the sign that announced 'Capetown, flight number SA45', he again felt a twinge of anxiety as he wondered what Tom would be like.

Lucinda's memories:

...It was at my father's house in Jo'burg during the summer holidays. He still has the house, a large mansion with sprawling gardens up in Sandton. These days, the house is rented out, and he lives in a small two-bedroom flat in Berea, so that he is very much closer to the heart of the city.

I was sixteen, and we were all at the house for the long summer break, leaving the Cape's cold spells behind us. It was hot, so much hotter than what we were used to, so we spent most of our time frolicking in the pool.

The neighbours to either side of us had children of about the same age, so it worked out that my younger brother James and myself were always with them. My older brothers, Alistair and Rodney, were off doing National Service at the time.

Apart from various girls and boys in the thirteen to fifteen age group, there were three boys in my age group. Hansie Grafenbauer was sixteen, as was John Mitchell, whilst Peter Mitchell was seventeen. They were all really nice guys.

One day it turned out that the Mitchells had gone down to the shopping centre, so that Hansie and myself were pretty much left alone for a few hours. We were by the pool and decided we needed cool drinks, so we strolled over to the pool house where there was a small fridge full of beers and soft drinks.

It was cool inside, and after the heat and glare outside, it seemed initially extra dark. We got ourselves a drink each. Hansie asked if he could see my breasts. I remember feeling really shocked, but a little amused as well. Then, and here I find it hard to believe it myself, I said something like that it was fine, but only if he was prepared to pay. Well, he did, he offered ten rand for a peep.

I looked at him in disbelief, and took my top off, feeling really embarrassed. He put a 10-rand note on the table and walked around me, looking closely. He then offered more money if he could feel them, which I did not agree to, and put my top on hurriedly. We never talked about the incident again.

The very next day, whilst sunbaking with John, I asked if he would be willing to pay to see a girl's breasts, to which he said that only low-life scum did that sort of thing. I felt such a rush of guilt at what I had done the day before, that I actually said that if he wanted to see mine, he could at any time, and all he had to do was ask.

Needlessly to say, this in turn led to us kissing and then later going off to the little house and continuing there. He was gentle, very gentle. All his moves were tentative and lacked any confidence. It was a voyage into unknown seas for both of us, and like Columbus we had preconceived ideas that the world was flat.

Well, it was a hell of an exciting journey. Self-discovery was so very thrilling for both of us. We were both virginal, and when I think back to the South Africa of 1983; we had no sex-shops ... even now Jo'burg has only one sex-shop, which advertises itself 'Joybar, sexy things for shy people' ... no pornography, no cinema on a Sunday, so we were very naive! The only sex education we had was what we had observed when in the Kruger Park, or in rare cases from liberal parents.

This retentive frigidity that the Calvinists imposed on us pervaded even our early sexual groping, for we were difficult, awkward and clumsy with each other, and felt as guilty as hell. Even so, we progressed, though the greatest difficulty was trying to be truly alone. Since there was always the chance of being discovered and time was at a premium, there was a sense of great urgency to all our meetings.

We did eventually have sex. It was painful for me, and a little distressing for John, as he tried to cope with my discomfort and his priapic state. All I can say was that it seemed so vastly overrated. Good, but by no means earth shattering, is how I felt. I guess I felt that somehow we had set sail, and although finding all sorts of lands, had failed to prove the earth was round ... this journey had vindicated Columbus!

During the next few weeks we had sex on various occasions, and it was pure chance that I did not fall pregnant. I was not in love with John, even though he had become my lover. He had become crazy about me. I still felt a little detached, though I did appreciate his kindness and consideration, for he was always the gentlest of people.

Shortly before the holidays ended, Peter asked if he could have a private talk with me. We were in the pool at the time, so I suggested we just go across to my infamous pool house. He said he would love that, but first he wanted to get rid of Hansie and John, which he did – though I'm not sure how, or what he told them. Anyway they sloped off and we went across and into the little house.

For whatever reason, I felt my heart beat particularly loud, and can even admit to a slight apprehension though I had no idea quite why at the time. He closed the door, and then turning to me asked if I was screwing his younger brother.

I gasped and told him to get lost, and what's more it was none of his business. As I moved to the door, he grabbed me and pinioned my arms behind my back with a fair bit of force. Whispering close to my ear, he said that it was his business, since he and his brother shared everything.

Telling him that he was sick and pleading to be let go, I started to struggle. He ignored my requests and continued to whisper and prevent me breaking free. He then said he wanted me badly, had always wanted me and was determined to have me there and then, with strength and if necessary force. I ceased struggling, ceased whimpering.

It could never be called a rape, for my capitulation was voluntary. I suddenly needed what he had to offer. Needed to experience and savour my own submission to a stronger male, who even promised force if necessary. A visceral fear was there, but it only added to the adrenaline flow that had already started my heart throbbing as we had entered the building.

Well. He moved fast, pulling down my bikini top so it stayed tangled around my middle, and rapidly removing my bikini pants. We almost fell to the floor as I struggled to remove his bathing suit. An indecent haste egged us on. There was no foreplay, no tenderness. He held my hands tightly together above my head pinned to the floor, and entered me there and then. It was an exquisite pain of surprising intensity, for I was not really ready for him yet.

His rough movements and the pain as he started to move inside were sending me delirious, for I had never been where I was now heading. These were again uncharted sensual seas, though the basic geography was there. I was gasping for breath as he moved harder and faster against me, and inside me. There was no question of him being considerate. I was swept along with his animalistic drive ... and I loved it!

Then, as my head was turned sideways, I opened my eyes. Framed in the window was Erasmus, the Ndebele gardener.[17] I gasped and tried to speak, but could not manage any words. I tried to loosen the grip on my hands, but Peter held them fast. As the intensity of the lovemaking grew, so too did my horror. Erasmus, in silence and displaying no emotion, continued to watch. I couldn't take my eyes off him, and unblinkingly continued to hold his stare as my first ever orgasm started to sweep through me. I started to arch my back involuntarily, and then to my surprise heard myself groaning ... and still I stared. I almost felt that his eyes riveted me to the floor.

As the orgasm peaked, and Peter screeched some obscenity in my ear, I blinked and surrendered to the delight of the tingling throughout my body. When I opened my eyes again ... and yes, it must have been a long blink ... Erasmus was gone.

What I felt was that it had added a further dimension to the storming of my body by Peter, a further fear. What the Afrikaners call the swartgevaar had swept through me.[18] Amazingly, I could have done nothing to protect my life, or Peter's had Erasmus so

[17]Tribe related to Zulus living in Zimbabwe and northern South Africa.
[18]Black peril.

wished to attack us. It was like a vision, I saw myself as vulnerable, totally taken, and powerless. What is more the threat or power was twofold: the aggressive male making love to me, and the apartheid-suppressed black male observing me. I'm aware that Erasmus never threatened me or hinted at anything at all ... other than perhaps curiosity ... but it's the liberal white South African conscience coming into play here, and it's guilt when faced with blacks.

Peter and I never had sex again, as school came to an end and we had to go our separate ways. The next year, during a clean-up of the sprawling squatter camps near Alexandria Township, some piccaninny shot him at point black range with a .22 revolver.

The little bastard was blasted away by some buddy of Peter's in the police, but Peter was paralysed from the neck down for life. When I went to see him at the hospital I just bawled my eyes out. The very next month, somebody put something lethal in his drip, so he snuffed it. There was a sort of inquiry, but everybody knew it was no mistake; he had arranged somebody to do it for him. Nobody was charged.

John never made another move, but that in part was from lack of opportunity, and I have no idea what has become of him. Hansie works as a businessman in Jo'burg, and I haven't seen him for years.

What Peter did, though, was to introduce me to a different aspect of my sexual nature. I felt confused as to what I wanted from a man. As such, he radically altered me.

As a final postscript, I now knew that what I had discovered with John, and what the cartographer Amerigo Vespucci and the explorer Christopher Columbus had thought, was all wrong ... I knew the world was round! I had launched myself as a woman!

Lucinda (Capetown)

She had showered, changed and combed her hair. She glanced at her watch. It was time to go, for the airport lay about twenty minutes outside the city. Almost on cue, she heard Tom taking the car out of the garage and closing the noisy garage doors.

She went downstairs and outside. It was a bright if somewhat windy day.

'Ready to go?' Tom enquired as came up to her. The car engine was running.

'Ja. I'll just get my handbag.'

'Good. I'll check that the house is locked.'

Lucinda picked up her handbag from the seat in the front hall and got into the car. She watched Tom lock the front door and check that the garage was properly closed. She watched him closely as he returned to the car, trying to judge his mood, after the morning's altercation. He seemed buoyant.

'Hope the N2 isn't too packed,' he said jovially.

'It shouldn't be. Saturday morning isn't a busy day heading out of town.'

'Ja. I suppose so.' He grinned impishly. 'Heck, I'm really looking forward to seeing that old bastard again.'

His high spirits were infectious, Lucinda felt buoyed by his mood. Her earlier black mood and anger evaporated. As the car moved down the drive, she again wondered how the meeting would be, and if Rick was anything like she expected him to be.

It was actually quite difficult to imagine him as anything concrete, as in reality all she conjured up in her mind was a mood, an 'ambience' as the French would say. There seemed to be a lot about Rick, a pool of calm and culture but obviously having a deeper current. It was impossible to give a real face to him, as the elusiveness was the salient factor. Perhaps on meeting him, the different impressions and moods he had somehow managed to engender over such a vast distance in the last few weeks would coalesce into a real form, a real person.

Tom glanced across at Lucie. 'Penny for your thoughts?'

'Oh, nothing really. Just a slow meandering.'

'You looked as if you were deep in thought.'

'Well, I guess I was thinking of Rick. What he's like.'

'I'm sure you'll like him, Lucie. In fact, I sort of feel you two will get on really well.'

'That's good.'

They drove on in silence, each locked in their private world, but at peace with each other again. The city with its bright colours and clean pristine air unfolded before them as they rounded the Hout Bay Road into Rhodes, and down into the city. They were heading down into the centre skirting the Lion's Rump. a part of Table Mountain, and cutting across to pick up the N2 de Waal freeway that started out of Jutland Avenue.

'It really is a beautiful city. I'm sure Rick will be impressed,' said Lucinda.

Tom just nodded his agreement. He put on the tape that had rattled in the tape deck. Toni Child's voice rang out loud and clear over the BMW's stereo system. They drove on in silence, listening to the music.

As they took the turn-off that led them to the DF Malan International Airport, they both noticed a SAA DC3 slowly coming down to land. Tom instinctively looked at his watch.

'I wonder if that's his plane?'

Lucie looked up at it. 'I would think that it is. I don't think that flights arrive here very close to each other. Perhaps it left Jo'burg a little bit early, or perhaps the tailwind was favourable!'

'I hope it is. It would be great not to have to wait around the airport.'

They turned into the car park that indicated Domestic Arrivals, and parked. There were few cars in the vast expanse of tarmac. The international airport section looked deserted.

The arrivals board was flashing 'landed' next to flight SA45. Tom and Lucinda quickened their pace and headed straight toward the baggage collection area. Bags were already being retrieved, and the first few passengers were leaving with the people that had obviously come to collect them.

Tom started to survey the crowd by standing on his toes. Lucinda held his jeans belt and looked around her at the happy milling throng of excited people. She saw him coming straight toward them, an almost sardonic grin gracing his youthful face. He looked so friendly, so very open. Even as he came up, she already had read the slight unease that permeated his very presence. She beamed at him.

'Lucinda, I presume,' he asked deferentially. He was asking in a rich plum-in-cheek voice, copying the classic line that Henry Stanley had used with Doctor Livingstone, when he found him in the depths of darkest Africa in 1871.

'Yes. Nice to meet you, Rick. Welcome to Capetown!' She

leaned forward and gave a kiss on his cheek. She shrugged, grinned, and added, 'Local custom.'

'It is best I get to know them as soon as possible!' he laughed. He turned to Tom who had been surveying the scene with a fixed and inane grin on his face. 'So, you big Afrikaner bastard, we meet again! It's good to see you!'

'You too, buddy.' Tom leaned forward and they embraced each other rather awkwardly. 'Have you got your luggage already?'

'I travel light!' answered Rick, and picked up the only two items of luggage he'd brought with him.

'Great. Let's go to the car. We have so much catching up to do. I'm really happy you've at last made it out here,' said Tom. They weaved their way through the throng and outside toward the car park.

As Rick felt the warm sun on his face, he smiled with contentment. He looked happily around him.

Lucinda watched him. He seemed so different from Tom's usual friends, but then he was a school friend, and he was English, not a local. As she looked at him again, he brushed his hair off his forehead and caught her eye. Just for a second, a quizzical look crossed his features, before dissolving in a smile.

This will be a travel adventure in itself, thought Lucinda, and I need never leave the house.

Three: Adagio Molto E Cantabile

The third movement is generally a minuet and trio, which may be in a moderate or fairly quick tempo. This movement varies in character from a courtly dance to a peasant romp to a vigorous piece that is hardly dance-like. Beethoven liked fast, energetic scherzos for his third movements.

> Life is Sensation – to feel that we exist – even though in Pain.
> *Lord Byron*

Rick (Capetown)

The car swept along the seaside road and turned off into the little village of Llandudno. Rick was awestruck at the breathtaking beauty of it all. The colours seemed so vibrant and so very alive, as if suffused with extra sharpness and clarity because of the clean ocean-sweeping winds. He presumed that the only conceivable pollution in the air, apart from contributions from passing ships, would be blown across from South America, and that was a vast distance away.

He debated on the different quality of the colours, for London's muted and drab hues were so very different from those he saw all around him. He wondered if it was the same everywhere in the southern hemisphere, and if the same would be found in Australia or New Zealand.

'Do you like the view?' enquired Lucinda, interrupting the flow of his thoughts.

'Bloody marvellous! I can hardly believe its beauty. It has a purity about it that's really wonderful. I was actually thinking about it at this very moment.' He looked at her; she was grinning at him with pleasure. Yes, he thought to himself, Tom has picked a real beauty here. Her dark medium length hair was held back in a ponytail, but the last part of the journey had loosened it, so that the open car window blew it across her face. It looked a little like a faint muslin veil.

'I'm glad you like it,' she said. She turned to see where they were, before adding, 'We're almost there. We have this view from the verandah, so you'll be treated to it with every evening drink session!'

'I must interrupt here. I don't intend to have you stay at home every evening. The view is always there. We must hit the town and have a jol!' laughed Tom.

'Jawl?'

'Jol. It's Afrikaans for a good time. A splurge if you like. It used to be summed up by the expression of "*drank, dagga, dobbel* and *vok*', which I'm sure Lucie will translate for you.'

Rick looked enquiringly across at Lucinda.

'I'm not sure why I should be left to translate, especially when he's the real Boer! Anyway, it translates as drink, dope – marijuana dope, that is – dagga is the local word, from I think the Indian. The next word means dice, and stands for gambling, whilst the last word, vee-oh-kay, is I'm sure obvious if you think that the Dutch, like the Germans pronounce their vees like effs … like in Folkswagen Beetle!'

They all laughed, as the car turned into and up the drive. Tom jumped out and opened the garage, whilst everybody climbed out. He looked like an excited big puppy, thought Rick.

'You guys live like lords,' he exclaimed, as he surveyed the house and view down to the sea. 'If I compare my little flat just off Clapham Common with this … well, I guess there just isn't any comparison.'

'Listen here, forget about comparisons and all that kak.[19] You can do all that when you get back; then you can sit back, remember, and analyse to your heart's content! While you are here, you've got to experience as much as you can. This means that I'll show where you can dump your bags, and then its straight away to a celebratory and welcome drink … and by the way, there is no rival to the South African wines, for it goes without saying that they are the best!' Tom laughed merrily and led the way into the house.

He took Rick through the house and into the back patio,

---

[19]Shit.

where he opened the door into the new guest room. It had originally been the servants' quarters.

It had a certain austerity about it, but was undoubtedly comfortable. The bed consisted of a thick mattress mounted on planks supported by bricks. Even the stylish bedside lamp, and the warm expensive glow of the Bokhara carpet, could not dampen the African feel of the room. It had a door leading to a small but basic shower and toilet. There were bars of soap, towels, and a basket of fresh fruit. It reminded Rick very much of a hotel 'welcome' message.

'I've put you in here, for a couple of reasons…'

'It's absolutely great, Tom. I'm really happy with this. It's great,' interjected Rick.

'What I wanted to say was that I've put you here, because it gave you a certain privacy. It has its own entrance, and should you wish to bring back some lady…?' He inclined his head inquisitively.

'Yeah, right!'

'Ja! Anyway, you can bring somebody in and have a ball without waking the household!'

'Well, Tom, as I said, it's great to be here. I'm genuinely happy with wherever I'm put in the house – with or without the lady!'

Tom lent close conspiratorially. 'Lucie is not a bit impressed, because these were the servants' quarters, and she feels it's a bit infra dig to put you in here.'

'Don't worry about me, I'm fine.'

'Ja, I knew you would be, but the problem was with her. Anyway in the long run it's unimportant.'

'If you feel it would make any difference, I'll reassure her myself,' suggested Rick.

'No, it's really not necessary … but if it makes you would feel better, I guess that it would be good.'

'As I said, I feel fine, but I shall do it as I prefer to pour oil on troubled waters. What is more I'll do it diplomatically.'

'Good.' Tom clasped his hands together as if undecided whether he should say something else or not. Deciding on action, he exclaimed, 'Right, man, let's go to the verandah and have that welcome drink.' He led the way out of the room.

Rick followed Tom into the house. Tom paused to have a look in the fridge and quickly realised that Lucie had already been there. He shrugged and then grunted with satisfaction.

'Already done,' he said and led Rick outside to the verandah. A platter of snacks were displayed on the coffee table, as well as two bottles; one of champagne that was stood prominently and almost expectantly on the table, as well as a second bottle of white wine in a bottle cooler. The glasses were all there ready to be filled.

Lucinda was leaning against the railing waiting for them. Her smile is also expectant, mused Rick. He grinned. 'This is so bloody marvellous, you can't believe how good this is to be here with friends, with such a reception ... and such a view!' he exclaimed as he looked out over the bay.

Tom opened the Veuve Clicquot '78 champagne. The cork came out with a large pop. Grinning with satisfaction, he poured the drinks, and handed a glass to Lucinda and then Rick.

'Cheers, Rick. Welcome to our home!' said Tom.

They clinked their glasses, and sipped their drinks. Rick caught Lucinda watching him again. It was a look of profound interest or curiosity. He wondered fleetingly if Tom had talked much about him, and if so, what he might have said.

'How was the room?' enquired Lucinda.

'Great. Really great. I'm really happy for any form of hospitality from friends. To be quite honest I would be happy to sleep on the floor or even in an old bathtub ... as long as the taps didn't drip!'

Everybody laughed. They all looked out across the sea. Various seagulls were swooping with what seemed great speed in the gusty coastal winds.

'Did Tom tell you about the *tokoloshe*?'

Rick turned to Lucinda and shook his head to indicate he had not. 'I'm afraid I haven't a clue what a toko-whatever is, and he certainly hasn't explained it to me.' He turned to Tom in anticipation.

'Well, I presume you noticed that the bed was up on bricks?'

'Yeah.'

'Well, it wasn't because we couldn't afford bed legs; it has to do with African folklore. It appears widespread among the two main tribal groups of Xhosa and Zulu. The legend says that should you sleep on the floor, there is a high risk of being bitten by the night prowling gremlin, the *tokoloshe*, who may then infect you with evil. It seems that the *tokoloshe* cannot climb, so by putting your bed up high, you are inevitably safe.'

'So the *tokoloshe* obviously hasn't a chance with me, as I'm a few feet up!'

'Ja, you are well protected. I should imagine that the tradition has a lot to do with the practicality of isolating oneself from all the creepy-crawlies ... or snakes that glide or creep on the ground. It ultimately is fairly sensible in Africa to be off the earth at night.'

They all contemplated Tom's words in silence.

Lucinda said, 'Why don't you guys sit down rather than stand around so awkwardly. I'm going to put on some soft music. I'm sure you've both got a lot of catching up to do.'

The two men smiled at each other and seated themselves on the garden chairs, as Lucinda moved back inside. They did indeed have a lot of catching up to do.

Tom's memories:

.. I've often wondered about that incident. It seems a little unreal to me. How to say it? A bit hallucinatory – or something close to that.

We had been horsing around, as we often did. The campsite was on a real lekker[20] site somewhere in Spain. The Mediterranean was right there, so nice and peaceful.

Anyway, at one stage we found that we had forgotten to buy some supplies from the local milk bar. He was saying that it was my turn to go back for them. The milk bar was about a kilometre away. It was actually his turn, but we decided to sort it out by flipping a coin.

I can't remember the result, but I think it was a no go as it landed in the sand. We then horsed around a bit and it came down to a wrestling match. It was all very jovial.

This of course was idiotic in itself as I was always much

---

[20] Nice, great.

tougher than he was. So right from the outset he must have somehow been planning it, or had at least an outline in his mind of how the scene would develop. It is so damn hard to know what people are all about, for what happened was a real surprise to me.

We wrestled, and as we were both wet from the sea, it was hard to get any grip on him. He manoeuvred himself so that eventually I ended up straddling him, and having him pinioned to the ground. I revelled in his defeat, for he had been a slippery eel to catch.

I sensed that he had given up, and that he somehow wanted me to dominate him. Looking back on this now it is easier to interpret, but of course it all happened so very fast. I felt triumphant.

'Sorry, sorry, sorry,' he said. 'I apologise and I'll get the milk. How can I make it up?'

Answering to the effect that of course he should be sorry, and anyway it was his turn, I laughed. I was out of breath and still above him.

Then, he started to wriggle beneath me, which was very ticklish. His head move closer to my crotch, whilst my knees were now doing the job of pinioning his arms. With my arms free, I tried to stop the movement. I was laughing. As he seemed so very vulnerable I was tempted to tickle him. In the struggle the coin fell between my legs.

He ceased all movement and lay still. The heat from his breath could be felt through my wet bathing suit. He then leant forward and placed a delicate kiss on my cock. I sat there in total shock. I knew then that he was a double adaptor,[21] and that he probably knew what to do from there. I was too naive and too straight to even know how we could continue being together.

Looking down at him I remember thinking that maybe he thinks this all one big joke. His eyes seem to be saying, 'give it to me, don't be afraid', but I couldn't and didn't. I got off him immediately and went for the milk myself.

I think he must have been hurt that I didn't respond to his approach, for he was very silent with me from then on. We never

---

[21]Bisexual.

talked about it, and I was fairly nervous of any moves he might make after that.

The reason this has disturbed me so much, even all these years later is that I found myself surprised. His kiss aroused me. I know he did this by the touch of his lips, which I could feel through the bathing suit ... which of course is disgusting ... but I was a hot-blooded young man at the time, and easily excitable, and easily led on. Luckily I resisted his advance, for God only knows where I might have ended up.

I hate him for creating a doubt in me about my sexuality, which I had never questioned until then. I'd never had any sort of sexual experience till then, other than occasional unsolicited erections. I know I'm straight, and I still like the guy, but there is no doubt in my mind, that he's a closet gay. He still manages to unsettle me, perverse as this may seem...

Lucinda (Capetown)

She looked out at them on the verandah. They looked awkward with each other. She knew that Tom was certainly ill at ease, for he had that same look about him as when he had visited her parents. The eyes gave her an almost desperate 'there must be a way out' look, whilst his body language gave off a 'fight or flight' air. He was certainly not relaxed, in spite of his warm words of welcome.

She turned to the music system, and decided to choose classical music rather than contemporary. Tom had a selection of light classical favourites that he loved as soothing background music, so she stacked three discs and pressed the play button. The beautiful sounds of Boccherini's Minuet filled the room.

The music drowned out their voices, so that only their gestures and hand movements could be seen through the fine curtains. She stood up and watched them from inside.

Tom appeared animated and excited now, as he described something with sweeping hand gestures. Rick sat more passively, with a gentle and tired look on his face, his whole body slightly slumped into the chair. She tried to work out what the topic could be, but found it impossible to guess.

Rick suddenly got up and, drawing aside the curtains, came

into the lounge. Lucinda was suddenly snapped out of her reverie.

'Oh, that's where you got to,' he said amiably.

'I'm sorry. Wasn't meaning to be rude, I was just lost in a little daydream, and of course listening to the music.'

He looked on the verge of asking something, thought Lucinda, but had then changed his mind. Was it a question as to what the daydream was all about?

Rick muttered, 'Loo,' and headed for the toilet.

Lucinda went back outside. Tom was standing near the railing, and was staring straight out to sea. He was lost in contemplation.

She went up behind him and put her arm around his middle. She felt him shudder slightly, and then relax as he turned to her.

'You okay, Tom?'

'Ja, fine. Why?'

'Nothing special. You still seem a little tense.'

'Well, I might still be. It has been a hard week. What do you think of Rick?'

'He seems a really nice guy. Very sensitive sort of character. He sounds so very, English though. I would almost call his accent an upper class English colonial accent.'

'To think that I sounded like that for a while. Luckily the army knocked it for six!' chuckled Tom.

They heard Rick come out again, and both turned to face him.

'I hope you haven't got anything planned for the weekend after next?' enquired Tom.

'No. I felt that I would do all the planning when I'm here in Capetown, and see what eventuates.'

'Well, I've got a friend who is flying up to Londonok Game Reserve for ten days and asked if we'd like to come along. It's a great game reserve, and it also gives us access to other parks in the area.'

'It sounds great, but where exactly is Londonok?'

'Right next to Kruger National Park,' said Lucinda. 'It is a great area, and well worth a visit. If you haven't got anything planned I'd really recommend you join us for the trip.'

'What's more, it's all free,' added Tom.

'It is sounding better by the minute. Is the de Beers Corporation footing the bill?'

'No, but my friend is very wealthy, and has his own plane. He would be happy for the company during the journey,' said Tom. 'What would be really great would be to then borrow, or rent a car, and take you around the Kruger Park – which we both know well.'

Rick smiled. 'It sounds a wonderful scenario. If your friend were happy to include me on this flight, I certainly wouldn't complain. What is more, seeing the Kruger with you two sounds a real bonus.'

Lucinda watched him as he talked. He had such a pronounced English accent. His posture had fluidity, a looseness to it that contrasted greatly with the somewhat rigid stance that Tom held. He frequently swept the hair off his forehead with his hand, or with a slight flick of his head.

Studying his face, Lucinda found him attractive. He exuded warmth, a friendliness that glowed from him. Just occasionally she found his eyes disconcerting. They were very direct – almost intrusive – and searching. They could be cold, but they also gave off certain softness, as if the soul reflected in them suffered.

Her mind returned to the night before and Tom's words that had so incensed her. She looked again at him. He seemed so stiff, so tense. The night had been so different, so out of character, that she found it almost hard to believe that Tom had been capable of the tenderness shown. She wondered whether the coming evening would be different in any way. She also wondered whether Rick's arrival would loosen Tom up, and finally have him relax and talk a bit more about … well, about whatever was on his mind and troubling him, she thought.

Mozambique

Estanislao looked worried as he squatted, wrapped in his blanket, next to Rodrigo. He kept looking over his shoulder as if he expected to be attacked. He was looking across at Rodrigo as he waited nervously for instructions, for he had come to him with the news that the woman of Manuel had disappeared in the night.

It was still dark, but the very early dawn light was changing the darks to greys. Rodrigo realised he had been lucky that the grief crazed woman had not slit his throat during the night. He must appoint a watch every night, as nobody could be trusted if they were as upset as the woman must have been. He had taken a great risk in trusting her, but she had taken a greater risk by fleeing in the dark.

He got up and woke Nkosi. 'Manuel's woman has gone,' he whispered. 'I want to see if we can find her trail before the others wake. If she does alert the authorities that we are headed in a certain direction, they might track us down. She must be stopped.'

All three of them left the other sleeping forms, and walked back along the path they had used to get into the small dry river bed, where they had made their encampment for the night. They passed Manuel's body with its head turned rakishly to one side. Blood had darkened the soil around him. Dark columns of ants radiated from the corpse. They strode out of the camp.

Once they were about fifty metres away, they spread out and started to slowly circle the camp, looking for tracks or any traces that might give away where the woman had fled. It didn't take them long, and they found the spoor easy to locate. Heading directly back toward the town was a set of footsteps with a scratched pattern next to it – the result of her blanket dragging in the soil.

Grunting with satisfaction, they all set off at a gently lope, following the easily discernible tracks in the ever increasing dawn light. They heard hyenas yelp in the distance, as well as the little staccato barks of jackals.

They had been running steadily with that effortless stride that so many Africans seem to have, when Nkosi stopped suddenly and pointed. In the sandy soil were the tracks of at least five hyenas; all were following the unfortunate woman's tracks.

They continued walking along the tracks, as if each needed to confirm their suspicions. There was no accidental crossing of paths; the hyenas were after her. They all knew that hyenas were really far removed from their image of being cowardly scavengers, and when in a pack will hunt and mercilessly bring down their prey. A lone human staggering through the bush would be easy prey, as soon as the pack realised that the human was not armed, and was probably panicking. They would sense her fear. Her only salvation would be to climb a tree that would take her out of reach of their powerful jaws.

All three stopped, and caught their breath. Up ahead they saw the bloodstained blanket lying by the track where it had been dropped.

'She is finished. The soldiers will never hear her story,' gasped Rodrigo. He continued to struggle for breath as he surveyed the scene ahead.

'I will follow some more. If I find her I'll – I'll – I'll do what you wish me to do,' stammered Estanislao.

Rodrigo and Nkosi looked at him, as if weighing up his words. Nkosi shrugged as if indifferent to this suggestion. Rodrigo nodded his assent. The hyenas would most probably have fed already, and would be very unlikely to attack a healthy male human who did not show any signs of fear, injury or illness.

'Do not waste time. *Kwaheri*.'[22]

'*Kwaheri*,' mumbled Estanislao.

They set off in opposite directions with Nkosi and Rodrigo starting to run back toward the camp.

'Do you trust him?' asked Nkosi.

Rodrigo was a little surprised at the original thought from his companion, and in turn wondered briefly if he could really trust him. There was a potential leader here, and a potential threat to his position. He had to make sure he not only watched him, but also used him correctly.

'No,' he replied, 'But he can do us no harm. He will return.' They ran in silence. He wondered what Nkosi was thinking, and if he had any further questions, and when none came, added, 'When we leave camp, we shall head in a south westerly direction to begin with, and try to cross near the road border, or even via Swaziland.'

'You know the way?'

'Yes,' lied Rodrigo. He made a mental note to keep a close watch on Nkosi, for he was potential trouble.

Just as they were about to come into the camp, they heard a shot. They stopped and turned to listen. There followed two

---

[22]Swahili for goodbye.

other shots, and the sound was coming from the direction they had come from. They ran down into the camp.

Everybody was already up and ready to go. Since nobody in the group had a gun, the shots could only spell trouble.

Rodrigo turned to address them. 'Half of you run along this side of the river, the other half along the other side. I want to show anybody trying to follow us, that we are heading west. After three hundred metres start moving down on to the rocks of the river bed. Then double back. We will head back down the river, going east. Keep on the rocks. No tracks. Leave all your blankets; we must travel light, and quickly. We can always live to have more blankets.'

He looked at the frightened group before him. 'Move it!' he barked.

They dropped their blankets and moved rapidly as directed. Nkosi took the lead on one side, Rodrigo on the other. They carried only their motley selection of spears, pangas and clubs. Rodrigo noticed with a pang that Mopete was running directly behind Nkosi. He looked back and was gratified to see how obvious the tracks were in the dusty dry African bush.

They soon doubled back and were again passing close to last night's encampment. The sun was now just up. Their blankets lay scattered around, and on the periphery of the site lay the already fly-covered body of Manuel. A jackal scampered into the bushes. They ran by on the stones in total silence.

After running for about an hour they all stopped to rest and catch their breath. They desperately needed water.

Rodrigo got them to go up a rocky incline of the river bank, and then in single file, head north. He took up the rear, and with a branch with leaves disguised their tracks. Once they were all about a hundred metres from the river bed, he looked back and with a grunt of satisfaction that he had done everything to disguise their tracks, ran on to join his group.

He decided to keep going north, till they had gone at least five kilometres, before they would turn again and head west toward the border. Their immediate concern though was to obtain water, food and if possible some more substantial weapons than the meagre array they currently possessed.

They were tired, hungry, and most of all thirsty. The most hazardous episode of their time together as a group would be in the days ahead, as they faced the perils of trying to cross the international frontier.

Rick's thoughts:

…It is always quite hard to really analyse what attracts one to a person. Is it musk, a scent that somehow is exuded and indecipherable to the normal mind, but is interpreted by the brain as a definite come-on? In other words, does a comparable process occur with humans as with dogs? We know that a bitch on heat emits an odour that is able to drive all male dogs wild in a fairly wide circle, so could the same be true for humans, except that we are unable to consciously read it?

Granted that in dogs the scent is non-discriminatory, and non-specific. Every male dog within a scent radius, whether it is a Chihuahua or Rottweiler, will be irresistibly drawn to an Irish wolfhound bitch in season. The human scent then must be different if indeed it really exists, but it still seems likely that some chemistry is there.

Attraction of course must also depend on a lot of other factors, such as behaviour, body language, and yet others such as ethnicity, social strata, language, etc. It does get difficult when it comes to attempting to apply the same criteria to those that seek out mates of the same gender. Perhaps here Jung's interpretation of the soul is relevant, where he interpreted *anima* as being man's inner woman, and *animus* being woman's inner man. If each sex is to fulfil its own sexuality, then an imbalance will make somebody lean too much one way or the other.

If I had to be brutally honest about myself I would say that I have chosen as a partner somebody who has too much animus, which of course could be interpreted as meaning the inverse – in other words that I have too much anima!

I was attracted to her by her good looks, and her slim figure … yes, you could almost say boyish. She had a certain haughty coldness about her that I felt was appealing. I felt that I could cruise along with her and never have a deep involvement, since the arrogance and stand-offishness that comes with her class permeates all the pores of her very being.

It was a guess that she would be good in bed, for she would probably approach the sexual scene with the same heartiness and gusto that she would put into any sporting activity. And yes, the bed scene was always good. What it lacked in imagination or diversity, it made up with in energy, and the basic sincerity of putting everything into it.

So it was a sort of swings and roundabouts situation, for what it lacked in one field it more than compensated in others. I was happy to have her on my arm, happy to be with her in company, and happy not to have too many demands made of me. I was happy she had a somewhat practical and cold personality that would not wish me to swim in any sea of sentimentality, nor would demand a passion from the relationship which I clearly did not seek. I never really have travelled very deep with her, and have often wondered what she really thinks of me, for we are so very different. She does however seem content, exhibiting a curiously unquestioning air of tranquillity and satisfaction, so very oblivious to the turmoil within me.

I don't feel I'm likely to be with her for much longer, for we have very quickly reached our limits. It has occurred to me that this is perhaps all she wants from a relationship, but then I'm not really sure. The horses occupy a lot of her energy and time.

A lot more is needed from a relationship for me to feel happy with it.

Lucinda (Capetown)

'So what do you feel about apartheid?' she asked as she faced Rick at the dinner table.

'It's always difficult to judge from afar,' he lied. He felt he had to be accommodating till at least he found where his host's sympathies lay, for he did not want a confrontation on his second night as their guest.

'And now that you are right in it, so to speak?'

'Still difficult, as I have hardly had time to judge. I've spent more time looking out to sea and daydreaming, or asleep, than I have being fully conscious!'

'Are your parents diplomats?'

'No. Why?'

'Because you are sticking to very diplomatic answers,' suggested Lucinda.

Rick smiled and declined to answer immediately. He took another sip of wine. 'Okay. Let me say this…'

'Rick,' Tom interrupted forcefully. 'Rick. I would like you to feel at ease here. Lucie can come on very strong, and it strikes me that she is being a little pushy here. So, if you …'

'Hang on a sec, Tom,' said Lucinda. 'I'm only curious as to what Rick thinks, and I'm sure he can speak for himself.'

She turned to look at Rick, who was surveying the scene from behind the protective glint of his pale Chablis. He remained silent.

'I'm sorry if it seems a little forceful, but believe me, I'm only curious, and am not going to sit in judgement on your answer – whatever, it may be. So, if you would rather not answer, fine. No skin off my nose.'

Rick smiled. She's certainly a fiery spirit, he thought to himself. 'Ultimately, I'm happy enough to reply – and yes, Lucie, you are right – I was avoiding the question.'

He paused, took another sip of wine and looked straight back at her. Her eyes had narrowed almost imperceptibly. Was she savouring her triumph in forcing an answer out of him, or was it an anticipation of what he might say, he wondered.

'I am against it. It seems to me that no matter how you look at it. No matter what sense there might be in protecting people's ethnicity and tribal lore, there is ultimately no justification in keeping a constitution that enshrines the moral, political and economic clout of one group over all the others. I feel it is evil, as it has kept the greater part of this nation repressed, uneducated, and without the vote, where a greater potential could have been realised all along.'

'Do you know what apartheid means?' asked Tom.

'Separateness, or something like that?'

'Separate development.'

'Yeah well, be that as it may, as I said, I essentially feel the system is evil. I feel the development of the white community has been at the expense of the majority of blacks.'

'Do you feel that this nation would be where it is today had the blacks taken over?'

'Where do you feel the nation is today? I would suggest it is in a hell of a mess. Do you feel – for instance – that not even having SAA being able to fly to the US or Australia; that companies like IBM, Coke and others have pulled out; that all sorts of embargoes and sanctions apply; that your passport cannot get you into many countries; that your beloved Springboks cannot play rugby or cricket except against themselves… constitutes being anywhere at all?'

Tom frowned with irritation. 'What I meant was … I mean, I didn't mean it like that. You saw the airports. You've briefly seen the roads and the development here. You know about the high medical standards, the massive mining achievements, the almost total self-sufficiency of the Republic, and the massive military and economic clout. With all the problems of this continent, here at least is a country that functions, no matter how flawed it may be.'

'Yeah, I agree. South Africa has gone far, and undoubtedly the whites have played a part …'

'A massive part!'

'Okay, a massive part, in the development of this country. But, it all needed the good fortune of finding the wealth below the soil, as well as the labour of the blacks.'

'That is *kak*! This country would have progressed fine without the blacks. We would have needed more immigrants that's all. What is more, the wealth below the ground has in part been responsible for the massive influx of blacks from outside, looking for work. If the English had not developed the mines, the hard work and intelligence of the whites who were the pioneers here would have still brought this country up.'

'Questionable, that last bit, as it is mere conjecture that the whites would be as well off without the massive wealth generated by the minerals. Anyway, more immigrants or not, the issue isn't that. The blacks are here, and always have been.'

'That also is not true. The Xhosa and Zulus are Bantu-Nilotic peoples that have drifted from further north, and have a similarity to the Ndebele of Rhodesia, the Watusi of Burundi, the Wagogo of Tanzania, the Masai and Samburu of Kenya, and others in Southern Sudan.'

Rick shrugged his shoulders and grinned, feeling he should set the tone to a lighter level. 'Well, you certainly know your African peoples!'

'Damn right I do,' exclaimed Tom grinning broadly. He sensed he had gained the upper hand. 'One thing for sure, you want to know your enemy.'

'Is that how you see them – as your enemy?'

'I certainly don't feel that Gorbachev poses any real threat to us here. The threat is from the black hordes on our doorstep, most of whom are committed Marxists.'

'And the black hordes – as you put it – within the door? Because the headcount would give them a high percentage in the numbers game.'

'The way I see it is this,' said Tom, obviously warming to his topic. 'Rhodesia held off the world for ten years after Ian Smith declared UDI. They were only two hundred and fifty thousand whites, up against the Shona and Ndebele of Mugabe and Nkomo respectively. The kaffirs – sorry, blacks – numbered seven million. That's a ratio of twenty-eight to one, and they still held on for ten years, and only really capitulated with SA's withdrawal of support which collapsed the economy. The UN imposed world sanctions were ineffective. Those Selous Scouts were the world's best.'

Rick wondered whether he should ask the basic question, could they have won, or would it have continued as a senseless slaughter, till demography changed the scene once and for all?

Tom looked across at Rick who watched him impassively, before continuing. 'Well, here the mathematics is this. We have five and a half million whites against something like twenty four million blacks, which makes it closer to a 'one against five' ratio. What is more, the Afrikaner has twice the determination of the softer Anglos up in Rhodesia.' He leaned back with obvious delight and pleasure at the speech he had just delivered.

Rick continued to look at him in silence. He was aware of how great the gulf between them had become. At school they had debated the issue, and had basically both felt that the system wouldn't work and was morally indefensible, but that was obviously not what Tom felt and believed now.

'Well, Tom, I've come to listen and learn, and I guess it is possible that I might change my mind. This trip is to relax, have a holiday and see for myself.'

'I hope you don't change your mind, because I agree with you,' said Lucinda. She had remained out of the debate till then, even though she had effectively instigated the exchange between the two friends. 'The system doesn't work. It has led to massive injustices being committed. These in turn have fuelled hatred and mistrust. The sooner the word apartheid, along with the system, is relegated to the trash bins of history, the better.'

'Lucie thinks like many of the Anglos up in Rhodesia thought. The problem with her thinking is that many of them regret it now that it has become a Marxist one party state. The lucky ones got out to SA, England or Australia, before Mugabe took over the reigns of office. If the real truth be known, apartheid is alive and well in many places in the world, the only difference being that it's not enshrined by law, but by economics and geography.'

Lucinda looked about to answer, but decided not to. Instead she turned to Rick, and smiled. 'As you can see, it's an emotive issue, and even divides this household. I personally find it hard to argue with Tom, as I feel that he very rapidly gets out of control. Since I started this topic, I shall now end it, and change tack. Tell me about yourself some more. You mentioned a lady – Trish, was it?'

'No, Tash. Short for Natasha.'

'Why don't you tell us about her? Are you guys a serious item? Are you really keen on her?'

Rick caught Tom's eye. He was looking straight at him with interest. Rick sighed and said, 'Okay. I'll talk about her, though like in all situations such as this, it's really hard to know where to begin!'

'Well! Are you really serious about her?' asked Lucie.

'Hey, Lucie! What is this, the seven o'clock quiz?' laughed Tom.

'There is a sort of yes and no to the answer,' replied Rick. 'I feel that in many ways we are well suited, but there are lingering doubts about her, in me at least. Curiously, though we talk long and deep about a whole range of topics and issues, we never really seem to talk about our relationship, or our feelings for one another. So … I'm unable to say how she really views me, or the relationship.' He sipped pensively at his wine. 'Somehow, I just feel that we are not destined to be together in the long run, though I have enjoyed my time with her. She's pretty, energetic and great fun to be with. I hope she waits for me!'

They all reflected on Rick's words. Another disc came on, and they were all treated to Schubert's *Ave Maria*. The music soothed them, and the silence continued.

Rick wondered about Natasha, and whether she would in fact be waiting for him when he returned, and guessed that she probably would be. He asked himself if it really was what he hoped for, and realised that the answer had to be no. There was an easy convenience to her, but if he was really truthful about her to himself, he wanted something different, even if he did not know quite what it was. Perhaps it was just another lady, more zest or excitement to his life?

'You certainly have a heavy frown on your face! I hope we haven't upset you in any way?' enquired Tom.

'No, no. Just a combination of things, the fresh air, the jet lag, and the great wine. I must confess that my first impressions of South African wines are that they are A1!'

'Just like our rugby teams. You should see how the Transvaal teams play. I'm sure the Springboks are the world's best!'

Lucinda rose to her feet. 'Well, guys, it seems to me that it's my turn to return to the kitchen. If we are to eat tonight, and before I become intoxicated with this heady wine, I shall exit and leave you to your sport.'

As she reached the doorway to the verandah she turned and remarked, 'Do you realise that the English historian Philip Toynbee fifty years ago commented on rugby? He said that if a bomb were to blow up the stand of spectators in Twickenham on a Rugby International day, right-wing politics and Fascism would be wiped out in England? How's that for something to chew on?' She laughed and went indoors, shutting the sliding door behind her.

'She's always got some sharp comment,' said Tom shaking his head disapprovingly.

Smart girl, thought Rick. She knows her history and has

thrown that in as a barb for Tom. 'I'd like to see some games and check them out for myself. Personally I don't believe they could beat the Kiwis!'

'*Kak*, man! We would walk all over them,' laughed Tom.

Rick smiled. I wonder, he thought. Maybe one day we'll see.

Rodrigo's memories:

...He remembered well how he had heard the voices in the little hut. They were raised in anger. His was a deep growl, full of menace. Hers had a shrill and indignant tone, with a touch of hysteria. He had no idea who they were.

His curiosity mounted to such an unbearable pitch that he decided to sneak out and see for himself what the commotion was all about. He was eight years old, small and quick on his feet. He had been working on repairing his mother's manioc sacks.

He looked around, and being sure that he was not being observed, slipped off and skirted his home via the ragged and messy banana trees, heading for the noise.

The couple were indoors, and were obviously becoming more heated with each other. They sounded drunk, he thought. He had heard grown ups talk in such a fashion before when they had drunk a lot of pembe, the fermented beer that tasted so bitter. They appeared to be arguing about her not wanting to give him something. He wondered why she didn't just give the object to him, rather than risk him becoming even more cross. I'd give it to him, and steal it back when he falls asleep, he thought triumphantly.

There was a sudden loud crash as a chair was smashed against the side of the hut. A loud scream followed, and then the sounds of slaps. Hard and vicious, they were like mini explosions. A gasp and then the door flew open.

A young woman ran out, her nose bloodied, and clutching her dress up to her bosom. With a shock, he realised it was Sofia. She ran right past him as he instinctively crouched. The man was soon also out of the hut. He looked enraged. His black face glistened in the heat. He was clutching his undone trousers around his waist.

He swore and gave chase. Sofia glanced back and screamed. He soon caught up with her and threw her to the ground. He started to beat her around the face. She was begging him to stop and screaming with fear and pain as the blows reigned down.

Awakening from the mesmeric state the scene had induced, Rodrigo jumped up and ran as fast as he could to the police station. Sofia was his aunt. Younger than his mother by many years, she was pretty, unmarried and popular. She had always been generous to her little nephew.

He got to the station and burst in. The two white policemen were playing cards and looked up casually through a cloud of cigarette smoke as he came in. Rodrigo gasped out his message that somebody was beating up his aunt in a little road, not far from where they were.

They jumped up and, grabbing rifles, followed Rodrigo to the scene. A small crowd of curious onlookers was watching from the shade of the trees. Rodrigo could not make out precisely what was going on, except that the man was on top of his aunt, who had her legs up in the air. Her dress was in shreds around her.

Rodrigo covered his face, he was sure that the man was killing her. He heard the policeman nearest him mutter something in Portuguese about animals.

One policeman stayed under cover, whilst the other walked up to the offender and kicked him viciously from behind. There was a cry of anger and rage as the man swung round off his aunt. He looked stunned for a minute and then jumped up and pulled his trousers up. He screamed abuse at the policeman, who backed off about five metres.

He then leant down and grabbing his aunt viciously by the hair, hauled her to her knees. He was still screaming abuse.

The first shot hit him in the chest. He looked surprised as the impact struck and somehow, perhaps instinctively seeking cover, pulled Sofia up as he fell back. The second shot spun her head around before it hit his neck. Both fell back with a thud. There was total silence before a loud piercing shriek went up.

Rodrigo crouched in fear. It was so very frightening. He realised it was his mother, and she was rushing forward to her sister.

He became galvanised into action and ran to join his obviously distressed mother. He saw that Sofia was still alive, but all her jaw and nose was a red and hideous mess. She was gargling incomprehensibly. He tried to hug his mother, more out of fear and confusion than to try and comfort her, but was brushed aside.

He noticed the policeman looking down at the bodies. He called out to his colleague that the medics should be fetched, as the whore was still alive, and the rapist was dead. Rodrigo listened in disbelief as he mentioned that it was a pity, as she used to be pretty.

His mother jumped up and tried to hit the policeman, who just pushed her away. He said words to the effect that they were both black offenders, and what was everybody getting so worked up about.

Honour was at stake here, and Rodrigo jumped up and started to pummel the legs of the policeman, screaming that he had killed them. The rifle butt swung round and sent him flying. He was knocked unconscious.

When he came round he was on the mattress in his hut, with a wet cloth around a huge swelling on the side of his head. The pain was terrible.

His aunt underwent emergency surgery and lived, but committed suicide about three months later. The facial disfigurement was dreadful, and she never came out of her deep depression.

Rodrigo hated the white man, and especially the Portuguese, ever since.

Capetown, South Africa

The noise could be heard from the road. There was a steady rhythmic beat coming from the nightclub. The Co-Zee was pulsating to the beat of Chaka's Clan, a Natal based group that included some Zulu musicians. A small group of young men were congregated around the two burly bouncers at the entrance, probably hoping for a free pass into the dark and inviting sea of people that swirled around inside.

Lucinda had linked her arm around each of her two companions. Both looked happy and walked with confidant strides toward the entrance. It was a Friday night and at Tom's insistence they were off to have a jol.

Tom led them through the crowd, paid the 10-rand entrance cost for each of them and pulled them toward the nearest bar. It was hard to talk above the din around them. He obtained drinks and then passed a Castle Beer back to Rick and a vodka and orange to Lucinda. He joined Rick with a beer.

'Well? What do you think?' he asked Rick.

Rick nodded his approval. 'It looks pretty good to me. I like the music!'

'They are pretty much a clone group,' said Lucinda. 'Have you heard of Johnny Clegg and Savuka.'

'Yes, but I can hardly claim to know them. They had a big hit a couple of years ago. Is that right?'

'Ja. It was called Third World Child. Here in SA, they have become really big with the youth – especially the liberal whites – as their message is very much an anti-establishment one.' She glanced at Tom. 'He doesn't like them for their words, but agrees the music is good! I think they are really good, with both the music and the words. What is more they have a good racial mix.'

'Hey, Rick. Take a shufti!'[23] interrupted Tom. He indicated two girls dancing.

Rick looked across at the girls. They were both whites, as were all of the clientele. Both girls were dressed in tight black dresses and had on dark red lipstick. They were doing an imitation of the Robert Palmer girls in the video clip doing 'Simply Irresistible'. Their duo act was sufficiently arresting for various other dancers to have cleared a space for them. They certainly moved well, thought Rick to himself. He particularly liked the look of the skinny girl, who had a sultry and moody expression.

He continued to watch her, and watch her pelvic thrusts and gyrations, and inadvertently caught her eye. She held his gaze for a moment with a haughty insolence but then turned away dismissively. He also turned back to his hosts, feeling a slight flush of embarrassment that he had been so fascinated.

Tom had his arm around Lucie and was grinning at him. 'You like the look of the SA girls, I can see that!'

'Yep. They are a nice pair of beauties out there.'

---

[23]Slang for 'look'.

'Which one do you like the most?'

'What? Of the two dancing?'

'Uh-huh,' grunted Tom.

Rick looked back as they finished dancing. The slimmer one was smiling, but soon returned to her smouldering Spanish look. Various men were crowding around them. 'The skinny one I guess,' murmured Rick in answer to Tom.

'Funny…'

Rick looked back at him. 'Funny? Why?'

'I would have been sure that you would have gone for the other one with the bigger tits. She's more curvaceous.'

'Cut it out, you two. Let him be, Tom,' said Lucinda in a humorous way. 'Rick. Be a gentleman. Take me for a dance. This one is a shy dancer!' she added, indicating Tom.

They handed their drinks to Tom and moved onto the dance floor. They danced to a steady African beat. Rick smiled at Lucie, and was entertained. She danced well, with a natural flow to her body. He wondered if she exercised daily, or had an aerobics workout routine.

He looked back to see if Tom was watching them, but in the melee of people, he appeared to have disappeared. He wondered about what was going through his mind. He seemed inordinately obsessed with Rick's sexual well-being, and at times seemed as if he was wanting to see him score, to make it with a woman. Was he imagining this, wondered Rick, or did these thoughts really inhabit Tom's conscious mind? He felt sure that it was important to Tom, to have Rick really enjoy himself whilst he was his guest in his home, but he also couldn't help feeling that a section of this was specifically to do with Rick having a partner. He wondered if this was purely a desire to see him in action, or a deeper distrust based on the events of their summer holiday. A shiver of unease swept through him, and he dismissed the thought from his mind.

'Rand?' shouted Lucie above the noise.

Rick looked puzzled. 'rand?'

She moved closer. 'You know. As in penny. Penny for your thoughts. Here we have rands!'

'Oh. Sorry, I was a bit slow there.'

'You weren't slow. You were far away. That's why the rand.

But don't worry – you don't have to answer.'

'Well, it wasn't anything really. You dance really well.'

Lucinda guffawed with laughter.

Slightly piqued, Rick inclined his head enquiringly.

Lucinda spoke. 'Listen, Rick, whatever you were thinking, I am really sure it wasn't anything to do with my dancing, for if it was, it appeared to be upsetting you, and that's not complimentary! Come on let's go and get our drinks. Can you see Tom?'

Rick felt unsettled. She seemed uncannily perceptive. He felt as if he'd been caught doing something bad. He saw Tom over by the corner of the bar. He indicated to Lucinda that he had located him, and led her in his direction. Tom seemed very serious, and lost in thought.

'You okay?' enquired Rick.

'Ja, ja. So sorry, man. I was miles away!'

'Rand?'

Tom laughed. 'I can see you have been around Lucie. I suppose I was thinking of the trip up to the Kruger Park. I'm really sure you'll enjoy it, and I could do with a break.'

'I'm really happy to be here, and believe me I'm really looking forward to the trip. It not often one has private guides!'

They all sipped their drinks contentedly. Rick surveyed the people around him. They all looked like the yuppie set from London, with a slightly different emphasis with the clothes. Most of the young men sported moustaches, and had a clean-cut look about them, almost as if they were all tennis players, healthy and tanned. Compared to the pasty pale colours of the sun-starved yuppies of London, this lot looked sickeningly healthy, thought Rick.

Tom led Lucie off towards the dance floor, grinning broadly. A frown crossed Rick's brow, as he wondered what Tom was up to. At that very moment he noticed the skinny girl whom he had been observing earlier, moving through the crowd in his general direction. She stopped in front of him and smiled.

'I saw ya watching me.'

'Yeah. You dance well,' said Rick, squirming with embarrassment.

'Thanks for the drink. Did the Jaime tell ya I like Rum and Coke?'

'Jaime?' Rick felt lost. He frowned with confusion fearing a dreadful mistake had been made.

'The big spider behind the bar.'[24]

'Yeah. Yeah, the spider,' mumbled Rick, wondering what she was talking about.

'Anyway, I know your name is Rick, and that you're a tourist – from England. Did ya ask the Jaime about me?'

'No, not really. I never got around to it,' he said as it dawned on him that Tom had set him up.

'Well, do ya want to know?'

'Yes,' answered Rick uncomfortably. He cursed Tom.

'Me name's Chrissie, short for Christina. I'm a door bitch.'

'A what?'

'A door bitch.' She looked at him quizzically.' Haven't ya heard that expression before?'

'No. I haven't.'

'You're not local, hey? Well. I hang around the door, in order to attract customers. Annabel and meself sometimes end up on the dance floor, doing a little number. That's when we become floor bitches!' She chuckled and took a sip from her drink.

Rick was amused. She had such a broad accent, and seemed so incredibly down-to-earth. Her sexual allure was almost overpowering; there was almost a heady musk in the air. He felt drawn to her, but doubted she felt anything at all for him. After all he mused, the function of a floor bitch must be to entertain the customers. She had finished her drink.

'Like another drink?'

'You trying to get me drunk or something?'

'No. I'm just offering another drink if you wish to join me.'

'Join you? Are you asking me out?'

'No. I'm sorry if I'm not making myself clear,' stammered Rick. 'I meant join me for a drink. Here! Where we are standing.'

She smiled provocatively up at him, and slipping her hand inside his shirt, drew him closer. 'Na. Can't. I can only have one

---

[24]Rock spider – slang and derogatory term for Afrikaner.

drink with a customer.' She watched his reaction, and when he shrugged showing that it was a pity, she added, 'So ya see I can't join you. I finish at midnight, though. Ya seem real nice. Can I join ya for a drink then?'

Rick grinned. 'Delighted if you would.'

'Before I go back to work… give me your hands.'

Rick looked mystified but brought his hands up. She glanced at them. 'No ring. Not married, eh?'

'No, not married.'

'Can't stand married creeps out for a screw on the side. Where are you staying?'

'Llandudno. With friends.'

'Transport?'

'No. I came with them.'

'No problem. I've got me car. Maybe we can go someplace – with or without yer friends – 'kay?'

'Sure. Look forward to it.'

'See ya later,' she said and turned back toward the dance floor. A slow number was playing. In no time Rick saw her in the arms of a burly man, who looked like a slightly shorter version of Schwartzenegger. He was nuzzling his head into her neck. As she turned, he noticed she was still chewing gum and looked decidedly bored.

Tom and Lucinda were dancing very close to Chrissie and her partner. Rick looked at his watch; it was already quarter to eleven. He felt ready for an adventure.

As Tom led Lucinda back to Rick, he was grinning from ear to ear. 'Like her?' he enquired, and laughed.

Rick smiled. 'Bastard!'

'What the hell are you two up to?' demanded Lucinda. 'Rick, please fill me in.'

'I'll answer for Rick,' said Tom. 'I watched him chatting up the skinny girl he was ogling earlier, and I find it amusing.'

'That's not the whole picture, but essentially that is correct.'

'So, where has she gone?' asked Lucinda.

'Well, I guess that here we may have a divergence of ways. She gets off duty at twelve.' He looked at his watch again in a reflex action. 'I'm sufficiently amused at this to want to stay and see where it leads me, but I'll cancel it all if you all had other plans.'

Lucie looked very amused. 'Rick, our plans are easy. Maybe we should keep you company till then and then leave you to it without us being in the way?'

'Personally I'd prefer if you stayed and were introduced as my friends.'

'I'm sure you'll be more comfortable alone. We really wouldn't want to cramp your style. You know our address, and I'll give you my key now, so if you get stuck, just get a taxi back. If you are really stuck, ring us!'

Rick thanked her and pocketed her keys. He looked back at Tom, who was staring straight at him. What are you thinking, Tom? he asked himself.

Lucinda's memories:

...I had been drifting for quite a while when I met him. There had been various relationships, each with its own merits and drawbacks, and each still lacking a magic ingredient that could really fire me. Looking back, it always later seemed that they were notable for what they lacked, rather than for what they contributed.

To be quite honest, this particular experience was so intense, and so brief, that I have never really considered it real. It was like a mirage, so it doesn't count as real. In fact when I've talked about previous relationships or people, I have consistently left this one out, as its fire burnt me at the time, and only the singed areas in my brain give any indication of the heat that must have passed through. This singeing was purely internal, so no visible sign ever showed.

I met him at a cocktail party, given by my family. There were lots of high society and rich people there. Some I knew from the newspapers, or by reputation, and others had been around at our house as dinner guests at different times in the past.

Not long before this particular evening, I had terminated a relationship, which had slowly drifted into ennui and routine. The vitality and spirit that the guy had shown when we had started off had long ago fizzled out. The only reason I decided to go to the party was that I had flown up to see my folks, and as their guest, felt a moral obligation to do the family thing. It meant that while I was there, I could also perhaps catch up with some old friends. They talked me into staying for the cocktail party, rather than spending the evening with my friends, as I would have preferred. I told them I would go out later.

It turned out as ghastly as I had always remembered my father's cocktail parties to be. I wandered around making small talk and chatting to the guests. I wasn't really enjoying it, and it seemed as if there was at least a twenty-year age gradient between myself and the youngest person there. Some of these older married men leered at me lasciviously, and one even attempted to pinch me as soon as his wife was looking the other way.

I had decided to leave early, in spite of having made promises to my folks that I would stay till at least the first guests were starting to leave. Then I caught his eye. He was standing in a group, dressed in a grey suit. He had quite a dapper and trim look, with a pale complexion, and pale fair hair. His eyes were sinister, totally cold and calculating, an icy cold blue. I guessed he was about forty-five. I hadn't seen him before.

I held his gaze. He was watching me intensely, and even though he was in a group of people, was obviously not paying any attention to them. Feeling coquettish, I decided that two could play this game.

I leaned against the wall and kept my eyes riveted to his. I must confess that I was getting edgy, and wanted to avert my gaze. I felt goose bumps all up my back. His look was so intense. He tilted his wineglass toward his lips and almost imperceptibly inclined his head to indicate a toast.

Suddenly, someone standing directly in front of me and asking me a question interrupted my reverie and steady gaze. It took me a few moments to return to earth, and answer whatever was being asked of me. I moved away as soon as I could and cast my eyes back to where he had been standing, and to my horror he was gone.

It must seem ludicrous that I felt nervous and even experienced palpitations when I could not spot him. I couldn't believe I had lost him. I calmed myself down and told myself that this was all ridiculous. I didn't know who he was, and he was probably just another married and horny male on the prowl, probably without his spouse.

I decided I would leave, as I had originally planned, but something – and God knows it's difficult to explain this – something made me decide to go one last round, to see if I could find him. When I couldn't, I felt devastated, totally pissed off! Inexplicably, I started to go round again, and still couldn't find him.

As I strode through the lounge again doing a final circuit and scanning the clusters of people, the door to the verandah opened. He was standing outside, holding the door open. With a flick of his head he indicated that I should go out and join him outside. I hesitated, and then to my own surprise, I followed him out.

We walked along in silence in the dark. He then stopped, turned to me and looked straight at me again. The silence was unbearable. I again I felt a heady cocktail of rising excitement laced with an animal fear. I couldn't take it any longer, so I made some inane comment to the effect that it was hot.

He didn't answer immediately, but took out a pen, and scribbled something on it. He handed it to me. It read, *Carlton Towers Hotel, suite 601, tonight.*

I flushed with confusion and embarrassment. I had never experienced such an approach. I then had a wave of righteous indignation, and turned to walk back inside. He still hadn't spoken.

His hand shot out and grabbed my arm, with a firm and hard grip. There was no mistaking the strength behind the grip.

He held me like that for a moment, before he said, 'I've got a wonderful air-conditioned room, a cold bottle of Möet, time, and a desire to hear you talk about your first ... experience.'

We stayed frozen in our gestures. His voice was deep, and foreign. It was calm and measured. He knew exactly what he was doing. I spun around to face him.

'What the bloody hell makes you think I'd come? I know nothing about you.'

'I don't ... but if you do, it is because of that.'

I must have looked puzzled. He explained, 'You are right. I don't know if you'll come. If, however, you do, it is only because you know nothing about me, and you are a gambler.'

I felt bewildered. He then said he would be rejoining the guests, as he would be leaving in another ten minutes. He guided me back in and then promptly left me. I didn't see him go, and remained in a fuzzy aura of muddled thoughts.

The evening suddenly dragged very badly, for I couldn't concentrate on anything except this strange and cryptic encounter. I had to be honest, it certainly was unusual and had a strange allure, but there was an element of extreme repulsion, which was a lame recognition that he regarded me as a sexual object – though it's strange to admit how thrilling that in itself can be! How contradictory my thoughts were.

I left when I saw some of the first few guests leaving, and got into my mother's little VW Golf. I drove toward my friends' house, but at the crossroad where I should have turned left, I kept going straight. My heart was palpitating really fast. I was ludicrously excited and yet simultaneously annoyed with myself.

I went into the underground car park associated with the hotel, and up into the lobby. There were few people about, as it was late at night. The receptionist looked across at me, but I went straight by her to the elevator, entered and rode to the sixth floor.

When I found his room I again felt a wave of panic, for I didn't even know his name. I fumbled for his card; it read *Bjorn Laerum, Volvo Aircraft Division*, followed by an address in Stockholm, Sweden.

I knocked. When he opened, I entered the luxurious room in a state of high anxiety. He was quiet, helping me remove my coat, and deferentially pouring me a drink of bubbly.

We spent an hour talking, and somehow he did manage to get me talking about my first experience – and old Erasmus watching it all! Bjorn kept gazing me all the while with his cold Nordic eyes.

He then came out with an order. It was direct and insensitive. It seemed out of place. He just told me to strip to my underclothes, just like that. It was totally unexpected. It was a non sequitur. When I objected he added that he wanted me to do as he said, and then reassuringly capped it all with, 'No harm will befall you.'

I stared at him feeling a rising animal excitement that I felt sure was betraying me. I stood, and while he dimmed the lights, stripped as I had been told. I kept telling myself that I must be truly mad.

He came over to me in the dark and, using a silk scarf, tied my wrists together behind my back. I didn't object or resist; I just felt a sense of belonging, of being part of his plan, a pawn to be moved, a part of the game. He then undid my bra clip and gently touched me. I became aroused. I felt ready for anything, and crazy though it may seem, I felt like he was my master, my controller in this sexual chess.

He made love to me, and for the next couple of hours I experienced a frenzied sexual passion, like I have never experienced before.

I was tied in different positions, got slapped and beaten, but the really peculiar part is that I wanted it all. I even went as far as asking him to hurt me! It is truly unbelievable the intensity of that weird and kinky session with Bjorn. All my rational behaviour went straight out the window, for I behaved with a wanton and depraved craving for further indulgences and humiliation. Any embellishment he could add to the session I eagerly sought.

He really didn't talk much or reveal much of himself, other than to express himself, with great ability, sexually. I was so very turned on by him, so confused at what had happened, and so ashamed that I had proved myself too weak to resist or influence the course of events. I was amazed at how low I had sunk, and blush even at the thought of what I said and did. There is no way I can explain my conduct or rationalise it, except to say that somehow the Pandora's box that was opened was a real surprise to me.

When Zeus gave that box to Pandora, he knew it contained all human ills. By helping in my self-discovery and opening that box, Bjorn allowed me to open up a section of inner self that I sometimes feel would have been better to leave dormant. It has made me compare, search and evaluate all relationships that I have since had against the yardstick that the evening provided. This is not meant to be a panegyric to him, as I'm sure Satan has danced with him.

Bjorn asked me to come back for either or both of his two remaining evenings. I said I would, but in the cold light of day, the next morning I knew I couldn't. I took off and went out to a friend's farm near Ventersdorp, and stayed there, totally distracted and distant, and in a state of considerable confusion. I did phone him, and when his voice came on the phone I panicked and hung up. I never saw him again.

It is a difficult exercise trying to evaluate all this, but I am sure that in the equilibrium that I've tried to maintain in my life, with basic goodness or kindness reigning supreme, there was a severe upset that night, for the devil had gained more than a foothold. The door had been opened when old Erasmus had watched, but was held ajar by Bjorn. This was no Achilles heel, this was a Trojan Horse, that has filled my subconscious with devils that subvert and undermine from within.

Mozambique.

They had been travelling for a few days now, and all were beginning to feel the strain of the journey. Nobody actually complained, but they were beginning to look depressed and sullen. They needed to rest and eat well before continuing the journey.

The dry bush yielded little in the way of food, and even water seemed scarce to come by. The last two wells had been severely polluted with dead game, so nobody had risked drinking.

They had noticed the fire up ahead. The smoke curled lazily up into the sky, before being dispersed by winds at higher levels. It meant that they were approaching a hamlet of some sort, or a command post that Frelimo had set up in the countryside to guard vital installations.

Rodrigo estimated that they were only about a kilometre away from the settlement. He decided to take the oldest man, Joaquim, as well as Mopete and Nkosi. The rest he ordered to stay hidden and rest in the shade.

The four set off towards the smoke, in single file and in silence. After a little while, Rodrigo talked quietly of his plan as they walked. They would use a previously successfully tested ruse, and alter it, if needed, as the encounter unfolded. It was risky, but they were getting desperate.

When they were only about three hundred metres away, Rodrigo and Nkosi slunk off to one side, and running in a crouched position rapidly disappeared into the dense bush. Joaquim and Mopete squatted in the shade of a tree and waited in silence.

After a wait of approximately a quarter of an hour, they both rose and headed off along the faint track toward the smoke. Mopete walked behind Joaquim. They soon entered a clearing, where all bushes had been removed, and all the trees had their lower branches cut away for firewood.

They shuffled on nervously, Mopete close behind Joaquim. Up ahead of them was a little shack with smoke trailing out from its small tin chimney, and on the ground in the shade sat two uniformed soldiers, absorbed in a game of cards. They were laughing quietly. Both wore the pale green fatigues of Frelimo guards.

One of them turned and spotted Joaquim approaching. He dived for his gun with a warning to his companion. Both rolled on the dusty soil and within seconds were aiming their assault rifles at the pair.

'*Tranquilo. Tranquilo*, easy, easy!'[25] shouted Joaquim raising his hands. 'We come in peace. We are alone.' As he approached closer, he turned himself around slowly. 'We have no weapons.'

'What do you want, old man?' shouted the younger soldier.

'Trade. Barter for food.'

'You have pesos?'

'No.'

'Then you have nothing to barter!' shouted the older soldier, and followed this with a string of curses and abuse. Neither soldier had put down his gun.

'I have something. Can we talk?'

There was a silence as the soldiers pondered this last statement. Finally the older one relented. 'Okay. Come no closer than ten metres and show us what you have. Any funny business, old man, and we shall blast you right out the world. Understood?'

Joaquim nodded sagely and shuffled forward with Mopete

---

[25]Portuguese for easy, calm.

close behind. When they had reached a distance of approximately ten metres from the soldiers they stopped. The soldiers barked out a warning to advance no further. They sat on the hard dry soil, still directly in the sights of the rifles of the soldiers.

'So, old man. Tell us what you have.'

'Can I tell you what I want? I want food for us, as we are all alone, and our village was destroyed by the MNR.[26] There is only my daughter and myself,' wailed Joaquim.

'We have little supplies. If you have nothing to trade, you move on. You cannot stay. We cannot feed all beggars that come here.' The tone was less hostile, as the soldiers were obviously recovering from their fright and felt less threatened.

'You are alone?'

The soldiers looked at Joaquim in silence. The younger one eventually spoke up. 'This is not your business. Go, old man, before we get cross.'

Joaquim turned to Mopete and gestured to her to rise. She did so slowly, with no sudden movements that might upset the edgy soldiers. When she was standing, Joaquim also got up, and went to stand beside her. 'I have my daughter to trade. She is a fine and young woman, who can satisfy any man, and well practised in the arts of love. She can make you happy for this afternoon – or for the whole night if you wish – in exchange for food.'

The soldiers appeared to be considering the offer, for the younger one had lowered his rifle and was no longer peering at them through the sights.

'What is more, what she has to offer as a woman is great – and – she is clean.' Joaquim slowly circled Mopete as he talked. He then lifted her rather tattered tee shirt over her head as she obligingly lifted her arms, revealing her naked upper torso. In spite of her youth and skinny appearance, she had large, full breasts. Her dark skin glistened in the bright sunlight. He continued to circle her. He then unclipped her baggy shorts and let them drop to her feet. She stepped out of them. A brief and soiled pair of red panties was all that remained on her. He looked back at the soldiers and could read the lust in their eyes; they were

---

[26]Movement of National Resistance, also called Renamo.

both entranced by the spectacle unfolding before them.

'We could kill you here and now and still have her you stupid old man!' said the younger soldier.

Joaquim nodded his head sagely. 'I know, but why bother? Why go to the trouble? You are not the MNR, and I present no threat – nor does my daughter. I appeal to you by the spirits of your ancestors.'

'Why would any man trade his very own daughter?' asked the older soldier. 'It sounds suspicious to me. What sort of man can you be?'

'A starving man, a man down on his luck,' whined Joaquim.

A silence followed. Joaquim looked back at Mopete. 'Like her mother, she is full,' he said, cupping and squeezing her breasts. He then pulled her panties down onto her thighs and, grabbing her pubic hair, added, 'She also has a good furrow. If you are potent men, you will enjoy her.' His slightly rounded shoulders shook as he laughed soundlessly, as she pulled her panties back up. 'Can we trade?' he repeated, with no hint of mirth in his voice. 'I only need food, water, and if you can spare some – cigarettes.'

'Come here, old man,' said the younger soldier. He rose from the ground, still keeping his rifle fixed on Joaquim. He squinted suspiciously as Joaquim shuffled forward.

When Joaquim was about a metre away he commanded him to stop and then ordered him to extend his right wrist. He attached handcuffs to the wrist and warily led him back to the tree, where he clipped the free end to an iron ring that protruded from a metal shaft sunk into the tree. The tree had obviously served as a makeshift prison in the past.

'Any move from you and we shall finish the girl, before we make sure that you have no further children. You understand?' He chuckled coarsely as he leered at Mopete. 'Of course, if she is good, you will eat.'

The other soldier was standing with his gun trained on Mopete, still looking a little cautious. His companion strode up to Mopete, and grabbing her by the hair, pulled her back into the shade near the entrance to the hut. He forced her to her knees, and unzipping his fly, withdrew his limp phallus. He grinned with delight as her lips enveloped him.

'Diego, this is heaven,' he moaned as his face contorted with pleasure. He withdrew suddenly and grabbing her hair again started to drag her inside. 'Help me, Diego! Grab her legs. I want to have this little she-devil of a gift inside. Hurry, compadre.'

Mopete half stumbled forward, as she was pulled inside, with Diego grabbing one leg and in crude desperation, ripping her panties into shreds. They were soon inside, and apart from the chortles of delight from the soldiers, only an occasional whimper could be heard from Mopete. The iron-framed bed springs squeaked as the two soldiers repeatedly took her.

Rodrigo and Nkosi were soon crouched either side of the entrance. On a signal from Rodrigo, they both rushed in. The previous sounds were interrupted by a couple of sharp thuds followed by cries of pain and dismay. There followed a series of muffled groans. Joaquim confidently stared at the entrance to the hut. He felt sure that the two soldiers were not prepared for any attack. Rodrigo came out with an arm protectively around Mopete. She was splattered with blood.

Nkosi followed soon after, with both soldiers shuffling forward on their knees, holding their hands on their heads. They were naked from the waist down. The younger soldier was bleeding down his neck and back from a large scalp wound, whilst the older soldier could barely see through his right eye, which was already very swollen. Both looked frightened. They were ordered to remain as they were, while Rodrigo went back into the hut for a search.

He came back out carrying the clothes of the two hapless soldiers. He removed some keys from the pockets and released Joaquim. He then reattached the handcuffs on the older soldier, pinioning his arms behind his back. The soldier started to whimper. Rodrigo ignored him, and re-entered the hut. He came out with a set of leg-irons and attached these to the younger soldier.

They raided the store, and took some tins, rice, pots and pans. Finding a packet of Camel cigarettes, they all lit one each, and in silence appreciated the smoke. They also took the meagre supplies of bullets for the two seized AK47 rifles, as well as two canteens full of water. One of the guns turned out to be a poor imitation fake which they discarded in disgust. They then sat and ate the bread they found on the table inside. Nobody said a word. Mopete had dressed, rejecting the remnants of her panties.

Rodrigo then questioned the soldiers about where the nearest outposts were, as well as the distance to the Limpopo River. Their relief party was due to arrive in four days' time. They also found out that there was a goat a short distance away.

Nkosi and Rodrigo put on the uniforms of the soldiers.

Joaquim went to retrieve the goat. Mopete found one further set of handcuffs folded near the bed. She ordered the soldiers to their feet, and snapped the cuffs around a wrist of each soldier. They were both sobbing with pain and fear.

Rodrigo restrained Mopete, who had found a knife and seemed on the verge of stabbing the unfortunate men. As it was they would have a difficult and awkward four days till help arrived, without further wounds being inflicted. The Frelimo commanders would be furious at the loss of the weapons.

When the small raiding party started to set off back into the bush, the enormity of their plight set in for the soldiers. They screamed and pleaded to be set free, falling uncomfortably to their knees in their appeal for clemency. They were ignored as Rodrigo and his companions faded into the bush.

'Maybe, with these weapons, we should follow the Limpopo, and cross into the big park they have. Kuga I think it is called,' said Rodrigo to his band. Nobody answered as they wearily trudged back to their group, leading the goat, and carrying all their new supplies.

Rick (Capetown)

He stretched lazily and looked down at Chrissie lying beside him. She looked so peaceful in sleep, and none of the wariness and air of suspicion about her was obvious. She looked young, he thought, and wondered if she really was the twenty-two years of age she claimed to be. Perhaps she said that in order to gain entry to the clubs, or be employed by them.

Her dark hair spread out on the pillow beside her. She was curled up in a foetal position with her knees drawn well up, which increased the look of vulnerable smallness. Her mouth had a slight pout, which even in sleep gave her a slightly sulky look. When this in turn was combined with the dark blue eyeshadow, it gave her a bruised look, which subtly made one want to bruise her more. The brazen sexuality displayed in her lean figure made her difficult to ignore. Rick understood clearly why the owners of the night-club were keen to have her employed there, for even timid patrons would cease being closet predators when they observed her.

Her parents were Portuguese, and had fled south when the independence of Angola seemed inevitable. They had been prosperous merchants in Luanda. They now had a retail business in Durban, but after a massive family row, she had fled to Capetown and was sharing a house with three others.

The night before, they had gone on to various night venues and had definitely drunk too much. Tom and Lucie had left earlier, so had not joined them. It had been a good jol, but the throbbing headache was testimony to the night's excesses. It had been fun, and certainly he had experienced a side of Capetown which he doubted that his friends were aware of. She had snorted coke at one of the little bars, which had been supplied by a thuggish-looking bouncer, who seemed inordinately pleased to see her, and decidedly less happy to see him. Rick had declined the snort, feeling a little uneasy about so openly breaking the law in a repressive society as South Africa's.

At about five in the morning, Rick was starting to feel that he couldn't continue this spree of merriment any longer and that he ought to say he was quitting, when Chrissie too decided that it was time to stop. She had asked about his room, and on hearing that it was the converted servants' quarters, offered to take him home to her place. He readily accepted, not so much out of lust or wanton desire, but out of a more pressing need to put his head down on a pillow, wherever it may be.

Once in her dimly lit and cosy little room, they had made love. She had been the instigator, and had managed to rouse him from the intense and nearly overpowering desire to sleep. They had both collapsed into deep sleep soon after.

Chrissie was curled over his outstretched left arm, which had lost all sensation. His fingers refused to acknowledge any commands. He gently tried to retrieve the arm and return it to life, without waking her in the process. She stirred and moved off him as he tugged, but did not wake.

Rick sat up and massaged his arm. The awful sensations of 'pins and needles' swept over him. He became aware of how thirsty he was. His mouth felt parched. As he sat there, there was an ominous rumble from his stomach, which in turn reminded him that his bladder was straining for relief. All in all, he felt a wreck.

Getting up from the bed, he checked to see if Chrissie had woken. Realising she was still sound asleep, he searched for his jocks and found them jumbled in with his jeans, socks and shoes. He got dressed and stepped outside the room to search for the toilet. He straightaway ran into a scruffy-looking girl in the hallway, who surveyed him in silence, before commenting that he looked rough.

Rick confirmed that he felt awful, and was in search of a toilet as well as a couple of aspirins. She indicated that the toilet was straight ahead, and that aspirins could be found in the kitchen's pantry, near the 'hair of the dog' supplies.

When Rick returned to the room, Chrissie was awake. Her big eyes were surveying him expressionless. A shy look came over her as she blinked, and then took refuge under the covers. Rick had been about to mumble a good morning, but thought the better of it. He sat on the edge of the bed, and carefully pulled back the curtain to look outside. The bright and startling colours dazzled him.

The view was not that spectacular, inasmuch as it was only of the back garden of the house. The lucidly startling colours of the profuse vegetation that had been allowed to grow untended or checked were almost an assault on his senses. The colours were so pure, so genuine, so undiluted, that even the mixtures had an essential quality to them that the muted colours of London could not achieve. The garden and the light were so intensely beautiful, so wildly exuberant, that they mesmerized him with an intoxicating spell. Primary colours were displayed in the wild profuse vegetation. Everything he had seen in the country so far provoked the same response, and that was that the pervasive light and the strong landscape were inescapable, and they in turn created a passion that embroiled all who lived in the land.

'You screw around a lot?' Her voice was drowsy.

Rick turned and looked down at Chrissie. 'No, not really.'

'Yeah? What are you doing here?'

He shuffled slightly on the bed. 'I liked you.'

She stared up at him, and then softening slightly smiled. 'Yeah, I remember liking you too. You bought me drink at the club, before we went to the bars. Right?'

He reddened slightly when he thought of Tom buying the drink, but felt sure it was wiser not to bring up the topic. He nodded his agreement.

'What's ya name?'

'Rick. Rick Graham.'

'You a Brit?'

'Yeah.'

'Don't like 'em much.'

'Why?'

'Soft on the kaffirs. It okay being liberal, like with dagga and that, but with them …what I think ya don't see is that soft is weak in Africa, and I know that for a fact. There is too much…' She trailed off and shrugged her shoulders. 'Anyway. I don't want to talk about it.'

'How are you feeling by the way?'

'Fine. You?'

'Bloody awful. I've got a bad headache.'

'Come and lie down in bed here with me. I've got some tricks up me sleeve which will get rid of it,' she said mischievously. She pulled the sheet covers back, and nodded to the space beside her.

Rick smiled and climbed back into the bed. 'I am genuinely out of action. My head is splitting.'

'What were you thinking – I wanted sex?' She looked irritated as a deep frown furrowed her brow. 'Fucking men! Insane bastards. All of 'em bloody think with their dicks. I was offering a massage.'

'Sorry,' he mumbled.

'*Ja-nee*, it doesn't matter.' She looked at him. 'Flip over, stomach down.'

Chrissie slid up on to his back and straddled him. Her bush nestled comfortably into the small of his back. She started to work on his neck. She was good at it, for Rick soon felt a great relief spread through him. She continued to apply force to all the tensed areas in his neck and shoulders, deftly and efficiently.

'You travelling around?'

'Yeah, thought I'd get about a bit and see the country.'

'Where have you been so far?'

'Actually, I've been nowhere. I've literally only been a week in the country, and all the time has been here in Capetown.'

'Have you much tom?'

'Tom?'

'Tom. Money. Bread.'

'Oh. Enough, I guess.'

'Where ya staying?'

'Llandudno. With friends.'

'Snooty folk?'

'No, not really. I knew him from school in the UK.'

Ja-nee. To live in Llandudno and to go to school in England, ya must be pretty loaded.'

'I didn't say they were poor. I said not snooty.'

'Mostly it's the same.'

Rick shrugged his disagreement. He felt the headache had receded as her fingers had worked on his tense muscles, but assumed that at least a little part of it was from the earlier aspirins. He noticed that her movements had become more sensual and less energetic. Her right hand had now strayed to his lower back and had made a few quick forays below the level of his jocks.

'When are you going travelling?'

'Next weekend, I think.'

'Want a partner? I'll pay me own way. And I can always relieve your headaches, and things.'

Rick chuckled and tried to swivel around, but she asked him to stay put. She deftly removed his jocks and using her legs spread his. The massage continued as she rubbed herself up against his buttocks. He felt her spread his cheeks and then suddenly and unexpectedly she inserted a wet finger into his anus. He reacted with surprise and turned over quickly, dislodging her, so that he was soon over her. He grabbed her wrists fiercely and held them against the mattress. He felt cross but soon found himself distracted by her big-eyed vulnerable look. Instantly he softened, she looked too impish, a little humorous scamp.

'I always like to see a man's reaction. I like it when they become animals,' she giggled.

Rick suppressed a smile. Her eyes were half closed and full of mischievous delight. He could see that Chrissie could make a wonderful travelling companion.

Lucinda (Capetown)

She woke and swept the hair out of her eyes. It hadn't been a late night, for they had returned shortly after leaving Rick at the Co-Zee Nightclub. She wondered how he had fared with the trim little girl he seemed to have latched on to. She wondered if Tom had anything to do with the drink that had been purchased for her, for that would explain the slightly amused hints that Rick appeared to be giving.

She turned over and found to her surprise that Tom had already risen. She glanced at the clock and discovered that it was only seven in the morning. This was most unusual, for Tom never got up early on a weekend, as it was his only chance to lie in.

She sat up to look across at the bathroom, but it was obvious that he wasn't there either. She got up and sneaking a quick glance in the mirror went downstairs. He was sitting in the lounge with his feet up, reading a book. He looked up as she came in.

'Morning, *Liefie*.[27] How is it?'

'Fine. What are you doing up so early?' asked Lucie. 'This is the weekend!'

'Ja. I just didn't sleep too good.'

'Why? What's up?'

'Nothing. Nothing.' He sounded irritated.

'You don't have to talk if you really don't want to, but you yourself have always said that it helps. No?'

---

[27]Love, dear heart.

'Well… it's nothing. I just kind of feel a little pissed off.'

'Why?' Lucie looked at him as she sat in the armchair opposite, and then decided to add, 'With whom?'

He looked up and smiled. He nodded toward the back.

'Our house guest?' she asked. 'What has he done?'

'He's been a little inconsiderate. Don't you think?'

'In what way? I felt he had been charming.'

'Well, you would.'

Lucinda raised her eyebrows in surprise. She had not expected an attack. She simmered in silence for a minute before giving vent to her feelings, 'What the fuck is that meant to mean?'

'I'm sorry. Just don't bug me. It's too bloody early in the morning.'

'No, I'm sorry! I want to know what you meant by that remark.'

'Okay, okay. It seems to me that he spends a lot of time looking at you. What with his charm, his proper English way of talking and all, I guess it would be obvious that you would be affected by his flattery.'

'It strikes me that you assume an awful lot. Yes it struck me that he liked me, but only as a friend. I certainly didn't see him in any other way, and I don't think he did either. What's more, if how he carried on last night is anything to go by, he already has other interests!'

'Ja, I know. I'm sorry, Lucie I don't know why I snapped at you. I have just got up on the wrong side of the bed.'

Lucinda smiled and walked over to him. She stroked the back of his neck. 'I really care for you. You know that don't you?'

He nodded in silence. She looked down at his glum face and continued to stroke his neck. 'I think a good massage would do you good, but first let me get us a coffee, and then I would like you to tell me what exactly is bugging you about Rick. What is more I'd like you to be honest.'

Tom (Capetown)

Honest, thought Tom to himself. Who the hell is really honest these days? Who of all his friends was really honest, or honest to himself? He felt that most of the time he himself was living a lie.

If he really expressed what he felt about the *swartgevaar*, he would be branded as an AWB[28] sympathiser, for everybody espoused more liberal ideas. He couldn't really say what he thought of Rick, either, for it would create a storm of protest. So, the answer to Lucie's request for honesty was that there was no place for such a clean and lofty ideal in such a soiled and earthbound reality.

He didn't really believe that Lucie was being honest with herself either. He felt her liberal ideals were ultimately only a facade, a veneer that hid the unease and fear that lay beneath. He remembered all too well her reaction when they had come out of the motel in Port Elizabeth. There was a Xhosa man sprawled vulnerably over the bonnet of the car, in a drunken sleep. He had defecated beside the car, as well as vomiting all over the windscreen. He lay there snoring raucously, oblivious to the world.

Lucinda had glowered at him, and then had swung her handbag and delivered a mighty blow to his groin. The man had regained consciousness, gasped in pain, and in his doubling-up reaction had toppled off the car. Lucinda had climbed in, swearing and muttering darkly about primitives and Stone Age people. Tom had felt convinced that she wanted him to drive over the hapless man. Tom had found the situation simultaneously both shocking and pleasing. The former because it was so very unladylike, whilst the latter was because it confirmed his suspicions that when it came to the crunch, all the whites were the same. It had been very revealing, even the rooineks[29] were verkrampt.[30] Africa had made them all Afrikaners. Within fifty years of the first Dutch settlers arriving at the Cape, the first generation were already calling themselves Afrikaners, and adapting to the rhythm of the continent and its indigenous peoples and natural hazards. The British had been around a slightly shorter time, but essentially had adapted, and in essence were also Afrikaners.

---

[28]Afrikaner Weerstandsbeweging, a right-wing fringe group espousing Nazi-like flacs, called the Afrikaner Resistance movement.

[29]Rednecks, a term used to describe the British.

[30]Narrow-minded.

He also felt sure that Rick was living a lie, because ultimately the man was a homosexual and was only pretending to be straight or normal. He disliked the fact that Rick had been unable to come to terms with his gay side and declare himself, rather than keep up a pretence and string along a girl as a smokescreen for his true nature. He felt angry that Rick couldn't be honest, for he felt that he himself could understand as a friend. He felt sure that Rick knew about himself when they went on holiday together, but had hidden his true nature from his best friend, in a bid to lure him into a relationship. A surge of indignation went through him. He felt that Rick should be taught a lesson…

Lucinda had returned to the room with the coffees. She placed his on the small table near him, and gently removed the book from his hands. 'Well? Are you going to talk?'

'I don't really have that much to say.'

'Aren't you at least going to tell me what it is that is irritating you about Rick?'

Tom turned to look at her. 'You realise that he didn't come home last night?'

'So?'

'Well – is he staying with us or not?'

'Of course he's staying here, but if he scores with a pretty dame, great stuff. He's had a triumph! A success!'

'That's not the way I see it.'

'How do you see it?'

'If he wants to screw around, that okay. But, he owes us the loyalty to return at night – even if he comes back in the early morning.'

'You actually sound like an old man, you know. I could have expected that sort of comment from my father, but it really surprises me coming from you – and about a friend.'

Neither spoke. Each diplomatically sipped their coffees.

'Didn't you encourage him anyway? You were asking him what he thought of SA girls and all. It doesn't add up!'

'Look, I just feel a bit peeved. I haven't thought this through very clearly…'

'I can see that.'

'Lay off, will you? Perhaps I'm not expressing myself well. All

I know is that it seems bad form, although I can't explain why. I'm also sure that the next thing that will happen is that the impish little tramp he picked up will latch on to him, and she'll be coming north as well.'

'So what? It's his holiday, isn't it? He wants to have a good time in his own way.'

Tom didn't answer.

Lucinda shrugged and picked up a magazine. Tom seethed and swore to himself that he would get even with Rick somehow. He felt great resentment toward him, and was acutely aware of the estrangement it had caused between Lucie and himself. Somehow and somewhere he knew he would have his chance to settle the score.

The Border of South Africa and Mozambique.

They moved cautiously toward the river bank. The mighty Limpopo was just ahead of them. The water moved sluggishly and eddied near the shaded bank where trees leant at precarious angles over the water. Both sides had steep banks that showed earth falls and erosion marks as a testament to the last wet season flooding that had swept through.

The cicadas kept up a deafening hum in the surrounding dense vegetation. The midday heat made everything look droopy and lifeless. As the group drew up on the steep embankment, the only sound noticeable above the insect's cacophony was a plopping sound as a fish leapt in the water, causing a series of ripples midstream.

The group all squatted in the shade, mesmerised by this peaceful scene. Across the other side of the river a lone male impala buck moved back from the water's edge to the denser bush behind. It was in dangerous country, for not only was it perilously close to a well-used crocodile slide, but the dense riverside bush would be the favoured haunt of the leopard. It faded into the bush and was soon lost from sight.

A fish eagle sailed by in its seemingly effortless flight. As soon as it was out of sight the stillness and tranquillity of an African river at midday returned. Most in the weary band were thinking how in other times to have a river like this near one's home would be a benefit. It would mean that there could be a great lifestyle to be had, for not only was there abundant water for crops, but the river would supply fish, game and trade with other communities up and down its length.

'How do we cross this mighty river?' asked Mopete. She sounded worried. 'I can't swim.'

'I also cannot swim,' added another voice, with a definite tremor.

'We shall cautiously follow the river upstream. In time I am sure we shall come across villages and shall negotiate for a boat to take us over, or if necessary steal a boat to cross. It is not important to cross now. Besides, the river shall be our provider.'

'The big lizards are plentiful,' said Nkosi as he pointed to the crocodile slide. 'We must be on our guard.'

'How many days, do you think…?' Joaquim paused in middle of his question. He inclined his head a little, listening intently. He suddenly dived for cover. '*Motor, motor!*' he hissed.

The group immediately took cover and looked skyward. They had slaughtered the goat only a day after the theft. Nkosi feared a small plane had spotted him while he was butchering it in a small clearing.

Small planes had flown over them three times in the last few days, so the group had assumed that Joaquim had heard another one. It soon became apparent that the engine was on the river, so they all shifted their positions to ensure that they could not be spotted from the water.

The noise of a strident engine grew louder, and soon the craft came into view. It was a light aluminium launch and it carried three Frelimo soldiers. It was powered by a small outboard that looked dangerously close to overheating, if the smoke fumes were anything to judge by. There was a long cord attached to the back of the launch and this pulled a little inflatable rubber dinghy. They were slowly moving midstream up the river.

The ripples spread out from the passage of the boats to gently lap at the banks. The two soldiers sitting in the prow were looking very alert and on guard, while the soldier in the stern appeared to be concerned with steering the boat, as well as keeping a watch on the dinghy being towed. The dinghy carried some dark shapes strapped together, which the band initially took to be logs but which were in fact three large crocodiles. The soldiers were obviously bolstering their income with some straightforward poaching.

The danger passed and the group relaxed as the sound faded. The hurdles they had to negotiate if the other side of the river was to be reached included not only the expanse of muddied water, but also soldiers and crocodiles.

Without any spoken word the group wearily got to its feet and quietly set off upstream, following the direction taken by the soldiers. Rodrigo took up the rear. For the twentieth time in the one day, he checked the safety catch on his assault rifle, to make sure it was off, and set off after his group of desperate refugees. He regretted that they only had a few rounds of ammunition. It seemed as if even the ammunition was rationed by the army to its soldiers these days.

Rick (Capetown)

He lay in the bed alone, drifting slowly in and out of consciousness. Earlier, Chrissie had wandered out with a wrap-around kanga. His headache had gone, but the tiredness remained. The lovemaking had been good. It had started slowly and tentatively, but her excitable nature and the pure passion she could muster had aroused him immensely. There was a reckless streak in her make-up.

He thought about Chrissie. Her Portuguese heritage with its mixture of Southern European as well as Moorish blood meant she was likely to be temperamental and volatile as well as passionate. Since Chrissie had been brought up in Africa, there were other cultural influences that Rick couldn't even dare to guess at, but it seemed to have created an explosive mixture. She was ludicrously shy about exposing her nakedness in front of him when she got out of bed to go to the toilet, but had come out with the most ribald comments and requests as they had made love. He found her lewdness extraordinarily exciting. He tried to imagine Tash talking that way, and found it impossible to do so. He smiled to himself. London seemed a lifetime away, and on a totally different planet.

He heard her come up the stairs, and turned as she entered the room. She was carrying the Sunday papers. She plopped them on the bed. 'I've put the kettle on. Wanna cup?'

'Please.'

''kay. Be back.'

'White, no sugar,' he called after her.

'No problem.'

He looked at the paper. The rapidly changing scenario in the Soviet Union dominated all the news. On the front page of the *Sunday Argus*, was an article about a brave if foolhardy lone black who was cheered by people in the audience, when he heckled Robert Mugabe of Zimbabwe into a stunned silence during a speech. He had stood up and loudly declared that 'Ian Smith was better' – a reference to the leader of the pre-independence, white-ruled government. The police had apparently bundled him off to jail, to face charges of insulting the President. Tom would love that article, thought Rick.

Chrissie re-entered with two mugs of coffee. She was beaming contentedly. '*Alles is reg.*'

'What does that mean.'

She shrugged. 'Fine, I guess. Everything is good.'

'Oh! I suppose I should have been able to work it out if I'd put my mind to it.'

'I've fixed it already.'

'What?'

'I just phoned the joint, and I've resigned. I'm free to travel.'

Rick smiled and raised his eyebrows. 'That easy, huh?'

'Ja. No problem.'

'You do want me to come, don't you?'

'Yes. Sure.'

'You don't sound very sure?'

'I'm just not one hundred per cent sure I can get you on this free flight.'

'Not a problem. If I have to, I'll meet you in Jo'burg.' She considered what she had just said, with her head inclined pensively to one side. 'Anyway, I'm keen to travel, with or without you – but preferably with you!'

'No worries. We'll sort it out somehow.' He extended his

hand. 'Welcome along, partner!'

They solemnly shook hands and then laughed. Rick looked at his watch. 'Listen, love, I think it would be a good idea to dress and we go off to my friends. I'd like to introduce them to you, but also inform them of the modification to the travel plans.'

Four: Presto

The fourth (often concluding) movement is fast. Lively and brilliant, it is somewhat lighter in mood than the opening movement.

I want to experience everything in life, so that in the journey to my death, my nights shall not be filled with regrets.

D H Lawrence

Rick (Capetown)

Chrissie dropped him off at the foot of the drive, and he walked leisurely up to the house. It was a comfortable suburban middle-class place, with its tidy garden and neat drive. Rick looked up at the house, and mused how the serenity of it all gave no insight to the turmoil or chaos that might be enveloping its inhabitants.

He thought about Tom and Lucie and how very different they seemed to be. Tom was possessed by a bourgeois spirit, which gave him a solid spiritual frame, a sense of belonging and made him sure of himself; it influenced his very outlook on life. His very grin had the rictus of certainty.

Undoubtedly, had he been born one hundred years previously, he would have been a farmer, solidly Boer, manifestly of the land and the Volk.[31] Whatever troubles he may have were based on any straying from the way that his cultural building blocks had determined for him.

Lucie on the other hand was the antithesis, for hers was an intellectual spirit that not only questioned many aspects of life and relationships, but was also restless and bohemian. There was no solid frame; rather a series of makeshift and ever changing abodes temporarily called home. It seemed to Rick that Lucie would never dogmatically stand her ground to the exclusion of any other

---

[31]People.

argument, for her very mental make-up allowed for other opinions. He wondered how good their relationship was, or if it was like his own with Natasha, where there was a definite attraction but little sustenance to be gained from the whole.

He reached the door and looked back at the view. The buttresses of rocks jutted out into the relatively calm sea; normally sharply delineated by the crashing white breakers, the scene was dramatic but tranquil. The day was hot and there was little wind, so that a haze hung over the view, tempering the beauty by blurring the focus. The idea of living with such a vista was so very enchanting that the very thought of returning to London became intensely unappealing.

He turned back to the door and rang the doorbell. It chimed inside, and was followed by a silence. Rick waited and listened for a sound. None came.

He searched through his pockets and found the keys that had been given to him by Lucie and opened the door. As he locked it again he glanced at his watch. It was still very early in the afternoon, and it would be very unlikely that anybody would be at home during a weekday at this time.

He went to the kitchen and made himself a coffee. He took it with him to the back door in order to sit by the pool for a while. He was surprised to find it unlocked. As he went out into the garden by the pool, he came face to face with Lucie as she climbed out of the water. He was startled, as he had thought he was alone.

She straightened and stood up on the pool's edge. She also registered surprise. She was wet and wearing a brief black bikini bottom. She instinctively brought her arms up to cover her breasts. She looked coy and shy.

Rick felt flustered and awkward, and all the more so since her look soon changed to one of composure. With great audacity, she slowly dropped her arms to her side.

'I rang the bell, but nobody answered,' he explained apologetically. Lucie didn't answer. He paused and then changed tack. 'How are you?'

'Fine. How is it with you?' she asked, smiling at him.

He felt relieved that her tone was friendly, though quite why he feared hostility he was at a loss to explain. Perhaps there had

113

been a sense of guilt as if he had shamefully tried to creep up on her and had been caught in the act. With an asinine grin he turned back to her and said, 'Fine. I'm really fine, thanks. Listen, I've just made a coffee. Would you like one.'

'No, but I could do with a soft drink if you are offering to fetch one?'

'No problem. Coke, lemonade?' He gestured enquiringly with his free hand as he put his cup down on the little table.

'A Coke would be great.'

'Okay.' He turned back to go inside. He fetched the drink from the fridge and returned to the kitchen bench to open the bottle. The window looked back over the pool. She was wrapping a pale yellow kanga around her body that defined her svelte figure. He turned away and opened the bottle. As he closed the door into the garden, she came up and took the drink from his hand.

'Thanks.'

'You're welcome.'

She raised the drink to her lips and tilting her head back drank long and deep. Rick sat down and sipped his coffee and then looked back at her.

Her dark hair was plastered to her head, and glistened with water. Her face looked tanned and healthy. He watched her as her full lips curled enticingly around the nozzle of the Coke bottle. Rick, blinked, a little shocked at his own thought. He dismissed it from his mind with a little involuntary shake of his head and looked back at the pool.

'That feel's a lot better.'

'Good.'

'You not going to join me in the pool?'

'Not with you looking like that!' laughed Rick.

She inclined her head coquettishly. 'Don't you like the way I look?'

'Yes. Too much. That's the trouble,' he warned. She was flirting openly with him. He wondered if he had ever given any signs that he was interested or that he harboured any designs on her.

'Hmm.' She looked skywards as if contemplating what she had

just said. 'Don't be worried. I'm a kept woman – or rather I'm almost a kept woman, for I do have my own job and identity. But what I mean is that here, I've definitely got a role to play, for I've been shown off to all of Tom's friends as his possession, his territory, so that they all keep well off, which means … well, it means a lot of things!' She grinned and sighed reflectively.

'You sound a bit depressed.'

'No, I'm not really. It's a sort of mid-afternoon, siesta time blues, that's all!'

'Oh.'

'Anyway, ignore me. Do have a swim should you feel like it. I shan't pounce on you.'

'Well, it does look fabulous. I might join you, if you don't mind the company.'

'Good. I'm now cool so I may not get straight back in. Please excuse me then while I go and lie in the sun. Join me when you are ready.'

She walked off to the grassy verge. The kanga had wet patches where it had moulded to her body. She unwound it and set it down on the grass. She lay down and stretched languidly. She closed her eyes.

Rick looked across at her and considered her beauty. He liked the look of her slender body, with its small pointed breasts. He felt sure that Tom was not appreciative enough of Lucie, and that he took her too much for granted. He drank his coffee and then returned to the kitchen to rinse the cup. He placed it back on the rack and after a last glance out at Lucie, went to his room and changed into his bathers. He went back outside to the pool.

She didn't move or open eyes as he approached. 'How's it going with your new lady?'

'Fine. She's a wild one. I like her a lot. Very –' he paused before continuing – 'upfront, in your face, and therefore… interesting?' The questioning tone invited confirmation. He placed his towel on the grass a discreet distance from her.

She chuckled. 'Ja. I'll bet! By the way, I almost forgot. There is a letter for you. It arrived today, and it's lying on the dining room table. Do you want me to get it for you?'

'No, don't worry. I'll fetch it. I'm at least dry, which means no wet patches in the house.'

He retrieved the letter and realised it was from Natasha. It seemed like an intrusion, an invasion of his newly created world. He felt as if he had spun himself into a new chrysalis, this in turn had shut out the light of the world that had constituted his reality. The newly created world was so stunningly different that it altered his perception of the future. He knew that it was only temporary and that he might be metamorphosed and re-emerge in a world that had changed since he was last there. Either way, he knew that he himself was undergoing change. The letter had the same effect as a pinprick on the chrysalis; it let in light out of all proportion to the size of the rupture.

He returned and sat himself down on his towel and examined the letter. 'It's from Natasha.'

'You sound gloomy. What's the word – melancholic?'

'Probably.'

'Guilty?'

'Not really. She wasn't waiting for me.'

'But you hoped she would be, right? Isn't that what you told us?'

Rick shrugged and then dwelt on her words. Yes, he thought, I did say that, but did I mean it?

'What's stopping you reading it then?' She turned her head to look at him. 'Don't mind me, Rick. I often tease, especially when I'm feeling bored.' She smiled and turned to face the sun again.

Rick looked at her again. She was definitely in a teasing mood, and exhibiting a flirtatious and mischievous side. She was playing a game, one in which he was not sure of his role, and which had all sorts of dangerous aspects. Ultimately all games between the genders were implicitly sexual, and this one was no exception. He turned his attention back to the letter, and opened it.

It was in Natasha's elegant and flowery writing, on her personal headed writing paper she had purchased at Harrods last month.

Dearest Ricky,

It has been a couple of weeks since you left on your travel adventure to South Africa. I did get a postcard from Capetown – thank-you.

The fact that you are actually not around has given me a chance to think about you, and what you mean to me. To my surprise, I really feel I'm in love with you. God knows why, since I dislike many aspects of your life, and certainly can't stand your politics (Daddy agrees, he says you are a misguided young man, but that you'll come right in the end!). Anyway, what I'm trying to say is that I love you, in spite of our obvious differences.

It struck me that you were always so very tolerant of my ways, my friends and hobbies, while I show a greater intolerance to the things that are important to you. I've resolved to correct this, and do better in the future.

I miss you a lot, and have thought about flying out and travelling with you for a couple of weeks. I have tentatively booked a flight on British Airways in a couple of weeks time – to Johannesburg – but will fly on to wherever you are, if it's a hassle to meet me. Can you ring me as soon as you get this letter? Do reverse charges if you are in the back of beyond! I would ring, but you never left your friends' number.

There really isn't that much more to say. I've had one mishap with Magical; he bruised his knee badly when he failed to take a jump well. The vet says it's a question of time before he's back in form again. I miss riding him. Maestra is such a temperamental mare.

Jonathan Outram has been around to see me and invited me out to dinner. I'm quite sure he wants to get into my knickers, so I told him to go and jump in the lake!

Looking forward to being with you again.
Much love,
Tash

Rick folded the letter and put it down beside him.

'She wants to come and join me.' He watched her turn and look at him. 'Turmoil appears to be a feature of my life,' he added in a desolate tone.

'Only if you let it be.'

'Yeah. Perhaps.'

'You don't strike me as the type who has chaos in his life, but perhaps that is only the impression you give! What do you think you'll do?'

'At this point, it seems the wrong moment for her to come out, and anyway, I'm not sure that there would ever have been a right moment.'

'This I presume is independent of Chrissie?'

'Irrespective of Chrissie.'

She closed her eyes and continued to sunbake in silence. He folded his arms behind his head and lay back to contemplate the letter.

'Fancy a drink of something a bit stronger?' she asked.

'Yes. I feel I need one.'

She chuckled, and got up. She didn't bother to cover herself. His eyebrows must have registered some surprise. 'Nothing you haven't seen before.' There was no response. She then added, 'What will it be?'

'I would quite like a beer if you have one.'

'Only a pleasure.' She went off to fetch the drinks, and soon returned carrying a beer as well as a gin and tonic for herself. She handed him his drink and then sat down cross-legged. She sipped her drink pensively, and then turned to look at him again. 'It seems to me you should drink up and let the beer start to have an effect … to pull you out of the doldrums. By the way, I heard a joke today, do you want to hear it?'

'Yeah. Go on.'

'Well, this lady was looking at her dog and realised that it had some really long hairs growing out of the side of its nose, which were not its whiskers. She had recently spent a fortune at the vets getting the dog treated for worms as well as having it groomed, so she felt reluctant to go back there. Instead she went to the chemist and asked if there was a depilatory cream to remove some long hairs. The chemist went to the back and returned with a cream. He took it out and looking at her, said, "It's really simple. You squeeze a little ointment onto your arm and rub it in. It will get rid of all the hairs on your arm. But, you can't wear a pullover for a couple of days." "It's not for my arm," she explained. "Okay, you rub it on your legs, and it will get rid of all the hairs on your leg. However, you can't wear long slacks for a couple of days." The lady smiled, and corrected him. "It's not for my legs. I don't think you understand. It's for my Chihuahua." "Oh," said the chemist knowingly, 'In which case, may I advise you that you cannot ride a bicycle for a couple days after you have rubbed it in."

Rick roared with laughter. Lucie was doubled up with mirth herself.

'Good one,' said Rick. 'Did Tom tell you that one?'

'No, I heard it at work. One of the cooks told me, and had me splitting my sides with laughter.'

'It's really good. I'm afraid I haven't any good ones to tell you! I seem to have an appalling memory for jokes.'

'Normally, so do I, but this one I had to remember.' She looked at her watch. 'Tom should be along soon.'

The mention of Tom seemed to have a sobering effect on both of them. Rick glanced around toward the kitchen.

'Does he make you nervous sometimes?' The question conveyed her changed disposition. She had become reflective.

'Who? Tom?' asked Rick. He looked startled.

'Yeah. Tom.'

'No, but I am surprised at the question.'

'Are you?'

'Yes. I've got a friendship stretching back a long way, and it really would be strange if I felt nervous with him. Why should I be feeling nervous? Let me put a couple of questions to you: Do you feel I have any reason to feel nervous, and do I look it?'

'For the first part, none at all, except that you seem very relaxed when we are alone together, but not really the same when Tom is about. I would also say the same of Tom. Ever since he heard you were coming, he has been on edge. He's definitely not the same person. So the second part is a qualified yes.'

'Being as analytical as you obviously are, what do you make of it?'

Her eyes narrowed slightly and then creased into a smile. *Bitch*, thought Rick. She obviously knows something, perhaps knows everything. It was obviously a cat and mouse game that she was playing and she was enjoying it. He wondered what Tom had said, and more important, how had he presented those distant but not forgotten events.

'Well, whatever I say would have to be guesswork. I would suggest that since you are one of the key players, it would be better that *you* talked; and then *we* talked.'

'What has he told you?'

'About?'

Rick squirmed mentally. 'About me, for instance.'

'Nothing derogatory, if that is actually what you are asking. He talked a bit of how good a friend you were. He said that you rescued him from many certain exam failures, and that you were always a bright pupil. He said that he always enjoyed your company.'

'Is that all?' he demanded curtly.

'Yes. He did mention that he was a little worried that you might have changed radically in the intervening years, so wasn't sure what you'd be like today. Stuff along those lines.' She looked skyward and frowned, as though engrossed with some inner troubling thought. 'He never specified how you might have changed come to think of it, and since I didn't know you, it never occurred to ask for specifics,' she added.

Rick reflected in silence on what had just been said. He felt a little like an animal being enticed out of its lair only to risk being pounced on by a hidden predator. 'Well, did he comment on whether I had changed? Was I different person? Had the intervening years brought about any big radical change?'

'He hasn't really commented at all. He did mention that you were very English and understated. He becomes moody when I have tried to get him to talk about you, and won't be drawn into the topic easily.'

'He seems very much as I remember him. Perhaps a little fatter. Certainly older or more mature perhaps would be a better description. However, he's very much the same person I knew all those years ago. My guess is that his reaction to myself is along similar lines.'

'Possibly, but it still hasn't explained the fundamental uptightness that exists between you two. Did you guys fall out over a girl? Was there a lady in all is?'

Rick's face broke into a smile. 'Well, it is either the beer working or the fact that I'm in good company, but I have no idea myself!' he lied. 'It certainly wasn't over any lady. English public schools leave little opportunity for girlfriends!'

'Sure.' She nodded her head knowingly. There was a mischievous glint in her eyes. 'A guy, then? A boy at school? I have heard what all these repressed and frustrated boys get up to! Or are they just scandalous rumours?' She laughed and was indicating that she was not to be taken seriously.

Rick shook his head. 'Nope. Sorry. You are sounding more and more like the female version of Herr Doktor Freud!' He tilted his head in a mockingly deferential way. He was squirming internally. He looked down at his empty glass. The conversation made him edgy, but was stimulating nonetheless. It had a slightly incisive aspect to it, an element of danger, an element of daring to play with fire for all its potential dire consequences.

'Well, it is beginning to cool down, so how about we dress and wander inside for some more drinks?' he asked.

She agreed. They both rose and took their empty glasses inside. There was still no sign of Tom.

Kruger National Park, South Africa.

The little dugout canoe was lying on the bank, unattended, and seemingly abandoned. Nkosi nodded to Joaquim, and they quietly continued down the path to reconnoitre ahead. It was very likely that there were villagers or fishermen on the banks nearby.

The rest of the group squatted patiently under the shade of the dense riverside foliage. There was a flash of iridescent blue as a kingfisher swooped fast and low over them. In the trees nearby there was a cackle of what seemed to be maniacal laughter. Some frightened vervet monkeys moved off, frightened by the presence of stationary men.

In the shallows near the dugout, a large bird waded slowly and carefully along the shoreline. It was a hamerkop, a bird distinguished by its hammer-shaped head, but otherwise remarkably like a heron. It was absorbed in its never-ending quest for food.

Mowa was the closest to the bird. He moved steadily and carefully removed the catapult that was tucked into his waistband. From his pocket he removed a smooth stone, and moving with the same steady flow, brought it up to aim.

The twang of the released rubber was followed instantly by a thwack, a flutter of feathers and a splash as the bird's body pitched sideways into the water. The stone had shattered its skull, but it still continued to kick and flutter feebly in the brown murky waters as if in protest at the imminent cessation of all movement.

Mowa darted out, checked that the coast was clear, and then raced down to retrieve the body. It would provide a tasty morsel for the evening meal. He squatted back in the shade with the dead bird at his feet. Everybody had watched the incident. Nobody spoke.

Presently Nkosi and Joaquim returned. They reported that there was no sign of any people nearby.

Perhaps the canoe belonged to hunters who had wandered inland, or fishermen who were scouring the banks with a motorised launch and had left this one as a back-up? In times of civil war and crisis, there were always bound to be strange happenings, reflected Rodrigo.

He quickly organised the group to cross in batches of four. He would be in the middle group, Joaquim in the first, Nkosi in the last. Mopete was to come with him. He would carry the only substantial weapon the group possessed.

Joaquim and the other three climbed aboard and pushed off into the still and brown murky waters. They lay low in the canoe and paddled with their arms over the sides. The current moved them fractionally downstream, but they made good progress.

The remaining group watched tensely as the canoe glided across the river. Rodrigo had released the safety catch on his AK-47. The canoe arrived safely, and they watched as Joaquim climbed out with two others. The remaining man, who had stayed in the canoe, paddled back furiously and soon returned to the original bank, his face a reflective sheen from his perspiration. He looked frightened.

Rodrigo and his three fellow travellers climbed aboard. The exhausted paddler rested on the return journey. They were also soon on the other side. A new lone paddler returned with the canoe.

As soon as the canoe had returned to the remaining group, Rodrigo could see that there was some sort of trouble. It appeared Nkosi and one man were arguing, and seemed to be coming to blows. Suddenly the man ran off into the bushes. Nkosi appeared to hesitate as if deliberating whether to pursue him or not, and then returned to the canoe.

They climbed in and started across. It was obvious that something was still not right, for one of the women known as Maria was sitting up and had begun wailing. The canoe was in midstream. Nkosi tried to get her to lie down prone. He lashed out at her in anger. The woman stood as if to run away, lost her balance and toppled into the river, capsizing the canoe.

The frantic splashing sounds and screams could be easily heard from the shore. Rodrigo grimaced in annoyance and frustration. There was little he could do from the bank except to watch the events unfold, and make a quick escape if the commotion attracted any unwanted attention.

Maria obviously could not swim, and in her panic was grasping frantically at Mowa, who seemed to be equally unable to keep afloat. The shiny upturned hull started to steadily drift away from the struggling group.

Rodrigo turned to look at his band standing safely on the shore. All were intently following the midstream events, and all were expressionless, no visible emotion flickered across their faces. Perhaps the calamities they had witnessed in the last few years had inured them to all future ones, allowing them to remain detached and aloof from the human tragedy unfolding in the water, Rodrigo reflected. He turned back to watch the outcome of the struggle.

The water was being churned frantically. Panic stricken screams could be heard. Mowa and Maria were losing the battle to stay afloat. They soon sank below the water, and did not resurface. The other man had struck out for the nearest shore, which was the one they had started from, whilst Nkosi was steadily approaching them. He was not a good swimmer and his progress was slow.

The far man seemed to suddenly slip under the water and did not reappear. Rodrigo presumed he had just given up. Crocodiles had not got him, or he would have screamed out his protests; it was more likely that he had just given up, exhausted.

Nkosi reached the shore. He looked tired and exhausted. Joaquim helped him up and then crossed himself.

Nkosi collapsed in the shade. 'I do not understand. First Sergio – first Sergio – he refused to cross,' he gasped. 'He said he could not go – go where – where the white men ruled. I think he was afraid of the water.'

As if to underline his point, a sad and forlorn figure appeared on the far bank. They all watched him. He looked dejected, even from a distance. He then turned and disappeared back into the bush.

Nkosi continued. 'Then Maria said – we must go back – go back and fetch him. She also was afraid – very afraid – she started to pray out aloud. She could not swim. Mowa also could not swim – even as he went down still had the dumb bird in his hand. What became of Tomas?'

Tomas was the other member of the group who had also drowned in his attempt to reach the shore they had started from. Nkosi had not seen what had happened.

'He is in the land of our ancestors,' replied Rodrigo. He turned to Joaquim. 'Did you hear the story Nkosi has just told you?'

Joaquim lowered his head abjectly. He knew why he was to be reprimanded. 'Yes,' he mumbled.

'You heard what Maria did?'

'Yes.'

'You heard that she appealed to the white man's gods?'

'Yes.'

'And she is dead. Drowned and not saved!'

'Yes.'

'And you make the sign of the cross, here? When you see there is no white man magic – there is no potency in their gods?'

'Yes. I'm sorry.'

'This should be a lesson to you all. The white man's gods are not for us. They eat the body and blood of their slain god every seven days. They called our African ancestors cannibals if they ate the slain warriors, but they eat their god, and call it mass. They have one god but there is a ghost and a son and a virgin. She is a woman who gives birth with no man. A god is born with no sex. We know this is foolish trickery, which they expect us to believe! They even say that the god was killed by humans, but was an example. This is all trickery. We know humans cannot kill gods. It is a trick to make us weak and not resist. This is a religion that has allowed us to be hunted and taken as slaves. In their own land they have a different religion, maybe not a Christian one for their own people. This religion is thought up for us, to enslave and keep us down. That is why we must reject it. We must return to our African ancestry and be true to it.' He paused and cast his eyes around. 'Christ does not travel with us!' he spat out venomously.

'Maria has paid the price for her stupidity, the white gods have not saved her.'

He got up and helped Nkosi to his feet. 'Let us follow the river for a few kilometres. We must get food, and we must remain under cover.'

The group dutifully followed in silence, moving along the river paths, on the lookout for game or humans. On the far bank, from the shelter of the riverside bushes, Sergio covered his face in his hands and sobbed as he watched his comrades melt into the bushes. The canoe continued to move slowly downstream. The shiny upturned hull was reflecting light from the hot midday sun.

The plane trip north

The voice of the air traffic controller came through the radio speakers. It sounded totally unintelligible to Rick. Not only was the radio transmission crackly, but the combination of technical jargon delivered in a heavy South African accent rendered it difficult to even understand the essence of what was being said.

'You guys all right back there?' shouted the pilot above the din of the engines starting up and revving.

Rick and Chrissie had been introduced to the pilot only a couple of nights ago, when they had all had dinner together at a smart seafood restaurant in Hout Bay. Gerard Pearson was a close friend of Tom and Lucinda, and was the owner of a successful chain of small supermarkets that had recently entered the black homelands of Bophuthatswana and Ciskei.

A few years ago he had taken a black worker who had shown business acumen, and had groomed his managerial skills. Eventually he was able to make him a full partner, and then allowed him to negotiate the deals that had seen his chain open in the black areas. He represented the more pragmatic entrepreneurs in commerce.

His company had diversified, and now also leased various small aircraft to the de Beers Corporation. Since he himself was a trained pilot, he had entrusted himself to the task of delivering the latest plane. He would be returning in two weeks' time with an older plane that was to be withdrawn from service.

Tom leant forward and gave the thumbs up sign. Gerard

nodded and started to move the small craft toward the control tower. The connecting strip that led to the main runway for the take-off began there.

They moved bumpily along, passing four large South Airways jets as well as various smaller parked commuter craft, bearing the logos of the prestigious companies that owned them. There was one BP craft, as well as two with the gold emblem of de Beers. An area that approached the size of a football field lay behind with many small aircraft, mostly Cessnas; a vivid testimony to the wealth of at least one segment of the population.

They were given the all-clear and soon taxied into position. Gerard gave the thumbs up sign and they roared down the runway. In remarkably little time, and making little use of the length of the runway, they became airborne.

As they climbed steeply Lucie turned and nudged Rick. She pointed out the Cape Mountains and the city nestled in around the harsh and severe natural splendour. The city sprawled like a white smudge in a sea of greens and blues that were sharply delineated by the azure sea. The only other place that Rick had seen which had comparable stark beauty and into which man was trying to accommodate himself was Rio de Janeiro. Both cities had the same severe and abrupt geography with mountains rising precipitously close to the sea. Though they were on different latitudes and therefore climatically different, both had the landscape softened by the green vegetation clinging to the abrupt cliffs and slopes, and both bore the scars of urban sprawl.

Rick stared out at the scenery as they climbed and banked to head north. He smiled contentedly to himself and turned to look at Lucie. She was lost in thought and appeared to be vacantly staring at Tom and Chrissie who were animatedly discussing something about the city below them. He looked at them. Chrissie was leaning across Tom and was pressed against him as they both peered out of the same cabin window.

Rick looked back at Lucie. She had noticed him looking at her. She shrugged and turned to look straight at him, as if studying his eyes. There was no jealousy there, thought Rick, just a slight hint of weariness, and perhaps a curiosity. She turned away and looked outside again.

'You looked as if you were about to ask something,' remarked Rick. He had to lean close to her and speak loudly to make himself heard. He involuntarily noticed the heavy musk perfume.

'Did I?'

'Yes. I thought I detected it in your eyes.'

'What? What I was about to ask?'

'No. The fact that you wanted to ask something.'

She smiled, and paused. 'Ja, maybe. There are always questions in my mind. I was not conscious of any particular one. Anyway, if it was a deep and meaningful, this would not be the appropriate place. Don't you agree?'

Rick grinned and nodded his agreement, and again looked out. It was funny how life seemed like a form of travel, and that the travel experienced by interacting with people was ultimately as important as a spiritual nutrient. It was as necessary as occasionally physically removing oneself from one's everyday surround and travelling to other countries, to observe their different cultures. The complex web of human relationships in this little aeroplane was difficult to unravel, and perplexing, but undoubtedly would be a feast for any analytical mind.

Gerard faced them all and removed his headphones. 'We've levelled out now. The Karoo will soon be below us. I'll point out any interesting features such as Bloemfontein or some of the big mines. You guys all right?'

'Ja dankie, alles is reg,' said Tom.[32]

Chrissie leant forward to ask Gerard something, which the noise of the engine prevented Rick from hearing. Gerard beamed and raising his eyebrows in approval or acceptance, moved to let Chrissie squeeze up beside him. He was obviously enjoying the close physical contact. Tom was helping her move up in the small cabin. Rick and Lucie were manifestly excluded from the conversation and the goings-on in the front of the aircraft.

She wasn't such a pretty girl, mused Rick, but somehow she had an aura that gave off a gravitational pull that would have had Galileo burnt at the stake had he tried to explain it in his day. The sum was greater than her parts. She also had that instinctive

---

[32] Thank you all, is okay.

female ability that she played so well, of appearing vulnerable, which brought out the protective side in males, but also excited them in spite of themselves.

Gerard Pearson was not a happy person. He was a man who was stifled by his own grim company. The evening they had gone out for dinner had seen him unexpectedly infected with smiles. The social side of the evening had lurched between two different planes, an earthy as well as an ethereal. On the ground level was the polite and intelligent discussion, which had been about the country and its directions. In the heady atmosphere there was the invisible and inaudible electrically charged level, akin to a tropical storm of lightning sexual strikes, crashing primarily around Chrissie. Gerard had become more and more animated, and somehow Tom had also become involved, in spite of his initial privately voiced dislike of Chrissie, so that they appeared increasingly like two bees who had found a pot of honey.

Rick and Lucinda had become quieter as the dinner had progressed, while the other three had become bawdy and rowdier. Chrissie had thrived on the attention. At one stage she obviously had decided that a limit had been reached, and she had abruptly turned, moved her chair up to Rick, and had proceeded to almost climb in his lap as she snuggled up to him. This had a severe deflationary effect on the other two males, and a look of wry amusement had crossed Lucinda's face.

The scenario was apparently repeating itself here in the plane, thought Rick. He then wondered if the ending would always be the same, or would it be different one day? Would she perhaps decide that she didn't want to reverse the flow and snuggle up again? Rick reappraised his thoughts and concluded that it really wasn't a question of would she – only *when*?

Londonok Game Reserve

The leopard paused in the shade of the tree, its tongue lolling out as it panted in the midday heat. It was obviously aware of the vehicle nearby, but chose to ignore its presence. It certainly wasn't hunting, for it made no effort to conceal itself. Small game, from duiker to impala, were initially driven into a panic at the smell of the feared predator, but soon relaxed, even if remaining very alert as they observed that the great cat was not out to hunt. The leopard needed stealth, concealment and cunning to be able to catch its prey; it could not outrun the buck or antelope like a fleet-of-foot cheetah could.

It looked back along the narrow track, its pale yellow eyes appearing dark in the shade, and then casually carried on walking with no obvious hurry. The chatter and howls of baboons nearby caused it to momentarily hesitate, for baboons could be abusive and aggressive, hurling objects at any enemy.

'Where is it headed, do you think?' whispered Rick.

'I should imagine it either has young nearby, or maybe a kill. Perhaps it needs water. The little spring is nearby,' answered Danie.

'There it is,' said Chrissie. 'The kill.' She pointed at a shape in the trees. A twisted set of legs stuck out at odd angles in the crook of a tree. It was obviously the leopard's meal, placed strategically for safety, so that scavengers such as jackals and hyenas could not reach it. It was an impala.

They watched as the leopard effortlessly sprang up the trunk and was soon high in the branches. It started to feed. It then appeared distracted and stared down and back. A spotted hyena tentatively came into view and sniffed around the base of the tree. It looked up wistfully. The leopard snarled, and then continued feeding. The hyena went up on its back legs and placed its front paws against the tree, unable to climb. The leopard continued to feed.

The small group continued to study the scene in silence in the Land-Rover. Danie, the white game warden who was their guide, spoke first. 'Well, what do you say – shall we get Gatsu here to lead us to some rhino?'

'Sounds great,' answered Tom.

'I can the black rhino, show you. Long horn. Also baby,' stammered Gatsu, the black driver appointed to the group by the Londonok Private Game Reserve. Danie agreed, and they set off gently down the bumpy track.

Rick studied Danie and Gatsu. They seemed to function so very well together as a team, he thought. It was obvious that they were good pals and that they not only shared a wealth of information about the animals in the reserve, but also obviously loved and respected them. They both seemed to know the land intimately. There must be some hope for the future if a full-blooded Zulu and an Afrikaner could work so harmoniously together, he concluded.

'Where are you guys off to next?' asked Danie.

'To the Kruger,' answered Tom.

'Will you be camping, or staying in the rondavels?'

'In the rondavels. We have bookings in Olifants, Letaba and up in the northern one, Punda Maria.'

'Ja, they are both good. There is a lot of game near the Limpopo as the drought in the North has dried up most of the waterholes. They had to cull quite a few elephant, as they were becoming too destructive of the riverside trees. You have to be a little alert up there as there is a bit of a security problem. There are a lot of our chaps in the hidden camps up there, mopping up the communist terrorists who slip across from Mozambique.'

'Have there been many such mop-up operations?'

'Who knows? Most of them are very hush-hush. I should imagine that with the open spaces up there they don't have much of a chance of slipping in undetected, and if they did, with a hungry lion population, how far will they get? Most come ill-equipped.'

'If they were terrorists intent on causing harm, why would they bother to come ill-equipped?' asked Rick. 'They must know that there are well-trained SA forces across the border. Are you sure they are not just refugees?'

'Well, that's not what the government says!'

'Governments, though, can be propaganda machines,' added Lucie.

'Ja, this is true. Who knows? But we don't want them in our reserves.'

Rick spoke again. 'What becomes of them?'

'"Mopped up" I think means "finished off". Who knows! Who knows why they come, indeed a lot of the time, who knows what the African actually thinks?'

Gatsu remained impassive, driving steadily on. Perhaps the friendship was just a veneer, and could not undergo any testing, contemplated Rick. Perhaps all the small appearances of Africans white and black working harmoniously together were wafer thin masks, a pretence that arose out of a genuine need to coexist. All appearances were ultimately deceptive, just as all solutions remained elusive.

Close to the border

They walked inland, keeping the river about two kilometres away constantly on their right. It was easy to keep going in the right direction, as the vegetation around the river was the only green in all the surrounding countryside. The vegetation was sparse, but sufficient to provide cover if a plane should pass overhead.

Two lone impala bucks were seen in the bush up ahead. They were too far away to be able to shoot them with the one assault rifle they possessed. The buck saw them and bounded out of sight into the bush. They all felt hungry, but the place with the most game was also the place with the most people. Mozambique's people were not only clustered along the river bank in order to flee the drought, but also to gain safety in numbers.

Nobody knew for sure which faction controlled which parts of the wild country. It would be likely that the border areas were under Government control, thought Rodrigo. However, since the interior seemed so much in Renamo hands, perhaps their supplies were coming across from secure border areas and these were in rebel hands. It was best to avoid both sides in the conflict, for each could be as deadly.

Joaquim, who was leading the group stopped. They all instinctively squatted. He pointed to a sign ahead.

Keeping low and hunched, Rodrigo scurried forward to read it. It said in Portuguese that the area was a prohibited military area. The lower half of the sign just read 'DANGER'. It was damaged by gunfire and rust.

'Take cover. We shall continue in the dark. This area might have many patrols. We must be close to the border,' said Rodrigo.

They all settled into shady spots under the trees and tried to find rest. Mopete came and rested against him. She idly used a stick to disturb a tsetse fly that kept trying to land on her leg.

The group had slowly drifted off to sleep when Nkosi, who

had stood watch, hissed an alert. Mopete moved off Rodrigo quickly as Rodrigo rapidly clicked the weapon into the fire position and looked toward where Nkosi was looking.

About half a kilometre away in the distance, an army truck had stopped on a track. Just ahead of it was an open army jeep. There seemed to be some soldiers standing near the lead jeep.

'What is happening?' asked Rodrigo.

Nkosi shrugged. 'They come quickly. Stop. Now they talk. Frelimo.'

Rodrigo nodded in agreement. He had noted the red star on the side of the truck, a government Frelimo marking. 'Get the group back with Joaquim. At least one hundred metres. Then come back and stay here with me. We must watch what they do.'

Rodrigo watched as the group moved back into the denser bush. Mopete was staring at him. He raised his eyebrows quizzically. She held his eyes and then turned to join the group fading into the denser cover. Rodrigo frowned. What was troubling her? Did she want to stay? Did she lack trust in him? Did she worry that he and Nkosi were about to make a dash for the border, and leave her and the group behind?

He closed his eyes momentarily as he recalled when he had first met her. He had found her in the little hamlet of Mbisi, near Chicomo in the Masinga district. He had gone to steal some maize from a farmer's hut, and had found her curled up in a foetal position in the back of the hut. She was bruised, terrified and close to collapse. As she had represented no threat to him, he had talked to her and heard how she had lost her family in the war, and was now travelling with the Frelimo patrol, which was currently stationed in Mbisi. A brawl had erupted the previous night, and two soldiers had lashed out at her, in spite of the fact that she was not involved in the original quarrel. In the ensuing chaos and darkness she had fled and sought refuge in the little isolated hut. She was petrified of returning. The mere fact that Rodrigo had talked to her civilly, and had not immediately made any demands of her, was enough for her to place her fate in his hands, if he was willing to accept it. She had made an impassioned plea, on her knees and begging. He had hesitated, but felt that perhaps she could be an asset, being small and lithe; and so his little group had started. They had developed an easy sexual liaison and companionship. She had remained a quiet and fiercely loyal member of the group. Her inner anguish sometimes revealed itself when she cried in her sleep.

Rodrigo opened his eyes and shook himself out his reverie. He glanced at Nkosi who was staring intently at the distant soldiers. They were getting out of the truck. There appeared to be about twenty in total.

'Sergio!' exclaimed Nkosi.

Rodrigo squinted intently at the distant group but was unable to distinguish anybody specifically. Feeling humbled he turned to Nkosi, 'Tell me. What is it you see? What is happening?'

Nkosi looked back at him quizzically. It was rare that a leader admitted to any form of defect. Perhaps his eyes were going? Perhaps he should not be the one carrying the gun?

'They have him bound, and he was with the group of soldiers in the Jeep. They must have found him near the river. He talked.'

Rodrigo agreed. He must have talked. They were in greater danger now as this meant that the patrols were out to look for them. Since they had not only assaulted the little outpost, but stolen the canoe and were fleeing the country, they would be classified as brigands and summarily shot if caught. Sergio was able to tell them that they were on this side of the river and their destination, so undoubtedly they were sending out patrols with trackers. Rodrigo cursed.

'We will have to move fast. Tonight we make the crossing.'

'How far is the border?'

'It cannot be far.'

'And the patrols?'

'We must be ahead of them.'

'I should have killed Sergio.'

'Yes.'

They both looked at each other. Rodrigo held his stare till Nkosi looked away. He is coming up to challenge me. I should get rid of him before he makes a move, thought Rodrigo. 'I will tell the group we shall be moving fast tonight. You keep watching the patrol. Let me know if anything happens.'

Nkosi nodded and turned to peer at the distant soldiers.

Rodrigo found his group again and quietly explained the unfolding events.

Kruger National Park

The game viewing had been great. Even as they entered the Kruger National Park, it was obvious that the great concentrations of game that could be found in Serengeti were also here, for they had almost immediately come across African wild dogs chasing a kudu. The whole pack of yelping dogs crossed right in front of them in tireless pursuit. It was rare to see wild dogs, let alone see them hunting.

Gerard had left them in order to return to Johannesburg. Just the four of them had continued into the Kruger. The atmosphere had been tense, though there had been no argument or incident to explain why, uncharacteristically Gerard's presence had been a jovial and light one, which had kept the mood buoyant. In his absence it seemed like the electrically charged, expectant feeling one has in the calm before a storm.

Tom turned the radio on and caught the end of the news that was reporting on disturbances in Los Angeles. 'Bloody Yanks! They are so damn quick to criticise, but they cannot even get their own house in order.'

'Couldn't agree more,' added Chrissie. 'Maybe a few more riots by the blacks there will shake them up a bit.'

'Hey Rick, I heard an interesting story, which I feel shows very much what the Yanks are like.' Tom looked in the mirror to see if he had caught Rick's attention.

'Yeah? What was it?'

'Well. Apparently the people in LA are now calling the cop cars "black and normals", rather than the "black and whites"! This is because the police chief, a white guy called Daryl Gates, apparently made some reference to the fact that the police no longer hold people in some sort of restraining way around the neck, as it has led to a couple of black deaths. Apparently he said there had never been a death with a normal guy, being restrained with his hold! How's that for racism, hey? Anyway, everybody now calls the black and white cop cars black and normals! I think that is damn funny!'

Rick smiled and looked out the window.

Tom frowned in frustration. 'What is it with everybody? I'm just trying to make light conversation, but it's like talking to a funeral party. Lighten up, all of you!' He glared across at Lucinda, who was sitting next to him. 'What's chewing you up?'

'Just tell me, Tom. What did you bring a gun for?'

Tom shrugged. 'That's my business. You know Africa, have you not felt at times that to have a gun is a good idea?'

'But you know they are not allowed in the Park. You told the Park Warden that we were not carrying anything such as a firearm.'

'*Ja-nee*. I lied. No big deal.'

'That's the problem, isn't it. Lying is no big deal to you.'

Tom did not answer, as he quietly fumed. She had the ability to make him feel foolish in public. He turned the volume up on the radio, which featured a talkback show. They all listened in silence as the scenery slowly slipped by with its wonderful complement of wildlife.

When the programme finished, Tom turned off the radio. '*Bo blink maar, onder stink!*' he muttered.

Chrissie looked across at Rick and smiled. She snuggled up close and translated, 'The top part may be clean, but underneath it's dirty.'

Olifants Camp, Kruger National Park

The large verandah of the Olifants Camp overlooked a small branch of the river. It was peaceful and beautiful as the sun slowly set. A lone bull elephant solemnly crossed the water and lingered in the shallow pools. In the distance a herd of blue wildebeest and zebra nervously approached the shallow ponds in order to drink; the evenings were always dangerous and a time when the predators were active.

They all looked out over the tranquil scene. A red-beaked hornbill stood on the edge of their table and edged forward hoping to claim some of the little morsels from the snacks that they had all indulged in. Chrissie tossed a little piece of bread from her sandwich and they all watched as the somewhat daring bird hopped along the table to get it. It craned its neck and reached the piece with its long beak, and then, inclining its beak upwards, seemed to virtually toss the bread into its throat. With a flap of its wings it returned to the ground at a safer distance. It then ruffled its black and white plumage before relaxing. Various smaller blackbirds with beady yellow eyes lined up on the backs of surrounding chairs, and waited expectantly.

Chrissie smiled at Rick. 'Cheeky li'l buggers, eh?'

'Yeah, they sure seem to be. They must be used to tourists.'

Tom agreed. 'The wildlife has become used to the cars, and to all intents and purposes, ignores them. It has what the Germans would call *Lebensraum*. You know the word?'

Rick shrugged. 'Well, I'm not one hundred per cent sure if I've got it right, but it's something like "room to live", or to that effect, no?'

'Ja, that's it. Room to live. A good concept.'

Lucie curled her lip sarcastically. 'It's an old Nazi term. Hitler and his cohorts all used it when they looked East at the lesser peoples occupying wonderful European soil; the Czechs and Slovaks, the Hungarians, the Poles, the Russians, the Ukranians, the Byelorussians, and on and on. These lesser, non-Germanic peoples were a hindrance to the chosen *Volk*, and therefore justifiably disposable if the Reich needed more breathing space. It's a concept that I'm sure the right wing of this country is ultimately familiar with, though not the wildlife!'

The vehemence of Lucie's outburst created a wall of silence which enveloped them all, and which nobody seemed willing to break. Rick sipped at his gin and tonic and decided that he at least would soon have to leave the table, as he had to make the phone call that he was so much dreading. He looked across at Lucie who was staring straight ahead with pursed lips. She looked ready to do battle. Tom's expression was not very different, just a little less grim. Chrissie seemed blissfully unaware of the tensions, or at least was choosing to ignore them.

'You'll have to excuse me, folks, but I must quickly make a phone call. I have the international line booked at the head office at six and it's nearly time. I'll be back in about ten minutes.'

Lucie grinned. 'Good luck!'

Tom visibly relaxed, and slouched in his chair. 'Ja, it seems to me you will need all the help you can get!'

'Relax, you guys, relax! I'm just making a phone call, I'm not out to wage a war.'

'You might as well be!' Tom was obviously finding it very funny, and laughed loudly.

Rick shrugged. '*Que sera, sera*.'

Chrissie sat up in her chair. 'I dunno what you all are talking about, but I'm off to get a drink.'

She stood up and walked off to the bar.

Tom looked across at Lucie, and decided not to say whatever had crossed his mind. He got up heavily, looked undecided and then with a simian walk started off after Chrissie. He muttered something under his breath.

Lucie looked up at Rick. 'What did he say?'

'I'm not sure, but I think it was something like "seems a good idea".'

'That follows. Whenever he's pissed off he turns to the daemon drink. The refuge of all who can't deal with reality.'

Rick smiled. 'I once heard it the other way around. Reality is the refuge for those unable to deal with drugs!'

They both laughed. She looked up at him. 'I like you, Rick. I'm glad you're here.'

Rick shuffled a little uncomfortably in acknowledgment of the compliment.

'Do you feel happy? Are you enjoying your holiday?'

'Yes. I am. Happy – and enjoying my holiday.'

'Do you not feel the tensions?'

'Yes, I'm aware of tensions… but I am at a loss to reasonably explain them.'

'Do they not revolve around you?'

'In what way revolve around me?'

'Well, it seems as if whatever it is that is bugging Tom, somehow has been set off by you. I'm sorry if I keep bringing this up, but somehow I know you are the catalyst. They say that a lack of normalcy is madness, but he's not mad, just chewed up. Unsettled by your presence … perhaps by your actions?' she suggested. 'Anyway, he's somehow unsettled by you. Yet you have no explanation?'

'Well I don't, really, not one that I could say would cause him to be troubled by me. If it's Chrissie…'

'No. I'm sure she's not the problem.' She looked vacantly in the direction of the bar. 'Perhaps she is a problem, but not the same sort of problem.'

Rick smiled and also looked across to the bar. Chrissie was clearly having a very spirited chat with Tom and was obviously enjoying herself immensely.

'You must make your call. I'm sorry to have kept you. One day I'd like to have a real good chat with you, about you, Tom, and … well, and things in general, I guess. I'm sure we have a lot in common.' She looked straight up at him.

He nodded. 'We'll find the time, I'm sure. See you later.'

She smiled conspiratorially. '*Tot siens*,' she whispered under her breath.

Rick walked off to the main office to make his phone call. He glanced again at Chrissie as he rounded the outside of the bar. Tom had his hand on her thigh as she sat on the barstool. They gave every appearance of a couple together. He stopped and observed them, and discovered to his surprise that he felt no emotion, no discomfiture, and no jealousy. He even realised that he had obviously somehow expected that they would get on … and probably be mutually attracted.

He looked right round to see what Lucie was doing. The gloom made it difficult to make her out, but he then realised with a jolt that she was staring straight at him. Unsettled, he turned and continued to the offices. He became aware of his increased heartbeat and sighed wearily. Life is such a mess, he thought as he entered the office. They were ready to connect his international call.

Kruger National Park – close to the border

Darkness had fallen and Rodrigo's group was still huddled in a watchful and uneasy silence under the trees. The army search party had fanned out and headed toward the river. They were combing the dense bush on the river banks and heading south from whence they had come. The two vehicles had disappeared from view; they had driven in the opposite direction, a northerly direction upstream.

Rodrigo stood up stiffly and stretched. He had spent many hours huddled and nervous about the possible developments of Sergio's capture. They would have to move quickly and quietly. The situation had changed dramatically, for the Frelimo authorities were not only actively searching for them, but also had a fairly good idea of the route and direction they had taken, plus knowledge of their great weakness – the lack of effective weaponry. With brusque hand movements he signalled his group to gather around him.

The shadows of the group all moved quietly from their respective shelters and shuffled up and around Rodrigo. Rodrigo could see the tension and fear in their faces.

'We move in single file. I want Nkosi to be the leader, and I shall be a little distance behind him. The rest of you are to follow. Leave distance between each of you and be quiet.' He looked around him. The whites of the eyes of his companions were virtually all he could make out in the dark. 'You have to be careful, and watch out for the enemy. Let's move.'

Nkosi came up to him. 'I'll keep to the paths, right?'

'Yes. You have good eyes. Be careful. The gun will be covering you. I'll walk with the catch off. Drop if you see or suspect anything at all.'

Nkosi nodded and turned. He set off at a steady pace along the little path. When he was about twenty metres ahead and almost indistinguishable, Rodrigo swivelled and patted Mopete tenderly on the shoulder and followed. As he walked, he undid the safety catch on the gun, and wondered if it worked all right. They had not had a chance to test it, and he hoped he wasn't carrying a dud. He swivelled round and confirmed that the group was following him some twenty metres behind, and in single file as he had instructed.

It was uneventful, but extremely dark. He stubbed his toes on various occasions against small rocks or branches, but apart from the distant cackle of a spotted hyena, there was no sign of any danger. They had stampeded a small herd of large hoofed animals, which had made them all drop to the ground in fright, but he assumed from the audible snorts that they were probably blue wildebeest. It became easier to walk as the light of the quarter moon eventually rose in the night sky.

Rodrigo started with surprise. Nkosi had stopped and was crouching. Rodrigo dropped instantly and gestured to those following to do the same. He swore to himself that he was becoming too lax, and had drifted into a comfortable reverie rather than remain alert as he had instructed everyone to be. He peered up at Nkosi, who was edging forward cautiously.

He appeared to be studying something ahead, but from where Rodrigo crouched it was impossible to make out what the danger was. Nkosi then turned and signalled for Rodrigo to join him.

When he reached him, the reason was obvious. Directly in front of them was a cleared area and a crude tarmac road with ruts, cracks and potholes in the surface. There was a more significant cleared verge on the other side of about thirty metres, and then there appeared to be some sort of hazy barrier, though it was extremely difficult to make it out clearly in the gloom. It was obviously a military area, and it was risky moving out into the open.

'Maybe a border road,' stated Nkosi.

'Can you see or hear any patrols?'

'No. It seems deserted.'

'You check the other side. I'll cover you.'

Nkosi nodded and slowly inched his way forward to the edge of the road. He remained hunched there for a minute intently looking in each direction for any sign of danger or of a border patrol. He then moved quickly to the other side and in a quick scurrying movement disappeared into the gloom.

In the dark he resembles a warthog, thought Rodrigo, so hopefully if anybody is watching, it's what he would be mistaken for. He had heard of binoculars that could see in the dark, and he worried greatly about these. He aimed the barrel of the gun down the road in one direction and then the other, but could see nothing.

The barn owl's sharp cry could be heard from the other side of the road, Nkosi's signal. Rodrigo peered into the gloom and could just see a beckoning movement from his comrade. He pivoted round and in turn beckoned Mopete.

In a whisper he instructed her to wait for his signal, and if the owl called twice, to cross one by one. If the signal was three hoots, they were to stay put and retreat into deeper cover.

'We are close. We must be careful. I'll go now and…'

The deep grunt of a lion was heard very nearby. Rodrigo froze in his tracks, and Mopete instinctively grabbed his arm and squeezed.

'The lion. It is close,' she mumbled.

Rodrigo turned to look at her. Her eyes were wide with fright. He had never seen her looking so visibly upset. The lion tailed off in a series of rhythmic grunts. It sounded as if it was very close to them, and just ahead.

'I am surprised to hear lion,' commented Rodrigo. 'I had thought they were all hunted by now. It has been many years since I've heard one. This is probably a lone male. When it smells humans, it will run. It will fear us more than we fear it.' Rodrigo did not feel as confident as his words, but felt safe with the gun.

'Keep a good lookout,' he warned, and crossed the road in the same scurrying way as Nkosi.

Moving quickly over the short grass he came to where Nkosi was crouched. Just behind him were rolls of barbed wire, followed by a high wire fence with concrete posts every ten metres. Every second post carried a sign reading 'Peligro. Gevaar. Danger.'[33] They could read the Portuguese, but neither could even comprehend the English or Afrikaans.

They moved closer and examined the human made barriers. The three coils of barbed wire formed a triangular obstacle, two coils ran parallel to each other, and the third on top linked the two. There was a strip of some ten metres before the high fence.

'We can get under the first lot, and climb the fence. Call the group Nkosi.'

'Do you think that there may be land bombs?'

'Mines?'

'Yes. The second cleared area. It may be dangerous.'

Rodrigo sighed. It was a risk they would have to take. He could see no option. 'It is possible, but the government has not

---

[33]Portuguese and Afrikaans for danger.

the money to pay for such expenses. We will cross. Call the others.'

Two sharp hoots followed. They looked back and watched as one by one the whole group reassembled near the fence.

'We must find a way under the first wires, and over the top of the second. Joaquim, you go for fifty metres to the right. Nkosi, you try for fifty metres to the left. Keep close to the wire. Look for a way through ... or under. Go.'

They all squatted and waited the return of the scouts.

Joaquim came sooner than expected. 'There is room. Under the wires. Maybe dik-dik he makes it. Not far.'

'Good. We shall follow you. Sokhela, you wait for Nkosi. Let's go.'

They followed Joaquim in the dark. He stopped and indicated a spot. Rodrigo moved forward to inspect it. There was a scratched groove in the soil, which indicated that some small animal such as a small antelope had used it as a crossing point to the other side, probably to graze on the slightly longer grass.

'Perfect! Mopete. You are small. You go first and push up the wire as best you can before we follow.'

Mopete crawled forward and started to squeeze through the small gap. She swivelled round on to her back as she pushed the barbed wire away from her. She got through easily.

Rodrigo sent Joaquim through next, and the party followed. Nkosi and Sokhela, who had rejoined the group, went next, and he took up the rear. He motioned them forward to the high fence.

The grass was longer here and various members of the group caught their toes in its strands, almost tripping up as they went forward. In the dark it was nearly impossible to see the transparent threads of nylon that were taut and criss-crossed the strip.

They reached the big fence, which stood about eight feet high and had wires with only about four inches between each strand. They would either have to scale it, or cut the wire. They were near a post, which had a sign, showing a bolt of lightning.

Nkosi looked back at Rodrigo. 'It's easy. I'll go over first.'

He stood up and grabbed the wire to start to climb. His body convulsed and he screamed as he fell back. A blue flash had come from the wire.

Everybody fell back in fright and turned to look at Nkosi. He was writhing on the ground, shaking his hands. 'It is on fire the wire. It burns.'

Joaquim started to moan and rock on his haunches.

'Shut up!' hissed Rodrigo. 'It is only electric. The white devils have put electricity in the fence.'

Nkosi had by now sat up and was examining his hands. They were still tingling. His heart was racing and his arms hurt, but he was otherwise unharmed.

They all listened intently. There was a distant deep boom. It was repeated only once.

'Thunder? Explosion?' asked Joaquim. 'It could be either. It is far.'

'Renamo operates in this zone, so maybe there is a confrontation,' declared Rodrigo. 'Whatever it is,' he paused as he examined the clear sky, 'I am sure we must cross over tonight.'

'Maybe we could use a log or a large stick to force the wires apart or break them?' suggested Mopete.

They investigated the surrounding area around but saw nothing that would help them.

'Once across we are safe. The Frelimo patrols are out looking for us. I will shoot the wire.'

They all watched as Rodrigo stood up and, holding the barrel close to a strand, unleashed a small volley of shots. The noise was deafening and was followed by a loud twang as the wire recoiled and whipped back. Looking terrified but keeping up the momentum, he repeated the same for three other strands and had cleared a gap of about one and half feet, large enough for them to slip through.

They went through rapidly, taking great care not to touch the remaining strands. Only Mopete got her shorts caught in the lower strand, but was able to free herself without incident.

They all ran into the denser bush, and kept on going for about one hundred metres. There was a dirt track, which they ran across and took refuge a good two hundred metres beyond.

Rodrigo grinned at his group. 'Well, comrades. We have made it to South Africa. We shall be okay here.'

They all permitted themselves a laugh and embraced him in turn.

'We should walk a little more tonight and then rest. We might have alerted a patrol. Let's go.'

They set off again in the dark. A weary, hungry but more buoyant group of stragglers, they had not noticed the sign in the dark by the road which read simply, '*Nasionale Kruger Wildtuin*'.[34]

Army HQ, Eastern Transvaal, South Africa

Luitenant Andries Homan smiled and shook his head in disbelief as he examined the data. 'Well, well. We have more monkeys in the mist.' An in-house joke that really meant guerrillas, from the film *Gorillas in the Mist.*'

He raised himself heavily from his desk. He was a large beefy man with a florid expression. He lumbered down the hallway of the Nissen hut to the room of Colonel Coetzee, and knocked deferentially.

'Ja. Enter.' The voice behind the door was curt and clear.

'Excuse me, Colonel. We have an intrusion just south of the Limpopo.' Luitenant Homan was almost obsequious, and was obviously ill at ease in the Colonel's presence. 'Here are the reports. I felt you should see them tonight.'

He handed the papers across to Colonel Coetzee who had stood up from the bunk bed where he had been reclining.

'How many?'

'They tripped eight of the wires, so our estimate is between four and eight. They cut two of the electrics, which suggests they may be armed guerrillas.'

Colonel Coetzee turned to look at the lieutenant. 'Pretty stupid place to cross, don't you think?' His cold blue eyes studied the now distinctly uncomfortable heavy man.

'Yes sir.'

'My guess is that they are amateurs.'

'Yes sir. I'm sure that's correct.'

'*Ja-nee*. Take two choppers at first light. Fourteen men. I'm only interested in the leader if he's armed. If so, I want him back at the John Vorster Square Security HQ in Jo'burg, a;ap. Understood?'

---

[34]Kruger National Park.

144

'Yes sir.'

'*Dankie*, Luitenant Homan. Goodnight.'

'Uhm, sir?'

'Ja?'

'The rest of the intruding party?'

Colonel Coetzee looked straight back at him. 'Whatever happens tomorrow, my instructions are to you, "Keep our house clean". Good night Luitenant Homan.'

'Good night, Colonel.'

Luitenant Homan bowed his head slightly, turned and let himself out. He mopped his brow when he was back in the corridor. The boys will like this he thought, and went off to the mess to inform the operational command.

Olifants Camp

Rick walked back toward the bar after the phone call. It had not been an easy exchange. Natasha had been very caustic and upset at first, and had immediately gone on the offensive. She had said that she regretted it all, and that she had to admit that she had decided anyway to finish with him, as she had found out that he was not a 'good bonk'. She claimed that since she had decided on a fling with her neighbour Ricky Outram, she had found how deficient he was as a man, and how inadequate his lovemaking was. She now felt, she had told him, that she had been wasting her time with a socially inept arsehole who had no passion, and was probably unable to experience real deep emotion, let alone something as involved as love. She had then run out of breath as well as ideas, for there had been a sudden silence on the phone. He apologised and wished her well. She shouted out that she wanted him to go to hell, and then added that she hoped it was where he was, and hung up. He lamented at how it all ended, and felt low and despondent. His insecurities resurfaced as he realised how unsure he was of his life's direction.

He reached the bar and looked in, expecting to see Tom and Chrissie. It was crowded, but the stools where they had been were now vacant. He walked in and cast his eyes over the tables and along the bar, but could see no sign of them. He decided to return to the rondavel when his attention was drawn to the tanned back with the hair pushed over the shoulder. It was Lucie. She was facing the other way and had not noticed him. A large, balding and jovial-looking man was talking enthusiastically with her. She appeared to be listening intently.

He strolled over and moved in front of them. He noticed the resigned expression on her face. She looked up and smiled as she recognised who it was.

'Rick. It's good to see you!' She sounded tipsy.

'Ah, I see your husband has turned up to join you. I'd better be going then,' said the other man. 'Nice to meet you.'

Lucie said goodbye, and shook her head dejectedly. 'All he wanted was a quickie before returning to his wife! Arsehole! The bloody nerve, the – the God knows – the *effrontery* of it all. I'm amazed how some people feel they can get away with it.' She turned to look at Rick again. She studied his face for a while and smiled again. 'So. It was awkward was it?' She paused. 'The phone call, that is. My guess is that you need a drink. Shall I be a good SA host and get up to fetch you one?'

'You sound inebriated, Lucie. I'll get one and return. Would you like a refill?'

She laughed. 'Inebriated! Why not bombed, loaded, smashed, pissed! It seems to me that the Brits always use long words when the shorter version would do!'

Rick grinned, for he knew he had a tendency to be pretentious with words. 'I'll be right back.'

He decided not to get her one as her glass was already full, so ordered himself a gin and tonic and returned to Lucie's side. 'Where have Tom and Chrissie gone?'

'Back to the rondavel.' She glanced at him. 'Don't be surprised, Tom can be like that. He was *katools*.'

He frowned with incomprehension. 'I have no idea what that word was or meant.'

'*Katools* is Afrikaans word. It means randy. Ja, randy! That's what he is tonight. randy! I'm sure he's turned on by Chrissie and wants to jump me.' She studied him again. 'I could use other words instead of jump, such as copulate or fornicate! Anyway … be that as it may, there is a but. And, the but is a big but. I said no! So he went off in a huff.' She took another sip of her drink and laughed. 'It means that he will be really cross tonight, or he's jumping Chrissie at the moment. I hope he takes her and not me. I feel in no mood for him, or for sex, or for anything. God, I feel miserable.'

'I'm sorry, Lucie. I wondered what the tension in the air was all about. You guys are having problems, I guess?'

'Yes, and yet … oh well, I suppose it must come down to a yes. But I don't … well, since you … I suppose I just don't understand.' She started to sob quietly.

Rick put down his drink and went over to hold her. 'I'm sorry to hear this. Really I am. I hope I'm in no way making matters worse by being around.'

She sniffed loudly and nestled her head against his comforting shoulder. 'No, Rick. You are not. It's my problem, and somehow I'll solve it. Somehow. I'm just sort of sorry that you're … well, that you're caught up in all this. I'm really sorry. You should be with Chrissie having a good time. Christ, you came far enough for a holiday.' She sniffed a couple of times and wiped her eyes. 'By the way, I'm sorry about what I said about Chrissie and Tom. That was really insensitive of me. I'm really sorry, and I'm sure she's waiting for you at the rondavel. Please forgive me.'

'It's okay. No need to apologise.' He continued to hold her for a while and gently stroked her hair. 'I'm sure it will all work out in the end. Most things do.'

'Like you and Tash?'

'Well, I didn't actually mean like that, but I guess that it's always a possibility. I hope not though. I really like both of you.'

'Do you?'

He hesitated before answering. 'Are you asking if I meant what I said then? In other words, do I like both of you?'

'Ja.'

'The answer then is yes.'

'You have little in common with Tom, but at least there is a shared past history, so perhaps you can pass on that one, but why do you like me?'

'Well, you've been very generous and hospitable, and … you're very likeable.'

'Do you find me attractive?'

147

Rick felt uneasy at the way the conversation was going, but decided to answer honestly anyway. 'Yes I do.'

She chuckled. 'It's comforting to hear a man say that even if he doesn't mean it.' She nestled in against his shoulder, making herself more comfortable. 'I'd like to continue this line, but I'm sure I shall end up embarrassing you, so I shall shut up. Thanks anyway.'

He continued to stroke her hair in silence. Yes, he had to admit, she was attractive. He found her both physically attractive and stimulating company to be with. She was a little like the iceberg, the little bit that was visible on top gave credence to the fact that there must be the greater amount hidden from view. He also suspected that like the iceberg, she may well be an object of great beauty, but was potentially dangerous to all shipping. The analogy ended there, for hers was not a northern pale artic beauty, there was colour warmth and passion in her. He reflected that he would like to know her better, and what's more he would like to continue this and spend the night with her. However, he knew this was an impossible and stupid dream for she was his friend's live-in girlfriend.

He was aware that she fancied him. Granted he had no concrete proof, but he also knew that he fancied her. He had felt the stirring inside of him, the pure animal attraction, made all the more poignant and intriguing because of its very forbidden nature. He recalled an expression that he had heard long ago, 'lust never sleeps', and how in essence this must be the basis of all he felt. Attractions and flirtatious encounters were all part of the chase, and still had the power to stir him, to perceptibly quicken his heartbeat. The very idea of returning to the rondavel and taking her with him to his room had suddenly become an overpowering but unrealistic fantasy. He shook his head to wake himself from his reverie.

He inclined his head slightly to gaze down at her. She seemed so very peaceful. He then realised she must have dozed off. The tensions, the tiredness and the alcohol had combined to send here off to sleep. He thought about adding the comfort and safety of his arms to the list, but smiled instead and shook her gently to wake her.

She opened her eyes slowly and with great difficulty, as if emerging from a deep sleep. She blinked and peered up at him mystified. 'Rick. Where am I?'

'We're still at the bar here in Punda Maria. You drifted off for a few minutes.'

'I'm so sorry. I must have been really tired.' She disengaged from his arms and stretched. 'I think I better head back to my bed. I've had it. What is the time?'

Rick glanced at his watch. 'Not too late. It's nearly eleven.'

They both got up and headed for the door. She slipped an arm around his waist; he protectively put his around her shoulder. She smiled up at him.

The African night sounds were very clearly heard once outside the bar. A pair of hyenas was whooping into the cool night air. They sounded close to the camp's perimeter. They walked in silence in the dark toward their rondavel. Neither noticed the motionless figure standing by the tree in the dark observing them.

The rondavel was dark. 'They must have retired already,' said Rick. 'I'll see you in the morning.'

'Thanks for … for being understanding, I guess!' She shrugged her shoulders amusedly.

'Goodnight. Sleep well.'

She nodded and smiled. 'You too.'

Rick climbed the steps to his little front porch and, feeling for the door handle in the dark, opened the netting door gently and entered. He looked across at the bed and could make out the recumbent form of Chrissie curled up tight into a foetal position, a sleeping pose she often adopted.

He undressed and climbed in quietly beside her. She stirred slightly but was otherwise quiet. He heard the door of the neighbouring room close as he lay in the dark. He involuntarily frowned. Can it be that she's going out again? he wondered. He raised himself on his elbows and listened. There was no further sound. He relaxed back on to his pillow. Perhaps she was just closing the door properly. He closed his eyes and sighed. They were due to make an early start tomorrow to drive along the tracks that bordered the mighty – but drought-affected – Limpopo River, so he'd better try and sleep.

The sudden sharp cry had been preceded by a sound rather like a slap. Rick opened his eyes again. He could hear muffled but angry sounding exchanges coming from next door. The bed squealed on the paved floor. There was another sharp cry and the unmistakable rhythmic shifting of a bed. It went on for about a minute before it stopped and there was a sudden hush. Rick turned on his side and tried to block out all thoughts.

Olifants Camp

Tom stood up and looked down at Lucie. She had not moved. Her exposed rump was over the side of the bed, her face buried in the ruffled sheets. She was sobbing quietly. Her tee shirt was pushed up near her neck and shoulders.

He found his underpants on the floor and put them on. He stood motionless staring down at the whiteness of her backside without saying a word, and then suddenly strode around the bed to the other side and climbed on it. He found an edge to the covering sheet and tugged it roughly to cover himself. She was forced to release some of the bunched-up sheet that her head was hidden in. He turned his head and watched her, expressionless.

She slowly raised herself onto her elbows and let her head hang down. The hair created a curtain right down to the mattress. After remaining like this for a minute, she straightened herself on to her knees. Even in the dark her face looked blotchy and crumpled. The moisture on her cheeks and around her eyes glistened in the dark. She sniffed loudly and slowly drew her hand across her nose.

Still kneeling beside the bed she removed her tee shirt and wiped her face with it. She then used the bed as a support and stood up. She was naked and still holding the crumpled tee shirt in her hand. An expression of disgust and scorn came across her face when she looked at him. She parted her legs and used the tee shirt to rub between them vigorously, still looking straight at him. She flung the shirt at him and went off to the small toilet. The door closed and Tom could hear the shower running.

He had fended off the shirt. He now grabbed it and flung it over toward the pile of clothes in the corner. He cursed softly under his breath, and turned on his side away from the bathroom door. The shower continued and he started to wonder if he should get up and turn it off, but dismissed the idea when he considered that she had very probably locked the door.

He continued to seethe quietly to himself as he contemplated the betrayal of his trust by both his girlfriend and his long-time friend and guest. He wondered if they had actually slept together, in all the afternoons back in Capetown when they had the opportunity to do so... Clenching his fist tightly, he told himself to calm down, he would find the time and place to teach Rick a lesson. He turned back to face the bathroom door to watch Lucie when she came out.

The shower stopped and a moment later the door opened. Steam streamed out. Lucie turned off the light and re-entered the dark bedroom. She picked up her panties, observed they were badly torn and flicked them into the bin. She walked over to their bag and pulled out a new pair of panties and tee shirt. Having put them on, she pushed her wet hair back off her face and looked down at Tom in silence. She picked up her pillow off the bed and walked over to the cupboard. She opened it, found a spare blanket and settled down on the floor.

He pushed himself up on an elbow and looked down at her curled-up figure. 'Listen. There are always scorpions and bugs on the floor. Come to bed.'

'Fuck off!'

'*You* can fuck off, traitorous bitch! You deserve much worse, you little slut. Stay on the fucking floor.' He turned on his side noisily.

'I shall. I prefer to take my chances with the scorpions than you.'

Tom stared out into the dark, consumed with visceral anger that blocked all chance of sleep.

Kruger National Park

They had all slept well, for the excitement of actually crossing the border into South Africa and being out of Mozambique had been very exhausting. They now felt safe, for the dreaded marauding Renamo gangs were behind them, and the ever-present danger of being picked up by the Frelimo border guards had faded the

151

further they had gone from the border fence.

The night had passed without incident. They were at least a kilometre from the fence, and had followed little tracks made by animals. They had crossed only one dirt road, which was really only a set of ruts, otherwise there had been no sign of any human habitation.

It was very early and the sun was barely making a faint glow in the East behind them. The sun will rise first on the country that has abandoned me, but in fact I have quite easily abandoned her for the time being, reflected Rodrigo. He continued to envision how in time he would return with wealth, find his mother in the Muanza refugee camp, and see her proud, and happy for her son's achievements. It was even conceivable that Mopete would be with him, and with a child, he mused dreamily.

'Comrade Rodrigo. It is time we move. The sun – it is close,' hissed Nkosi in the dark. 'Nkosi is right.'

Nkosi was crouched beside him in the gloom. Rodrigo raised his head to peer around him.

'We should make much distance. Half a day of walking, before we relax,' continued Nkosi.

Rodrigo disengaged his arm from beneath Mopete's shoulder. He felt piqued at all the gratuitous advice. He was the leader. 'I agree. We must move, but we shall move in a north direction. Water is almost finished. The river will not be too far. We must also find food. The next hamlet. We shall rob and move quickly. Get everybody up. Let's go.'

Once everyone was raised. Rodrigo signalled to Nkosi to lead. They would carry on in the same formation as yesterday, whereby he would carry the gun, some twenty metres behind. Nkosi started off with an almost jaunty simian gait.

Twenty minutes later Nkosi signalled that there was danger ahead. He crouched low and waited for Rodrigo to catch up with him.

'What is it?' whispered Rodrigo.

'Road. This one is better. More used. More people.'

Rodrigo squinted ahead and saw the carefully graded dirt road. It was as Nkosi said, better maintained and therefore a greater danger. It ran at an angle to their present direction, slightly north-west. It probably leads to the water and villages, Rodrigo guessed.

'Let us cross it and then follow it, some thirty metres in the bush, on the other side. I think it will lead us to the river ... but also to people. We must be careful.'

They both froze when they heard the breaking of the twigs. There was somebody – or something – very close by. They turned slowly to peer into the gloom to their side see if they could make out what had made the noise in the dense surrounding bush. Rodrigo raised his gun to shoulder level and again checked that the safety catch was not on. They stayed totally motionless.

The twigs cracked again followed by the rustle of slow movement through the bush. The enemy was probably only ten metres away. Rodrigo looked quickly at Nkosi and raised his eyebrows twice in rapid succession, at the same time nodding in the direction of the bush away from the group huddled close to the ground behind them. Nkosi understood.

He picked up a stone very steadily and carefully. With one last glance at Rodrigo to verify all was right, he lobbed the stone into the bush some ten metres to the side.

As soon as the stone clattered through the bush and hit the ground, Rodrigo stood and peered down the sights of the gun, ready to fire. He heard a snort and the sound of something scurrying through the bush away from them. He relaxed. It was probably a warthog, judging by the noise it was making.

He smiled at Nkosi sardonically, and let out a sigh of relief. 'It always pays to be on guard.'

'I worry about the South Africans. They are very rich and very strong. All the Zulus, they fear the Dutch ones. They are very tough.'

'We have nothing to fear. We are of this land. We are black. We know the ways of the people. No white man can know Africa like we do. Have we not survived so far.'

Nkosi managed a grin, but looked unconvinced.

It started with what seemed to be a puff from a steam engine, and was instantly followed by the crashing sound of something hurtling through the undergrowth. Nkosi's eyes opened wide with fright, and his jaw dropped open revealing a set of white teeth that had at least two missing from the centre. He looked paralysed with fear.

Rodrigo spun around and raised his sub-machine gun to his shoulder as he did so. He had levelled it at the dark object hurtling toward them and fired off a volley before he even realised what was attacking them. The noise in the stillness of the night was deafening. Yellow-blue tongues of light leaped from the barrel as the rapid volley was fired.

The black rhino stumbled with the impact of the high velocity bullets and buckled on to its front knees. It emitted a short, single, high-pitched squeal. It then stood up and shook itself as if disbelieving it had been hit, before pawing the ground once and starting to charge again.

Rodrigo had regained some level of composure and had put in a new clip. He had not expected the beast to continue its charge. He fired off a second volley, but to his horror on about the third or fourth bullet the gun jammed. He looked up in horror at the rhino.

It had stopped, and appeared confused. It staggered to one side. It then swayed as its great head sunk lower to the ground. The rapid pants changed, and now took on a liquid quality, and became gurgles. Its vital lifeblood flowed in torrents from its massive wounds into the parched soil. With a rasping gurgling sound, the great animal eventually sank to its knees. Its head attempted one last effort at fighting the ever-weakening neck muscles, but gave up and hitting the ground rolled to one side. The last remnants of life ebbed away. It was only ten metres away from them.

Nkosi was jubilant, and warmly congratulated Rodrigo. The group all surged forward from the dark bush. Only Rodrigo felt in no mood to celebrate, for the sole weapon for their defence was jammed. He decided to examine it in the morning light. He moved slowly forward toward the dead rhino.

Nkosi had already started to hack off the horn, whilst the rest were starting to dismember the carcass. It represented meat, even if it would be tough.

The crashing noise in the bush made the group scatter and dive for cover. Rodrigo swung round and again raised the gun to the firing position but with the sinking realisation that he was doomed, for there would be no protecting volley to save him this time. Then he saw the young rhino cub run in a panic through the bush and quickly out of sight, and relaxed. He lowered the gun, and managed a nervous chuckle. It must have been the cub they had disturbed earlier, and mother had seen fit to charge.

'It was good you didn't fire. Why waste bullets?' Nkosi patted him on the back approvingly, and returned to his self-appointed task as rhino-horn remover.

Rodrigo clenched his teeth together. He did not like what he felt was the patronising attitude of his comrade. He represented a real threat to his leadership.

'We shall cook in the morning. Fires at night may attract the enemy. We shall sleep here. Rest well. We shall have a feast of meat before we go to seek water in the morning. Let there be a constant guard.'

He saw Mopete looking at him appraisingly, and he wondered how loyal she was. She was poised, knife in hand, above the carcass, holding a bloody strip of meat in the other. He turned to find himself a place to curl up. He must get some rest and be alert; above all he must keep the gun next to himself, and fix it with the first light.

Kruger National Park

They had risen early and the game viewing had been spectacular. They had seen giraffe, kudu, impala, zebra, wildebeest and elephant. A herd of Cape buffalo had moved quietly out of sight into the tall but dry grass not far from the river's banks as they had approached. The mighty Limpopo River itself, although showing very clearly that its water level had dropped, was still home to a huge herd of hippos, and the smooth mud slides on the steeper banks testified to the presence of the ever dangerous crocodile.

Lucie had remained sullenly and obstinately silent. She had occasionally taken a drink from a canteen with fresh juice, but otherwise had hardly shifted in her seat, and viewed the wildlife with complete disinterest. She remained distant behind her dark glasses. Chrissie meanwhile had drifted off to sleep in the back seat, with her head cradled on Rick's lap. Only Tom and Rick were talking.

As they moved slowly along in the rented Land-Rover, Tom

spotted a van ahead. It was a white VW camper van, and was pulled off the road in a viewing spot near the river. Tom indicated he was going to have a word with the owners.

They pulled alongside, and a pleasant-looking sandy-haired young man, the driver of the van, chatted amiably with Tom. They had spotted a pride of lion just off the road about three kilometres further along the track in the direction that Tom and his party was headed.

'They were about six in all. All lionesses, with about three cubs, I think. I guess there may well be a lion around, but we didn't see him, did we, Faye?'

The woman sitting next to the young man agreed. 'By now they will probably be near the waterhole, on the right hand-side of the road. They might even have got the African by now.'

'What African?' asked Tom.

'Oh, just some down-and-out terrorist from across the border, I guess. He was near the waterhole. He had a wound on his leg, and was crouched near the water, in the shade on the left of the water as you drive in,' answered the man.

'Was he armed?'

'Didn't seem to have anything with him, but you never can tell with these guys.'

'What did you do?' asked Rick.

'Do? Nothing! What do you expect me to do?' he answered defensively.

'Well, you said he was injured,' replied Rick.

The man squinted at Rick. 'You English or something?'

'What is it to you?' snapped Lucie.

The man rolled his window up rapidly, curling his lip up in disgust. 'Fucking *kafferboetie*![35] he shouted as the window closed. He turned his back on them inside the car.

Tom drove off slowly. 'Well, you guys certainly rubbed him up the wrong way.'

'Fucking arsehole,' said Lucie.

'Ja. Everybody who doesn't agree with you always is,' said Tom with venom.

---

[35]Lover of blacks.

Rick cleared his throat. 'Before we have a full scale argument here, the guy was a prickly character who immediately took offence at my question … and went on the attack.'

'Well, your question was offensive, or at best provocative.'

'Why? I asked what he did about it … about the injured African that she mentioned.'

'What did you expect him to do about it?'

'I don't know, perhaps offer some assistance, perhaps organise to contact the Park Rangers so that he can be picked up. I realise that it may be impractical to take him along, but at least offer some help. Christ, Tom, the guy is a human being and there is a pride of lions heading for him!'

'Right,' intoned Lucie.

'It doesn't work like that. You cannot trust the Africans. This guy may well be a genuine refugee, but he could easily be a terrorist, and it could have been an ambush.'

'There is little cover offered by the surrounding bush near these waterholes, so my guess is that it's probably easy enough to check out if there was really any danger. Anyway, we're becoming sidetracked. What he did or didn't do is not the actual issue. The ethics of doing nothing and leaving the individual to be a possible lion pride's meal is something else. The issue is why the hell the guy should have been so offensive – or did he actually have a guilty conscience?'

Tom drove on in silence and then tentatively started his answer, 'Okay. I guess I feel it wasn't that, it was the way … the way you asked your question … the way Lucie…'

'Jesus Christ!' said Chrissie from her curled up position. She sat up, and rubbed her eyes. 'The guy was a bloody racist. The questions were upsetting to him, because he would have to publicly admit out loud his racism. He hates the fucking kaffirs, and did not expect anything but support from youse all. Fuck, he's an Afrikaner. Probably AWB,[36] and he sees youse all as *kafferboeties* … which in case ya don't know what it means, Rick, is nigger lover. There is nothing more to discuss.' She lay down

---

[36] *Afrikaner Weerstand Beweging*, an extremist right-wing militia group led by Terre Blanche.

again. She then added petulantly, 'Wake me if there is any good wildlife.'

Tom smiled and drove on in silence. Rick and Lucie had also been stunned into silence. Chrissie's emphatic outburst had left a conversational vacuum.

The silence persisted. Tom slowed down and looked as if he was about to turn into the track leading to the waterhole that the couple had talked about, but obviously decided against it. Nobody commented.

'A lot of vultures up ahead,' observed Tom.

Rick lent forward and peered up at the sky. There were about ten vultures slowly circling the sky just ahead of them.

'There must be a large kill ... or death, for so many vultures to be about.' Tom shrugged. 'Maybe an elephant has keeled over.'

Lucie grunted and then suggested, 'Or the lions have got something.'

'Could be. The ... the uhm ... the fucking arsehole, said they were around here.'

Lucie glowered at him, but decided not to further inflame the situation by adding anything.

'See?' Tom pointed to a tree ahead of them just off the road. 'That tree ahead seems to be carrying the main load of the vultures around here. There must be a kill nearby.'

Chrissie sat up and they all peered into the surrounding bush. She removed the lightweight binoculars from its case and studied the bush near the tree. Tom drove very slowly. Nobody spoke. The windows were all down.

'Bloody hell! Is that a braai?[37] I smell meat cooking!' said Lucie, looking surprised.

'Shit! Oh man, shit! Tom, keep the bloody car moving! There are kaffir poachers out there. I've spotted at least two.' Chrissie kept her eyes glued to the binoculars.

'Bloody terrorists,' muttered Tom and leant forward to open the glove compartment. He pulled out his revolver, and taking his hands off the steering wheel briefly, unbuttoned the protective holster, took the gun out and placed it on the dashboard in front

---

[37] Barbecue.

of him. He kept driving steadily and pulled off the road, some fifty metres ahead behind some thicker bushes.

'What the hell do you think you are doing?' asked Lucie. 'If you are intent on any heroics, I beg you to forget it. Only you are armed, and there may be twenty of them for all we know.'

Tom shrugged, checked that the gun was fully loaded and then filled his pockets with spare ammunition. 'I will go and check it out. If I cannot deal with it I shall return. You stay. The car keys are in the ignition.'

'Do you think you are bloody Rambo? Come to your senses man!'

'This is my country, Lucie! I realise that you are not sure if it really is yours, but it is mine, and bloody hell, sometimes we must stand up for it!'

'This is putting all of us in unnecessary danger, whilst you arse around playing soldiers.'

'I know what I'm doing. I was in a *Koevoet*[38] in Namibia. If I can't deal with these terrorists, I shall return.'

'I'll come with ya. I'm small and I can stay out of sight,' said Chrissie.

Tom looked back at her and nodded. 'Good. Let's go. Rick, get into the driver's seat. Lucie, watch through the binoculars. Okay?'

'I don't believe this, you are mad.' Lucie spoke with a resigned tone.

Tom and Chrissie ran quickly and crouched low into the surrounding bush. Rick climbed over the seat into the drivers' seat, and looked back. He had not said anything during the recent exchange, but rather like Lucie, felt that this couldn't really be happening.

Kruger National Park

Nkosi felt sure the engine had stopped. He listened intently, but could not hear it any more. He pushed some bushes gently aside, but the vehicle could not be seen. It had either stopped on the track at some distance, or had continued down some sidetrack, for

---

[38]Crowbar, the name of a type of armoured car, also a specific counter-insurgency unit that operated in Namibia.

he had a view down the main road ahead, and it was not to be seen.

'I am sure they stopped.'

'Were they soldiers?' asked Rodrigo.

'Not all. One was female. White.'

'More than four?'

'I think four.'

Rodrigo peered back over his shoulder. The small smoke-free fire that they had cooked on was out, covered by soil. There had been no smoke. It must have been the vultures that had attracted the white man.

He looked to the side, at the remaining six in his group. They were all lying flat on the ground, studying the bush for any sign of the white people. He wished he had some weapons.

'I think we must start a fire. The wind is gentle, but it will destroy evidence, and is in a direction away from the river. The bush is dry. There will be smoke and it will allow us to continue on to get water.'

'I think they know we are here,' muttered Nkosi.

'Are you sure?'

'I think …'

'Stop thinking. Did they see us?'

'Yes.'

'Let us stay low a little longer and then we light a fire,' grumbled Rodrigo. He felt irritated. The day had seen them all have a good feed, but the vultures had come with extraordinary speed. The white man had come quickly to see what was happening.

He looked back into the bush, and decided that they must have driven on. He noticed Nkosi turning round with a bewildered look on his face.

A wave of panic swept through him as he heard the strong male voice bark out something unintelligible behind him. He shuddered involuntarily, and turned slowly.

A tall blond man was standing about ten metres behind them with his legs spread apart and his arms outstretched toward them pointing a gun. He repeated his meaningless command and kept covering them all in a slow sweeping motion. Rodrigo was still stunned and continued to stare with awe.

'Put your hands above your head. Lie face down, and spread your legs,' said a clear female voice in Portuguese. Rodrigo gaped. A small white lady was crouched near a tree to the left of the man.

'Do it or we shoot!' shouted the female.

Rodrigo turned back slowly and groaned. It was all over.

'Do it now,' hissed Nkosi.

Rodrigo looked at him. Nkosi's veins stood out with tension and his eyes glowered with hatred.

'Do it now,' he repeated. 'It will soon be too late.'

Rodrigo looked down. It would be suicide to try and turn on this man.

Nkosi suddenly leant across and snatched the AK-47. Rodrigo was so surprised that he had no time to react or stop him. Empty-handed, he was sidelined and could only watch as the events unfolded. Nkosi rolled twice in the dust and raised himself swiftly to a crouching firing position with the gun pointing at the white man.

Rodrigo had heard the white man's shout, and heard the two rapid reports. He looked back at Nkosi. He had turned on to the small of his back and was curled with his legs in the air. He still held the gun tightly to him. Blood was already spreading across his grubby tee shirt. He was nodding his head in disbelief and seemed to be saying something like 'Why?' He coughed, and blood appeared at his mouth and nose.

Rodrigo ducked instinctively as he heard another sharp report. He heard a scream. He raised his head cautiously and saw Sokhela thrashing around on the ground with a serious leg wound. The white man had moved to a crouching position a little to one side from where he had been standing. He could not see the white woman.

He turned to look at Nkosi again, and realised that life had flowed from him and with it the spirits. His eyes were still open, and still registered surprise. He had not known that the gun was jammed.

It was at that moment that Rodrigo heard Mopete's shrill girlish voice. 'My comrade is wounded. I have no gun. I will attend to him. He also has no gun. Do not shoot.'

He heard the white man and woman discuss something in a foreign tongue and then the white woman answered, 'You can help your friend. Anything funny and you will be shot.'

Rodrigo watched Mopete get up slowly and stand proud. She looked strong and self-assured. Did she have a plan? He wondered. She moved across to Sokhela's side in a slow and steady movement. She looked like a wild animal in its prime. How had she kept this aura about her with their meagre and erratic food and water supplies, all the while enduring such physical hardship? Perhaps the answer lay entirely with her youth, Rodrigo speculated.

The sudden deafening noise made him cringe with fright. The vultures had all taken flight as the massive helicopter swept low seemingly only just above the treetops. It hovered fractionally to one side. A loudspeaker boomed out a voice in Portuguese, 'You have entered South Africa illegally. Lay down all your weapons. You are covered. Lie with your hands above your head. Do not resist. This is the South African Security Force.'

He stared up at the chopper in disbelief. He could clearly make out a man behind a large machine gun that was trained on them. He heard the white man shout something but it was lost in the din.

Suddenly the helicopter moved away and seemed to go to the road to land. It was then that he realised that he was surrounded by about ten well-armed troops. They were all white. He put his head down into the dry dusty soil and resigned himself to his fate.

Kruger National Park

Luitenant Homan introduced himself to Tom, and patted him on the back. 'Bloody marvellous, man! You certainly showed these black bastards what you were made of!' He laughed out loud.

Tom turned to his new-found friend, 'Luitenant …'

'Call me Andries.'

'Andries. There was a black girl. A young one. She ran off when the chopper arrived. I shouted at her to stop but she did not and was very quick.'

'Not a problem. We will round her up easily, and if not, the big cats will get her.' He chuckled. 'They have developed a taste for human flesh, some of these cats. Constant clean up job they have.'

'Ja, by the way, back at the waterhole …'

'We have him already in the second chopper. A lone refugee. The lions nearly got him.'

Tom nodded and watched as the soldiers searched and bound the hands of the sorry band, making them stand huddled close together near the tree. Rick and Lucie were making their way toward him accompanied by a soldier.

'What will happen to them?' he asked.

'Well, the leader goes straight to Jo'burg for interrogation. The rest, well …' his voice trailed off and he shrugged.

'Returned across the border?'

'Sort of. Shit man, you understand we don't want more garbage than we already have?' He chuckled.

Tom smiled. He watched the soldier come up to them. He was carrying an AK-47. He spoke in Afrikaans.

'They only had one weapon, Luitenant. A jammed Soviet assault weapon. Very easy to fix, but these dumb bastards couldn't! Apart from that they only had slingshots and knives.'

'Do you know who was the leader? Is it the stiff over there?'

'No. It is the guy who looks close to tears over there.'

They all looked across at the huddled group of prisoners. Rodrigo stood a little apart with his head bowed and his body partially slumped forward. The rest looked subdued but not too concerned. Sokhela was a little to one side and being attended to by a military paramedic.

'Bring him over.'

The soldier fetched Rodrigo and escorted him back. He stood in front of Tom and Luitenant Homan with his head bowed.

'What is your name?' asked the Luitenant in Portuguese.

'Rodrigo Gusmao.'

'Where are you from?'

'Near Maputo.'

'You realise you are in South Africa?'

'Yes sir.'

'Who sent you?'

'Nobody.'

'Are you the leader?'

'Yes sir.'

'What was the name of the girl who got away?'

'Mopete.' A flicker of a smile crossed his face.

'Are you terrorists?'

Rodrigo shook his head forlornly.

'You are wearing some Frelimo items of clothing. Are you deserters?'

Rodrigo did not answer, just raised his head to look at his interrogator.

'Why were you armed with a Soviet weapon?'

'With what?'

'A Russian, a communist weapon.'

'We stole it.' He shrugged and turned to scrutinise Tom.

'I don't think they were real poachers, just a bunch of bandits,' reflected Luitenant Homan. 'Probably surprised the rhino and were starving anyway.'

Tom looked at the bunch rounded up by the army personnel. They carried no hatred, no intense animosity, thought Tom. They were a little curious, but above all the expression was one of tired resignation. Poor bastards, he thought and wondered what would become of them.

The soldiers led Rodrigo to the second helicopter, and started to load the others on to the first helicopter. Tom caught a glimpse of an emaciated black man already sitting in the chopper with his hands bound behind his back. He presumed he must be the refugee who had been picked up at the waterhole.

'Well, Tom. It was truly a pleasure. My congratulations.'

'Thank you.'

'Two things, though. One is that I prefer if nobody talks of any of this to the press; and two, we need a statement from you. I think the easiest thing is to get that from you at the Lodge. Where are you staying?'

'Punda Maria.'

'Good. I'll pass by this evening if that is okay?'

'Ja, no problem. Look forward to it.'

'Mention what I said to your friends, and keep the gun out of sight. It is of course illegal to have one in the park!' He laughed and set off after Rodrigo.

Rick and Lucie came up and surveyed the scene. Chrissie also joined them. Two soldiers had just finished placing Nkosi's body in a plastic casualty bag that they immediately zipped up and hauled off unceremoniously to the waiting chopper.

'Well done, Tom,' said Chrissie and extended her hand.

'Thanks.' He smiled and then added, 'I'm glad you came along. Where did you learn Portuguese?'

'Angola. Basically from Mum and Dad.'

'Well, it sure came in useful!'

'Did you kill that guy in the sack?' asked Lucie doubtfully.

'Ja. He drew an AK-47 on me.'

'You are so lucky to be alive. Christ we had no idea what the hell was going on!'

'Well, I'm sorry about that, but as they say, "All's well that ends well." Let's return to the car.'

They all walked back to the vehicle and had to protect their eyes from the dust storm the choppers made as they took off. As soon as the deafening roar had faded, the silence seemed to suddenly envelope them as fully as the dust previously had. They walked in silence.

Rick stopped and looked down. A dark, bloodied object lay in the dust, with flies gathering all over it.

'What the hell is that?'

Lucie who was closest turned away in disgust. 'A rhino horn.'

They had all stopped to stare at it. Chrissie picked it up and disturbed a swarm of flies. She examined it and chose to speak. 'The Arabs pay a high price for the horn to put as handles to their daggers. The Taiwanese pay a high price for the horn to make a powder to increase their potency. The Kaffirs kill the rhino for just the horn and will sell to any bidder. This bunch were amateurs. Probably just poachers.' She then tossed the horn off into the bush.

They all returned to the car in silence.

The horn landed with a thud in the dust. For a second Mopete thought she had been discovered. It had landed just behind her. She was curled up and was virtually covered with soil and some loose branches. A warthog had dug the hole in search of succulent roots and it now provided her with a perfect cover.

She heard the engine start nearby and drive off. She felt very alone.

Punda Maria Camp

They all sat at the table in the bar and said nothing. There had been an almost complete silence since the disturbing incidents in the morning. Nobody had felt like further game viewing and they had returned to lounge by the pool at the Punda Maria Lodge. They had been the only ones there all day; as all the other camp residents were out viewing game.

Lunch was served by the pool, and somehow even the food had not broken the aura of gloom and introspection. In the afternoon they had each read their own books, and lain in the sun. Separate, distant and silent, the time had past till the evening bell had rung to announce the first servings of dinner.

Rick sipped his gin and tonic and sighed. 'Well, that was quite a day. I must agree I don't feel like further game viewing, but it seems a little idiotic to throw it all away because … because of ugly incidents like the one this morning.' He took another sip and studied the condensation patterns on the glass. 'Perhaps, if you all agree, we should keep away from areas near the border so we can continue the trip?'

Chrissie disagreed. 'No. Well, I dunno, but I've had enough. I phoned Gerard this afternoon, Rick … and he's happy to put me up in Jo'burg at his flat. I've bought a Comair ticket from Phalaborwa Gate back and have organised a ride early tomorrow on a bus to Phalaborwa. The bus leaves early – at five – and the plane at five in the evening. Gerard said he'd meet me at the airport – at the other end.'

'That's a bit drastic, isn't it?'

She shrugged. 'I can do what I like.'

'Undoubtedly. I'm just a bit surprised, that's all.'

'So? You don't own me. I can do what I like.'

Rick looked exasperated. 'I didn't say I was trying to stop you. Go. Please go if it makes you happy.'

'I will. I already said I would.'

'Fine.'

Tom cleared his throat. 'If you don't mind, Lucie, I think I feel it would be best if I also went. I also was on the phone, and because of my past with Koevoet, the SA Defence Force guys and the Veiligheidspolisie[39] ... the security blokes in John Vorster Square, said they would like me to drop by, and receive a thanks in person. I've talked briefly with Luitenant Homan, and he's keen that I go, so I've got the option of driving there or taking the Comair flight with Chrissie. It seems sensible to fly.'

Lucie had studied him as he had spoken. 'I presume your plans only extended as far as yourself?' she asked. Her eyes took in Chrissie and the eyebrows raised inquisitively as she continued, 'Or is it plural?'

Tom looked uncomfortable with the insinuations and the tone of his voice revealed his mounting irritation. 'I alone felt it better to do that and suggest that you help Rick drive back to Johannesburg, or perhaps stay a further few days in the Kruger, and then drive back to get a free flight with Gerard?'

'Gee, thanks!'

'Am I being unreasonable?'

'No, it's okay. You buzz off to the social security of your tribe. I'll stay if Rick wants to stay on, but I don't think I want to rush back to fly back with Gerard. I've a few more days up my sleeve, so I for one may well stay with my folks and then take the train back.'

'And you, Rick?'

'I would very much like it if Lucie did stay on, but certainly not if it's under duress.'

'It's okay. I'd love to stay if you want me to.'

'Yes – why, yes. I'd enjoy the company. That would be great. I'd be happy to take the train back as well, as it's another way of seeing the country. I've also got a couple of contacts in Jo'burg who could probably put me up for a couple of nights ... and it would be good to see him.'

'Don't be silly. If we need accommodation, you can stay with my family, and still go out to see your friends.'

Tom looked at Lucie. 'Will you guys get us to Skukuza, or

---

[39]Security police.

shall we take the bus?'

'We'll take you,' volunteered Lucie.

'Good. Anybody want another drink?'

They all nodded in agreement and Tom left to fetch a new round. He returned carrying a one-day old copy of the *Johannesburg Star* on the drinks tray, which he placed on the table. The headlines loudly proclaimed the horrendous events surrounding the massacre of various black ANC workers in the Natal Province by presumed Inkatha loyalists.

Tom peered down at it and then swivelled it around for Rick to read. 'A legacy of the past, or a foretaste of the future?'

Rick shrugged. 'My guess is that it's a bit of each. Machiavelli's doctrine is at work here; as long as your enemies are not united, you can rule in peace.'

Tom chuckled. 'Is that what he was all about? I've heard the name often enough, but always been too shy to ask!' His expression turned sombre. He looked at Rick. 'Seriously though, do you disapprove of what happened this morning?'

Rick shrugged his shoulders. 'Not *disapprove* exactly. I felt you were a bit reckless. There was tragedy already inasmuch that somebody died, but we could have all ended up as casualties.'

'I don't think so.'

'No I gather you don't. But as I see it you took a risk...'

'Which worked!'

'Yes. But you have to allow for the possibility, however remote it may seem to you, that you might have failed, and there would have been a greater number of casualties, including all of us.'

'These people are unable to fight effectively. They are peasants who are not properly trained and poorly armed.'

'They may be, but demography dictates that there are enough of them to count. You had no idea how many there were, nor how well armed they might be.'

'I went on a recce – a reconnoitre trip. They weren't many, nor were they well armed. The demography argument does not count. They are not well-armed people.'

'Agreed. The numbers equation is in a broader sense, I agree. But still, it would be wiser to make peace with them, rather than continually confront them. What happens if, one day, Mandela and Buthelezi decide that enough is enough and truly unite their forces?'

'Unlikely. The Xhosa and Zulus have always hated each other.'

'Like the British and the French? Or the French and the Germans? They are all together today in the EC.'

'For every example you have of peaceful coexistence, there are others – the Serbs and Croats, the Greeks and Turks, the Jews and the Arab Muslims, and so on. We have to plan to survive this. If Aids doesn't decimate them, then we shall have to hold the line. Man is in part a function of what he believes, and we are moulded by what has happened to us … as a people.'

'History is a lesson, and those who ignore it are condemned to repeat it, but life moves on. The confrontations of your ancestors in Africa are all in the past. Be wary, but move forward. You can't read the writing on the wall, because I believe you collectively have your backs to it, but it seems to me that you only have to step away a little to be able to see. Some of your gifted poets and writers … Afrikaners such as Breytenbach, Brink and Coetzee … have seen it years ago.'

Tom shook his head negatively. 'You are such a typical Anglo. Always so bloody tolerant,' he paused for dramatic effect, and then added, 'until you find something you can't stand!'

Chrissie laughed. 'Ja. Spot on!'

Tom looked revitalised by her support. 'I feel that an incident such as this one you saw should not leave you un-moved. I grant that there was an element of risk, and even that we might not have emerged from it, but …' he shook his head disbelievingly…'don't you feel revitalised, almost reborn, now that good has triumphed over evil? The West has held the line against the Communists and terrorists. Isn't that a triumph?'

'I'm moved, all right. I'm saddened.'

'That's a pity.'

Lucie stood up. 'Let's have dinner and drop this topic. There will never be a solution to your arguments. I believe that all problems carry the seeds of their solution, but we certainly don't have the means to germinate them. Chrissie, shall we go and find a table and let these guys follow?'

Chrissie stood up and linking arms with Lucie strode off in search of a dining-room table. Neither of the menfolk stirred.

'I'm sorry if you are upset.'

'I'm not. Just a little stunned. A little confused.'

'You feel I shouldn't have done it, but—'

'It's okay,' interrupted Rick. 'No need for any apologies. You are at least being true to yourself.'

Tom stared straight at Rick. Rick kept the stare for a moment and then looked away. 'What?' he asked.

'Are you?'

Rick looked down as if considering the question. 'Intellectually, yes. Emotionally … I'm not sure.'

Tom considered this and looked puzzled. Without words they rose and went off to join the ladies.

'So that's the end of your Capetown lady, eh?' enquired Tom.

'It seems so. Endings are often beginnings … I don't know, but perhaps it's better this way. I can begin my travel in earnest – unencumbered!'

'Beginnings, eh?'

Rick frowned and looked quizzically across at Tom as they walked. His brow was furrowed as if he was grappling with troubling thoughts.

Five: Chorale

Beethoven's concluding movement tends to be more triumphant and heroic in character. It is meant as the climax of the whole symphony. A theme in one movement will only rarely reappear in later movements. Beethoven's Ninth being an exception. But a symphony is unified partly by the use of the same key in three of its movements. More important, the movements balance and complement each other both musically and emotionally.

> Ah Love, could thou and I with Fate conspire
> To grasp this sorry Scheme of Things entire.
> Would not we shatter it to bits – and then
> Re-mould it nearer to the Heart's Desire?
>
> Omar Khayyám

Tom

'Shall we have a drink in Mopani Camp first?' asked Tom. He looked round at Rick and Chrissie in the back, and they both nodded their agreement. Lucie was staring fixedly out the window and chose not to even acknowledge the question.

The fork ahead had a sign indicating the airfield, but Tom drove on. The Camp was a further three kilometres off the main road.

They parked in the large area shaded by the jacaranda trees and walked over to the air-conditioned bar. It was mid-afternoon and only a handful of people were at the bar.

'Beers all round?' asked Tom.

They all nodded. Rick moved forward. 'Let it be my shout. I'm fairly sure you ended up paying the bill last night, as I certainly didn't!'

Tom smiled. 'It still seems to me that it's a pity that it should all end like this. Has anyone any change of mind?'

'What sort of change of mind do you have in mind? We all fly with you two and leave the Rover here? Good one Tom!' quipped Lucie.

'No I meant …' his voice trailed off. 'Stuff it. Who cares what I meant!'

They all drank their beers and stared absently about them. The small Indian barman made a lame attempt to chat with the group, but feeling out of place and uncomfortable, quickly moved away.

Rick glanced at his watch. Chrissie took his arm. 'Ja. It's time. Let's get to the airfield.'

They returned to the car. Rick drove to the airfield, and parked alongside various minibuses with their tour drivers waiting to pick up passengers. The Comair operated daily shuttle flights between Jan Smuts International Airport in Johannesburg and the Phalaborwa Gate near the National Park; in one hour, international passengers arriving in South Africa could find themselves in the wilds of the largest park in the continent.

The two passengers checked in and handed over their small travelling bags to be stowed in the cargo hold. A smartly dressed young lady attended them behind the small counter. 'The flight is on schedule, and should be here in about fifteen minutes,' she said as she handed back the two tickets. 'I hope you have a pleasant flight.'

Tom turned to Rick. 'Where were you planning on staying tonight?'

'I suppose Skukuza. I'm fairly sure they would have some vacancies, but I'm not too bothered. Whatever Lucie thinks. She'll have to be tour guide for the next few days.' He shrugged his shoulders resignedly.

Lucinda smiled wanly and agreed, 'Skukuza tonight if there are vacancies, but if not perhaps Satara Camp, which is not too far.'

'And then?' persisted Tom.

Lucinda shrugged. 'Wherever. Probably follow the Sabie River for a day and then head down to the Malelane Lodge … it's meant to be great, and right on the Crocodile River. I'll see what Rick wants.'

'Good. I hope it all goes well. I know it will be fun.' Tom nodded sagely. 'No sense in you guys sticking around. Better go and sort things out before it gets dark.'

Rick held out his hand and they shook. They said goodbye and agreed to meet up in Capetown next week when Rick would pass through to retrieve his rucksack, and continue his trip. They wished each other well. Rick was distracted by Tom's clenched jaw. He remembered it clearly from his schooldays when they were about to play rugby; he had had the same look when he was about to do battle.

Rick turned to Chrissie. They embraced wordlessly and nodded their goodbyes to each other. She kissed her fingertip and placed it gently on his lips, and then turned away. He felt a twinge of regret; this wild, turbulent and impulsive female was walking out of his life; the unpredictable card was simply leaving. He studied her face one last time and realised how much he still admired that sultry look that had first attracted him to her. He turned away.

Lucinda and Tom were looking extremely clumsy together. His arms held her, but hers hung lifelessly at her side.

'Tom. Please let me go.'

He released her and stood back, looking offended.

'Tom. I would like to say this now. When I return, I shall be moving out. I've thought a lot about it, and I really feel it's for the best. Okay?'

'Fine. Nobody is holding you back. It strikes me as the best solution as well. *Tot siens, slet.*'[40]

Lucinda watched him turn to find a seat. She sighed deeply and turned to Rick. Her eyes were brimming with tears. 'Let's go, you still have a holiday to … to enjoy.' She managed a morbid chuckle.

They walked back to the car and started to move off. The Comair flight was just visible above the far end of the runway coming in to land. Neither spoke. Each had their own gremlins to deal with.

Kruger National Park/Transvaal

---

[40]Slut.

He saw the shadow move quickly into the bush, and wandered what it was. It had looked too bulky to be any form of buck, but could possibly be a very large male baboon. Nxongo slowed his truck from the permitted fifty kilometres per hour speed limit down to twenty and scrutinised the bush. The arid conditions meant that a lot of the vegetation had thinned out and the grass was short and sparse. It was easy to spot any large game, in spite of the slight shimmer the heat caused.

He was a driver who delivered supplies to the various northern camps from a large depot in Louis Trichardt, a country town in Northern Transvaal, and drove the route every week through the small nominally independent homeland of Venda. Nxongo himself was a Ndebele tribesman. Cautious and middle aged, he was proud of his job, and very keen to make sure he kept it, as his two wives and his seven children depended solely upon him.

He enjoyed his work immensely, and especially the drive through the Kruger National Park. He found it the most fascinating part of his journey, for he always felt spiritually at home. He loved to see the wildlife; to see the game that his aged grandfather had talked about, when life had been a constant struggle against nature, before the Boers had really changed the landscape. He had never been the least interested in politics, and unquestioningly accepted the status quo. Any challenge to it could result in him losing his means of support and his livelihood, so all his life he had adopted a cautious and non-confrontational attitude. Perhaps because of this, his Afrikaner boss liked and respected him.

The fleeting shadow had aroused his curiosity. It may even be a baby rhino, he mused. As he drew level with where he had seen the shape, he quickly checked that there was no tourist traffic in sight, and slowed down to a crawl. He hung out of the window and shielded his eyes from the setting sun.

He saw her crouching behind the bush. She had not had enough time to find good shelter and was now desperately trying to hide. Even from the twenty metres that separated them, Nxongo could see the fear.

Instinct told him to drive on; a lone black girl out here could only be up to some mischief and cause him trouble. He sat back in his seat and started to accelerate, berating his luck and life in general. He glanced in his rear-view mirror and saw the pathetic little figure stagger and fall. He pressed the brakes gently and slowed to a stop. He continued to watch her in the mirror. She got up again and limped heavily into deeper bush, she seemed exhausted. A wave of pity swept through him, she looked so frail and vulnerable.

There was no vehicle in sight. He reversed till he had drawn level with her. She had stopped and was squatting, looking back at him. She was expressionless, the hunted look he had fleetingly glimpsed earlier had gone. She was resigned to her fate, whatever it may be, and defiantly held her ground.

'Who are you? What are doing here? Don't you know this a wild place?' he shouted in English. She did not answer. He then repeated his questions in Ndebele and Afrikaans, but still she didn't respond. He wondered if he should just drive on, but the fact that she looked so young made him try one last tack. He held out a bottle of water. She stood up and watched him.

'Come and drink, girl!' he shouted and poured some out onto the parched soil.

The girl moved forward cautiously and eventually came to the side of the road and stopped.

He looked at her. Pretty young thing he thought, even if she is bedraggled and dirty. She appeared close to total exhaustion. He shook the bottle for her, indicating it was hers to have.

She eventually moved over and took the bottle. She drank avidly and had soon emptied it. Nxongo watched in awe, she had drunk a litre of water without even stopping for breath.

'Do you want some more?'

She shrugged and passed the bottle back. She stood there staring desolately up at him.

'Where you from?' he enquired. She shrugged again. 'You don't speak at all?'

Mopete explained in Portuguese that she didn't understand a word he was saying. Nxongo stared down at her looking perplexed, but passed her a second bottle. She drank half of it.

'I don't know what you saying. This some other white man

talk.' He felt confused. 'Okay you come to the park border. The animals, they eat you here. Get in.' He leant over and opened the passenger seat door.

Mopete did not hesitate. She moved around and climbed in. She smiled in gratitude as she took her seat.

Nxongo smiled in acknowledgment and passed her a plastic container with some biscuits. He watched as she devoured them with obvious relish. The girl was thirsty and hungry. He wondered where she was from and how long she had been in the bush.

They drove in silence, unable to communicate. Two neighbouring Africans unable to find a common language, but having the colour of their skin in common. They did not feel threatened by each other, and were comfortable with the silence.

The darkness was rapidly encroaching. He looked across at her and realised that she was fast asleep. Her head seemed to be able to remain upright in spite of the rocking motion of the vehicle. He would be reaching the park border soon. There was no way he would be able to keep her with him in the front cab. It would surely cost him his job, as he would be breaking company rules as well as park rules. He could however, store her in the back of the truck, and she could hide among the crates, mostly containing empty bottles. It had been a very long time since anybody had looked in the back and actually climbed inside the truck for a random check, so the chances were not very great. He also knew that in the evening it was mostly the black rangers who were on duty; the white ones had already returned to their families.

He fretted as to whether it was the right decision, as it did entail taking a risk, but was simultaneously shamed at the very idea of leaving a young and defenceless girl out in the wild. The risk to him was less than the risk to her, he concluded.

He put his hand on her shoulder and she was instantly awake. She looked very wide-eyed and for a second, like any young girl who finds herself in unfamiliar surrounds at night when woken from a sleep. The frightened look quickly changed to a distrustful assessing gaze, accompanied by a slight narrowing of her eyes. She was on guard and suspicious of him.

Nxongo laughed. 'Easy, missy! I don't mean harm.' He

stopped the truck and left the engine running. It was dark outside. The headlights lit up the road ahead, but the surrounding bush only gave a hint of surrounding hills against the dark azure sky of a cloudless evening.

With a nod of the head he indicated she should follow him. They went around to the back of the truck. He opened the door, and reached out to pick up the torch which hung on a bracket just inside. He shone it inside and then made covering type gestures to indicate she should cover herself inside. He handed her the torch.

He pointed ahead in the darkness. 'Police, police!' he said emphatically. He gestured again to the back of the truck. She hesitated for a second, and then smiled as she climbed in. She went to the back and crouched behind the crates.

Nxongo put his fingers to his lips and hissed a 'Shhh', hoping she understood that he wanted her to keep quiet. She seemed to understand. 'You be good now, you hear!' he muttered as he closed the doors. It would be very dark inside there, and he hoped she wouldn't panic.

As he approached the park border he realised his heart was racing. He mopped his brow and tried to calm himself. He looked around and noticed to his dismay the two young whites with moustaches and combat fatigues talking to Simon, the black Ranger. They looked like soldiers. Never before had he seen the presence of troops in the park. He wondered if he should declare his passenger in the back as he stopped and turned off the engine.

Simon strolled over. 'Nxongo, how is it?'

'Good. Really good.' He felt his voice betrayed his guilt.

'Punda Maria as usual?'

'Yes.'

The white man moved forward. 'How often are you on this run?'

'Once a week, baas.'

'You see anybody in the bush?'

'No, baas.'

The man walked alongside the truck and banged on the side. He moved back under the driver's window. 'What's inside?'

'Empty bottles, baas. From the Punda Maria Lodge, baas.'

The white man stopped and looked back at him. He seemed to

be studying his face. Nxongo resisted the urge to mop his brow, and remained impassive. The white man banged the side of the truck again. 'Who's your boss man?'

'Mr Petrus de Koker, baas.'

'He a good boss man?'

'Yes, baas.'

'You got nobody in the back?'

'No baas.'

'Okay you can go. If you ever see anything strange, you tell Simon here. Okay?'

'Yes, baas. I tell Simon all.' He grinned and nodded at Simon.

'Good man. Mr de Koker has a good man.' The white man waved him on.

Nxongo vowed that this would be his one and only effort to ever help somebody where his job was on the line. He drove out and sighed with relief. He glanced in the rear-view mirror and saw that there was no sign of anybody following him. He did not trust the soldiers, and he felt sure the one who had talked to him had sensed something.

Ten kilometres further on, he stopped at a small wayside African inn. He sometimes stayed the night here. He parked in the darker area, and turning the engine off, studied the other parked trucks. He recognised one that belonged to Themba, who often drove down to Lydenburg and Sabie. Themba was a good-natured young Xhosa, with a strong avaricious streak, and there was little he would not do for money.

Nxongo entered the café and located Themba. He bought him a drink and they talked rapidly in Fanagalo.[41] They shook on the deal.

They returned to their trucks, and Nxongo opened the back to let the girl out. She came out, blinking at the nearby lights. He smiled at her and taking the torch back led her across to the nearby truck.

'Missy, this here is Themba. He take you from here. Here is some tom.' He gave her twenty rand, and opened the door for

---

[41]An Esperanto language of Southern Africa with a mixture of Zulu, Xhosa, Tswana and English.

her. She shook his hand and climbed in. He walked around to the other side and paid Themba with a 50-rand note. He looked very happy.

Nxongo followed Themba out onto the road and allowed him to pull ahead. Half an hour later he saw his lights turn South toward Giyani and Lydenburg. Nxongo carried on straight toward the Venda border.

The police car appeared out of nowhere and put on its blue flashing light and siren. Nxongo swallowed hard and pulled over. He got out of the truck. There were two white policemen and the second white man whom he had seen at the park border.

They claimed he had been weaving slightly on the road, so would like him to submit to a breathalyser test. Since he had just had a beer with Themba, the reading was high, and the policeman claimed it was on the limit.

Nxongo was crestfallen. He knew this was unjust, but also knew it was a no-win situation. He would probably lose his job after all. It was best to just cooperate and play along. The soldier asked to search the truck, so Nxongo opened it for him. They spent some time rummaging inside.

'Have you got anything?' shouted the policeman to his colleague and the soldier inside the truck.

'*Ek het vokol!*'[42] said the soldier.

The policeman smiled patronisingly at Nxongo. 'Right. We'll let you off this time. Any more dangerous driving and you'll be in big trouble. You understand?'

'Yes baas,' mumbled Nxongo.

As he drove off he watched the police car race back toward the park border. He thanked the gods for his safe delivery.

Tom

He looked at his watch. The flight was on time, it had taken off on time and it was only an hour's flying time from the little runway at Skukuza. It was ten to six in the evening and they were beginning the descent and slow circle into Jan Smuts

---

[42]I have fuck-all.

International Airport. He looked out of the window at the country below.

The country was bathed in different hues of red and brown. There was a profound drought, and the red soil of the Transvaal was showing through the sparse covering vegetation. Around the great city were numerous spoil tips, a visual testimony to the mining spree that had brought people and money to the African bush the previous century. The large skyscrapers were bathed in warm colours from the setting sun and occasionally sparkled as the plane caught the reflections. A smoky pall of polluted air hung over a large section of the surrounding country where no tall buildings were to be found, and where many roads appeared small and unpaved, the notorious South-west-township, or Soweto. It was the troubled and turbulent home to the thousands of black workers who came to work the mines and run the city for the European settlers.

Tom stared down at it and felt an involuntary frown cross his brow. *Swartgevaar*, the fear of the blacks, who so evidently were the numerically superior people swept through him. Demography and time were against him, he reflected with regret.

Police HQ, Johannesburg

The officer watched as the prisoner was brought in. He was sitting behind a desk in a sparsely furnished room. There was a chair in the centre of the room and another near the door. The only decorations were two pictures on the walls; one depicted an early voortrekker[43] wagon heroically – or foolishly – attempting to cross a swollen river in pale water colours, and the other a black and white print of Paul Kruger, the austere Calvinistic hero of the nineteenth-century Boers.

There was a lot of smoke in the room, which caused the fading sunlight to be clearly defined in rays. The windows looking out on to downtown Johannesburg were heavily tinted and this in turn enhanced the gloom in the room.

The room was interview room number nine, on the seventh

---

[43]Resolute Dutch settlers who tekked north to the Transvaal in the nineteenth century.

floor of the security police headquarters in John Vorster Square, Johannesburg. Sitting behind the desk was Colonel Coetzee and flanking him stood two uniformed security police. A third security policeman had brought in the prisoner, who stood bowed and seemingly was about to collapse.

'I think you better get him to sit,' said the Colonel. 'He looks like he's had it.'

The policeman nodded. 'It has been a long day for him, sir.' He pushed the prisoner on to the chair.

Colonel Coetzee turned to the man on his left. 'The man responsible for the apprehension of this terrorist sounds a very interesting character. I would like to meet him when he comes in. I gather some other top brass will also be present, but please inform me.'

'Yes sir,' replied the security police officer.

The Colonel's attention turned back to the prisoner, and he studied the broken-looking man before him. His eyes were almost swollen shut and even the dark skin showed all the signs of bruising and lacerations. His hands were handcuffed behind his back, which caused his shoulders to appear strained. He slumped forward, breathing heavily through a partially obstructed nose.

'Has he added anything since, to the report?' asked the Colonel, lifting and then dropping the document back on the desk.

'No, sir. I feel that the story he gave is most likely the truth, and they were just a small band of brigand refugees, sir,' said the policeman in reply.

Colonel Coetzee looked at the closed report and pondered awhile. He then lit a cigar and turned to the man on his left. He was now speaking in Afrikaans. 'It's smoky in here. Please open the window, Piet. Make sure the courtyard is clear.' He turned to the other one and nodded at the prisoner. 'Rob, he has not seen the view, and that's a pity.'

The security policeman answering to the name Piet opened the window and breathed in deeply. He then casually looked down before he swung around and winked at his partner. The other two picked up the prisoner under the arms and walked him over to the window. He looked resigned until it suddenly dawned what was about to happen, when his face contorted into a rictus of disbelief and horror.

Rodrigo gave one piercing scream as he was lifted slightly and then tumbled through the window. He tried desperately to hook his feet on the sill as he started to move over, but the momentum was too great, and he only fractionally stayed his fall.

'Leave to report a suicide by the prisoner, sir,' said the policeman.

Colonel Coetzee gave his approval and requested reports from all present as to the circumstances that led up to the tragic suicidal death of the infiltrating terrorist. He walked straight out without even glancing back at the still open window.

Rick

He drove on in silence. He had been caught up in his own thoughts and presumed that Lucie was similarly distracted. As they arrived at Skukuza Camp, two VW Kombi vans were disgorging their tourists who were excitedly comparing notes on the day, the game spotted, the routes taken, the videos filmed, and the general exhilaration of it all. They sounded American. If they notice us at all, thought Rick, they probably see us as a couple who have just had a row and aren't talking to each other.

They walked over to the main reception, and on entering the air-conditioned room effectively blocked out the excited din the tourists were making outside. With its large posters, detailed maps and pamphlets explaining the different delights of the park, the office was a little oasis of calm. A pleasant-looking girl in khaki uniform came up to attend them.

'Can I help you?'

Rick answered. 'Yes, if you would. We need accommodation for the night. We haven't got any reservations. Do you have anything available?'

'For just the two of you?'

'Yes. Just the two of us.'

'Well, you are in luck. We have one rondavel left. It is a small one.' She paused and seemed to be considering her statement and then added in confirmation, 'Our smallest, in fact. It only fits the matrimonial bed and little else besides, but it does have that, the verandah, the shower and toilet facilities as well as the fridge. Would that be okay?'

Rick ran his fingers through his hair and looked across at Lucinda. 'I guess I can always sleep in the car, or...'

'Ja. We'll take it,' interrupted Lucie emphatically.

The girl nodded, though she had given them a quizzical look when Rick had spoken. She turned to fetch the paperwork and retrieve the keys. Once it was all completed she handed over the keys and bade them a good night.

When they located the rondavel that had been allocated to them, it proved to be as the girl had said. A basic, small, clean room dominated by the bed, which barely fitted the space. They placed their bags on the end of the bed.

'Not much space, huh?' chuckled Lucie.

'No, there isn't!'

'I guess we were warned.' She looked at him.

He shuffled uncomfortably and shrugged. 'Look, I can always sleep in the car.' He averted her eyes.

'I'm sure you can, but why? We're both adults. You take one side, and I'll take the other.'

'Well ... if you don't mind?'

'Should I?'

He looked directly back at her and they held each other's gaze for a few seconds. A psychic charge was building within him, which gave him an almost visceral pain. Still holding her gaze he answered, 'No. I can be trusted.'

A smile slowly spread across her face. 'You know, Rick, you took so long to answer, I almost felt the opposite!' She laughed for the first time since the airfield. 'How about we go over to the canteen for some drinks and food, before retiring. It would be good to have an early night if we are to achieve any serious game viewing. That sound okay to you?'

Rick agreed. They grabbed their pullovers and locking the door behind them set off in the rapidly encroaching gloom to the bar.

Johannesburg

Gerard was waiting in the hall. He had a trolley ready with a black porter, who relieved them of their entire luggage in an obsequious manner. Tom felt irritable. He had mentally branded the porter as a potential source of trouble.

Tom shook hands with his friend and politely stepped aside as Chrissie in turn came forward to greet him. Gerard greeted her as he would a long-lost love and embraced her fondly. His hands pulled her to him and Tom could not help but notice how one hand skimmed her pert little backside in a cupping motion. Tom was dismayed. Lust never sleeps he reflected.

'So you guys have had enough of the bush, huh?' laughed Gerard.

By way of an answer Chrissie chuckled and twined her arm around him. They gave every appearance of a couple in love, Tom thought. He felt acutely irritated, and discomfited. He knew very well that Chrissie owed him no allegiance and that he had absolutely no right to expect anything from her, but somehow her behaviour seemed almost treasonous. She was a free agent and had no commitments to anybody, but he had been the one who'd brought Rick into her life, and subsequently also brought her into contact with Gerard. He felt almost like a child who is promised a sweet if he does a good deed, but finds that the adults keep forgetting to reward him, and remains in that excruciating limbo of feeling cheated. The sweet is deserved but the embarrassment is great enough to actually prevent the asking. A frustrating misery endures way beyond the fleeting moments of pleasure the sweet would have brought. He snapped out of his reverie when he suddenly realised with a jolt that he was being spoken to. He stammered in his confusion to gather his thoughts, 'Sorry – what was it you were saying?'

Gerard smiled. 'Where were you, Tom? With Lucie?' He cocked his eyebrows mischievously. 'Or just miles away?'

'Just miles away,' he answered somewhat curtly.

'How is Lucie, by the way?'

'Fine. Just fine. She's making her own way back and showing Rick a bit of the surrounding countryside.'

They reached the car, a rented Toyota Cressida sedan. Gerard unlocked the doors and pressed the lever that sprang the boot open. The porter made a great show of placing everything extra neatly in the boot. Tom looked him straight in the eye, and to his surprise the man held his. He speculated about this and realised it was a sign of the times, the underprivileged and repressed class were beginning to show their muscle in the very heart of Afrikaner country, the Transvaal. The fish was rotting from its very head.

The porter asked if there was anything else to go in the boot, and could he close it.

'It's okay. Close it,' said Tom. He continued to regard the man.

'Yes baas.' The man turned and carefully but forcefully closed the boot. He then stood up straight and squared his shoulders. Their eyes were level.

'What's your name boy?' asked Tom as he took out a tip.

A hint of a smile that turned into a sneer crossed the porter's face. 'Gift.'

Tom looked straight back at him. 'Gift?'

The porter nodded as his whole expression turned scornful.

Tom gave him his tip and thanked him. He turned away. The charged atmosphere was almost palpable. There was an ominous and persistent feeling of danger. The porter's insolence had struck a raw nerve, he felt his very existence was challenged. He knew the man needed a *kafferpak*[44] to sort him out. He wondered if he shouldn't join the security forces, where he at least felt that the issues were being dealt with, and leave his comfortable life in Capetown. He climbed into the car, aware that his heart was racing.

Gerard had started the car and was already driving when he turned to address Tom. 'Hey listen, you are welcome to stay with me, man, but my apartment is a single-bedroom place, so you would be relegated to the couch. Somehow I feel …'

'It's all right. Drop me off at any central big hotel. I'll be fine.'

'You sure that's okay?'

'Of course. I appreciate the lift.'

'Chrissie and I are hitting some the night spots after dinner tonight. Do you wish to join us? You're welcome to tag along. It might help wash away all the tension from the events that you two were involved in … and by the way, I'd like to hear all about your heroics sometime.'

---

[44] Beating of a black.

'I'll pass on the evening. I'm pretty bushed.' What is more, I would not like to cramp your style, he added mentally. He then did add, 'It sounds like you have given some serious thought to the evening!' He knew his remark was caustic and vowed to try and keep his cynical side under tighter rein.

Gerard laughed and wagged a finger in an admonitory way. 'Listen, man, there is nothing more serious than play!'

Chrissie laughed and affectionately put an arm on his shoulder. Tom stoically remained staring at the passing scenery.

When they were in the centre of the city, Tom alighted at the Carlton Towers, having wished his friends goodnight. He was fuming, and decided to avoid Gerard in the future.

As he checked into the hotel he rediscovered the telephone number of the Security Police that he had been given. They had requested that he ring them on arrival in Johannesburg. He decided to call that very evening.

Lydenburg, Transvaal

Gatsu watched her as she walked along the road and stared up the road-sign. She looked lost and was almost certainly from another country, or from a very rural area. She had almost got herself run over as she had crossed the road in Lydenburg, the bus had blown its horn and braked to avoid hitting her. This could only mean that she was stupid, or very unused to traffic, or came from a country where they drove on the other side of the road – such as Mozambique.

He decided to follow her and see what she was up to. She seemed after all to be heading out of town. He crossed the road and soon caught up with her. She looked at him distrustfully as he drew level. He noticed the poor clothing and her tired expression.

'Where you going?' he asked in a friendly tone.

She stopped walking and looked him up and down. She then shrugged and smiled and started to walk again.

He stood where he had stopped and called to her in Fanagalo. As she didn't answer, he tried Portuguese and she stopped. Bravo he said to himself, a refugee, spot on. He walked up to her smiling and continued to talk in basic pidgin Portuguese.

Gatsu's past was far more complicated than his present part-time day job working in the van Loewe Bakery in Lydenburg suggested. He had spent time in a training camp in Angola, where the cadres had been MPLA (the Communist backed Popular Movement for the Liberation of Angola); East German, Cuban and Soviet advisers assisted the officials from Luanda. Portuguese had been an essential language if the best was to be gleaned from the foreigners. He had been a star pupil and had been rapidly promoted into the security department of the ANC (the African National Congress) the *Mbokodo*, the boulder that crushes. As a Zulu, he felt unhappy about the ever-intensifying clashes between his people, who mostly backed the Inkatha Freedom Party, and the Xhosa-dominated ANC. The leadership directly above him felt he had divided loyalties, so he was demoted to a non-active cell of the Umkhonto we-Sizwe, the military wing of the ANC, called the 'Spear of the Nation.'

He had a month's leave now and was returning to Tembisa, a township just north of Johannesburg, to see his comrades-in-arms before his trip back to Natal to see his family. They were always looking for new recruits, especially those that had a sense of dedication tinged with desperation. A girl like this refugee was probably willing to do anything for just being able to live and survive in the country she had almost certainly entered illegally. Either way, whatever her story, she needed some form of help, and it was worth the time of day to try and find out who she was, what she was up to, and what her future plans were. For a square meal, companionship, and a place to lay her head without fear of arrest she was probably prepared to do a lot, reflected Gatsu.

He talked to her and persuaded her in very little time to join him in the journey to Tembisa. He graciously offered to organise her transport – in other words join him in a crowded African taxi, which consisted of a grossly overloaded VW Kombi van.

They sat together huddled into ludicrously little space and endured the discomfort and lack of space impassively. Gatsu had warned Mopete to not talk in the taxi as this would only draw more attention to herself, so it would be better to act dumb and let him deal with everybody around them.

As they hurtled along the wide roads leading toward Johannesburg and then veered north toward Pretoria, Gatsu was lost in thought and distracted by the festivities that he knew were to be on the coming weekend. There was to be an ANC rally followed by various soccer competitions between different hostels and their teams. It was likely that the mother of the nation, Winnie Mandela, would be addressing the crowds.

He looked across at Mopete, who had drifted into a doze and he could see them both dancing and drowning in a torrent of unleashed tribal energy. The pulsating African rhythms would subdue individuals into a single entity, a vibrant pulsing force of energy, which would then come to that realisation, a staggering one for a repressed people, which was that they were invincible. A smile drifted across his features; the future was theirs.

Skukuza Lodge

She giggled as they unlocked the door to the small rondavel and virtually collided with the bed before they had switched the lights on. It had been a subdued evening, with both of them feeling a little sombre after the day's events and the parting of ways of the little group. They'd both been concerned with their own thoughts and had not really felt like conversation or any frivolities. At the bar for after-dinner drinks they'd seemed to drift into a daze-like state. Some lively American tourists had briefly managed to stir them out of it when they started asking a series of politically involved questions about the country. They felt relieved to be on their own.

'Christ, there really isn't much room,' she said. 'I'll climb across the bed and use the loo first – if I may?' She winked. 'Lady's prerogative!'

'Certainly. You go first.'

'After all the smoke in there I feel I also stink! If it's okay I'll carry straight on and have a shower. You're not desperate for the toilet are you?'

'No, no. Go ahead. I'll just read the Park Guide for this area, and have a shower after you. I feel I need to turn in early tonight. The drive from Punda Maria and...' he seemed lost in contemplation as he spoke... 'and everything that has happened today, have made me ready to crash out.'

She nodded in agreement. 'Ja. Me too. A good hot shower

followed by a good night's sleep are what I need.' She was standing at the bathroom door. 'See you in a minute. I'm going to start the ball rolling!' She closed the door.

Rick lay back on the bed and contemplated the thatched ceiling. The truth was that even if he did have the energy to read, as he said he would, it was nicer to unwind and lie back listening to the shower running next door and the sounds of the African night outside.

The shower stopped. He heard the squeal of the shower curtain being pulled back.

'Rick? Rick, can you do me a favour?'

Rick sat up on the bed. 'Yes, go ahead,' he answered to the closed door.

'My towel. I forgot to bring my towel in. It's in my bag.'

'Hang on. Be right there.' He climbed across to her bag and opened the zip. Her beach towel, with Umhlanga Rocks blazoned across the top, was folded neatly down the side. He pulled it out and dislodged some clothes. Two very small G-strings in a smoky grey were among the items accidentally revealed. Their briefness and the small twined rear section immediately made him imagine how they would look on her. He hastily put everything back before he moved across the door and knocked. 'One towel, ma'am.'

There was a chuckle. 'Watson? Is that you?'

'Yes ma'am.'

'Pray enter then, Watson.'

He opened the door and steam poured out. She was partially concealed by the shower curtain, but had her head round the side glistening with water. He passed her the towel. 'Shall I – uhm – retire then, ma'am? Will that be all?'

She laughed. 'Ja. Piss off, Watson. If I need you I'll ring the bell!'

He started to close the door as he moved out.

'Thanks, by the way.'

'You're welcome.' He had closed the door.

She spoke through the door. 'Christ, there really is so little room to manoeuvre in here. The Park Authority must have ended up with some spare materials, but not enough to build a normal rondavel!'

Rick chuckled. He pulled his towel out as the door opened. Steam flooded into the room. She climbed on to the bed and moved to her bag to retrieve her nightclothes.

'All yours, Watson.'

'Shan't be too long. I need a good relaxing shower. A real hot one to ease up the tension.' The bathroom was wet and steamy. The hot shower made him feel good and helped ease some of the stresses that so clearly manifested themselves in the knotted muscles of the neck. He dried himself and, after putting on a light tee shirt and fresh underpants, brushed his teeth and re-entered the bedroom.

Lucie was curled up at the far end of the bed under the covers. She was facing him. 'Feel better?'

He smiled. 'Much. It has relaxed me.'

'Me too.'

He turned the light out in the bathroom and closed the door. 'I presume you are also ready for sleep?'

'Definitely.'

He grinned at her. 'Okay – lights out time.'

'Fine.'

He turned the bedroom light off and climbed under the cover on his appointed side. 'Goodnight Lucie.'

Goodnight, Rick.'

He lay on his back and stretched his legs. It was nice to be in a comfortable bed at last. It had been a long day. A hyena yelped in the near distance.

'Hyena,' she said.

'Yeah, I guessed. It is entertaining to hear them around you at night, when you know you are safe and sound in bed.'

There was a long silence before she continued. 'I feel safe with you.'

'You mean here in bed?'

'No, well yes, that as well. I didn't mean that I felt safe from assault here in bed, but just not threatened by you … in any way. Intellectually, physically, whatever. A sort of all encompassing safeness … is there such a word as safeness?'

'I think there is. It sounds right. Either way, I'm happy you feel that way.'

'With Tom there was always an underlying aggression, which could be a turn-on, but somehow never seemed to really go.'

'He's sure tough in his own way.'

'Ja. He can be tough all right.'

'The events in the bush yesterday. He took it so much in his stride. It was incredible. I don't know what to think of it all. I haven't really sorted it out in my brain yet!'

'He's a product of Africa. A product of his *Volk*.'

'Yes, I guess so.'

Neither spoke for a good minute before Lucie spoke again. 'Do you miss her?'

He fleetingly wondered if she meant Tash, but concluded Chrissie was being referred to. He contemplated what it meant not having her with him before he answered. 'Not a hell of a lot. It sounds a bit brutal, doesn't it? A sort of callous heartlessness.'

'Not really. It seemed fairly obvious you weren't in love with her.'

'Yes, I guess. Do you miss Tom?'

'No. We were becoming alienated from each other anyway. An ongoing process that had been going on for a long time.'

'Are you really going to move out?'

'Ja, of course.'

'Where will you go?'

'I'll sort something out.'

'Jeez, I really hope I wasn't the catalyst for a lot of this.'

'No, not really.' There was a brief silence. 'Rick?'

'Yes?' He turned to look at her, even though the darkness could not allow him to make her out clearly.

'Please cuddle up to me.'

He didn't answer but moved across to her. Her hand found his and wrapped his arm around her as she turned. They lay up against each other with Rick on his side pressed up against her back. He gently moved her hair out of his face with his free hand. He enjoyed the warmth of her body and the closeness.

She still held his hand in hers up against her chest. He felt her kiss it gently and squeeze it. 'Thanks,' she whispered in the dark.

By way of reply he gently returned the hand squeeze and soon felt waves of sleep carry him off.

Security Forces HQ, Johannesburg

Tom took a sip from his Castle lager and looked at Colonel Coetzee. The man had arrived late at the small gathering of top brass at the Security Headquarters who had gathered to say thanks to Tom, and had made a direct beeline to him. Even now, as the whole group was beginning to break up, the Colonel remained limpet-like next to him, chatting amiably.

The man was likeable and had a friendly personality, but did have very uncharitable eyes. The eyes, reputedly mirrors of the soul, seemed to lack all warmth and kindness. They were a vivid arctic blue, reminiscent of the iciness of the frozen and near lifeless areas of the world. It was peculiar, he mused to himself, for the eyes said one thing, but the manner was different, a living South African version of Jekyll and Hyde – the big difference being that both sides were visible at once. They had chatted about all sorts of trivia: his family, his business, even Lucinda, but he never came close to offending or seeming to intrusive, just jocular and talkative. The eyes remained Tom's source of concern.

'It was quite a daring little exploit you carried out, Tom,' said the Colonel. 'You obviously felt sure of the situation, and had appraised it correctly.'

'Yes, on both counts,' answered Tom.

'I like a man who is sure of himself. We need men like that.'

'Need for what?'

'To meet the challenges of the future – and the present ones.'

'You mean in politics?'

'Yes, partly. Politics plays its part, but actions speak louder than words.'

Tom gave him a questioning look. 'What exactly do you mean?'

'That men of action,' he inclined his head back, in a 'you do understand don't you' manner, 'who are on the right side can positively influence the outcome of events for the better. I meant right as in ethical or correct, of course, rather than specifically politically speaking.'

Tom laughed. 'My girlfriend would say something like, "how do you know it's the right side?"'

'*Hou links gaan regs verby*! The common road sign you see

throughout the dual carriageways in this country says it all. Keep left, but overtake on the right. I believe this is correct, and not just for the roads.'

Tom chuckled but did not comment. The Colonel shrugged and continued, 'On a serious note though. I maintain certain truths are self-evident. Would not the world have been a better place if Lenin or Stalin had been struck down early in life before they could wreak all the havoc they caused? What if somebody had murdered Marx, would we have a Marxist philosophy today?'

Tom had stopped laughing. 'I'm not convinced. Wasn't Engels also involved in the theory? If there were no rotten Tsar, would Russia have thrown up a Lenin? Anyway, most people would pull you up for not mentioning Hitler. Does the same apply there?'

'Certainly, Hitler did a lot of damage. The pity with him was that he became too ambitious, and overextended himself. He wasn't all evil. Ideally he should have been shunted aside in 1943 and then the whole outcome of the war would have been different. I cannot dislike the man entirely, he had some good ideas. It was a pity that his ruling clique became so blinded by events that they couldn't alter course slightly, well before the tide had started to change. The fate that befell Germany, and the subsequent course of history, could have been very different. We would probably have a world dominated by the Teutonic peoples rather than the Jewish-WASP coalition in America.'

'A lot of food for thought there. I'm not sure I agree with it all, but anyway. Go on,' he urged. 'What about today?'

'Well, even the Americans would feel happy if Saddam Hussein were despatched, wouldn't you agree? Yes? So, it seems to me that once upon a time the CIA and the American Establishment had the backbone to carry out such deeds if they were necessary, and nobody would say the perpetrators were bad assassins, just men fighting a just cause. Today we are left with the greatest and most powerful nation on earth, acting out a liberal and stupid charade, and lacking the backbone to confront evil.' He paused to sip his drink and assess the effect his words were having on Tom.

His audience of one was mesmerised by the words and the message. He continued, 'Governments are elected fundamentally by people who view humans from one aspect or the other. Let me explain. You either believe in the magnificence of the human spirit, and feel that liberal freedom will allow it to develop to its full potential, or you believe that human nature is fundamentally evil and corrupted and needs laws and society to keep the anarchic mayhem and chaos under control. The Americans believe in the former and now pay the price with their LA riots, a deluge of crime, unbelievable murder statistics, the immigration problems and the Mafia. The decay and corruption started and became visible when their hero and spokesman, Kennedy, came in with his madcap ideas, whores and liberal confusion. The Americans are paying now. But the Israelis and the South Africans – some South Africans – well, we are virtually the only ones who know better. We have looked the serpent in the eye, and we know what he is capable of. What is more, he is writhing on our very doorstep. Consequently MOSSAD and BOSS[45] have assumed the true mantle of the West and confront the devil, whilst the CIA and the MI5, bow and scrape to appease him. There is a big difference.'

Tom nodded in agreement. 'I basically agree with what you have to say, and have even thought of rejoining the forces.'

'Good. I'm happy we see things the same way. I know...' he looked around the room... 'I know the top brass have honoured you here tonight, but I would like to send a couple of my men to meet up with you back in Kaapstad. Would that be okay?'

Tom looked confused. 'Is this part of the Broederbond?'[46]

'No. Boere Kommando. We are a group that is highly placed in terms of the leadership and need recruits in both the military and the civilian walks of life. If you are interested my men will explain further. If not, I will issue a single warning and request, and that is not to talk about this conversation to anyone, not even your girlfriend.'

Tom straightened up and sighed. 'I'm glad I had this chance to meet you. It would be only a pleasure to meet up and see your men.'

---

[45]MOSSAD, BOSS: Israeli and South African Secret Services.

[46]Broederbond : Secret South African group dedicated to the Afrikanerdom.

Colonel Coetzee grinned, and brought his heels together. He put his glass down on the table. 'Good. I will be off then.'

'Colonel, before you go, there was something I wanted to ask.'

'Ja? What is it?'

'The postscript to the incidents in the Park. The men for example, what became of them? Did you catch the girl?'

'Ja-nee. The girl has vanished, but I do not believe for one minute she made it far. The big predators have developed a taste for humans, it seems. She was far too weak, and I really don't rate her chances. As for the men, well they were dropped off back in Mozambican territory.'

'Dropped off? By the helicopter?'

'I would not use the word by.'

'From? Ja, of course, from.'

'Refugee brigand scum.'

'Ja, of course.'

'The leader was a man called Rodrigo. A communist sympathiser turned brigand. He was coming to spread his revolutionary message. Today he felt so suicidal he terminated his life before he could be restrained.'

'How?'

'He jumped from the seventh floor, I think. I haven't got the details yet.'

'So the whole gang "jumped" in one way or another.'

'Correct. But waste no sympathy. They were devoid of human feelings. Scum.'

'I'm sure,' said Tom in agreement.

'Anyway. I look forward to our next encounter. Goed dankie. Tot siens.'[47]

'Goeienag,[48] Colonel,' replied Tom. A hint of inner amusement could be seen on his face as he politely bade farewell to his hosts and left the building. He toyed with the idea of going to the nightclub his friends had spoken of to see what was happening.

As he walked out, he felt his mood change. There was a gathering storm within him, a surge of frustration and anger,

---

[47] God bless.

[48] Goodnight.

which threatened to burst out and lash uncontrolled like a cyclone on a tropical coast, a huge demonstration of violence and force was needing to be released.

His thoughts drifted back to Chrissie, and it dawned on him that he was hurt that she had so markedly chosen Gerard and not himself. He needed and wanted her tonight; that she could be the answer to his pent up frustration and anger. He hailed a taxi and asked to be taken directly to the nightclub.

It was noisy and smoky, and charged a nominal entry fee. To his relief it wasn't too crowded. He moved through the crowd slowly and directed himself toward the nearest bar, illuminated by a blue incandescent light. He ordered a beer and having paid for it turned to look around him and watch the people on the dance floor.

She was there, a Latin cork adrift in a sea of Anglos and Afrikaners. She danced well, he observed, and remembered how he had first noticed her when he had arranged the meeting with Rick in Capetown. She was also supple, so she could bend and move with great ease. Hell, he swore to himself. If he was being honest with himself, he wanted her in bed. He berated Lucinda for having been in the way.

He continued to observe her as she danced. She caught his eye and acknowledged him without registering any surprise. She was dancing with a group of girls to Seventies rock music, and gyrating in the fashion of the time. He reflected that she was able to make it seem that she was dancing exclusively for him, but also realised that every male observing her probably thought the same.

He noticed Gerard move on to the floor and hold her close as the music changed tempo. He folded her in his arms as he shuffled in slow circles to the music. She noticed Tom's intense stare and held it each time her face came round toward him. In Gerard's arms her head rested comfortably against his chest, and she appeared not to notice or care as his hands wandered lasciviously over her rump. The hands grabbed, stroked, explored, pinched as they moved around, occasionally pressing in, and clearly defining the petite backside that Chrissie called her own.

As the mauling continued throughout the song, he decided that he would not let his friend discover his presence. He turned his back on them and moved into a darker corner, where he would be able to observe, but was unlikely to be spotted. She was searching to see where he had gone, he realised, for she occasionally tilted her head and scanned the crowd.

They left the dance floor and returned to the table where they had drinks. They had obviously joined up with some friends of Gerard's who were all drinking and talking animatedly. Some of the girls who had been dancing with Chrissie were there. She seemed indifferent and occasionally turned to survey the crowd. Gerard's arm still hung protectively around her.

She detached herself and, putting down her drink, moved off from the group. She was heading for the toilets at the rear. Tom moved swiftly and caught up with her just before she entered. He grabbed her arm and pulled her forcibly away from the door. She didn't resist.

He took her in his arms and pressing her against the wall kissed her passionately on the mouth. She offered no resistance, but no enthusiasm either. Her arms exerted no pressure, just resting on his hips.

He pulled away, and still holding her in his embrace, studied her face. It looked back at him dispassionately. 'Why did you let him maul you?'

'Because he's my man,' she answered quietly.

'Ja. Your man. Your man of two days!'

'Shame! What's it to you?' she retorted angrily.

He scoffed accusingly, 'You have this ability to jump from one man to another very easily.'

'Like you. Don't tell me you didn't screw Lucie recently, cause ya did. I fuckin' heard ya! And now what? You want me?' she asked venomously.

He blinked and stared at her. 'Ja. Sorry.'

'So ya should be. What's this all about. You wanna jump me too?'

He pulled away from her, and shook his head in confusion. Her arms hung loosely by her side as she watched him.

'I'm really sorry. I don't know what got into me. I just … well, I saw you out there, and I just …'

'Wanted to fuck me?' she added.

He looked at her with a sense of relief and gratitude. 'Ja. If I'm honest, that's right.'

'You saw me as a possible little highlight as you were feeling low? Right? A way to cheer yourself up by having a screw with me?'

A reward in the carnal fallout, he brooded. Where had he heard the phrase? She was right, he admitted to himself. Making an audible sigh he answered, 'I hadn't quite thought it out in such terms, but I guess you could say that it's possible.'

'Bullshit, Tom! Did I look surprised to see ya tonight? I wanna put the record straight for ya. When I also saw you, I knew instinctively you were my type. Call it female intuition if ya like. You also saw it, but you was hitched with Lucie-babes, right? I came along with a sense of curiosity, adventure, and what the fuck, Rick was a good guy. But, I also came to check you out. What did I find? Somebody that attracts me to the point where I feel weak at the knees, but also scares me. You have a violent and unstable part to ya. You would hurt me. I feel ya need a victim. You're burning inside Tom, and I don't want to feel those flames.'

Tom had placed his hands on his hips and was staring at the floor. 'Heavy stuff. Have you finished.'

'Almost. Find your victim. Burn her, not me, and then ... if the fires only singe, look me up. I'll be whatever ya want me to be. I'm sure ya know what I mean. It's a genuine offer. You can always find me.'

He watched her as she moved through the crowd and hesitated at the toilet door. She looked round at him and smiled before she entered. Tom took a deep breath and left unobserved by his friend. Fuel had been added to his erotic fantasies.

Kruger National Park – Barberton, Transvaal

The impala buck twitched nervously and raised its head. It was skittish and not well. Its flank on one side had a deep angry-looking graze, probably the result of a fight with the lonely younger bucks who were always reappearing from out the bush in order to challenge its supremacy, and its domination of the harem. In one of the recent tussles, the challenger had obviously managed to score a hit of sorts, but the buck still remained in charge of its does.

It moved briskly around the perimeter of its herd. The does automatically huddled closer, but continued to graze on the sparse grass, seemingly content to leave all guard duties to the male. Only the very young were oblivious to the warning signs that the buck was giving, obviously still unable to interpret the buck's strut as being a 'come-on, huddle-together'-type command.

Having completed its circuit, it stopped and regarded the Land-Rover in which Rick and Lucie sheltered as if assessing if it was the cause of its unease. Its tail flickered incessantly as it contemplated the vehicle.

'Perhaps it's unsettled by us?' queried Rick.

'It could be,' answered Lucinda, who was slouched in the passenger seat with the binoculars. 'The wound looks pretty nasty. My guess is that his supremacy is in serious jeopardy.'

'Poor guy,' sympathised Rick.

Lucinda put down the binoculars and smiled at him. 'Nature,' she stated, 'can be cruel. Can't it?'

He nodded slowly and held her gaze for a few seconds before averting his eyes. Then on a sudden impulse he brought them back up and stared back at her. They held each other's eyes for nearly a minute before she blinked and, laughing, turned away. Rick felt glad he had held his ground, no matter how silly it seemed.

'I think your idea was a good one,' she said.

'I hope it is,' said Rick.

'Well, it seems to me that if we leave now we should be in Barberton by about four this afternoon, and we can see what your Mr van der Linden is like.'

'Right. Let's go.' Rick started the engine, which immediately caused the impala to scatter in a wild panic, bouncing high and jumping into the denser bush. Several of the impala does were pronking up to two metres vertically into the air. Rick turned the four-wheel drive around and headed along the road that indicated the southern exit of the Park, at the Crocodile River.

They reached Barberton by four in the afternoon having stopped briefly for lunch in Nelspruit. Rick phoned the man whose acquaintance he had made on the flight into South Africa, and was immediately invited over to stay. He noticed when he mentioned that he had a lady with him that the tone had cooled considerably, but he suspected it was all in his imagination.

They followed the directions out to the tobacco farm and were welcomed by the whole family. The were all assembled to greet the guests; Breyten, his wife Anna, the four children, an aunt, two nieces, and a wizened old grandmother bent nearly double with age. Her sparkling blue eyes had not seen their native Holland since her infancy. The welcome was effusive, and this was followed by an insistence they be shown the farm before an early *braai*.

Breyten and one of his daughters drove them around the farm with its well-tended fields and its sullen-looking black field workers. He stopped to show them the tobacco plants, the manner in which it is cultivated, the means of determining quality, and how to pick the correct leaves. They stopped at one point, when they noticed a small crowd helping up a collapsed worker. The workers and Breyten spoke in rapid Fanagalo, Breyten's large bulk and great height towering over the slender and undernourished looking blacks. The crowd then shuffled and helped load the ill looking young man into the back of the *bakkie*.[49]

The workers all looked sullen and quiet, occasionally giving them surreptitious malevolent looks; Breyten seemed oblivious and unconcerned. He talked in a paternalistic tone about Joshua, who slouched disconsolately in the back. He explained how he had admonished him about spending all his money on women of ill repute in the big cities. His advice was that he should save up to buy himself a second, fertile, wife back in Swaziland; his first had been unable to bear him children. It didn't seem as if he was talking about a human, but more like an occasionally errant but tolerated dog.

Their personal family isolation on the farm, and the future developments in the country, inevitably developed as topics of conversation. Breyten acted unconcerned and talked how he had shot a man dead a few months ago, someone who had tried to burgle the house. He had, with police connivance and physical help, moved the body back inside the house's fence boundary,

---

[49]Ute, utility van

knowing full well that shooting an intruder on your property is automatically dismissed by the courts as self-defence. He showed no remorse, not even a hint of regret that somebody should die so violently at his hands.

They drove off the farm to a little cluster of houses nearby where Joshua was dropped off at a small first aid clinic. Breyten told the receptionist that he would be back in a couple of hours to fetch him. Joshua slumped on to the floor, a forlorn and obviously unwell individual. The other black patients regarded Breyten with blank and expressionless faces.

'Hope he bloody well hasn't caught Aids,' remarked Breyten. 'It will, of course, clear a lot of people off the face of this earth. The blacks here, the degenerates in the West. It is already spreading like wildfire in Uganda, Kenya and Tanzania, and now has a firm foothold here.'

'Yes. It's a terrible disease. It's called "slim" in East Africa, due to the rapid weight loss of the victim,' said Rick.

'God's punishment,' retorted Breyten with an air of finality.

'It is rather extreme to assume that the people who have Aids deserve it for some ungodly wrongdoing!'

'I might have guessed you'd be a *pinko*,'[50] laughed Breyten. 'Somehow I felt you were, but because you were from East Africa originally I felt … no … *hoped* … you might be different, but I guess you're not. You regard people like F W de Klerk as heroes I suppose?'

'Yes, I respect him,' Rick stated strongly.

'I thought as much. Well, let me tell you, the whites of this country who support him are like lemmings. They have a lemming mentality, and like those silly animals are prepared to follow him over a cliff. They are all scared. Scared of the blacks, scared of death. There is no need, God is on our side, and we shall triumph in the end. I for one, along with most of the Afrikaner nation, am not prepared to commit communal suicide.'

'But nobody is asking you to. De Klerk is trying to make peace.'

'Peace is fine, but at what cost? To have these people rule over

---

[50] Socialist.

me? To have a Joshua have the same vote as me?'

'Why not? He's human, and entitled to a say.'

'*Human* eh?' Breyten's rising ire was obvious. 'Can I tell you a little story?'

Rick shrugged resignedly.

Breyten continued, 'The couple next door in the farm called Paraiso, were a mixed marriage. She was Portuguese from just across the border, and came across as a young girl when her parents fled the chaos in Mozambique. He was an Anglo from Northern Rhodesia, now Zambia, who also had parents who'd fled chaos. Well, they met in college. He somehow avoided call-up, and they bought this farm, determined not to repeat the mistakes their parents had made. This was to be a new beginning.'

They had arrived back at the farmhouse. Breyten parked the car, and turned the engine off. He wanted to finish the story before they got out of the car.

'Well, it started well. They made a profit, and shared some with the workers, and paid for the education of the children of their workers. One night about a year ago, they were coming back from a Rotary meeting late at night and they had a full on collision with an African taxi that had veered across the road. The impact was terrible, but fortunately the Fultons were wearing seat belts. When he came to from the daze, Mike realised that his left shoulder was broken, and that he was severely wedged against the steering wheel. Maria, his wife, who must have been sitting cross-legged on the passenger seat, was unconscious with her head resting on the bonnet of the crumpled car, with facial lacerations from where she had hit the windscreen. Also on the bonnet was the black driver of the other vehicle, who was dead and whose head was inches from hers. Mike had difficulty moving. He heard people and realised some of the passengers were all right. He shouted for help. A couple of young blacks with bruised faces appeared. They proceeded to remove his watch, wallet and possessions. Any *tom*[51] they could find they took. They did the same with the other driver and his wife. They made no move to help, just loot. Mike recognised one of them. He had helped pay

---

[51] South African slang for 'money'.

for his education, he was the son of an employee. He begged for help, but had difficulty talking. He had many broken ribs. The boy recognised him but proceeded nonchalantly. The little bastard even pulled up Maria's dress to her waist, and I'm sure would have raped her had he had access. Once done, the two started to try and set the wrecks alight, but were scared off when by chance another vehicle approached and interrupted them. Mike and Maria owe their lives to the occupants of the other car. A few days later when they came out of hospital, all bandaged up and taking heaps of muti,[52] they gave up! These liberals had had enough, and within the year they had sold out and left for Australia. Like all true liberals they voted with their feet. Paraiso has gone to my other neighbour. So, my friend, tell me now: what do you think of those black guys and what they did?'

Rick sighed and cleared his throat. 'First off, I agree, it's a shocking story. I also agree that the young lads acted callously and cruelly, but they are from a deprived, repressed and uneducated class …'

'Mike paid for his education,' interrupted Breyten heatedly.

'To what grade?'

'He completed primary!'

'Big deal. He left school a kid, able to read and write. But he also had parents, uncles, relatives, cousins and friends, all brutalised and underprivileged, so I'm sure he saw no justice. I'm not for one minute saying what he did was right, but the crime has a context, an overall picture that frames it. It is not excusable, but perhaps understandable.'

Breyten nodded his head in disagreement. 'That is *kak*[53], man. These people made a sacrifice, partly in the name of socialism or justice and for their basic humanity and belief in fellow men being equal. But it wasn't worth it. Not many sacrifices of that nature are. They fled. Hurt. Pissed-off. Disillusioned. Ex-Zac de Beer's supporters.[54] They are in Australia now. And –' he wagged

---

[52]Muti – a Zulu word meaning 'medicine' widely used in South Africa in English an 1 Afrikaans.

[53] Afrikaans for 'shit'.

[54]Zac de Beer: liberal opposition leader of the Progressive Party.

his finger in a meaningful way – 'and they left believing that the Africans were *animals*, not much more than a fraction above a vermin rat.'

'Well, I believe that is sad and terrible. If the wealth and resources of this country were equitably distributed, I don't believe such incidents would occur, and the sad part is that this country has such potential.'

'Dad, I feel you should mention that the people who saved the Fultons were blacks, and that the two young guys who did the looting were killed in what seemed an execution killing about a week later outside Nelspruit. Perhaps there are blacks out there who knew they had done great evil?' the daughter suggested.

'Or that neighbours of the Fultons arranged to have them shot?' chipped in Lucinda.

Breyten sighed deeply. 'My friends, I think it would be better if I booked the best hotel in town for you and your lady friend, all at my expense of course, because I don't think you should stay under the same roof as my family. We are all God-fearing people, and I feel you are Satan's friend.'

There was total silence whilst they absorbed his harsh words. Breyten sighed again. 'Ja, this is hard, but is the honest way. It is the Boer way.'

'Papa! How can you do this?' gasped his daughter.

'Quiet!' snapped Breyten. He swivelled round to face Rick and vehemently added, 'I will have your bags brought out to your car. Please do charge me for the stay there, I wish it to be my account.'

Rick had paled visibly. 'Fine, we'll move on. I'm certainly not keen to stay where I'm not welcome – nor, may I add, do I wish to take up your offer. You can keep your generosity. If you really feel generous, perhaps use the money you might have spent on us, helping your sick worker, Joshua, or any other such worthy scheme. We can pay our own way, and believe me, we are happy to do so. If nothing else, this has been educational as an insight into Boer culture, and I'm sorry you ended it this way.'

They all climbed out of the car. The daughter strode off angrily, Breyten calmly barking orders to his servant, Rick and Lucie walked awkwardly in silence across to the Land-Rover. Their bags arrived shortly afterwards, and were loaded into the back. Nobody seemed to be around; it was as if the place was deserted.

Rick drove off down the red-earthed dirt drive. They both looked across at the house with its green and lush garden. In the shade stood the old grandmother and Breyten's daughter. The girl gave a furtive wave. Lucinda waved back. The old Dutch lady watched their departure through her watery blue eyes.

They turned through the gates and drove in silence toward Nelspruit. Lucinda laughed, 'Well, you now know the meaning of the car sticker which you can see in Natal; "Support wildlife, hug a vaaly". Some of these guys out here are a law unto themselves! The Transvaal is our Wild West!'

Rick

He yawned and stretched his arms. He placed the book on the bedside table. He had been reading Rian Malan's book about Africa, *My Traitor's Heart*, and was finding it very interesting and relevant. He glanced across at Lucinda in the neighbouring bed, with the idea of asking her about the book, but she appeared to be asleep.

He studied her relaxed face. Her lips appeared to be pouting as the pillow was bunching the face together. Her hair was spread in a dark storm of shiny tresses partly across her face and back over the pillow. Her bare shoulders were hunched together as she was not only lying on her front, but also had her arms folded under her. She looked so very attractive, he reflected.

Reaching across, he turned off the light and sank into his pillow, to go over the day's events, with all the drama of leaving Breyten's house. They had driven to Nelspruit where they had found a moderately priced hotel, and had eaten in the hotel's dining room, before retiring early.

'You sleepy?' came the voice from the dark.

'A little, yes. Why?'

'I've got a backache.'

'Oh,' he commented, and then added,' Do you want me to get you something for it?'

'You could do something for it, but only if you are not sleepy!'

Rick chuckled. 'What? Can I guess? You want a massage?'

'You got it! But only if you are not too tired.'

Rick got out of bed. He was wearing a tee shirt and underpants. 'How do you SA people say it? Only a pleasure?'

'Ja. That's it.' She laughed. 'There is some moisturising oil in my make-up bag.'

Rick turned the bathroom light on and located the oil. He decided to leave the light on as it threw a soft glow across the room. He climbed on to the bed and squatted next to her whilst he opened the bottle.

'It will be better if you sit on me,' she said. 'I'm sure you are not too heavy.' She threw the covers back and in so doing gave Rick a glimpse of her small, well-rounded breasts. She was only wearing a pair of black panties.

Rick climbed on top and sat, effectively on her rump. An involuntary thrill of excitement ran threw him as he mentally savoured her close physical presence. He poured some of the cream up and down her back, making what seemed to be Ndebele tribal line patterns: decorative light lines painted against a dark background.

She shuddered, for the cream was cold on her skin.

He rubbed his hands together vigorously after he put the cream bottle down, in order to warm them. He apologised for his lack of practice in the massage field beforehand and then started at the shoulders to rub and gently knead in the cream. Her skin felt smooth and soft, and her body responded to his hands. At times she would moan with pleasure, or ask for a bit more strength to be applied. He reflected that she was a lot like a cat enjoying a luxuriously long and gentle stroking session; she almost purred.

'God, this is heaven,' she murmured, as his hands worked the various knotted muscles between her shoulder blades.

His hands move down inexorably to the small of her back and the lumbar region, just above the pelvis. Rick shifted down on to her thighs, to be able to properly apply pressure. As the hands moved on to the pelvic region, they detected the slight push back as the rump was raised slightly.

He dismissed it from his mind and continued to massage in silence. When he looked up he noticed that her hands, which were spread wide on either side of her head, were now clenched, holding the sides of the pillow. It dawned on him that she was expectantly tense. A thrill swept through him as he tried to ignore the adrenaline that had started to course through his system. Hell, I'm getting excited, he realised.

He looked down as his hands worked her lower back and watched as they strayed fractionally on to her rump. She responded almost imperceptibly, but he was sure she was reacting. He swallowed hard as he faced the fact that he seriously wanted to bed her, and knew that he'd wanted to for some time.

Gently taking the panties on either side, he pulled them down to the top of her thighs. Her backside was white, and clearly delineated by the tanned skin. He thought he detected a sigh. She hadn't objected or resisted. He gently put one hand under her pelvic bone to raise her rump further, and then used the other hand to bring the panties further down, to half-way down her thighs.

She whispered in a voice muffled by the pillow where her face was buried, 'What are you doing?' The tone was inquisitive, almost offhand, certainly not hostile or vexed.

Rick leant forward and whispered back conspiratorially, 'I'm fixing your back, which means I'm giving you a massage, and will make love to you.'

There was a long silence before she replied, 'That's nice.'

Rick smiled and didn't answer. He continued to massage her rump, alternating between soft and hard, gently gripping each cheek in his hands. Then using his left hand to once again raise her backside up slightly, he gently explored between her legs with his right. He went around her anal passage with his finger, gently, without forcing any entry. It made her squirm slightly in response.

His fingers then went further down and gently stroked her lips before moving around to the small mound. He gently kept a rotary movement on her clitoral mound, till a moan escaped her lips. He then pressed harder and, parting the lips, inserted finger into her moist interior. Her rump had now moved up off the bed and moved with his inserted finger.

He released her and withdrew his finger in order to pull his underpants down, and free his erect member. She tried to spread her legs, but was prevented from doing so by the panties that were only halfway down her thighs, and by his legs which were either side of her.

Falling forward on to his elbows on either side of her, he pushed his erect member between her legs. He pressed forward between her legs and soon found the welcoming moistness, which allowed him to enter. She groaned with pleasure, and he sighed with relief as the warm interior enveloped him.

Her arms came up to grip his body to hers, whilst his hands moved to her shoulders for support, and strayed to her breasts which were pressed to the bed. She started to move gently to his thrusts, as she felt waves of pleasure sweep through her.

'Oh God! Don't stop. It's so good. Just don't stop!' she gasped, raising her head from the pillow.

He wrapped his legs tightly around hers and wrapped his arms tightly around her shoulders. 'This is great and you feel so good! God, how I love this. I've wanted this so much.'

Lucie giggled. 'You bastard! I've wanted you too. Why the fuck didn't you tell me?'

'Don't know! Perhaps I was waiting for an Afrikaner to throw us together,' he chuckled.

'Christ, I love this!' she groaned.

He pulled her rump upwards and effectively forced her on all fours, all the while remaining inside her. He continued to move gently behind her, and in her. His torso was pressed tight against her back. He felt her breathing increase in frequency and the intensity of her movements grow. He maintained a steady rhythm, till he felt her sudden sharp jerky movements announcing her orgasm. Wetting his finger, he pressed it against her anus, which caused her to shudder violently.

He withdrew and managed to finally remove her panties. She turned over. He lowered himself on to her and they kissed passionately. Her legs spread and allowed him to rest between them. Her hand then went down and guided him back into her.

He started to move rhythmically again. She raised her legs and he grabbed them tight and started a strong thrusting rhythm. She was breathing in shallow gasps as her face contorted in the waves of intense pleasure. His look was that of a surprised and angry person, intent upon achieving a hard task.

It flashed through Rick's mind that she looked incredibly beautiful, gasping below him, in his embrace. He had a sudden sense of belonging, of being where he ought to be. Could it be that he had always felt he should be with her? He felt ecstatically confused.

As the frequency and strength of their synchronised movements intensified, they both had their fingers intensely gripping each others' shoulders, holding their union together. Rick suddenly felt out of control as his orgasm came and he felt the hard jerking movements as he released into her. She was gasping as her second climax was reached simultaneously.

He felt an overwhelming feeling of relief and physical collapse, intermingled with gratitude and love. Clearly this was why the French called it *le petit mort*, the little death.

They collapsed together, out of breath, laughing uncontrollably. They were both hot and sweaty. They looked at each other and continued to laugh.

'That's what I would call a cosmic fuck!' she laughed. 'I really needed that.'

'Me too,' he agreed. 'Come and sleep in my arms, I'd really like that!'

She moved her head on to his shoulder and sighed. 'What about the bathroom light?'

'Stuff the light.'

They both felt at peace. Neither spoke again that night.

Rick felt her twitch a few times as sleep overcame her. He smiled to himself. For the first time this holiday, he mused, he felt really happy.

Rick (Capetown)

A week had gone by and Rick was back in Capetown. It was time to collect his goods and continue his travels. It was time to experience more of South Africa. There was a lot to see. On his list was Natal, the heartland of the liberal Anglos and their opposition Progressive Party, and perhaps include a visit to Ulundi, the Zulu capital. Also on the list were visits to either of the two Xhosa homelands of Ciskei or Transkei, or a visit to one of the other two larger ones of Venda or Bophuthatswana. If time would allow he also wanted to visit the nation states of Swaziland and Lesotho. The idea was to travel, absorbing what he could of the culture, atmosphere and politics of the land that was so much in flux and swaying so precariously above the abyss of a civil war. There was so much to see, and so much to experience, that any involvement in personal relationships almost seemed a travesty of the original design of the trip. He felt pleased with the decision to continue the trip.

He had contacted Tom, who had insisted that he stay the night and leave the next day, rather than leave that very evening. Since he still had a house key, he would be able to let himself in. Tom assured him he would almost certainly be late as he had a dinner to attend, but was looking forward to meeting him later on at the house, for a drink before retiring. Rick agreed to wait up for him.

Lucinda had left him at the train station in order to go and organise her flat, she said. They had said goodbye there, as it was not a certainty when or if they would meet again. She told him she wasn't sure if she would be around at the house that evening, but would certainly try to meet up with him the next day. She had given her work number, for him to contact her in case he left the house early.

They had continued to enjoy each other's company during the return trip to Capetown, and had made love on several further occasions. Their arrival in Capetown had made them re-assess, both felt that time should elapse before any form of travel together or indeed any form of relationship could be contemplated. A sense of angst prevailed.

Perhaps, pondered Rick, it was the imminent parting of the ways, or the possible bad scene that could result when Lucie came to fetch her belongings from Tom's house. Or perhaps it was the sense of guilt: guilt at finding happiness; guilt at spending time with Tom's girl; guilt at perhaps being the catalyst that led to their break-up. He knew that he must, but he did not feel like meeting up with Tom. He had the distinct impression it might well be a tense encounter.

He entered the house, finding it shrouded in darkness. There was a note on the kitchen table addressed to him, from Tom. He read it. It said only that he should make himself at home, and that there were two good bottles of Groot Constantia wine from the Cape in the fridge, and that he should get started on one, but leave the second for them to drink together. He signed off with an underlined statement that he was really looking forward to their meeting.

Rick opened the fridge, found the bottles, and removed one. There was a corkscrew on the table, along with two glasses. He opened it and poured himself a glass. It was a fine Rhine Riesling. He savoured the delicate taste. He looked through the darkened doorway and could make out a picture of Tom and Lucinda that sat on the mantelpiece of the living room. He studied it from a distance before he moved over and picked it up.

The picture was taken with a flash, at night, at a party. It showed them dancing in the midst of a lot of people. They were not posing, merely moving to a beat and obviously enjoying themselves. The picture froze them with a glint of reflection in their eyes and on their clothing from the flash. Both were in formal dress. Rick studied their respective faces. Lucinda looked lost, happy and vacant, as if giving herself completely to the music and the occasion and probably Tom, he mused. Tom looked more restrained, for although there was a smile, there was alertness, a cagey look about him, that gave away the fact that he wasn't fully relaxed. Rick languished over her image, and acknowledged her beauty with a deep sigh, before he replaced the picture. He fleetingly wondered if he was likely to see her again in his life, or whether she was really just a companion along the way, destined to take a different path.

He took his wine to his little room and started to tidy up the books, guides and maps that lay strewn around the room. He gradually managed to pack into his rucksack all his belongings. He changed into a pair of casual shorts and a tee shirt, and sat down to watch the evening television, on the small set placed there for guests.

Tom arrived about eleven o'clock. Rick who had started to feel dozy, noticed the lights go on in the kitchen. He sat up and rubbed his eyes. The bottle was almost empty, and the alcohol had certainly made him happier and drowsy. He stood up, and leant across to switch off the set. Whatever the show was, it was not riveting material.

There was a knock on the door, and Tom entered. 'How is it?' he laughed. He had the flushed looked of someone slightly intoxicated. He was carrying the second Groot Constantia bottle.

'Fine... fine,' mumbled Rick. 'It's good to see you.'

'Ja. I bet,' said Tom. He sat down heavily. He picked up the nearly empty bottle and chuckled. 'Good. I see you can drink. Let's kill this second bottle – for old times' sake!'

Rick agreed and sat down opposite him. Tom had removed his tie, shoes and socks, and was now with great determination removing the cork from the bottle. He succeeded with a loud 'plop' as the cork came free, and grinning from ear to ear, poured himself a full glass before filling Rick's glass to the brim.

'Drink up, *Meneer*. Tonight we dust away the years and relax. *Gesondheid*! Cheers! Prost!'

'Cheers!'

They raised their glasses in a toast and clinked them together. They each sipped in silence.

'Good, eh?'

'Yes. I like it a lot.'

'South Africa has everything going for it. You know sometimes I feel we shouldn't pity the past for what it did not know, but perhaps feel sorry for ourselves for what it did. The old Hottentots and Bushmen, they really knew this land, but their savvy has gone with them.'

'Yes, it's a pity. What about the other more populous tribes? Don't they have knowledge of this land?'

'They are just Kaffirs. I can respect the Zulus as warriors, but not the rest. They all arrived at the same time as we did.'

Rick smiled. 'A debatable point, but let's not argue tonight.'

Tom stared down into his drink and remained silent. He wore a heavy frown.

Rick watched him in silence for a while and then spoke. 'Are you all right? You seem upset.'

'No, I'm not upset, but I do want to ask you something. Did you sleep with Lucinda?' His eyes were cold and burned with an inner fire, as they fixed on Rick.

Rick swallowed hard. So there was a problem, he thought. 'Yes, I did.'

'Really?'

'Yes.'

'I mean sleep as in fuck.'

'I know what you mean Tom. Yes, we did.'

'I find that hard to believe.'

Rick cleared his throat. 'Well, we drifted together. We were both outcasts. Flotsam cast adrift. I'm not trying to convince you, and God knows I don't wish to upset you, but it is the truth.'

'You know why I don't believe you?'

'No, but it's irrelevant anyway.'

'No, it's not. I'll come back to it. I want you to tell me why Chrissie left you.'

Rick frowned with confusion. 'I don't know. We didn't hit it off that well. Perhaps we were too fundamentally different? It seems to me you would have to ask her.'

'I did.'

Rick studied Tom's face. 'In which case you can tell me.'

'Because you are a poofter, a queer. What we call here a turd-burglar, and can't get it up with a chick.'

Rick blinked and sat up. He had visibly blanched. A doubtful frown crossed his face. 'I don't believe you. She wouldn't have said that,' he said, his voice quavering slightly in shock. 'I just do not believe you.'

'What don't you believe? The truth?'

'First off, it's not the truth, and I just don't believe she said that. Why should she say such a thing? There is no truth to it, for God's sake.'

'Well, I believe it. I also believe that there isn't a Natasha. She's just a front for you. A cover, if you like, just like I also don't believe you jumped Lucie. I believe you are a cocksucker.'

Rick stared at him. 'You really are an offensive bastard, aren't you?'

'What is it? The truth upsetting you?'

Rick got up. 'I really feel it's time for me to go. I'll leave tonight. I can't believe what I'm hearing, and I'm certainly not keen to listen to any more perverted insinuations of yours.'

Tom also got up. 'Insinuations – is that what you call them? Did you or did you not kiss my cock when we were on holiday in Spain?'

Rick glowered at him, and took a deep breath, 'That's what this is all about isn't it?'

'Answer the question!' said Tom raising his voice.

'Okay. Yes, but ...'

'Come again, come again,' interrupted Tom. 'Did you say yes?'

'I did, but I would like to talk about the incident, and at ...'

'Nothing to talk about. You are a faggot, who pretends to jump my woman. Well, I have a plan. I would like to make it a happy ending for you. I want you to be real happy, so get on your knees and suck my dick.'

Rick gaped at him. 'You must be insane!'

'No, I'm serious.'

'Tom – just fuck off, will you,' said Rick backing away from him.

Tom put his drink down. 'Listen, buddy, I want to finish this. I'm going to make you if I have to.' He advanced threateningly toward Rick.

'Tom, just back off, will you! You are deranged! This is not funny.'

'No, it's not funny, but it will be fun. I be able to compare you to Lucie, and you ... well, you can just enjoy it.'

Tom was now laughing insanely as he advanced on Rick. Rick tried to push him away, but Tom grabbed his arm and twisted it suddenly and violently, forcing a yelp of pain out of him. He spun Rick around and pulled his body against his, whilst encircling his neck with his free arm. Rick was gasping with pain from his twisted arm.

'Good,' laughed Tom in a daemonic voice. 'I see we can understand each other. There is no use fighting me, I can make you submit, so relax and enjoy while you can. Sink to your knees.'

Rick reluctantly sank to his knees, groaning in pain. Tom released him, causing him to slump forward.

'My commands should be easy for you to follow. Just turn around and sta—'

'Fuck off!' yelled Rick.

'We could do that to,' said Tom derisively. He grabbed Rick by the hair at the nape of his neck and pulled him upwards.

Rick grimaced in pain, and half-turning swung hard at Tom. Tom deflected the blow away from his face and on to his shoulder. He pushed Rick forward and released the hold on his hair. Rick staggered and turned to swing at him again. Tom easily sidestepped and putting in all of his weight drove a hard punch into Rick's stomach area.

There was a gasp as Rick crumpled forward, completely winded. He was struggling for breath. The room was spinning around him as he crumpled forward. The next thing he was aware of was blood coming into his right eye, which was level with the floor. Tom's large bare foot right next to his face came into focus.

He felt himself being hauled up, but was obliviously to everything except his pain, his lack of breath, and the blood, which has caused him to close his right eye. His lungs continued to seek air frantically. He felt himself fall and was vaguely conscious of landing on the bed. He curled up into a foetal position, still struggling for breath and clarity of mind, which was eluding him.

An arm was roughly pulled away from where it clutched his stomach, and was forced behind his back. It was held in place as his other arm was wrenched around and also forced back. This in turn forced him on to his belly, and caused his legs to straighten. He tried to protest, but no voice came, and he felt something encircling his wrists tightly, pinioning them together. He tried vainly to pull them away, but was unable to muster any force.

A great weight suddenly pressed down on his lower back causing him to panic and try to scream, but again no sound came. He tried to twist, but the weight kept him firmly in place. His ankles were now firmly bound together.

The weight was suddenly lifted and Rick felt a gush of air enter his lungs. He was starting to recover. Laughter flooded the room.

Lucinda (Capetown)

She looked around the room. It seemed so very cold and

impersonal. Her touch was no longer there; it had left with her when she had moved across to Tom's house. The poster was faded and had started to warp. As it pulled away from the wall with its drying blue-tack, it was looking distinctly forlorn. It was a picture showing children running from gunfire, a poster from Richard Attenborough's film *Cry Freedom*, about the white reporter Donald Woods and the murdered black activist Steve Biko. *Cry Freedom* had been banned, but somehow college activists had obtained posters advertising the film.

She stared at the poster and tried to rekindle the embers of her idealism, which had become distinctly cool, as life and a creeping sense of unease and cynicism overcame her. The feeling was deep and visceral, and like maladies of the gut, difficult to identify and pinpoint. She felt as if nothing much mattered, as if she had entered a cosmic black hole, which was able to suck all emotions into a void, without seemingly to have any impact on the environment or life.

The time spent with Rick had been a happy one, she realised. He had been tender, loving and caring, with a strong sentimental streak through him. She remembered how Carl Jung had postulated that the psyche of any human contained both the animus and the anima, the male and female consciousness within it. A very macho, aggressive male would have a low anima, but a lot of animus, whilst someone like Rick probably had more anima than the norm, but this in turn explained his amiable nature.

She wondered what he might be doing at this very minute. She looked at her watch. It was ten past eleven. She felt a sudden surge of warmth toward him and was overcome by an impulsive desire to go and see if he was up. She hesitated a moment as she wondered how a meeting with Tom would go, but decided to drive by, and if the lights were on, enter; if not she would return unannounced.

She drove there distractedly, listening to an evocative trumpet solo by Maurice Andre. She felt her impulsive almost festive mood turn to one of introspection and reticence. She felt in no mood to confront Tom, however much she might feel like seeing Rick. It would be an uncomfortable situation.

As she arrived she pulled into the drive automatically and

turned off the headlights. There were lights on inside the house. The mood music carried on. She surveyed the house and found herself thinking about the many scenes, good and bad, that had occurred within its walls. She smiled to herself as she turned off the engine, but continued to listen to the music. Tom wasn't all bad, she thought. He did have some good points to him.

She froze. Out of the corner of her eye she noticed a shadowy human shape moving. It seemed to move in a crouched position from some bushes in the garden, to somewhere behind her car. She also was sure that someone else was moving in the bushes too. She felt anxious as she swung around to look more closely, but couldn't make anything out. She glanced back at the house. The kitchen and the hall lights were on, which meant that somebody was home.

Toying with the idea of starting the car and revving it up before reversing at great speed, she decided against that and, grabbing her keys, ran for the front door, praying that it hadn't been bolted on the inside. She opened it frantically and was flooded with relief as it swung open. She glanced out into the gloom as she rapidly closed it, and then bolted it. There was nobody to be seen out there. A foolish thought crossed her as she contemplated the possibility that she had imagined the shadows. She dismissed it as idiotic. There had been a person – or persons – out there.

She looked around. The place was silent. She could not imagine Tom going to bed with the lights on. She moved to the foot of the stairs, and glanced up, but no lights were on. As she moved into the kitchen she realised Rick's lights were on. She walked out and across to knock on the door.

Rick (Capetown)

Rick had started to regain his breath. His thoughts were clearing even if the blood blurred his vision. He tried to free his arms, but was unable to do so. His ankles were equally well secured together. He twisted his head around from the wall that it had been facing to survey the room. Tom was standing by the bed, with a glass in his hand. He was grinning inanely and wearing only his briefs.

'I'm sorry about the cut above the eye. You should never have taken a swing at me.'

'Cut it out, Tom. Let me loose.'

'No way. I know you enjoy this – and hell, do you need any proof I do?' He revealed his erect penis.

'I don't enjoy this, I swear. Please let me loose.'

Tom just laughed and climbed onto the bed. Rick felt his shorts and underpants being violently dragged down to his knees. He tried to twist around but was forced back by a broad hand slamming down between his shoulder blades.

'Fuck off! Let me loose,' he screamed.

By way of reply he felt his whole body suddenly pulled by the ankles down to the edge of the bed. His knees and feet hit the floor. He again vainly tried to protect himself by trying to reach down with his hands, but they were too securely bound to be of any use. He felt what he presumed to be the wine being poured over his backside. His buttocks were crudely separated and suddenly a hand grabbed his genitals in a firm and hard grip.

'You bloody well relax, hey? I can squeeze you so hard that you will black out, so bloody relax,' hissed the voice.

Rick winced in pain, and squirmed. He involuntarily bucked and tried to straighten and pull away. The sudden sharp pain in the centre of his back from Tom's blow made him gasp. He slumped and unwillingly relaxed.

'That's better, you little faggot. I have waited so long to have you. I don't think you have any idea how much I have wanted to jab my cock into you since Spain. I should have done it then, but I was too immature. But I'm grown now.'

Rick groaned.

'Please. Oh God, please don't,' he pleaded. He tensed. He was as rigid as a plank, and was only vaguely aware of the threats to relax. He felt a series of dry, racking sobs well in his throat.

Rick felt his body being clasped tight as Tom brought his head close, in order to whisper coarsely in his ear, 'You have got to relax, but perhaps we should continue where we started so many years ago?'

Tom started to chortle. 'I can't believe it, I've got you at last. I like it that you put up a fight, but you can relax now, you are under my control, and I won't hurt you. I've only ever done this to a female … in England, funnily enough.'

'*Are you fucking mad?*' screamed a voice that made Tom sit up in shock. Rick arched and bucked. A series of dry, racking sobs escaped his throat.

Tom grabbed his trousers and held them over his privates as he stared wild-eyed at Lucinda. He appeared speechless.

She stared at him with a look of disgust and loathing. Her hands were on her hips defiantly. She was dressed casually in a flimsy cotton floral summer dress. She looked across at Rick, who was writhing slowly and groaning on the edge of the bed. She shook her head in disbelief and turned back to Tom who had since regained his composure and had slipped on his underpants. 'I know I'm repeating myself, you bastard, but are you fucking mad?'

Tom grinned inanely. 'Perhaps a good answer would be, only incidentally.'

'Quit fucking around, you arsehole. What the hell are you up to?' she bellowed at him.

He surveyed her with a look of disdain, and then calmly walked toward her. She raised her arms self-protectively, immediately sure he was about to hit her, but he moved around and closed the door. He locked it, and turned. 'If you are going to act like a fishwife in my house, I want the doors closed,' he said scornfully.

She gasped in exasperation. 'Fishwife? What the hell is going on here? What are you up to?'

'What does it look like?' he shot back.

She turned to look at Rick who had his face averted, but was obviously still in a lot of pain. Tom moved dangerously close to her, so that she felt immediately threatened, her space was being invaded. She backed away and then deftly stepped around him to attend to Rick.

'Like a bloody … brutal … rape, if you ask me.'

'It is not rape if you have consent.'

'You fucking bastard, Tom. That's shit!' yelled Rick vehemently.

Lucie shook her head in disbelief. 'I can't believe you did this Tom. Help me release him… please,' she pleaded as she struggled with the tightly knotted belts.

Tom remained silent, glowering at her.

As she continued to struggle he unexpectedly knelt and undid the belt that fastened his ankles, and started to rub them. Rick pulled his legs away forcefully.

Tom stood up and glared at Lucinda. 'In case you didn't realise it, he likes this.'

'I do not—'

'Shut up!' snapped Tom. He turned to Lucinda again. 'He likes this. I know this for a fact.'

'It sure as hell doesn't look that way. Not only is he trussed up, it appears you beat him up and have caused him pain. Does he look happy?' She managed at last to free his hands.

'Did you hear me? I said I *know!*'

'You know fuck-all, Tom!'

He gave an exasperated sigh. 'I know he's a faggot. He likes men. He has kissed my cock before.'

'And what does that make you?'

'I didn't enjoy it. He did it to me,' protested Tom.

'You are so full of shit, it's a wonder your eyes aren't brown.'

'Listen you caustic little bitch,' said Tom scathingly. 'Let's find out the truth. Answer me this. Did he jump you when you were alone these last few days?'

'Is that what this is all about? The revenge of the jilted lover?' She stood and faced him as Rick straightened himself and wiped his eye.

'Answer the bloody question!'

She fixed with an incensed glare, then answered quietly, 'I would state it differently, Tom. He made love to me, not jumped me!'

Tom looked surprised and stared at her. 'I don't believe you. I think you made it up to protect him.'

'Bullshit. Why would I say such a thing?'

'I can think of several reasons.'

Lucinda glanced back at Rick and saw the cut above his right eye. The smeared blood on his face dramatised the injury. 'Oh Christ, Rick, what has he done?'

Rick winced, and slowly started to move his arms round and

to the side. He was obviously in a lot of pain. Lucie stood up and put her hand on her forehead in disbelief.

With deceptive speed Tom lunged forward and grabbed her around the waist and pulled her back in a flash. She screamed in protest and tried to disengage herself. He had deliberately caught hold of the lapel of the dress, so that her violent movements ripped it open at the front. She stared down at her ripped dress in consternation and alarm. Before she had time to gather herself, he had grabbed the other side and with one strong tug had not only removed it from her, but had toppled her to her knees. She swore and jumped up, but as she lunged for him, his hand shot forward and clamped her around the throat. She flayed her arms in an effort to dislodge him, but was clearly unable to do so.

He let go his grip and with the other arm quickly encircled her neck and pulled her tight to him. She tried desperately to kick and claw at him. He swung round and faced Rick with her, who had risen from the bed and was lurching unsteadily toward the fracas. He dragged her back to the small table and with his free hand grabbed his penknife, which had a corkscrew on it he'd been using. He deftly brought the blade out. He noticed Rick gasp in disbelief.

'Sit, you faggot, or I'll really harm her,' he ordered Rick.

Rick slowly lowered himself on to the bed. Tom staggered back with his victim and allowed himself to collapse back into the armchair, with Lucie sprawled between his legs, and his arm still firmly around her neck. She had ceased struggling when she saw the knife.

There was silence. Tom and Lucinda were breathing heavily, whilst Rick continued to cough and wince.

'Good,' said Tom. 'I want to find out the truth once and for all.' He leant forward and using the knife cut through Lucinda's bra. As he reached down and tried to cut her panties she brought her legs up self-protectively. She yelped as the blade superficially cut her thigh. He succeeded in cutting the panties free. Lucinda had started to remonstrate under his stranglehold.

Rick had started to rise. 'Stop, Tom – for God's sake stop!' he implored.

Tom ordered him to sit, and the menace in his voice was very real. Rick sat down again. Lucie continued to cry gently, with her arms stretched down to cover her privates.

'Okay, okay. Here's what I have in mind,' said Tom. He scrutinised Rick. 'If you can jump her, I'll release you both unharmed. If you cannot, it means I'm right and I'll do what I please with you both if needs be. Don't, I repeat don't, don't try to leap at me. I'm capable of seriously harming you guys.'

'So what is it you want?'

'Jump her! Fuck her! *Now*. With her on me.'

Rick gawked with his mouth open. 'I can't believe you want me to make love to Lucie. Just like that? In the state I'm in, after what you have done? On top of you? After all you've done? You must be kidding, you sick fucking son of a bitch!'

'No, man, I'm not kidding. *Poes is koning, maar piel is sy baas.* That's Afrikaans for pussy is the king, but the prick is always the boss. I want you to prove that to me. But the truth is I know you can't.'

Rick sat as if paralysed. He was in a state of shock.

'Come on, man! What's the problem?' laughed Tom. He turned his gaze back to Lucie, and moved the knife up and down her belly. 'Drop your hands, slut,' he ordered, and she let them fall by her side. He chuckled. 'See? She's hot. She's always liked a little of the rough stuff, has Lucie. Perhaps there was a peasant ancestor in her line? Who knows? But I know she can enjoy this. She enjoys being manhandled.'

He brought the blade down to her pubic region and ordered her to spread her legs. She did so slowly. He grinned lewdly at Rick. He deliberately turned the sharp end away from her and started to spread her lips with the knife. 'Look, man, she can't wait all night. Her pussy is wet now.'

Rick looked at Lucie's eyes. They narrowed slightly as they looked at him, and then widened. Tom was right. She was ready, she was beckoning him, whether for self-preservation or because she had become excited he could not tell. He closed his eyes and hung his head for a few seconds.

He then looked up again as if to confirm that the scene was really true, and it was. She still lay across Tom, naked and with her legs spread, with her neck firmly encircled by his muscular arm. His other arm rested across her body and still had a penknife with a blade playing gently in her dark pubic hair.

'*Carpe diem* is one of her favourite sayings, so go ahead. Seize her. If you can, that is! What do you want her to do? What are you going to do?'

Rick looked at her again. She was breathing short sharp shallow breaths. The eyes had a sensuous beckoning look, a look of pure female sensuality. For the first time he felt a stirring of arousal. He cleared his throat. 'I want her to play with her breasts. To gently finger her nipples.'

Tom gave a quiet ribald chuckle, and withdrew his arm. Lucie gradually brought her hands up and started to caressingly feel her breasts and play with her nipples. Her mouth opened slightly. Her eyes remained fixed on Rick's.

Rick crawled forward and started to run his hands up and along her thighs. There was blood on his hands – his – and blood on her thighs – hers. He began to gently play with her, and with great tenderness inserted a finger into her moist interior. He moved to gently massage her in her dark furrow. As soon as he perceived that she was beginning to move slightly to his probing and massaging finger, he moved up and inserted his now erect penis into her. She had raised her hips slightly to accept him.

He started slowly, but her responses urged him on. He increased the tempo, oblivious to Tom and the extraordinary situation they were in. He started pounding into her. Her pelvis was moving violently to meet every thrust. She started to gurgle with the mounting pleasure, and then suddenly screamed aloud as a strong and pulsating orgasm flooded her whole body. Unable to contain himself, he also felt a flooding release of concentrated pleasure that momentarily eradicated all the cares of the world. He spasmodically jerked a few more times and equally abruptly, stopped. They were both out of breath, it had all been so quick but so intensely strong.

Tom looked aghast and set her free. She slipped forward and embraced Rick. He sat back on his haunches and she straddled him, with him still inside her. They hugged and cried into each other's necks. Neither even noticed that Tom had dressed, and with tears streaming from his eyes, left the room.

Lucinda stopped crying and looked around. 'Where has he gone?'

Rick wiped his eyes and shrugged.

Lucinda jumped up and, grabbing her torn dress, ran out after Tom. He was in the hall and about to leave. His eyes were red, his expression confused.

'Tom! Tom! There are blacks out there in the garden. Don't go out.'

He smiled weakly. 'That's just the gardener with his girl. They often hang out under the front bushes. They are harmless.'

'Oh.'

'Listen, Lucie. I'm so, so very ashamed and sorry. I can't even begin …'

'Don't. Don't say anything. I am in a state of confusion and shock. I don't know what to think.'

'I'm leaving the house. I want to be alone in a hotel tonight. Stay with Rick. Tell him …'

'It's okay. Just go. Be careful.'

He nodded and left quietly. His tears had left shiny streaks down his cheeks.

Lucinda turned back to the room. She knew that she would spend the night with Rick, but after the evening's events she also knew that it would take her a long time to work herself out, and that was something that she had to do on her own.

She entered the room. Rick smiled a faint smile of welcome. He was standing and had at least made himself decent. The cut above his eye looked hideous, but he had moved beyond the pain. He was celebrating life, even if he was doing it a bit weakly at the moment.

Tom's thoughts:

What the hell was it all about? What possessed me to act in the insane way that I did?

I'm not sure that I can answer that to myself. I feel a sense of disbelief, a sense that it couldn't really happen like this in life; that only deviant and perverted minds would come up with such abnormal behaviour, yet I have never felt myself to be a deviant. I have been aware that there are games that I have played, which many people may only fantasise about, but does that mean I fall into a degenerate bracket?

Perhaps life has moulded me. Perhaps abnormal pleasures kill the taste for the normal ones. Could I honestly say that the incident back in Spain really upset me?

The answer to the last question would have to be no. It didn't upset me, but it did disturb me, for it brought out into the open, the cauldron of murky thoughts, attachments and liaisons that exist in a schoolboy's mind. I could not acknowledge to myself that the incident actually gave me pleasure, for – ludicrously – it did. I don't feel it set me off on a deviant path, but it did arouse my curiosity and awareness that there were other ways that could be followed in life. I don't feel warped, but perhaps my weakness in the academic field combined with the strength in sport made me feel possessive and embracing towards Rick. I should admit it. Perhaps I was infatuated…

I'm not sure about the second thought dealing with abnormal pleasures killing the taste for the normal ones. I feel that the violence I displayed with them both was the daemons getting the upper hand, shaking an already confused mind and steering it in a self-destructive way to display all its worst traits. I was under their power, and I guess I'm frightened by it. I'm still not sure about Rick; there are elements of unfinished business, rage, frustration and curiosity all blended in here. I do know that I was shocked to find myself watching them make love and enjoying it. So the voyeuristic and the power play were exciting to me, but I do feel that I can keep both under control.

I feel as if life has so many stupid rules, and my passage through it has been to take timid steps obeying them and trying to respect them. Well, I feel changed. I know I can be whatever I want to be within reason, and that in my own little way I have pushed the rules and the very boundaries to one side. *Finis coronat opus* – the end crowns all. While not condoning what I did, I have learnt from it, even if Rick and Lucie never forgive or understand it. Most important, I can recognise my daemons, so I am capable of being happy in the future … whatever it may hold.

Lucinda's thoughts:

My God, what do I make of it all? Did I really go through with all that?

I can't explain myself fully, nor can I truly understand how I came to enjoy it at the end, when there was so much real violence and coercion. Tom's force and intimidation were very real. My only feasible explanation is that like in all games of domination and sadomasochism the real power ultimately lies with the masochist rather than the sadist. As long as it remains within the parameters of being only a game, then the perpetrator is really only carrying out the wishes of the victim. At some non-definable moment it had changed status from a rage in Tom to a game, and he had re-balanced enough to be alert to the game's sensibilities. Even if it apparently hadn't changed outwardly in any form or manner, the crucial point was that he had.

I have always wanted to burn in divine conflagration, and burn I did. I emerged, bruised, cut, violated, but at peace after my climax. So much at peace, in fact, that I even felt I wanted to warn Tom of the potential dangers outside. I had been ready to instantly forgive and offer absolution. But burn I did, and the sexual inferno that engulfed me has left me tired and a little confused, because the fires appear to be hellish. I'm not sure if Satan himself lit them, but the blaze was not a heavenly one. Its charred embers, which still smoulder within me, talk of perversions and aberrant behaviour. It is as if the erotic nerve ignites this violent and destructive craving, and the sexual impetus hurls me forward, oblivious of all save my own satisfaction.

Without knowing how or why, I sensed that something like this might happen, the moment I walked in the room. I also knew that in the passion of rape, and enmeshed in its lust Tom would not be amenable to reason.

Strangely, I don't regret it at all. I feel my weirdness was verified. It was a confirmation of sorts, and as such I can accept it. I know this might inhibit many aspects of what society feels I ought to be; such things as exemplary wife, mother, member of society, worker, grateful and humble recipient of a male partner's sexual mood, cook and whatever else that goes with a female white Anglo-Saxon South African. But I cannot fully embrace any of these things fully. I now know my path is different, and perhaps I shall never be a mother or wife, but I don't care. I have gone through a voyage of self-discovery, and feel more balanced and happy about life.

I shall remain Tom's friend if he can face me again, and may well organise to go and spend some time with Rick in London. I feel deeply for him but am confused emotionally as well as bewildered by the events. My future is here, I suspect without a permanent partner. I suspect it will entail a nomadic sexual future, wandering in the marginalized sexual sidetracks that cross the main highways. My future also lies here in this turbulent land, and with its uncertain future.

Rick's thoughts:

I guess it falls into two distinct questions, the one being, what *should* I feel about it all? While the second would be, what *do* I feel about it all?

The answers are difficult to express clearly, but would need to include a few emotions: pain, confusion and anger, as well as relief, surprise and a little something of gratitude. Mixed together they would make a peculiar recipe, and I'm sure most people would say it isn't one flavour or the other. But I'm sure when one deals with the human psyche, it cannot be so clear cut, so well defined that only one flavour dominates, a mixture would have to be the norm.

Yes, what Tom did was painful, and there is no doubt in my mind: it was wrong. I felt a sense of disbelief and intense anger. I'm sure that I would have used the knife at one stage to protect myself, had I been aware of its presence on the coffee table. What he actually did was humiliating and really painful, but at the end of it all there is a tinge of relief. There had always been a deep-seated lingering doubt and confusion about what or who I am. Was I a repressed homosexual, waiting for the 'out of the closet' scenario, or a non-liberated bisexual, perhaps? I now know that whatever may have happened back in Spain, it was transitory and perhaps developmental in my life, but is certainly not a part of my present, only a relegated episode from my past. I feel heterosexual, and I love Lucinda. I know we shall be taking different paths and I shall never be sure if what she did was for me, or did she really enjoy the whole lurid episode as Tom lewdly suggested. So, a little bit of gratitude is there for the clarification, even if the getting there was so very difficult and traumatic. I can now safely package the Spain incident into personal history under the bracket of boyhood experience.

There is curiously no residual anger or hatred towards Tom. I would quite like to remain his friend, if that is possible. Time needs to elapse before we could ever be comfortable in each other's company again, but realistically, our paths may indeed never cross again. The living history here in South Africa is akin to a cauldron bubbling over, and the broth that spills out may be harmful to all, as well may be the daemons who keep the fire going.

My confusion lies in the sole aspect of having experienced such a strong orgasm under such circumstances, where, I to all intents and purposes, violated a woman – even if she was my lover – held against her will. I remember reading somewhere that the quality of an orgasm is defined by the number of people involved in getting one there, and thinking that it was a peculiar statement. Perhaps it isn't so peculiar; maybe there are many others out there who have experienced such highs. All I know is that it was tremendous and exhilarating in the extreme.

Like I suppose all experiences of this intense nature, it does question the very foundations of society and what you are led to believe and expect. Sometimes the foundations don't seem so firm, and I get a visceral feeling that they may well be built on shifting sand. Perhaps all generations felt that, not just those here and now in the South Africa of the Nineties.

But I feel ready to continue. I hope that Lucie will join me along the way, and perhaps in London. I feel now that all I owe life is the obligation to live it and celebrate it to the full.

1996 Natal, South Africa

The police officer looked down at the carnage. Both of the dead were unrecognisable. They had obviously gone through a horrific ordeal before being 'necklaced' by their attackers. They looked as if they had deep cuts to their limbs. These were probably inflicted by hard blows with the Zulu traditional sword, the assegai,[55] he surmised.

With a sigh he beckoned the police photographer who placed a face mask on and then stepped forward to record the scene. Many of these crimes remained unsolved but all the correct motions were carried out in case there was ever to be a trial and evidence was needed.

The stench of charred flesh mixed with burnt rubber was horrendous; a smell that once experienced was difficult to ever forget. He looked at the surrounds; a scorched and broken little hut had served as the execution chamber. The horror must have been dreadful he thought, as he tried to imagine the scene. The crudely painted slogan on the outside of the hut denouncing the ANC indicated that in all likelihood they were Zulu thugs, loyal to Chief Buthelezi, who roamed at large and seemed answerable to nobody.

He had seen many such scenes in the new South Africa that had been born two years previously. Natal had become a killing field that often pitted ethnic groups against each other in their bids to gain political power. He hoped this essentially was a legacy of the past rather than a foretaste of the future, because if it was the latter, the future looked bleak.

He looked at the two photographs that the offices of the ANC in Pietermaritzburg had given him. Gatsu Simbalesi and Luther Mowanga, both Zulus and active members of the party, had not returned last night after declaring that they were going to visit some friends who were holding a political meeting and had invited them to come along and officiate. They had not returned last night and the office already had feared the worst.

So, once again it was Zulu pitted against Zulu, and ideology rather than ethnicity divided them. The officer hoped that the turbulent transitional phase the country was going through would not last, for he felt too tired and too sickened by the events to feel he could really keep going. He looked across at the young black officer who was clearly distressed and slowly walking around the

---

[55]Short Zulu sword.

horrific scene. He had apparently known Gatsu, whom he claimed was a great man and very dedicated to his people.

He wondered briefly if he should retire early and make way for the up-and-coming junior officers in the force. It was after all a very different country since the elections of April 1994, and he no longer felt sure he truly belonged. Despondent and tired, he walked back to the car to radio in his initial findings.

South-West Angola

The train was travelling on the section between Munhango and Luso heading for the Atlantic coast port of Lobito via Benguela and Nova Lisboa. It was a dangerous run. The Popular Front for the Independence of Angola government soldiers (MPLA), were locked in a power struggle for the land with the opposing rebel forces of the National Union for the Total Independence Of Angola (UNITA). It was easy to see the struggle in terms of ideology, the reality being far more complex. It was a heady mix of power, guns, ethnicity and religion. UNITA was led by its Protestant leader Jonas Savimbi, and had outside support from the West, whilst the MPLA, based in the capital, Luanda, relied on Cuban and former Soviet bloc support. Many close to the combat saw the war as a power struggle for ethnic dominance. The UNITA rebels were primarily Ovimbundu, whilst the MPLA forces were mainly Mbundu.

The war had been deadlocked for many years and showed no signs of cessation. Casualties long ago dehumanised by the Western media were reported purely as statistics. The stalemate meant that the country was literally paralysed economically.

The railway line was under nominal government control. MPLA troops protected the line and until recently a contingent of Zairean reinforcements actually rode on the carriages, bristling with weaponry and effectively making the train seem like a modified armoured troop carrier.

Zaire in turn was convulsed with civil war and unrest in the eastern provinces bordering Rwanda, Uganda and Burundi. A mixture of forces espousing different ideologies, ethnic loyalties, banditry or witchcraft had destabilised the region. Summoned back home, the remaining Zairean troops had departed. Active Cuban and Soviet help had long ago ceased, so that the vacuum created had been filled with regular MPLA troops.

Tom surveyed the scene through his binoculars as the train came closer to the packed charges that were well camouflaged on the tracks. The train with its heavy load laboured slowly up the slight gradient.

He could clearly make out the gun-toting soldiers on the roof of the carriages. There would be further reinforcements inside. The mind-numbing heat had undoubtedly lulled them into a false sense of security. They looked tired, dusty and disinterested.

The old-fashioned Russian-manufactured charge detonator was resting on the small rocky ledge in front of him. He just had to wait for the most propitious moment to set off the blast. Even with the heavy armour plating that protected the ponderous locomotive, the blast would be big enough to destroy it and derail the carriages in tow. The noise of the blast would bring out the many bitter and hardened UNITA rebels that were hiding in the scraggy bush and behind the outcrops.

A small rock hyrax moved into view just below the rocky ledge. It was oblivious of the human presence and went about its business foraging for small green shrubs and roots. In the drought stricken areas of the South of the African continent there was not much nutritious sustenance left, as most of the green had long ago become brown dry and wizened.

The hissing and chugging noise of the steam engine could now be clearly heard as it drew laboriously closer. It was edging closer to the lethal charge, and its human cargo would soon be in the deadly sights and range of the guns that awaited their arrival. The squeal of the metal wheels on the rails was occasionally deafening; a metallic protest at its cumbersome duties that could be heard far and wide.

Tom involuntarily shuddered at the noise. He even felt sorry for the poor soldiers, who along with heat and the ever-possible threat of ambush, were forced to endure it all day long.

He shifted slightly to ease the discomfort of lying on the hard rocky soil, causing the hyrax to freeze momentarily when it realised the close proximity of the humans. It scurried off to the safety of the rock crevices.

'Sensible dassie!'[56] muttered Tom under his breath.

Joseph, the UNITA commander by his side, inclined his head quizzically, but Tom's dismissive nod made him turn back to watching the train.

Tom turned to watch his companion. He was checking the safety catch on his M16 assault rifle. He then double-checked the ammunition clips on his belt, and then – as Tom knew he would – closed his eyes and frowned. He was praying, something he did without fail before any combat.

Guns and Christianity… here in Africa they went and in hand, mused Tom. He wondered whether the prayer was a plea to survive the ordeal and come out unscathed, or a prayer for the souls of those soon to fall in combat. Whichever it was, there was no doubt that Joseph was a great and committed soldier, and that religion played a great role in his life.

The seconds passed. They were suspended between conflict and calm, a transitional space between the two states.

The train drew level with the charge and Tom depressed the detonator handle as he lowered his head. The noise was deafening. There seemed a slight lull before the hiss of steam and screech of metal followed, along with a shower of small pebbles and dirt.

Tom and Joseph jumped up and raced forward. There was a lot of dust, steam and smoke. Most of the soldiers who were riding on the roof had been thrown to the ground, as the first three carriages had not only been derailed but buckled and toppled over on to their sides.

Through the smoky confusion Tom could make out troops staggering with shock and bewilderment as others raced to try and retrieve their weapons. In their panic some were already trampling over one another in order to escape. A few were clawing the ground in desperation. The UNITA rebels had already leased a deadly barrage and were racing in with machetes and other weaponry.

A hideous, blood-curdling scream came from the smoke

---

[56]Rock hyrax.

ahead. A man staggered forward carrying what appeared to be his own entrails. He had no time to even register surprise at seeing them as Joseph unleashed a lethal volley at him.

They ran past his crumpled body and up to the train. Shards of metal and debris lay everywhere. They slowed down and moved forward cautiously through thick palls of cordite smoke and dust. A machine-gun that had started to chatter had fallen silent and there was now only the odd shot, or scream, in the ensuing quiet. Steam still hissed in the charred and twisted wreckage of the grand old locomotive.

It was over very quickly. Resistance was silenced. A few had surrendered and were cowering on the ground, unwilling to die for their regime, whilst others had panicked and had dropped all weapons in order to dash towards the bush. Very few made it up the surrounding slopes.

Tom took out his revolver and hung the Uzi[57] on his shoulder. He walked forward tentatively, as Joseph raced off to co-ordinate the prisoners taken and the systematic looting of the train. There was likely to be gold bullion on board, hidden in with all the bauxite. His spies had already informed him this was the case.

A set of dentures lay in the dust, looking like a stage prop for a future comedy. The owner of the dentures was not far away. An old and wizened grey-haired African, he had managed to crawl a short distance before death had overcome him. He wore the overalls of a railway employee. He lay face down in the centre of a large and dark pool of blood that was slowly sinking into the parched soil. A genuine casualty of war, or 'collateral damage' as the Americans would term it, reflected Tom.

He felt weary. The bloodshed never stopped. No continent had an unblemished history, but Africa seemed particularly brutal in its killings and bloodletting. Most warfare these days was conducted by sophisticated technology insulating the combatants from their enemies. The gore and the demise of real human beings were hardly ever visible, but Africa still had wars where the killing was all too apparent.

He looked across to where a handful of MPLA troops were

---

[57]Israeli manufactured hand-held sub-machine gun.

cringing on the ground huddled together. They had already had their uniforms stripped from them and were now having their wrists pinioned by plastic handcuffs. A crowd of jubilant and jeering gun-waving rebels celebrated their victory and systematically hurled abuse at their captives.

Joseph was attempting to maintain some degree of order and was desperately trying to establish his authority over the mob. He looked a little ashen and grim, and Tom then realised he had been wounded in the arm. His left arm hung limp, and even at a distance seemed bloodied. He wondered how the wound had occurred.

Tom sighed. Any flesh wound out here was serious, as the medical services were dismally rudimentary. Infections abounded and could easily prove fatal in remarkably little time.

His mind went back to Colonel Coetzee, who two years ago had talked Tom into joining him on this mercenary venture. He had died only five days earlier from infective meningococcal meningitis. With his body covered in large purple blotches, the local Africans had refused to come anywhere near the dying man. They feared he was contagious and suspected that it might even be the deadly Ebola virus. He had drifted in and out of consciousness before his death.

In the hope that his friend would overcome the illness, Tom had had him transported to Menongue on the Cubango River where he purloined a small thatched hut with an army camp bed to lay him on. He mopped his brow and tried to keep him clean and cool, but without medications he knew at the time that the care was only palliative.

In a rare moment of clarity on his deathbed, Coetzee had looked up and apologised for bringing Tom into the hell they found themselves in. He had gasped and wheezed and even looked frightened at times.

'Tom, I am so very sorry for everything. This is a hell-hole and you deserve a life. Leave while you can. Forget Africa, the continent is doomed. The problems are insurmountable, our aims incommensurable. Death, disease, destruction and disaster. It is all here. And … despair. Yes, despair. To die this way, *Gott*…' his voice trailed off, and he wiped his eyes. 'Listen, man, you never know where your journey begins or where it may take you, but you have a chance. Leave this damned place, leave Africa and make your life somewhere else. Live and be happy!'

Coetzee had shook his head from side to side. His expression was a mixture of pain and what looked like disbelief. It registered his surprise that the tiniest of organisms could bring him, a great warrior who had endured so much, to his knees. He knew his body had been conquered and his spirit was vanquished. He had never regained consciousness again and had died within a few hours.

Tom had had him cremated and scattered his ashes over the harsh and desiccated soils of Angola. He was of Africa and the land was claiming its own back again.

Tom reflected on the old man's words. Were they sagacious? It was his powerfully convincing argument that had brought him to Angola in the first place. Perhaps the dying had greater insight and perception and should be heeded. He mulled over his thoughts.

It had been difficult leaving his civilian life in Capetown for this adventure. He knew from the outset how very much every journey was likely to overturn the established order of life, but this journey was radically different with its high pay and risk. The events during Rick's visit had left him with an emotional paralysis that had not really left him. It was ameliorated by the fleeting moments he had spent with Chrissie.

Lucie had left South Africa and he had not heard from Rick again, but Chrissie had briefly re-entered his life. He did not find contentment with her. She made him happy and nourished the illusion of stability and contentment, and what life could be.

In the midst of the detritus that now surrounded him, Tom felt keenly the suffering and desperation that abounded here was likely to drive him insane. He was riddled with disillusion. The violence and killing had no end. This war was not his. He had already lost his fight, for the white tribe of Africa, his tribe, no longer held sway. History was totally ruthless in its verdict; the illusions had been shattered and his country had changed. The judgement of the world was harsh, judging the white tribe as mistaken racist supremists. It was time to leave, restore his life ard save his soul.

Mbabane, Swaziland

She crossed the street, running carefully with her small child wrapped in the sarong sling. She looked nervous. Mopete felt unused to traffic after so many days of trudging north along small back roads.

She had crossed Natal and climbed the hills to eventually reach Swaziland. She felt weary and unnerved by the possibility of discovery, as she had no documentation of any sort on her. Her despair was such that she felt unable to shake the gloom that had engulfed her. She had no fixed plan except that after Gatsu's violent death she knew she had to leave. She did not want to belong in the South Africa that had risen like a phoenix from the old. Dreams and aspirations had perished along with him. Life for her was slowly passing away and her spirit was drifting off. The remaining fight in her was for her child, who was only eighteen months old.

The little market hawking African crafted products to the wealthy foreign tourists also had a section devoted to small fruit vendors. She desperately needed some food for Steve, and there was always the possibility of scrounging some discarded or overripe fruit.

She moved into the bustling African crowd. She noticed some European tourists ahead who were looking at the fruit. She knew that everybody would watch them so the likelihood of detection would be reduced. A crowd had already gathered around the foreigners, curious to see what they would buy.

Mopete moved in closer and, feigning curiosity, allowed her garment folds cover some fruit. She quickly lifted a couple of apples. The fruit stall owner was uneasy at such a crowd around her produce. She shooed people away. Mopete sauntered away and headed outside into the shade of the large jacaranda trees.

She noticed the man with the limp out the corner of her eye. He was approaching fast. As he drew level he reached out a hand and grabbed her shoulder. She felt too weak to stop him or shake him off.

'Please come with me,' the voice boomed in Swazi. Her acquired knowledge of Zulu meant she understood him.

She followed him meekly as he kept a firm hold on her

shoulder. Once in the shade of more remote trees, and away from the crowds, his grip relaxed.

'What is his name?' The inquisitive voice was friendly and in Portuguese.

Her eyes widened in surprise. She turned to look at him. He looked impassive at first, but then grinned from ear to ear. She recognised him: Sergio. The one they had left on the far side of the river as he was afraid to cross and who had been picked up by the Frelimo security forces. He had survived.

She stared at him with a sense of disbelief. Sergio smiled benevolently and repeated his enquiry.

'Steve Biko Simbalesi,' she responded. After a pause she added, 'His father was killed in Natal not long ago.'

'You are alone?'

'Yes.'

'Hungry?'

'Mhm.' She nodded in agreement slowly and pensively.

'Mhm,' he said by way of reply. His foot traced patterns in the dust. He almost looked shy.

'Rodrigo?'

She shrugged to indicate her lack of information. Pointing to his leg, she tipped her head enquiringly.

He followed her gaze and shrugged. 'Frelimo. They put a bullet through and told me to go home. I did not. I came to Mbabane.'

She grinned. 'Life – it is good here?'

'Mhm. Good. Yes, good. I am an immigration officer. I process the illegal refugees.' He bowed his head and continued to shuffle where he stood.

Mopete shuffled uneasily. She had blanched on hearing the news. 'Well, I must go.'

'Wait.' A long silence ensued.

'I have…' his voice trailed off and he shrugged awkwardly again. 'I have no woman. I am lonely. Maybe you could…'

She grinned.

'I have money and I can look after you and Steve. If… if you want that?'

'I want that,' she whispered, grinning sheepishly.

He beamed and, beckoning her to follow led the way. The African crowd swallowed them anonymously and communally into its midst.

Blantyre, Malawi

Lucie glanced out at the sun-drenched streets of Blantyre. They looked pretty even with all the jacaranda trees dropping their flowers. It had a quintessentially African feel. It reminded her of Pretoria. There was little traffic in the early morning and the scene was tranquil.

She looked back at her new acquisition, a small laptop computer by Acer. It was quick and powerful and she was impressed with its speed and performance. She stared at the letter on the screen. It was a personal and brief account of her life and events since leaving Capetown four and a half years ago.

She read it back to herself:

Dear Rick,

A veritable blast from the past!

It has been a long time since I last communicated with you. The last time I saw you was in Capetown when I left you at the station and you were about to take a train up to Windhoek. Apart from the one postcard from Etosha there has been a huge silence. I know they say that silence speaks louder than words, and perhaps you don't wish to hear from me, but I'm hoping this is not the case. I presume you made it back to London and settled back into work. Did you get to see all you hoped to see?

I have no idea if you even want to hear from me after all this time, and perhaps the email address you gave me so many years ago is no longer valid and this will just bounce out into cyberspace after all! From my point of view, you have never really been far away in my mind. In spite of the passage of time your impact on me was huge and I regret aspects of the tumultuous events that led us down the path they did. I don't regret meeting you, as I feel I've gained from meeting someone like yourself. I learnt that love was possible and that it was a very real emotion. However, I regret losing touch with you and not maintaining the contact. The time we spent together was good, albeit a short and tumultuous time – and it was meaningful for me. We communicated and I found a soul mate – I hope reciprocated.

My reason for re-establishing contact after so many years is simple and selfish. I wanted to hear what you are up to, what has become of you, and generally hear about how life has treated you. I am guessing you are probably married now and hopefully outrageously happy and contented with the standard 2.4 kids! It would be good to hear from you and get an update on you/your life and perhaps become long-distance pen pals? I haven't great expectations that this email will even reach you. I understand if you don't wish to reply – it has after all been a long time, and perhaps too much water has flowed under the bridge. Should there be silence I shall never know the reason for it (email lost or email deleted!), though my sentiments already expressed remain unchanged! I shall assume that perhaps you don't wish contact and I shall respect it. I did think on various occasions that I should try and locate you in London, but it always ended up in the 'too hard' basket! *Mea culpa* as I was there for the odd business trip.

In case you do receive this and feel curious about what became of those you left behind including me, I'll fill you in.

Tom went through a very emotional roller coaster and eventually left for Jo'burg and then I think emigrated. He seems to have disappeared off the face of the SA scene. We met once in Pretoria by chance about two years ago and had a coffee together. It was awkward and he seemed very withdrawn and austere. His comments were very acerbic. I even think he hinted that he was seeing Chrissie, though he did not confirm this. It was not a comfortable meeting, and I haven't seen him since. Have you kept in touch?

Gerard left for New Zealand where he joined some tourist organisation that flew small craft over the peaks or something like that. He seemed very happy when I last saw him three years ago. Chrissie I spotted twice. Once on the arm of a Japanese businessman at the airport, and on the second occasion she was with a well-known de Beers executive in an outrageously expensive restaurant. Both encounters were in Jo'burg. I know she recognised me the second time, but when there was no acknowledgement I felt it was wiser to move away. As you know she's a real live wire and it certainly appears she's having fun!

My life certainly doesn't include such fun, but I shall fill you in on what I have been up to. After you left, Tom and I split. I'm sure you know this much! I moved out and buried myself in work. I promoted the idea of getting the small family restaurants that I had been managing to expand north. The Tavern was becoming a very successful chain in SA and I felt I could take it a stage further by taking it into neighbouring countries. I spearheaded the move into Botswana and Malawi.

It wasn't all smooth sailing. I had extraordinary and unforeseen problems in Gaborone when the manageress – a white – had an open and very public affair with a flamboyant local black politician! Her husband was outraged and then threatened to kill him. The business very nearly folded with all the ensuing scandal that erupted over the affair. The cuckolded husband eventually returned with the kids to Durban. She stayed on but at least had the decency to resign from our employ before moving in with her new lover! What a kerfuffle!

My life has otherwise been uneventful. The business has expanded as I predicted and we now have a chain of restaurants that are currently being franchised and like Nando's are to be found everywhere – at least over here. I have established new ventures in Malawi (where I am currently based), Namibia, Swaziland and Lesotho. I am currently working on the possibility of Mozambique – incidentally a more settled place since Samora Machel's demise, Renamo's defeat and since you were here. So, as you can see the challenges of the business side of my life keeps me occupied. It is going well.

On the personal side, there is precious little to tell. I am in essence enjoying myself, as there is nobody else to enjoy! I have not had any serious relationships, so have remained avowedly single. I had a brief dalliance with a businessman who visited from overseas, but right from the outset we both knew it was short-lived. No real challenges, attractions or events of note – which all sounds revoltingly boring.

The manager of a large commercial enterprise in Zimbabwe that owns The Wave Rafting Adventures has been keen on me for some time – ever since I fell into the water during a white-water rafting trip on the Zambesi. I suspect he fell for the wet and clinging tee shirt look rather than myself! My lack of interest has dampened his ardour. Unrequited love and all that! He has started to wane, citing troubles in Zim. I haven't seen him for quite a while!

Anyway, Rick – it would be great to hear from you – and I'm hoping I will! My apologies if this all seems a little garbled, but I found this quite hard to write. It is the difficulty of talking to someone you are not sure even wants to receive the letter you are sending. I never had difficulty talking with you in the past, but this has not been easy.

All the best.
Your friend, Lucie.

Satisfied that it set the right tone, she typed in the email address ricklg@hotmail.com that she had retrieved from her battered old address book. She wondered where he might be. Emails seldom gave any hint of where the person resided. There were sometimes a few clues, but not in this case. She added her 'signature' which immediately added at the bottom:

Lucinda Beresford,
Apart. 3,
4th Floor Nkrumah Building,
Banda Avenue,
Blantyre,
Malawi
tel. (265) 7534-2889
lucieb_1992@yahoo.com

She sipped her coffee and stared vacantly into the street below. She then leant across and pressed 'send'. The computer whirred and a notification informed her the message had been sent. She logged off and closed the laptop.

A smile crossed her face. She wondered if she would get a reply, or even if he would receive it?

Johannesburg

Chrissie waited in the room as she had been told. She went straight to the fridge and picked out two American Dry ginger ales and some ice cubes. Distributing the ice cubes to two whisky glasses, she poured a small Johnny Walker red label whisky into each and added the ginger ale. She placed one drink on the table, waiting to be claimed. She immediately started on her own. She considered having another one straight away in order to get an alcoholic shot before her consort for the night, Ryutaro Sasagawa, came to her.

He paid her well and was always very considerate to her, but tonight had seemed a bit brusquer with her. Perhaps the business deal with the Americans was not going quite as planned. It was the first time she had been ordered up to the room to await him. Normally he came along with her and was quite affectionate, almost loving. He was different tonight.

She craved a cigarette, but decided against it, as she knew Ryutaro disapproved of her smoking. She sighed and walked into the bedroom from the connected lounge. The phone ringing startled her.

She picked it up and listened.

'Halo you there? Chantelle, is that you?'

She smiled languorously. 'Did you expect to find another lady here?'

'No. No. Very funny!' He laughed in his own inimitable way. 'You are sometimes very funny.'

'Yes,' she replied and thought about all the destinations that Sasagawa Enterprises took him in any one calendar year. How many women would there be who catered to him when he was away from his wife? There obviously would be other women in different locations, who also waited in hotel rooms and who he also found funny.

'Tonight I have special job for you. I pay extra. You know that yes?'

'What sort of special job?'

'I explain later. Pay you big money to make you happy. Ryutaro always look after my special Chantelle. Not so?'

'Yes you do, darling. What sort of special job? Are you wanting what you said was forbidden in Japan?'

'Ah yes. Yes. I want forbidden stuff. Forbidden means good. But tonight, special job. Put on special outfit numba one. Yesa, numba one is very fine. I am there very soon.'

'I can't wait, darling. See you soon.' She hung up and pondered the special job that he'd mentioned. He had two outfits he loved her to wear. Number one was an ankle length see-through nightgown, whilst number two consisted of a schoolgirl outfit. Perhaps the special job was a variation on a scene. She walked over to the cupboard, took out the nightgown, and draped it over the bed. She undressed and put on a G-string of lacy black before slipping into the nightie.

She dimmed the lights and wandering into the bathroom, sprayed some of Guerlain's *Jardin de Bagatelle* perfume on her shoulders and neck. She lay down on the bed. She began to think about little Tomas who was home with her mother in Durban. It was a symbiotic arrangement. Tomas had a surrogate mother, and her mother had company, as her husband had passed away. Tomas was so cute and so very much like his father with his big blue-green eyes and blond flaxen hair. He was a lovable child.

Her thoughts drifted on to Tom. She wondered what life would be like if he actually knew about the child. How would he be? Would he be possessive and demand time with Tomas? She even wondered where he might be this very moment as she lay in a luxury hotel waiting for her Japanese client.

She had last seen him when they had spent a week together about three years ago. He had unexpectedly turned up in Jo'burg when she had been living with Gerard. She realised he must have known Gerard was away for two weeks, but was nonetheless delighted to see him and, undaunted, let him in. After an initial awkwardness they had genuinely started to enjoy each other's company.

They knew that their liaison was sinful, but nevertheless they had fallen into an intense and passionate week together. Both acted as if there was no tomorrow, and the intensity of their passion left them spent and exhausted. It had been a short and bright fire, which burnt out just as quickly. When he left, she knew he had plans that he had not revealed to her. He may never return. She felt intuitively that he would never return to her.

When Gerard came home it was no longer the same Chrissie who met him at the airport. She was no longer the same girl. Tom and Gerard could represent two bald men fighting for a hairbrush. She was the hairbrush and she didn't belong to either man. A defiant streak had risen to the fore and summoning up all of her courage, she walked out on Gerard within a couple of days. She felt that she could not live a lie and had to be true to herself. Even then, she suspected that her destiny lay in the dangerous profession she had currently chosen.

By the time she had returned to Capetown she was already sure that she was carrying Tom's child. She made the decision to keep it and keep the knowledge to herself. Tom would never know the truth. Her mother would have to help in its upbringing, as she needed to go out and earn enough to support it.

After his birth, she had him christened Tomas, and within a very short time had joined an escort agency. Her first savings went into enlarging her breasts. 'Bust augmentation', they had called it. Her friends had laughed and called it a boob job. She smiled at the memory. She had silicone implants put in that enhanced her bust considerably, and straight away she was aware of the impact on men. They immediately noticed her.

About one year ago she had moved up to Jo'burg and worked as a private escort. She adopted the name of Chantelle. It had proved lucrative and very soon she was popular and in high demand.

She heard the door open and the sound of Ryutaro talking to somebody in the corridor. She waited for him to enter. He was always good to her. In some difficult to define way, she knew that he had given her the consolation of believing in another world, in another possibility of what could have been or what could still be. In her own way, she cared for him deeply.

He came into the bedroom and grinned lasciviously. He looked as if he had been drinking. He closed the door.

The soft bedside lamp threw up soft and golden hues.

He came and sat on the bed. He smiled a lopsided grin and asked her to stand.

She got up and stood in front of him.

'Walk aroun' so I can see my beauty. Walk aroun', roun' and roun' so I can see!' His speech was slurred.

She paraded slowly and sensuously in front of him.

'My sexy lady. You are so beautifu'. In Japan, they would kill to have you. To possess a white girl. So curvy. So beautifu'.' He chuckled. His mirth was infectious. 'Come sit on my knee. My beautifu' Chantelle.'

She felt totally acquiescent and sat gently on his knee. She briefly remembered the drink she had prepared for him but decided to forget it as he had obviously drunk enough this evening.

He kissed her on the lips gently and placed her left arm over his shoulder. His left arm curled around her waist whilst his right hand explored her. It sought out the curves, the rounded and silken contours of her body. It sought out the slender waist, moved on to the full female soft breasts, and lingered on the now erect nipples. It wandered to the cleavage, to the slightly moist and warm flesh pressed against flesh. It ran back down over the discernable ribs and to the lacy contours of the G-string, over them and to her soft thighs. The fingers pressed between the thighs which compliantly parted slightly. His very touch elicited a soft moan as it ran higher.

He had a surge of happiness that she was all his; an amazement that his money could buy such beauty.

He turned her over and gently placed her face down over his knees. He pulled the nightie up and caressed her rear. He then gave her a few symbolic slaps. She gasped in mock pain.

She started to slip off his knees and on to the carpeted floor. She knelt at his feet and parted his legs. She moved forward. She deftly undid his trousers' zip and undid the belt. She gently reached in and released him. He was hard and wildly excited.

She gently stroked him with her right hand and used her left to move inside his trousers and stroke his buttocks. He moved his hands and entwined her hair in them. He gently encouraged her head forward.

She took him in her mouth and slowly moved her tongue around the head before taking in his shaft deeply into her. He was almost totally in her and could feel himself bump the back of her constricted throat.

He gurgled with delight and as the warmth, wetness and suction started to bring him to the edge. Her tongue was massaging him assiduously whilst he was in her. He suddenly knew he was on the very brink so started to control her head and move it vigorously. She offered no resistance and allowed herself to be controlled, as she instinctively knew he wanted.

Her mumbled groans made him ejaculate. He thrust up and simultaneously pulled her head down. His pleasure was almost unbearable and he sputtered in delight. He kept her head down on him till he started to go limp. He loosened his grip.

She raised her head and smiled. 'Was it good, my love?'

'Yesa, oh yesa! You are soo good. Nobody in Japan gives

headjob like you. You are best headjob girl ever. Sooo good.' He chortled with delight.

She smiled and got up from her knees to lie next to him.

A frown crossed his forehead. 'You make drink? You make drink for me?'

She nodded and started to get up to fetch it. He pushed her back down. 'No I fetch.'

He zipped himself up and tidied himself in the mirror. He looked unsteady on his feet. She frowned in confusion. Why tidy himself up?

He opened the door to the lounge and she heard him talk to somebody. She leapt up off the bed. Three stocky Chinese men entered.

'What the hell is this?' she demanded. She glared at Ryutaro, slowly crossing her arms over her bust, as she was now aware of the smirks on the guests' faces. Her tone changed from anger to hurt. 'Ryutaro, please. Tell me this is a joke. It can't be so?' she pleaded. Her voice had become more high-pitched.

'No joke. No joke,' sniggered one of the Chinese men. 'You are part of the package!'

'What package?'

Ryutaro looked sad. 'These gentlemen clinch deal only as long as I provide you for the night.' He hunched his shoulders and added in a near whisper, 'I had no option. No deal if no you. I had to agree.'

'I'm part of the deal?' she sounded incredulous. 'The American deal?'

'We are Taiwanese representing American interests, but now baby you are our interest!' one of them chuckled lecherously.

'Mr Sasagawa said you give best blowjob!' added another. 'The best in Africa, he assures us!'

'We all want a white woman to fuck. You lot fucked a lot of folk for a long time. Our time to fuck you guys now,' sniggered the other as he closed the door behind Ryutaro.

Ryutaro sat down and hung his head. He heard a slap, sounds of ripping, and laughter followed by a squeal. He noticed the drink that had been poured for him. He gulped it down and went out for a walk, ashamed of his own moral turpitude.

He returned about an hour later and the door was still closed though he could hear muted noises from behind it. He sat down and waited. He started to fall asleep with his head on his chest. The excessive alcohol was starting to take its toll.

The door opened and the three businessmen came out adjusting themselves. They looked hot and somewhat haggard but pleased with themselves.

The all bowed slightly and thanked him. 'Very good entertainment. Good night, Mr Sasagawa.'

Ryutaro walked slowly into the bedroom. The bed was a mess. Chrissie was sprawled over it on her back. Her nightie was partially wrapped about a wrist and was torn. Her breasts looked red and almost raw. She looked scratched and mauled. She raised herself on one elbow and looked straight at Ryaturo. Her eyes were red, one showing signs of a bruise. Her lower lip was swollen, cut and bleeding. She looked a mess.

He gasped and fell to his knees. 'So very sorry, Chanta' – so sorry.'

'Save it, you shithead. You absolute lowlife! To think I even cared for you. You fucking bastard! You are the worst. A real piece of scum,' she sneered.

She slowly got off the bed and grimaced in pain. She went to the bathroom. She gasped as she saw her reflected image. Without closing the door, she slowly and steadily started to clean herself up.

She emerged about half an hour later. Ryutaro was not around. A bulging envelope lay on the table. She opened it. It was crammed with US dollar notes of high denominations. She snorted derisively. Sasagawa guilt money, she surmised. It would all go straight to her mother. She placed it into her Louis Vuitton handbag.

She put on her coat and shoved her belongings into her small bag before leaving the suite and heading down to the basement car park and her black BMW 320i cabriolet. She headed out and into traffic.

As she stopped at the first intersection before the dual carriageway, she noticed the young black jauntily come up towards her. He was carrying a gun. She assessed the situation and decided to try and hit him with the car. The tires squealed as the car lurched forward and veered straight at the young man. He looked terrified and raised his gun. He made no attempt to flee or dodge. Perhaps his astonishment kept him firmly on the spot.

The impact of his body against the bonnet made the car shudder. The windscreen shattered. Chrissie felt winded as she hit the steering wheel. As she accelerated she was in turn thrown back into her seat. The car straightened and at great speed entered the dual carriageway. The wind entering through the gaping hole where the windscreen used to be blew her hair back in disorderly fashion. She laughed at her survival.

Her dress felt wet. She put her hand up and felt her neck. It was wet and sticky. She looked at her hand. It was dark and glistening. She realised it was blood. In dismay she felt again and realised that blood was pumping from her neck.

She started to feel faint. The car veered to the left and hit the curb. It mounted the edge and careered into a municipal park before stopping in the middle of the manicured grass. She opened the door and literally fell out onto the ground. She was aware of people running towards her. She vainly felt around for her handbag but she could no longer see and had no energy left. She grasped that her lifeblood was flowing into the soil around her. The bullet from the gun had hit her after all.

She desperately wanted to wail, not in pain but in the dreadful knowledge that Tomas would be without a mother or her vital support.

The first rescuers that came racing up found her already dead beside the car. She lay on her side with her coat partially pulled off and one blood-covered breast revealed. Her left arm seemed to be reaching for her bag on the seat of the car. A relatively small bloody hole was visible in her neck. Her face wore a strong grimace as if protesting furiously at the injustice of the world. A large dark stain of blood covered the green and tended grass.

Jan Smuts International Airport

Tom picked up a copy of the *Star*. He had already read *Die Beeld* but needed to fill in the time till his flight departed. The main story dealt with news about the newly convened Committee for Justice and Reconciliation under Bishop Desmond Tutu. He skipped to items of lesser significance.

Under a small caption that read 'Crime wave soars in City of Gold' he read an article about the depressingly high crime statistics. It claimed that all aspects of criminal activity, from murder to aggravated assault, from burglary to carjacking were increasing at alarming rates. It mentioned how Johannesburg had areas where to even wear a watch and walk alone down the streets was to invite attack from the roaming gangs of young thugs. It went on to compare other cities in the world where crime was a great problem and how Johannesburg had surpassed all of them, and finally it had extracts of a speech a Police Commissioner had recently given on the very subject; how the security forces were drowning in this tidal wave of violence and crime.

Tom sighed with resignation. It was perhaps inevitable with the huge population numbers around the city and the inability of businesses to rapidly absorb them into employment. Freedom fighters were rapidly reinventing themselves as criminals in vast numbers and a multitude of rival gangs. The elections had brought Nelson Mandela and his African National Congress Party to power. People's expectations were high, but there was a palpable sense of frustration as they realised they were not being met. It was not that the promises made were insincere or even unrealistic, but change was happening slowly and there was no likelihood of any sudden transfer of wealth from one segment of society to another.

He read the smaller news items. There was a catalogue of violent robberies and an article dealing with the much-publicized rape of a young Australian tourist. Under all of them was an article that read:

Police are appealing for help from the public after the discovery of a near naked white female in an abandoned petrol station on the outskirts of Johannesburg. She appears to be the victim of violent crime and police have not ruled out a sexual motive. The perpetrators appear to have removed all identifying clothing and effects from the scene. The forensic department has assessed her to be in her early twenties. Please call the Police at Sandton on 11-835-447 if you have any information that may lead to the discovery of her identity and help catch her killers. Anonymity will be respected.

Tom looked up at the departure board. Alitalia Flight AL 783 to New York via Rome was now flashing 'Please proceed to Departure Lounge'. He walked over to the rubbish bin and dropped the newspaper in. It was a conscious gesture. He was leaving South Africa behind. He did not even look around him as he strode forward into the departure lounge. A very short distance away, South African Airways passengers from Malawi were entering the airport, including Lucinda Beresford.

He thought of Colonel Coetzee as he walked forward. Andries had lived and died by his beliefs. He held sacred a creed, which stated that it isn't enough to just succeed, others must fail. Involuntarily, Tom shuddered as an image of him on his deathbed flashed in front of his eyes. He shook his head and dismissed all his morbid thoughts. He looked around him and focused on his surrounds.

He passed through passport control and proceeded straight to the area in front of the designated departure gate. He watched the three Chinese businessmen who were all talking animatedly. They were laughing at some photos. He caught a glimpse and realised they were pornographic pictures. He smiled to himself and turned away to await the final boarding call.

Lucinda sat down and sighed with irritation when she realised that the flight back to Blantyre had been delayed. She had made the effort to be well in time, as requested, but there had been no call from the airline that there was a delay, in spite of the fact that she had kept her mobile on. There were times when life in the new South Africa was seemingly moving rapidly close to the laissez-faire complacency of the rest of the continent.

She walked past the small shop selling African curios and souvenirs to a coffee shop and settled in to read the paper. Most of the news she had heard endlessly repeated on the radio, so she gravitated to smaller items and advertisements to entertain herself and help pass the time of the enforced wait.

Like Tom one week previously, she read about the crimes and troubles that were besetting Johannesburg. She scanned down and came across a short article entitled 'Police still need help'. She read the article:

Police are still anxious to gain any information from the public about last movements of Ms Chantelle Neuman who was last seen eight days ago in the lobby of the Charlton Hotel. Ms Neuman was positively identified by her mother. It appears she was the victim of a sexual assault and robbery. Her body was found last weekend outside of Johannesburg. Police are anxious to gather any information that may lead to the solving of this crime. Her car, a BMW 320i 1995 model cabriolet, registration TJ 20065 has also been stolen. Ms Neuman leaves behind a small child of eighteen months who is currently in her mother's care in Durban. Please contact the Sandton Police on 11-835-447 with any information that may be of help.

Lucinda sighed again as she contemplated the huge number of murders occurring in South Africa. It had become a country with alarming statistics.

The following article dealt with the equally gruesome facts about how death from violence and accidents was being outpaced by the ever-mounting casualties from Aids-related disease. Health care workers were predicting that death from Aids related disease were likely to reach the astronomically high figures of 300,000 per year by the time the century had ended.

She shook her head in disbelief. The numbers were almost too large to realistically comprehend. It would mean a death rate of 6,000 per week, she calculated. At that rate what would become of South Africa? Whole communities – if not cultures – would succumb to the deadly virus and change the ethnic geography permanently.

She shook her head again as if negating the thoughts and placed the newspaper straight in the bin. It was ultimately too depressing to read.

The newspaper fell into the bin and crumpled. Unseen by Lucinda was the page where it had opened on the death notices. Under a heading saying 'In memoriam' was a picture of a young and smiling Chrissie. There was a cross above her name. It read as follows:

In memory of Christina Maria De Oliveira, also known as Chantal Neuman, born 12/6/1970, died tragically at the hands of unknown assailants 3/10/96 in Johannesburg. Loving daughter of Maria Estela, she leaves behind her little son Tomas. Into God's hands, we commend you.

Lucinda did not see it as she rose to walk around and pace away her frustration at the delays.

She spotted an Internet kiosk and directly walked over. She placed a few rand into the machine and accessed her Hotmail account. There were various messages from a spectrum of countries that were all business related. Amongst them all was a message from Rick. Her heart skipped a beat and she giggled involuntarily in surprise. It was titled 'Gooday'.

She inhaled deeply. It was amazing that she had an answer! With a degree of nervousness and expectation, she opened the letter.

Dear Lucie,

What a surprise and delight it was to hear from you! I just couldn't believe you had made contact after all these years. I think I read your letter about four times just to assure myself that it was real and there was no real likelihood of a hoax!

Anyway, I'm amazed (and happy) you kept my address and I'm also relieved I didn't somewhere along the line change it! Where to begin? There seems so much to talk about! What a pity you didn't try to contact me in London. I must have spent approx. two years somewhat half-heartedly working there before deciding that adventures and travel still awaited me!

How fantastic that you have expanded your business as well as you have. You must feel really chuffed. I think it's really brilliant. You certainly have got the stuff I always felt you were made of – stern go out and get 'em South African stuff! Just kidding and bullshitting around! It sounds really good and enterprising, but tell me – is the food also good? I never did get to try it whilst I was out there.

I don't really know where to begin? I took off for New Zealand and spent some time there involved in an architectural venture in the capital, Wellington. It wasn't too strenuous and of course allowed me to see the country (Mt Cook, Franz Josef Glacier, Milford Sound, etc.) – and watch some brilliant rugby. The Maoris are fearsome opponents in these matches. Great to watch them on home turf.

Australia beckoned in the form of more work and better pay, so I crossed the Tasman Sea and have sort of settled here in Perth. Work is good. The Aussies are a laidback mob (local lingo!) and easygoing. The lifestyle is quintessential California with the

Californians taken out of the equation!

And – when I say settled, I have nobody in my life. I spent some time with a Kiwi girl but she was too parochial and wedded to NZ. It meant that she could not/would not consider travel elsewhere, hence the parting of ways. Since arriving here about a year ago, I've settled into a somewhat hedonistic lifestyle with yachts, wine, scuba-diving and the like, but alas no women – it seemed easier to live alone. Friends are always trying to matchmake but I've politely declined.

I did think of contacting you on so many occasions but there was an ethereal make-believe quality to you in my memories. At times it seemed totally unreal – all the SA experience. A sort of nightmare and wet dream blended into a holiday. What a weird and strange holiday experience it was. And I guess that was why the silence. It struck me you were perhaps part of a holiday romance – though this didn't sit well with me – but unreal as it all seemed – I have never forgotten you and you're often in my mind.

As time went by, though, you did seem increasingly remote – and difficult to get hold of – I don't think you had an email address back then, did you? I had lost contact with Tom and realistically I had no idea where you might be.

Since you are without a partner, can I say with all sincerity that I would just love to catch up with you. I am due (or in need of!) a holiday. How about Mauritius? Salubrious climate, indulgent lifestyle. Do you fancy catching up there? I could get a room for twin sharing (I am not expecting you to jump into the cot with me) and we could catch up? I would really love that and I'm hoping you'll agree. I'll even send you the ticket to you in Blantyre – my treat! Think about it – no strings attached – honest!

Yes… Tom. I have no idea what has become of him. Have not heard a word since Capetown. I never felt inclined to write, so have just let it be.

Chrissie also disappeared into the big blue and off the planet, but then I'm not surprised. I can imagine her in Jo'burg, she had aspirations to be a social butterfly! (I think, but in truth I never knew her that well!)

I'm surprised I never ran into Gerard, but probably some day will – the antipodean scene is too small not to meet up by chance.

I'm sure SA has changed drastically, but I'd rather be sipping a gin and tonic on some tropical locale with you and listen to you tell me all about it, than have emails – so here's hoping your reply

will be 'Yes, I'm coming.'
Love,
Rick
R L Graham,

5 Hoxton Rise, Carine,
WA 6020, Australia
w. 61-8-9881-2108 h. 61-8-9448-1274
mob. 61-409-560-021

PS: I'll be checking my emails more frequently from now on. If I
don't hear from you soon, I'll give you a ring.

Lucie grinned from ear to ear. How unbelievable she thought to
herself. Time had stood still, it's almost as if they had only just
parted instead of there being a gap of almost five years. She
already knew she would meet him in Mauritius, or wherever; she
would be happy to just see him again.

She closed her Hotmail passport and still grinning impishly
went back to a seat near the departure board to await her flight.
She would reply from Blantyre after she had got over her initial
excitement.

> I consider perversion and vice to be the most
> vibrant forms of thought and action, just as I
> consider love to be the only attitude worthy of
> a man's life.'
>
> Salvador Dali,
> 1930

1998: Vancouver, British Columbia, Canada

Tom laughed as she span around and modelled her new dress that
showed her outline so clearly. Annalore was small, very pretty and
she was his wife. The pregnancy was already visible and this made
both of them incredibly happy.

She was a young Canadian of German descent, who Tom had
courted and married. A fresh and young girl with parents who

lived on the land, she had succumbed to Tom's charms and left the farm to live in Vancouver.

Their happiness was fulfilling. She felt secure with him, and Tom felt settled and happy with her earthy and robust sexuality. She gained a serious and hard-working husband with similar cultural values and he was able to adopt her extended family as his own and finally leave Africa out of the equation.

He had come to realise that Andries had been right. For the sake of his own salvation it was best that Africa and his roots there were left in the past. He adopted everything about his new home and slowly he even started to sound Canadian. He would never leave this new land. His passionate loyalty to his wife, in-laws, and most importantly his future child, were bordering on the extreme.

He had almost stopped reading the international news and assiduously avoided anything to do with South Africa. He no longer even followed rugby or the progress of his previously beloved Springboks. He never dwelt on the past or even thought of Rick, Lucie, or Chrissie, for mentally he had metamorphosed. Tom had reinvented himself and felt vigorously positive and happy with his life.

Mbabane, Swaziland

Mopete smiled as Sergio came back into the room carrying little Enrique in his arms. He was such a proud father and was literally beside himself with joy since the birth of their son. They had been happy together and had even managed to successfully sort out legal papers for Mopete. They had since married and were now celebrating their first child.

Steve had been adopted into the family as if he was Sergio's and it seemed unlikely he would ever truly miss his dead father, as he had been too young to remember or know him. They had all adopted Swazi nationality, which had been granted them by the Royal Court.

Neither parents ever saw themselves returning to either Mozambique or South Africa, or immersing themselves in any form of politics. They were just content to be together as a modern nuclear African family. Neither had extended family back in Mozambique and were happy with their new adopted homeland. It seemed a small oasis of calm in a turbulent continent and both were happy to be there and saw the future as positive.

Perth, Western Australia

Rick looked up at the board again in Perth's new International Arrivals for the Qantas flight QF 9 from Harare. It had the ETA as 10.15 and next to it was flashing the cryptic message of 'on time'. He looked at his watch; it was 9.55, so he was too early. Even after arrival there was always immigration, baggage retrieval and customs which could add a further three-quarters of an hour. He paced up and down and decided to have a coffee in the small cafeteria that allowed him to watch the runway and the arrival of the plane he was waiting for.

He decided to try and distract himself and ordered a cappuccino and distractedly read the local edition of the *Australian*. The worsening events in Timor and across Indonesia occupied the main news. He continued to read distractedly.

He saw the plane as it gently coasted down from the clear blue skies of Western Australia. A large Boeing 747 it looked gleamingly white with its red bouncing kangaroo clearly visible on its tail. It was a perfect day with the best of Perth's weather on show. A great day to arrive.

He remained leaning on the barrier as the people streamed through. Smiles, whoops of joy and screams of delight greeted each new batch of arrivals.

Then he saw her. She had that jet lagged and confused look that people often have after a long intercontinental flight. She looked around with a half smile and quizzical expression as her eyes scanned the crowds lining the barrier. She moved her baggage trolley slowly forward and then she spotted his frantically waving arm. Her smile of recognition and pleasure lit up her face as she confidently moved forward towards him. Lucie looked joyful.

Rick felt ecstatically happy. Here coming toward him was the answer to all his lascivious dreams and the soul mate he had sought in his life. He had never been so sure that this woman and their destiny were hopelessly interwoven and had a feeling that a wonderful new life was about to begin. Every step she took towards him brought her closer to the embrace he was so longing to give her.

Mauritius two years ago, and the one-month extended holiday together in Kenya last year, had both been outstanding successes. At the end of the last holiday together he had proposed to her. On the sun-drenched island of Lamu in Northern Kenya he had produced the Argyle diamond and gold ring from Western Australia and asked her to be his wife. She had choked with emotion at the time and accepted.

'Lucie! Christ, it is so good to see you!' He stepped forward and took her in his arms in an almost smothering embrace.

'It is so good to see you. I am so happy.'

'So am I. I just couldn't wait to see you again. I love the way your whole face lights up when you smile. I love you.'

'I love you too, darling,' she chuckled.

He kissed her passionately on the mouth and folded his arms around her. She kissed him back.

The pressure of the crowds behind forced them to move on and they slowly moved towards the exit doors.

'Jeez, it is really cold here,' said Lucie as she rubbed her bare arms.

'Wait till you get outside. Like the Yanks, the Aussies use their air-conditioners too much. Welcome to WA,' responded Rick. 'I am so happy that you are finally here. There is so much to show you and so much to do together.'

She looked up at him and grinned. 'Believe me, darling, I can't wait!'

He laughed. 'Let's go home!'

Finis coronat opus

Perth,
Western Australia,